Also by J  ...ian

HISTORICAL FICTION

The Jacobite Chronicles

Jacobite Chronicles Stories

i

JULIA BRANNAN

Jacobite Chronicles Novellas

Dealing in Treason

CONTEMPORARY FICTION

A Seventy-Five Percent Solution

The Baronet's Tale: Anthony
Part II

A Jacobite Chronicles Story

Julia Brannan

DISCLAIMER

This novel is a work of fiction, and except in the case of historical fact, any resemblance to actual persons, living or dead, is purely coincidental.

To all my wonderful readers.
I wanted to dedicate the last book in this series (probably) to all of you. Without your support I would not be living my dream. Thank you, from the bottom of my heart!

Acknowledgements

Thanks to the long-suffering Mary Brady, friend and first critic, who reads the chapters as I write them, critiques them for me and reassures me that I can actually write stuff people will want to read, and to my beta readers Angela, Claire, Susan, Ashelle and Anna for their valued and honest opinions. I can't stress how important you are!

Thanks also go to Mandy Condon, who sends me useful articles, has already determined the cast list for the film of my books, and who has been a wonderful and supportive friend for over thirty years. I moved house recently, and Mandy, along with her husband Pete were wonderful! Everything was unpacked and in its right place in four days. They made a stressful event fun, too!

My gratitude also to fellow author Kym Grosso, who has been extremely supportive and has generously given me the benefit of her experience in the minefield of indie publishing. I value her friendship and support enormously.

A big thank you also to the hugely talented Diana Gabaldon, who wrote a fabulous review for my books, and who is a kind, supportive, and very interesting person.

And thanks as always go to the talented and very patient Najla Qamber, who does all my covers, puts up with my lack of artistic ability, and still manages to somehow understand exactly what I want my covers to look like! Thanks also to Beathag Mhoireasdan, who translated various phrases into Gaelic for me in record time, and toRichard and Helen, who helped me achieve the perfect Anthony pose for this book.

To all my wonderful and loyal readers, who not only buy my books, but take the time and effort to give me feedback, to review them on Amazon, Audible, Goodreads, and Bookbub and recommend them to others, by word of mouth and on social media – thank you so much. You keep me going on those dark days when I'd rather do anything than stare at a blank screen for hours while my brain turns to mush...you are amazing! Without all of you I would be nothing, and I appreciate you more than you know.

A special thank you to Anna MacRae MacDonald, who does a fabulous job of running the Jacobite Chronicles Reader Group on Facebook, and to everyone who's joined it so far, and who make it a warm and welcoming place to be.

I also want to send a huge thank you to Inverness Outlanders, a wonderful, intelligent, kind and friendly group of women who've not only made me very welcome and part of the community since I moved to Scotland, but who are always willing to help me with research too! You are wonderful friends to have.

I want to also show my appreciation for Angela Hickey, who runs Queen Bee's Outlandish Hive, and who is featuring my books in depth in her Facebook group at the moment. She does a lot of interesting features about Outlander too, so if you're an Outlander fan you might be interested in taking a look. And also look at Global Girls Online Book Club, who featured me as Author of the Day. A friendly place to find new books of all genres!

And finally, to Bob and Dolores. You are wonderful people and I love you.

PROLOGUE

Scotland, March, 1737

Alex sat at the top of the hill, arms wrapped round his knees, watching the sun set over Loch Lomond. He had spent the last couple of hours sitting here, making excuses for not setting off on the final leg of his journey home, a journey that had taken him far longer than he'd wanted it to.

It was ironic, really. He'd spent over a month in a state of almost constant impatience, desperate to be where he now was, just an hour from home, expecting that when he *was* here he would merely glance at the glorious view before running down the hill and along the path to the settlement, where his brothers would be waiting for him.

Where his clan would be waiting for him.

And that was the reason why he was still sitting here. It was not because he was tired, although he *was* a little weary. Nor was it because he needed to think or to prepare a fitting entrance as chieftain of the clan. He had had plenty of time to think about everything on the way home.

In truth it was because sitting here he was Alex MacGregor, who he had always been, a person he was sometimes pleased with, sometimes ashamed of, but nevertheless someone he knew well, and was comfortable being. But once he arrived in the settlement he would immediately become chieftain of the clan, who he had never been, who he did not know at all, and in many ways was terrified of having to be.

1

He was being silly, he knew that. The clan would not expect him to become his father. He would, in time, make the role of chieftain his own. They would understand that it would take him a little time to adjust to his new responsibilities, just as it must have taken his da time to, and his grandda before him. They would support him, as they were certainly supporting Duncan now.

He would head down. Just another minute to prepare himself, and then he would head down.

When he had arrived at Scolastica and Ashelle's on that terrible evening, he had been determined to be strong and practical, as befitted a new chieftain of a clan, but to his horror had disintegrated completely the minute he'd seen the loving, sympathetic faces of his friends.

And they had done everything right. Highbury had soothed and consoled him in the way any father would his beloved child, managing to make him feel that there was nothing weak or embarrassing in breaking down as he had. In fact, the earl had said, when Alex was capable of listening again and had gulped and sobbed his apologies, he would have thought less of the young Highlander if he *had* been strong and practical at such a time, would have thought him maybe cold and unfeeling, instead of loving and grief-stricken, which were the proper emotions to feel at such a time.

"I could only wish that Daniel would react as you are, when he learns of my death," he had said softly, almost to himself. But Alex had heard, and in that moment had hated the unknown Daniel more than he thought possible.

The women had withdrawn temporarily, aware that their friend needed time alone with the man who had become a second father to him, reappearing only after he had calmed enough to be able to plan his next move. Between them they had managed to dissuade him from leaving Paris immediately, making him see that another few days would make no difference to Duncan, who, from all Alex had told them about him, was certainly making a good job of standing in for him.

They were right, he'd realised, once he was thinking sensibly. It would be better to plan his journey home, make contingency plans for extreme weather, which was likely in January.

So instead of dashing off into the night, he had stayed in Paris for another couple of days, had explained to the rector why he must leave, had said his farewells to his friends, and had spent a final evening at *L'Accueil Chaleureux* with them, even doing a final caricature of the long-dead Beauregard, to rapturous applause. He had had no desire to partake in a riotous drunken evening, but he knew his friends meant well, and he wanted their last memory of him to be a good one, so he had gone along with it, telling himself it was good practice for when he arrived home and would need to conceal some of the emotions that he felt, now he was chieftain.

Meanwhile Highbury had persuaded the coachman Jean to take Alex to Calais in the coach. Then Jean could spend some time with his family, because the earl intended to stay in Paris until the summer and could certainly manage without a coach until then, as he did not intend to travel outside the city. He also insisted Alex take some money, overriding the Scot's refusal by telling him that it could be expensive to find a captain willing to cross the channel in mid-winter, and a generous bribe might make all the difference between him getting home quickly or languishing in Calais until the spring.

Alex had seen the sense in this, and as Highbury had pointed out, they were close friends now, and close friends should never be embarrassed about either giving or accepting help from each other.

So he had taken the money, and had been very glad he had, because when he arrived in Calais there was a gale blowing and absolutely nothing was going out of port, and was unlikely to be doing so for some time, he was told.

He had thought about travelling to another port in the hopes of persuading a fisherman to take him to England, but had been advised by numerous sea-faring men that anyone who would agree to take him across the sea in this weather would be a fool of the highest order, and if he wanted to commit suicide there were easier and cheaper ways to do it.

Having listened to various versions of the same advice Alex had accepted the wisdom of it, and had found a cheap room in the fisherman's area of the town to wait it out. He had written letters to Highbury, and Ashelle and Scolastica, had thought about writing to Duncan and Angus, but then realised that he would certainly arrive home before any letter did, and had then spent ten days alternately sitting in his room reading books and brooding, or wandering around the town, spending hours staring frustratedly at the colossal storm-driven waves crashing onto the shore, while the almost constant icy horizontal rain soaked his clothes and body, his mood as dark as the heavy grey clouds looming over the raging ocean.

Home was *so* close; or rather not home, but England. He was told that when the weather was good you could actually *see* the coast of England from Calais, although he didn't believe this.

On the tenth day, having seen nobody except his landlady and the servers at the places he'd bought food in, he decided to go for a drink. The evening would probably pass more quickly in company, he thought.

There was a ramshackle-looking tavern in the next street, its rusty sign proclaiming it to be *Le Chat D'Or* and although neither the exterior nor the sign looked as promising as Claude's tavern had, Alex doubted the interior could be much worse. It would be nice to converse with someone, or at the very least be in the company of others for a short time. It would be a change from brooding alone in his room or staring pointlessly across the sea.

The tavern door had creaked loudly as he'd forced it open, announcing his arrival to everyone in the place, who all immediately stopped whatever they'd been doing to stare at him. He glanced around, seemingly casually, but taking in as much as he could, glad that he had three weapons available should he need them.

It was not a promising place for a jolly evening; the interior was as ramshackle as the exterior, the lighting consisting of two candles burning in a pile of wax on the table to his right, round which sat half a dozen men nursing tankards of alcohol and looking at him warily. There seemed to be no one else in the place apart from a man standing behind the bar, although the staircase at the far end of the L-shaped room told Alex that any number of men could be upstairs.

He sighed inwardly. Whatever this place was, it was not one that welcomed strangers as Claude's tavern had, and there would be no food available, not even watery soup and rock-hard bread. He thought rapidly. If he just turned and left he would broadcast fear, encouraging them to follow him and try to rob him of whatever they thought he might have on his person.

He assessed them as best he could in a few seconds. Both the pervading smell and their looks told him they were probably fishermen; weather-beaten skin, strong, muscular bodies. Hard men, accustomed to danger then, but not skilfully trained warriors as he was. As long as he made sure they were never between him and the door he should be safe, he decided. These men would know the weather, and they would know the name of anyone who might be willing to take him to England the second it was possible to do so.

He nodded to the men, then made his way to the bar, asking for whatever they were drinking. The man took down a tankard from the shelf, wiped it on his dirty apron and filled it with wine. Alex took his tankard and made his way across to the table, where one of them immediately asked him his business in Calais.

He had sat down, relaxed and at ease, told them he was a Highlander, but not his name or the name of his clan, and had said he was in France on business for his father.

"And what manner of business might that be?" one of the men had asked.

"It doesna signify now, for my da has died, and I'm needing to go home as quickly as I can," Alex had said, speaking coarse French with a distinct Scottish accent, rather than the fluent educated French or English he'd been mainly using for the last months.

"What made you come in here?" another asked.

"I'm staying in a room nearby," Alex had replied, coming to a sudden decision. "I havena a great deal of money wi' me, just enough to get home and a wee bit more. I was here for my father, to find someone who could maybe help him buy...certain necessities, and get them home for him."

A younger man's face immediately brightened, and he opened his mouth, but whatever he'd been about to say was quenched by the scowl from the man opposite him. Alex was right; they *were* smugglers, or if not smugglers themselves, well acquainted with them.

"What manner of necessities?" the scowling man asked.

"Well, no' wine, anyway," Alex replied, having taken a gulp of the coarse liquid in his tankard and grimacing.

"My wife makes the wine," the barman objected hotly, when the laughter this comment attracted had died down.

"You might get her to wash her feet between tending the pigs and treading the grapes though," another put in, to more laughter.

The tension in the room abated, and Alex thanked God that he seemed to have unknowingly stumbled on this tavern's equivalent of Raymond's soup in *L'Acceuil Chaleureux*.

"As I said, at the moment I'm only thinking to get home, although I'll almost certainly be back at some point. It's no' goods to sell on we're looking for, but goods to use, shall we say, should the need arise. Although I wouldna say no to some fine cognac or claret, when it's available. I was hoping to at least find a contact to discuss it wi', but everything's changed now. Have ye any notion when ye might be able to cross the sea?"

"Not yet," a man at the far end of the table said. "We're as frustrated as you. If we don't fish, we don't eat. But even when the weather improves enough to fish, none of us would venture that far. Maybe in spring, but not in February."

The others nodded.

"No one would cross in this," the scowling man told him.

"Except Gabriel and his men," the young man said. "And—"

"Yes, well, they're not here, so it doesn't matter, does it?" the barman cut in roughly, causing the young man to blush furiously and subside. An interesting silence fell on the group for a moment.

Alex was wise enough not to ask anything more about Gabriel, whoever he was, and instead sympathised with their inability to fish, saying Highlanders had the same problem if the harvest failed. He asked them about their lives, and then told them some tales of clan life, chosen to let the men know that although the dangers they faced were very different, they had one important thing in common – they all lived a dangerous, adventurous life, on a knife edge between sufficiency and starvation.

By the end of the evening they were reassured enough to tell him he should call in again, and that if he told them where he was staying, they'd let him know if they found anyone willing to take him across *la Manche* to Dover.

It had been a successful night, he had thought. Although the drink had been disgusting it had been alcoholic, and had dulled the edge of his persistent grief and impatience. He had had an interesting conversation, had not even had to think about drawing his pistol, dirk or *sgian dubh,* and had managed to put out feelers regarding a smuggling contact, in case he should need one.

That had been an impulse decision. Although his father had bought goods that had been smuggled into the country, as just about everyone in Britain did, he had never participated in smuggling expeditions. But if Prince Charles lived up to his promise, then one day the clans would need a lot more weapons than they currently possessed, so it would do no harm to have the right contacts.

He had no idea whether this Gabriel man was a smuggler or just a suicidal sailor, but hopefully if he made a few more visits, he could find a safe way of contacting the man.

In the end he had not needed to do this, because two days later his landlady had told him there was a man asking to see him, and on descending the stairs to the street, Alex had been confronted by the scowling man from the tavern, who told him that he had found someone willing to take him to Dover, probably in a couple of days, as a temporary lull in the weather was expected.

And so it was that Alex had crossed the sea a few days later surrounded by an assortment of barrels and crates, about which he wisely asked no questions, although he did help to both load them at Calais on a grey afternoon, and unload them at a beach a short distance from Dover in the dead of night. He had been given the address of an inn in a place called Stockwell, to which he could address a careful letter to one Gabriel Foley, should he wish to. And in return he had given a name which was not his, and had said that any mail to him could be sent to the post in Glasgow.

And then he had set off for home, deciding to walk as much of the way as he could. Not because walking would be quicker than the coach, although in this weather it probably would be, and not because he could not afford to take a coach. It was because he was very aware, from how much his muscles were aching after loading and unloading cargo, of just how unfit he was.

He had intended to regain his strength and fitness in Paris, in between studying and spending pleasant evenings with Highbury, Ashelle and Scolastica. But now he had to try to do it between Dover and Loch Lomond, for he wanted to arrive home as capable of being the chieftain as possible, physically, if not mentally. If he built his strength and endurance, then Kenneth would make sure his fighting abilities were brought up to scratch as quickly as possible.

So he had walked the whole way, stopping at farms or in villages to buy food, and sleeping in barns or under hedges.

And now he was sitting on a hill as the sky darkened and the icy wind freshened, still reluctant to take the final steps that would lead him back to his old life, to his new life. By the time he got home it would be night and the clansfolk would all be in their homes, unless Duncan had invited them to a ceilidh in Da's house.

In his house, now.

Sighing, he stood and stretched. He could not imagine Duncan voluntarily holding a ceilidh. Angus, maybe, but not Duncan. An idea suddenly occurred to him which lifted his spirits a little, and then he shouldered his small pack and prepared to go down the hill, his *féileadh mór* blowing around his legs, his feet clad in the *brògan* he'd made in Lyon, and which he had not worn since crossing the Alps.

He smiled sadly then, remembering Highbury wearing them and both of them splashing in the river, giggling like small boys. In all probability they would never meet again, which saddened him. He would miss him.

Then he shook off all thoughts of the past, and focussing on the future, headed down the hill to the loch, and home.

CHAPTER ONE

KENNETH CAME OUT OF the chieftain's house, closed the door behind him, then stood outside it for a few moments, debating whether to go straight home to his wife or to head down to the loch and freshen up first. It was late and he was very tired and cold too, and wanted nothing more than to be in his bed, warm and snug, with his wife curled up against him.

It had been a strange three months since Alexander had died. Everyone had expected it to be a little different, but had assumed that initially things would carry on pretty well as they had before, especially as it was winter, when everyone in the Highlands generally focussed on homely tasks, and on surviving whatever the weather threw at them. It was not a time when the chieftain would normally be needed to make life-or-death decisions. If Alexander had to die, he had chosen the best season of the year to do it.

At least he had if his heir had been around to take up the reins. But Alex was not around, and for the hundredth time Kenneth wondered when he would arrive. There was no doubt that once he received the news he would return home as quickly as possible; everyone in the clan knew that. Duncan had sent three letters, hoping that at least one of them would reach its destination. All they could do now was wait.

Except that Duncan, who of Alexander's three sons had always been the patient one, the contemplative one, the one who couldn't care less what others thought of him, had found himself unable to just passively sit and wait for his brother to come home and take over. Instead he seemed to think he had to make everything as perfect as possible, to show Alex and the clan what a competent deputy chieftain he was.

Because of that every house was in perfect repair, every knife, dirk and sword sharpened, every ounce of oatmeal, every apple accounted for. When there was nothing left to do, Duncan had searched for tasks to occupy himself with.

And both Duncan and Angus, without even realising it, had relied on Kenneth. Kenneth had expected that; as the tallest and strongest man in the clan by far, everyone looked to him to help with heavy work. But Duncan and Angus had needed a different strength – they had needed a father figure, someone they could trust, ask for advice, and receive reassurance from. They had looked to him, and Kenneth, moved beyond words, had given them that, to the best of his ability.

Duncan had also needed someone he could show his vulnerability to. He knew the clan looked to him now as their chieftain, albeit temporarily, and a chieftain could not show fear, could not show weakness, for if he did the clan would doubt his capability.

Alex, when he returned, would no doubt hide his vulnerabilities even from Kenneth. But Duncan, grieving the loss of his father and absence of his brother, needed support, needed to ask for advice, and to receive sensible suggestions when he did.

The clan were only in the habit of asking for Kenneth's muscular assistance, and he hadn't been sure he was capable of providing the intellectual help he was now being asked for. But Duncan had asked him, and so Kenneth had done the best he could in that capacity too. And to his absolute astonishment, not only had Duncan listened to and adopted many of his suggestions, but over time other clansfolk had started coming to him for advice too. Which told him that Duncan, whatever his worries about appearing weak, saw no need to claim the credit for ideas that were not his own, as many a lesser m an would.

Although Kenneth never had, and never would have the slightest interest in one day becoming the chieftain, this new respect from the clan members gave him a new sense of purpose, a spring in his step.

So it was that when there had been a sudden warm spell a few weeks ago, and much of the snow had melted, Kenneth had suggested that it might be worthwhile checking whether there was any unusual move-ment at Inversnaid barracks. Duncan had immediately agreed, and had sent him, Allan, and Angus along on a reconnaissance expedition. Which had told Kenneth that not only did Duncan trust his advice, but also trusted him to look after the person he treasured most apart from his fiancée and his absent older brother. It was a very good feeling indeed, to be so trusted, so respected.

He had just delivered the exhausted but over-excited Angus home, along with the reassuring news that nothing at all was happening at Inversnaid. What soldiers there were were all huddled in their rooms round their fires, it seemed.

Kenneth stretched and yawned, then making a sudden decision, headed in the direction of the loch. A quick dip in the icy waters would wash off the sweat and dirt of the last week and wake him up a little, both of which Jeannie would certainly appreciate when he arrived home. He had missed her in the last week, and was sure she'd missed him too.

Once at the loch he began to unbuckle his sword belt, then froze. The hairs on his arms rose, and not just from the cold. Although he had neither seen nor heard anything, he suddenly knew he was not alone. It was late and very cold; all the clan members were in bed. Anyone who was not would have greeted him as he passed, not hidden from him. Very slowly and silently he turned from the loch, drawing his dirk as he did, his nostrils dilating as all his senses went on full alert.

Then he saw it; the slight movement of a branch although there was no wind, and then a shadow broke free from the trees and started to make its way towards the settlement, being very careful to make no noise.

Too late, laddie, Kenneth thought grimly to himself. He waited a moment to be sure there were no others, and then he ran with incredible speed and lightness for such an enormous man, reaching the figure just as it became aware of him and started to turn. He seized the intruder in a bone-crushing hold, and laid his dirk against its throat.

"Kenneth?" the intruder croaked, and then staggered forward as he was released as quickly as he'd been grabbed.

"Alex?" Kenneth asked incredulously. "What the hell are ye doing skulking around in the trees? I could have killt ye!"

Alex was bent over, hugging his bruised ribs and fighting to get enough breath in his lungs to reply.

"Christ, man, ye havena lost your strength, at any rate," he gasped finally. "Ye'll have no difficulty bringing my fighting skills back up to strength either, I'm thinking."

He straightened up carefully, and Kenneth took an instinctive step forward to embrace him, then stopped, uncertain.

"This wasna exactly the way I'd planned on greeting my new chieftain, when he returned," he said.

"Aye, well, that's why I was skulking in the trees," Alex admitted. "I was hoping no' to be greeted as the new chieftain tonight."

"Ah," Kenneth said, a world of understanding perfectly expressed in that one syllable. "Well, if ye're willing, we can forget this wee meeting altogether. Ye'll no' be seen, for everyone's in bed. Everyone excepting your brothers. Angus'll no' be sleeping yet awhile. I've just come back from Inversnaid, and was away down the loch to wash myself."

"Inversnaid?" Alex said, suddenly alert. "What's amiss at Inversnaid?"

"Nothing's amiss. That's what I've been to find out. I took wee Angus wi' me, although he isna so wee any more. Will I look out for ye, to make sure no one else has thought to come out and sees ye?"

He glanced across, to see Alex smiling at him, the tears in his eyes sparkling in the moonlight.

"Christ, Kenneth, but I've missed ye," he said shakily. And then Kenneth, no longer uncertain, stepped forward and took him in his arms.

"We've all missed ye too, laddie. I'm sorry ye had to come home this way, but awfu' glad ye're here," he said. "Duncan's been a mighty fine chieftain in your stead. Away hame. I'll no' tell a soul I've seen ye, so no one'll ken ye're back until ye want them to."

"Thank ye," Alex said, and then Kenneth let him go. "I dinna think my ribs'll forget the wee meeting for a while though," he added, grinning, and then was gone.

Kenneth undressed, smiling, remembering Alex's reaction to the mention of Inversnaid.

Aye, ye'll be a fine chieftain, as I always kent ye would be, he thought. And then he plunged into the loch, to wash off the sweat and dirt. He no longer needed to wake up.

"We couldna see *anyone*, even after we lay at the top of the ben for *hours*. There was snow all the way down to the barracks, but we couldna even see a footprint either. I wanted to go down, and see if maybe they were all dead or had gone away, but Kenneth wouldna let me, for there was smoke coming from some of the chimneys," Angus said, munching on a bannock, while Duncan stood over the fire heating water to add to some whisky to warm his brother up.

"I'm thinking Kenneth wouldna have let ye anyway," Duncan said. "For there wasna any need to, and it's awfu' stupid to risk your life for nothing."

"Aye, he tellt me that, but—" Angus continued, and then stopped as the door suddenly opened and Alex walked in.

There was a moment of stunned silence as the two brothers stared in disbelief at their sibling, and then Angus let out a whoop of joy, and dropping his bannock on the floor leapt at his brother, driving him back against the now closed door with a thump.

"I canna believe it!" he cried. "Ye're home!"

"*Ist,* laddie," Alex said, returning the hug and trying not to wince. "The clan dinna ken I'm home yet." He looked over Angus's shoulder to Duncan, silhouetted against the firelight, holding a poker in his hand. "I dinna want them to, no' until the morrow."

Duncan nodded then.

"I'm thinking ye'll be wanting a bannock and a wee toddy then, if ye've just arrived," he said.

"That would be wonderful," Alex replied, gently disengaging himself from Angus and moving over to the *sèis,* where his youngest brother, after retrieving his bannock from the floor, immediately plopped down next to him.

"What have—" Angus began excitedly.

"Gie him a wee minute, Angus," Duncan interrupted. "We've all night to blether, I'm thinking," he added, aware that Angus would not let them sleep for hours yet, even if they felt inclined to.

"Aye. I met Kenneth by the loch, or rather my ribs did," Alex told them laughingly. "I was trying to sneak in wi' no one seeing me, but he caught me. He'll no' tell anyone though, so we've as long as we want together, if I dinna go outside."

"I'm so happy!" Angus said, leaning his head against Alex's shoulder.

He could lean his head against Alex's shoulder. Not his elbow, or his bicep, but his shoulder. Alex swallowed down the sudden lump in his throat. All that precious time missed that would never come back, wasted learning lots of things he'd never need.

"Christ, laddie, but ye've grown," he said.

"Aye. I'll be thirteen in April," Angus replied proudly. "Duncan says I'm going to be taller than Da! Ah, I'm sorry," he added. "I didna mean to mention Da."

"Dinna fash yourself. Ye've had three months to adapt to it. And he'd want us to talk about him. I want it too. I dinna want it to be like when Ma died," Alex said.

Duncan poured whisky then hot water into three cups and handed them out before pulling up a chair to sit opposite his brothers.

"When did ye get my letter?" he asked.

"No' till the end of January," Alex replied. "I'd been in Hanover wi' the nobleman, learning German, so that if I ever met yon German lairdie I'd be able to speak wi' him in his own tongue. As soon as I read it I set off for home, but it was awfu' difficult to get across the sea, for there was a storm at Calais and nothing was going in or out. So I had a wee bit of time there to come to terms wi' Da then. I finally came across wi' a band of smugglers. They were the only people willing to risk it."

"Did ye come to terms wi' it?" Duncan asked quietly.

"I thought I had, aye. No' wi' being chieftain – I havena a notion how I'll do that, but wi' Da being gone. But I realise now I havena, because when I walked through the door, I expected the three of ye to greet me, and there's an awfu' big space where he should be."

Angus wrapped his arm round Alex's waist, while Duncan watched him over his pewter cup. Alex had forgotten how comforting Angus's exuberant affection was, how calming Duncan's clear grey gaze was. He relaxed, just a little.

"Ye'll grow accustomed," Duncan said now. "It's no' like when Ma died. We'll never be like that wi' each other."

Alex smiled then.

"No," he said. "We never will be."

While they drank Duncan told Alex what had happened since he'd written the letter, about everything he'd done as the temporary chieftain, and how helpful Kenneth had been.

"In truth everyone's been helpful," he said. "For I hadna a notion what to do. They've been awfu' kind to me. But Kenneth has been amazing. He'd be a grand right-hand man, if ye ever needed one. No, I'm no' leaving," he added quickly, seeing Alex's sudden startled look.

"No, but he is—" Angus stopped, and flushed scarlet.

"He is what?" Alex asked, then looked at Duncan, who, to his surprise was blushing too. Duncan *never* blushed. He wiped his hand across his eyes, then glared at Angus.

"I wasna going to tell ye tonight," he said.

"Well whatever it is ye're going to have to now, for I willna rest until I ken," Alex told him.

"I've asked Màiri to marry me, and she said aye," Duncan admitted.

"Ah, but that's bonny news!" Alex cried. "Why were ye no' going to tell me?"

"I was, but no' the minute ye arrived. I thought I'd let ye settle in a wee bit first."

"I'm sorry," Angus said insincerely. "But he asked her months ago, and he hasna tellt *anyone*, and I've kent about it for *so* long! I thought I'd *die* keeping it a secret."

Alex looked at Angus, whose tone and face were deadly serious, and then at Duncan, whose expression was a mixture of irritation at Angus, joy at Alex's reaction to his news, and relief that he'd finally told someone. Then he started laughing, and standing, bringing Angus with him, he stepped across to embrace Duncan too.

"It's going to be all right," he said, as the three of them stood wrapped in each other's arms. "As long as we've got each other, we can do anything."

They stood like that for a while, both comforting and being comforted by each other, by the knowledge that nothing but death could break their bond, and maybe not even that.

It was a very good feeling.

They sat up half the night then, Alex giving them a brief but very personal view of his last three years in Paris and on his tour, sharing the parts he would not tell the clan when he held his first meeting as their new chieftain.

He told them about Beauregard, about the nobleman he'd met, although even to his brothers he did not reveal Highbury's name, nor even his title, for he'd promised the earl that he never would. He told them about the meeting with Charles, and the great impression the young prince had made on him. And he told them about his misgivings regarding James, and that if *he* ever made another attempt, king though he was, Alex would hold the clan back to see what happened.

"For while he might have the personality to be king, I dinna think he's a man who could inspire the clans to fight for him, and hold them together while they did," he admitted.

"But ye think Charles is," Duncan said.

"He seems to be, aye. He's certainly got magnetism, and the confidence and enthusiasm to go wi' it. He sees it as his purpose in life to regain the throne for his da. But he's only fifteen, and he hasna the experience of battle, though he's trying to get it."

"Fifteen," Angus said. "That's only two years older than me."

"Aye. Could ye imagine leading the clans in battle against yon German lairdie in two years?" Alex asked.

Angus shook his head.

"I couldna imagine leading *this* clan," he admitted. "Duncan's done a wonderful job, though. I've never seen him so busy. He didna sit and gaze at nothing for hours *at all!*"

"It's called thinking, ye wee gomerel," Duncan growled in mock anger. "Ye'd no' ken what that is."

"Well then, he didna think *at all*," Angus amended. "I thought ye'd need to think something powerful if ye're chieftain, but it seems he managed it without that. So maybe I could be chieftain one day. But I dinna want to be," he added.

Angus had either developed an incredibly dry sense of humour in the last three years, or was deadly serious. Alex started laughing, even as he felt a pang at the realisation that as well as learning how to be chieftain, he also had to learn how his youngest brother had changed since he was ten.

They continued talking, putting more peat on the fire, making another hot drink, trying to pack three years of experiences into a few hours.

"So when we get up in the morning, I'll show myself and call a clan meeting," Alex said. "Have ye been doing them up in the cave, or here?"

"In the cave, for the weather's been awfu' cold until last week," Duncan said. "I've tried to keep things as close to how Da did it as I could. I didna make changes, for I didna ken what ye'd want to do when ye came back, or how soon that would be. I thought that would be easier for ye."

"I dinna ken what I want to do, either," Alex admitted. "I'm thinking I'll keep everything the same until I've settled in again. But we should go to bed now, for I was walking all day, and I'm wanting to have my wits about me tomorrow."

"We can sleep as late as we want to," Angus said happily, yawning, "for no one kens ye're here."

That was true. It would be good to sleep under a roof, in a bed, with his brothers beside him.

He smiled, not just with his mouth, but with his heart.

"I canna believe I agreed to do this," Alex moaned a few minutes later. "Ye were a wee bairn last time!" Duncan was in the box bed, pressed uncomfortably up against the back of it, Alex lying next to him, while Angus sat on the edge trying to work out how to fit his body into the six inches of space left.

"We didna agree to do this," Duncan pointed out.

"But we *have* to," Angus reasoned. "It's a tradition! Whenever we've been apart for a long time, we *have* to sleep together on the first night. And we'll no' be able to do it when Duncan's married, for he'll be sleeping wi' Màiri then, so this will be the last time!"

"Thank God for that," Alex said, groaning as Angus pushed his way into the bed, his elbow driving into the exact spot where Kenneth had crushed his ribs a few hours previously. "I'll no' get a wink of sleep the night, after all."

"See! I tellt ye we could do it!" Angus said triumphantly, leaning over to blow out the candle before overbalancing and landing on the floor with a thud.

The next day, although Alex felt he'd hardly slept at all, between waking up choking to find his mouth full of Angus's hair, carefully shifting position to ease his cramped muscles from being crushed between two bodies, and waking up every time Angus fell out, as he ate his breakfast porridge and prepared himself for the day ahead, he felt more awake, and very much happier than he had in months.

He had dreaded this day, had worried endlessly about it ever since he'd read that terrible letter, but now that it was finally here he found that, in a strange way, he was looking forward to it. It was his destiny after all, to lead the clan. Just as it was Charles's destiny to one day lead the Jacobite army.

He was home, where he belonged, and where he would stay for the rest of his life, he hoped.

And he had his brothers beside him. And Kenneth, too.

He could do this, and he would do it well. He would put everything of himself into it. Everything was as it should be. He was ready.

Or he thought he was ready, but after his third drink and second bowl of porridge, he realised that although he *was* hungry, having not eaten properly for days, the only reason he was ridiculously considering a third bowl although he was already full was because he was looking for reasons to delay announcing his presence to the clan, to having to become a different person.

Last night had been wonderful, sitting with his brothers chatting, being intimate in the way you could only be with people you'd known and loved forever. He would never be able to be whatever a chieftain was with them, he realised, or not fully, anyway. But when he thought about it, Da had been different with Ma to how he was with the clan. He remembered lying in bed as a child, listening to their voices as they murmured in the boxbed, sometimes hearing the words too. His da had confided in his ma, had shown his vulnerability to her as he had not to anyone else, not even his children.

Alex hadn't understood that as a child, but remembering now, as he prepared for this new phase of his life, he realised with a great surge of relief that he did not have to become remote from his brothers, to stand alone, as he'd always believed he would have to – as his da had in fact told him he would have to.

It was that more than anything he had been worried about, he now realised; never to be able to share his doubts, his vulnerabilities with *anyone,* no matter how much he was struggling. He did not have to do that. Even his father, who he had admired more than anyone, had not done that. And when he'd tried to, after Moira died, he had become a m onster.

He would never become a monster; he would *always* be able to show all of himself to Duncan, and to Angus too when he was just a wee bit older. They would not judge him for it, would not think him weak, would not challenge his authority because he confided in them, because he trusted them.

"Why are ye grinning to yourself like a loon?" Duncan asked, breaking into his thoughts.

"Am I?" Alex said. "I was just thinking it's maybe time to call the clan to the cave."

"Oh, that's a shame," Angus said. "Duncan tellt me to leave ye alone to prepare yourself, and we just had a wager to see how many bowls of porridge ye'd eat before ye finally decided to go outside. I said four."

"Aye, well, I said three, so we've neither of us won," Duncan pointed out.

"I'm thinking that—" Alex began, and then the door opened and Màiri walked in.

"I kent ye'd both be awake by now, for it's late..." she said, and then her voice trailed off as she realised she was not addressing two, but three people. "Holy Mother of God," she breathed. "I'm sorry," she added, flushing scarlet. "I'll away and—"

"No," Alex said. "Come in and sit down, for Duncan's tellt me your news, and I'm wanting to speak wi' ye both before I tell everyone I'm home."

She moved into the room hesitantly.

"When did ye get back?" she asked.

"Last night," he replied. "Màiri, I'm no' unhappy that ye're marrying. I'm overjoyed, in fact. I canna think of a better match for Duncan than yourself. Or a better sister for me and Angus."

Màiri let out a great sigh of relief then, and sat down on a stool Duncan had brought across for her.

"Did ye think I wouldna be happy?" Alex asked.

"In truth I didna ken," she admitted. "Duncan said ye'd be happy for us, but I dinna really ken ye well enough to be sure."

"We'll have to remedy that," Alex said, leaning across and taking her hands in his. "Ye have my blessing, both of ye. He tellt me he wrote a letter to me, that he tellt Da the day before he died, and that Da was going to call a meeting to announce it."

"Aye, he did. But Duncan didna feel right to send ye the both letters, and we were going to wait until ye came home before we married anyway, and then there was never a time when it felt right to announce it, somehow," she said. "I'm awfu' glad you're home, Alex!" she added, smiling.

By God, but she was bonny, Alex thought, smiling back at her. He'd never noticed just how beautiful she was. He suddenly felt a great wave of joy wash over him, as he realised his first task as chieftain was going to be to announce a wedding to the clan, and such a perfect match. What a wonderful way to start his leadership! And thinking on that...

"Duncan, sit down a minute too, for I'm wanting to ask ye something. Ye tellt me Da said he'd look for a good tree for roof timbers, and then build ye a wee house in the spring, and then ye'd marry as soon as I got home, in the summer."

"Aye, but that was before everything changed," Duncan said, sitting next to Màiri.

"So what I was thinking is, were ye waiting until the summer for any other reason than for me to come home?" Alex asked.

"No," Duncan admitted, and then both of them flushed a little.

"Good. For I'm thinking the trees are bare now, so we can find a roof timber, and then build a house the minute the weather's good enough to. And I'm home now, so ye can marry whenever ye want."

Duncan and Màiri looked at each other.

"But...we thought ye'd need time to grieve for your da, and to become the chieftain first," Màiri said.

"I do need time to do that, I'll no' deny it. But I canna think of a better way to start my life as the chieftain than by telling the clan that my right-hand man is going to marry, and then planning for it! I havena had as long to accept it as you have," he admitted, "for I didna ken he'd died until the end of January. But I wouldna keep ye from marrying while I sit about grieving. Da wouldna want that either. He was happy wi' the match and so am I, so wi' your permission I'll announce that you're betrothed today, and then we can maybe have a wee ceilidh to celebrate both that and me coming home. I canna think of a better way to settle in. But if ye dinna want to, then I'll wait until ye're ready."

"I've been ready since the moment she said aye," Duncan admitted.

"I've been ready since the moment ye asked me, even before that," Màiri said.

"Good. Ye've just given me a reason to delay telling the clan I'm home for another few minutes," Alex said. "Angus, get the claret out, will ye? Let's have a wee toast."

"Ye dinna want another two bowls of porridge?" Angus asked hopefully.

"No, I dinna, ye wee gomerel," Alex said. "When we've drunk the toast, we'll call the clan to the cave. And then ye can decide when ye want to marry, and when ye have, we'll set the date, and see if we can find a priest to marry ye. If we canna, ye'll need to decide if ye'll accept a handfasting."

"Aye, we will," Màiri said immediately, "for it's a legal wedding and I dinna want to wait any longer than we have to."

"I'm awfu' glad we dinna have to wait until summer," Duncan said.

"Aye, they said they canna be alone together in Susan's. I thought they'd want to be alone to talk, but they dinna, it seems," Angus said innocently. "But they can be alone at the loch. I've seen them there many a time."

Duncan and Màiri both flushed crimson at this and Alex nearly spilt the wine he was pouring into four cups.

"Who tellt ye that?" he asked, trying not to laugh, and failing.

"Duncan did. Well, he didna tell me, he tellt Màiri when I was in the next room," Angus explained. "He said, 'I'll be awfu' glad when we're wed and can be alone together, and I dinna have to leave every time Susan goes out'. So I'm thinking it'll be a lot easier for them, for if it's raining they'll be able to sit together anywhere they want, no' just by the loch."

How could he have forgotten how wonderful it was to be home? Chieftain or not, this was where he belonged. He would never become a spy, never have to live in England with cold-blooded pompous aristocrats. He could not imagine how he had ever thought he could do such a ridiculous thing. He must have gone daft in the head.

He handed the wine to his three companions.

"To being home, and new beginnings. Happy new beginnings," he said. "*Sláinte!*"

They raised their cups and drank, and then Màiri and Duncan set out to call a clan meeting, while Alex, who until now had been dressed only in his shirt, donned his *féileadh mór,* and prepared himself for his first speech as chieftain of the Loch Lomond MacGregors.

He was home, where he belonged, the only place he could feel whole. And, God willing, he would never leave again.

CHAPTER TWO

"Aye, THAT'LL DO FINE," Allan said, looking up to the top of the tree and then quickly down again, immediately white-faced.

"Ye dinna need to do this now, man," Alex said, feeling as light-headed and queasy as Allan, although he was doing his best not to show it.

Allan looked up again, clearly measuring the roof timbers he could see contained in the tree's trunk, and then sat down suddenly on a nearby rock.

"Aye, I'm thinking ye've the right of it," he admitted. "It was a fine ceilidh, though."

It had indeed been a fine ceilidh. The whole clan had shown such unfeigned pleasure at having their new chieftain back with them that Alex had found himself relaxing, even almost enjoying his first clan meeting as their leader.

He had told them a little about his time in Europe, in particular his meeting with Prince Charles, but had cut short any debate about possible future scenarios, saying that there were more immediate things to discuss – as the prince was only fifteen, it would be some time before he did make any attempt on the crown, if ever.

And then, as everyone had been so very welcoming, he had decided, on the spur of the moment, to be an honest chieftain. He would be ruthless when he needed to be, as all leaders were at times, and commanding too, when the occasion called for it. But he also wanted to be fair-minded and approachable. He had no desire to be a leader that his people were afraid of. He wanted respect, yes, hoped to earn it. But never fear, not unless they'd done something to be fearful about.

So he had spoken honestly with them, had told them that he had no idea how to be a chieftain, but then Duncan hadn't either, but had made a good job of it anyway. Everyone had agreed with this, to Duncan's embarrassed pleasure.

"I'm wanting to be the manner of chieftain my da was," he'd said then, "for I'm thinking he was a good man, and a fair one. I canna be exactly like him, for I'm no' the same person, although I'm sure ye all ken I tried to be, for many years!"

The older members, who remembered his childish attempts to mirror Alexander had all laughed then, which Alex had taken as a good sign. They were relaxed with him. They would not be afraid to give him suggestions or advice if he needed it.

He also needed them to obey him without question when the occasion called for it. That was something that would come, once he had proved himself as a leader. And that would be the hard part.

But it was not something he could achieve in his first clan meeting. It would take time. So he pushed that thought to one side for now.

"I promise ye now, I'll be the best chieftain I can be, and I've a fine right-hand man to help me," he continued. "But there's one thing I want *you* to promise *me*."

He waited until he was sure he had their attention, and that they realised he was being serious now.

"I remember well the way my da was after Ma died," he said.

"Ye suffered the most for it," Barbara said, and others murmured agreement.

"No, I didna. Aye, I suffered for it, and my brothers too. But ye all suffered, for in his grief he lost the ability to lead the clan. Alasdair spends his days in constant pain because of a pointless raid that Da never should have led ye on. He was the best chieftain imaginable, but in grief he became a tyrant, and none of ye felt ye could tell him so. So I'm wanting ye all to promise me now – if I ever become unfit to lead ye, tell me. All of ye together, if I willna listen to reason."

"I'll tell ye," Duncan said softly.

"So will I, when I'm old enough to," Angus added.

Alex smiled.

"Aye, I ken ye will, and I'm glad of it. But I dinna want ye ever to fear me in the way ye did Da. I need ye to follow me from respect, and because I deserve to be followed. I need ye to fear me if ye've done wrong and deserve my anger. I dinna need ye to fear me because I've lost my way and am putting ye all in danger."

A silence had fallen on the clan for a few moments then as they all absorbed this speech, as they all realised that, as good a chieftain as Alexander had been, his son already seemed on course to better him.

"I'm thinking ye'll never be like your da in that way, laddie," Kenneth said finally. "But if ye ever are, then I'll no' let ye take us on a raid like the one ye're talking about. I'm thinking none of us will, now ye've tellt us that's what ye want."

"Thank ye, Kenneth. I'll hold ye to that," Alex told him gratefully.

"He'll likely be the only man who can," Susan added. "Ye've grown again while ye were away. Ye're a lot taller than your da now, and broader too."

Was he? It was true he'd been an inch or two taller than Alexander three years ago, the last time he'd been home. But he didn't realise he'd grown even more.

"Ah, well. I might be taller and broader, but I couldna practice the fighting while I was travelling wi' yon nobleman," he said, pushing away the memory of the duel and how effortlessly he'd amputated the fool Joseph's hand. He had not decided which parts of his travels he was going to share with the clan yet. And no Highlander worth his salt would be proud of beating such an inept foe anyway. Beating him had been no great achievement. "Tomorrow I'm hoping to have Kenneth start to bring me up to standard again. But first of all, I've some bonny news to share wi' ye. Or rather Duncan and Màiri have. Ye tell them," he'd continued.

They had, standing hand in hand, and the whole clan, who had been wondering when they were going to declare the news everyone had been expecting to hear for at least a year, cheered. And then cheered again when Alex had announced a wee ceilidh, wi' claret and whisky and whatever food they could summon up, to celebrate both his being home and the prospect of an imminent wedding.

But now, sitting next to the ashen-faced Allan, Alex realised that there was no way on earth he would be able to practice his fighting skills today. His head was banging like a drum with every move, and even the thought of food made him want to vomit.

It had been a wonderful ceilidh though. Alasdair played the fiddle and Dugald the pipes. The old man was now teaching his grandson to play the fiddle, and he hoped one day to be as good as his grandda, but said he wouldna inflict himself on the clan as yet.

They had sung, and danced, laughed and joked, and drank.

My God, had they drank. Alex closed his eyes for a moment, then opened them again rapidly as the world tilted on its axis. Kenneth and Jeannie had danced together most of the night, and Kenneth had surely drunk a good deal of whisky. Hopefully he wouldn't be wanting to fight, either.

"Let's give it up for today, man," he said to Allan then. "We've found the right tree. Duncan and Màiri'll no' die if they have to wait an extra day for the house, but I might if I have to help ye cut yon tree down."

Allan laughed and then clutched his head, and in mutual agreement they abandoned the chore and went home.

When he got home Susan and Màiri were there, having just finished clearing away the remains of the previous night's revels. They looked annoyingly healthy, and Angus, who Alex *knew* had imbibed a good deal of alcohol, was positively bursting with vitality.

Alex went and sat down on the *sèis* next to Duncan, who at least had the decency to look as fragile as Alex felt. He was taking sips from a cup, in which was a clear liquid. Alex observed it with interest.

"It's a cure for surfeits," Susan said, observing Alex's pallor with amusement. "I'm thinking there'll be no tree felling today then."

"No, but we'll make a start tomorrow, I promise," Alex replied. "What's in it? It doesna smell of anything."

"I'll make one for ye now," Susan replied, causing Màiri to giggle. Alex looked up suspiciously as Susan brought a cup over to him.

"Dinna fash yerself. I'm no' going to poison the chieftain," she joked. "It's water."

"Water? Is that all?"

"Aye. When I was in Edinburgh I used to take a long time making some cordial wi' all manner of things in, brandy, poppies, mint, wood betony, figs...I canna remember the rest. It took hours, and then it had to stand for a fortnight. But I found that drinking as much water as ye can has just the same effect, without all the effort. In Edinburgh I used to put a few wee leaves in so they'd believe it was medicine, and they'd tell me it was powerful good. And then as soon as ye can, eat a bannock to settle the stomach."

"I'm feeling a wee bit better, after three cups," Duncan admitted. "I havena managed a bannock yet, though."

"I've had three," Angus said brightly. "Màiri made them."

"How many cups of water has he had?" Alex asked, sipping from his cup. His stomach grumbled, then settled.

"I havena had any. I felt good this morning. Well, I had some wi' the bannocks, but I always do," Angus told him. "Ye look dreadful," he added helpfully.

"Would ye help me fetch some more water from the loch, Angus?" Màiri asked, seeing that neither of the brothers were appreciating Angus's glowing health and energy at the minute.

"I canna understand it," Alex said when his brother had departed. "I saw him drink most of a bottle of claret myself, and he's no' thirteen yet. I thought he'd be in bed the whole day!"

"It didna seem to affect him at all," Susan said. "I was watching ye all. I'm thinking ye'll no' want to be drinking quite as much at your wedding as ye did last night, Duncan."

"I'm thinking I'll never want to be drinking again, at the minute," Duncan admitted.

"Ah, we all say that. Keep drinking the water. Ye'll be much better in a while. I'll make some more bannocks for when ye are."

Although Alex and Duncan were initially sceptical about the effectiveness of mere water in curing such powerful sickness, by the afternoon they were both feeling a lot better. Much better than they had after previous drinking sessions. As it was too late to make a start on the tree, instead the three of them rowed across the loch to Inchcailloch Island, where Alexander was buried. It was something Alex felt he needed to do.

In his head he knew his da was dead, but even so, every time the door opened he expected Alexander to walk through it. When he came down the ladder from the roofspace where the three of them slept, he half expected to see his da sitting by the fire. In the clan meeting, at times he'd felt like an impostor, expecting Alexander to walk in and ask him what he was doing.

He thought that seeing the grave would help him to truly accept his father was dead, and not just away on a raid or a visit to another clan. He'd intended to go to the island on his own, but when his brothers had offered to accompany him, he'd agreed.

Now he was very glad he had, because on seeing the bare mound of earth currently topped only by a simple wooden cross until the ground settled, when they would erect a stone, the stark truth of it hit him like a hammer blow. Underneath that mound of earth lay his father, cold and dead. The warm loving man whose arm he could still feel across his shoulders, heavy and comforting as they had sat by the loch together, the memory of which had helped to sustain him through the last three years, was gone. He would never hear his laugh again, never hear him tell his fireside tales, full of humour, never see him again. Never.

Then the grief felled him, and he dropped to his knees at the side of the grave, not in reverence as strangers might have thought, but because his legs were suddenly unable to take his weight.

He braced his hands on the ground, bowing his head and gasping for breath as he fought the wave of unbearable grief and despair that washed over him. His brothers, who were not strangers and knew what was happening, moved to his side and knelt down next to him, sheltering him from the icy wind with their bodies and comforting him as he lost his fight for mastery, sobbing and moaning like a man possessed.

In his room in Paris he had been aware that others might hear him; on the coach, the ship, and the final walk home he had known he could not let emotion take him, as he had to have his wits about him. Even with Highbury, who he trusted implicitly, he had not been able to show his grief as openly as he did now. Since he'd arrived home the grief had been abated by his joy at seeing his brothers, and then his need to make a good first impression with the clan.

Now, with the two people who understood him completely, loved him completely, he could, finally, let it all out, to his utter, utter relief.

He had no idea how long he knelt there with his brothers. He only knew that when at last he came back to himself it was dark, the sky was sprinkled with stars, and the wind had died down a little, although it was still bitterly cold.

He sat back on his haunches then, wiping his face with his hands, after which Angus moved away a little and sat down on the grass, hugging his knees, while Duncan pulled his plaid over his head against the chill. He did not apologise for his outburst as he would have done with anyone else. There was no need for that here.

"Ye've accepted it now, then," Duncan said softly after a while.

"Aye," Alex said. "I have. I needed to do this. And I needed ye with me."

"We kent that," Angus told him. "That's why we wanted to come wi' ye. We saw him when…we saw him. But ye didna. I went in to wake him in the morning, and I didna want to see him later, for I kent that once I did, I'd have to believe he was gone. It was Kenneth who tellt me I needed to do it, and so Duncan came in wi' me. I dinna think I could have done it without him. So we wanted ye to have us wi' ye too."

They sat there a while longer, just being there with their father, although he was no longer there, or not in the way they wanted him to be, and never would be again.

"I'm ready now," Alex murmured, almost to himself, and Duncan and Angus nodded, and standing, they made their way along the track back to the boat.

And then they rowed back across the loch, Angus swallowing fiercely as they did, and walked home in silence, but not alone.

Never alone, while they had each other. Their mother had given them that, and their father too, although some of the ways he had helped them to bond were not ways he would have been proud of, and not ways that they would have wished for.

But nevertheless, bonded they were, for life. And that felt very good indeed, salving Alex's grief, and giving him the courage to face whatever lay ahead.

Late March, 1737

The clan stood around the finished house, admiring the drystone walls and heather-covered roof, its flue positioned in the centre to allow the peat smoke to escape. It had two windows and a perfectly fitted door in the middle, thanks to Allan's carpentry skills. Outside was a wooden bench, where the couple would be able to sit of an evening stargazing, something both of the intended occupants loved to do.

"Oh, it's beautiful!" Màiri cried, clapping her hands together with joy.

"It isna finished yet," Alex said.

"No' inside, but the outside is," Duncan replied.

"No' quite. I'm away to Glasgow in a few days, to pick up any mail and learn of any news, and I'll bring back my wedding present to ye."

"I thought the house was your wedding present," Duncan said.

"No, that was Da's present. Ye tellt me that yerself."

"Aye, but as ye're the chieftain now, it's your present instead," Màiri said.

"And a bonny present it is, too," Barbara added.

"No, the house will be Da's last present to ye. I'd no' take that away from him," Alex insisted. "My present will be glass for the two windows."

"Real glass?" Màiri cried, eyes sparkling. "But will that no' be awfu' expensive?"

"My brother will only be married the once," Alex said. "Yon nobleman paid for my travels, and I had the money to live in Paris until June but came back early, so I've a wee bit to spare."

Duncan opened his mouth to object, but Alex held his hand up, his first, if unconscious, authoritarian gesture since he'd become chieftain.

"I'm wanting to buy ye a bonny present," he said. "For ye've done a wonderful job as chieftain while I was away, and I couldna be happier wi' your choice of wife. I didna ken what to get ye until yesterday when I saw Allan putting in the wee frames."

"Will I be needing to make wee bars for the panes to sit in?" Allan asked.

"Aye, but no' till I'm back, for I havena a notion of the sizes of panes of glass. It isna something I've ever had to think about."

"Ye'll have looked out of yon glazed windows though, I'm thinking," Simon commented. "When ye were wi' yon nobleman. What was his name?"

"Aye, I did, but I didna measure them! I even had a window in my wee room in Paris, although I'd have done better wi' a few peats to block it, for the view wasna worth looking at and the wind blew so hard through it I had to put stones on my essays to stop them blowing round the room at times," Alex remarked. "Ye'll be wanting furniture for the inside now," he finished.

"I'm helping Allan make a boxbed for them, and some kists," Angus said. "But I've my own present that I'm making. Allan will help me wi' it. It's a secret," he added after a moment, as everyone was looking at him expectantly.

"Will we leave ye to go inside and plan what ye want and where it'll go?" Susan suggested. The happy looks on the faces of the lovers gave them their answer, and everyone set off for home, pleased with the week's work, for it was a bonny cottage and everyone was providing something for it, so it would be ready to live in within a couple of weeks, although the date for the actual wedding had still not been fixed.

Once inside Duncan and Màiri waited for a few minutes, until they were sure that everyone had gone and no one was about to come in with a furnishing suggestion, and then Màiri grinned from ear to ear and let out a cry of unutterable joy. Duncan reached across and embraced her, and the two of them stood in the middle of the room for a few minutes, just enjoying the wonder of being so very much in love, and of being alone, in their own home.

Their own home.

"It feels real now, finally," he murmured into her hair.

"It does!" she said. "I canna believe it! I think I'll die of happiness."

"No, ye willna!" Duncan said sternly, feeling a stirring down below and willing it to subside. "I feel as though I've waited half my life to be your husband. Ye'll have to contain yourself, at least until after the wedding night."

She laughed then. Such a beautiful, joyous laugh she had, and he held her even tighter, overwhelmed by love for her.

"Will we set the date?" he asked. "Or are ye wanting to wait until we can find a priest?"

She wriggled a little then, because his embrace, while wonderful, was so tight as to be almost painful, making it impossible to hold a conversation, which this was clearly about to become. He let her go reluctantly, and they sat down on the only items of furniture they currently possessed, two small stools placed around where the fire would be.

"By the way ye are now, it wouldna be fair to ask ye to wait any longer than we have to," she observed, grinning. "And I'm wanting to spend a lot of time in here wi' ye, making it cosy for when we're wed, without a chaperon."

"I can control myself," he said indignantly. "I respect ye. Ye can trust me."

"I ken that, ye loon," she replied. "It's myself I dinna trust. I'm wanting to be with ye so badly, I canna bear it. When d'ye think Alex will allow it? Wi' your Da dying, I mean. I dinna want to set a date before he's ready, for as ye said, we've had more time to grieve than he has."

"If ye're happy wi' a handfasting, we can marry as soon as we're wanting to," Duncan told her. "We went to Da's grave last week, and when we got back and Angus was in bed, Alex tellt me he was ready now, and he didna want us to delay the wedding due to him, or due to Da, for he doesna think Da would want us to wait any more, or be miserable. He'd want us to go on wi' our lives, as it should be."

"Even though he couldna do it himself?" Màiri asked.

"Even more because of that, I'm thinking. When he came back to himself, he was awfu' sad that he'd missed so much of our growing, that he'd almost lost us – me and Alex at any rate. He wasted years grieving, and he kent that Ma wouldna have wanted it that way. She would have been horrified."

"Did your da tell ye that?" Màiri asked. She had always been a little fearful of Alexander, her first impression of him as an aggressive tyrant never quite being erased by his later mellowing.

"Aye. I was sitting by the loch one night, while Alex was still in Edinburgh, and he came down there and sat wi' me. He apologised for what he'd done, and tellt me what I just tellt you. I never spoke of it till now, for it was private. But he loved ye, and I dinna think he'd mind ye knowing. No' the now, anyway."

"He loved me?" Màiri asked, feeling suddenly ashamed of her fear of the formidable man.

"Aye. He tellt me he couldna imagine a better wife than yourself for me, and that he thought we'd love each other as he and Ma did."

Màiri smiled at this, for although she'd never witnessed the love between the former chieftain and his wife, it was almost legendary in the clan.

"I wouldna have ye become as he did, if anything—" she began.

"*Ist,*" he interrupted. "Nothing's going to happen."

"No, but..."

"If it does, I willna become as he did. But it willna be for many a year, and we'll have our bairns, and their bairns to comfort whichever of us dies first," he said. "I dinna want to talk of such things. This is a happy day."

He was right, it was. The *happiest* day, except for the one they needed to set.

"Will we marry next month, then?" she suggested shyly.

"It's almost next month now," he said.

"Aye, I ken. But I'm thinking we'll have all the furniture we need then. And I canna wait much longer!" she finished a little desperately.

"April," he said in wonder, as though it was the most beautiful word in the world. "Aye, that'll be bonny."

She stood then, and coming over to him plopped herself down on his knee, almost overbalancing him in the process. The stirring down below, which had started to subside, now became alarming, causing Màiri to laugh, and then blush crimson.

"I'm thinking...that is...if ye want to...we could..." she said hesitantly, looking round the room.

"I thought ye wanted to wait," Duncan said.

"I did, but only because I didna want to face the priest, or the clan, wi' a swollen belly on my wedding day. But Alex is home, and even if we marry on the last day of April I wouldna be showing, even if I got wi' child immediately."

"That's true," Duncan said, fighting to maintain his composure, because he had never wanted anything so much as to make love to the beautiful woman sitting on his lap. "But fornication is a sin."

"We could declare ourselves man and wife now, could we no'?" Màiri said, putting her arms round his neck. "Then it wouldna be a sin, would it?"

Every nerve in Duncan's body was on fire. He thought he would die if he didn't take her, right now. Her lips were so close to his, and she was so warm, so willing, and he wanted her so very badly. The words of agreement to this proposal filled his mind, and then his mouth. But ...

"Aye, it would," he said in a strangled voice, "for it isna official unless we declare it publicly. And I want our first time to be beautiful, in a bed wi' a mattress and new white linen sheets, wi' wine, and maybe cakes. No' rutting on the floor. It wouldna be right. I love ye too much for that," he added, although right now he was so close to dragging her down onto the dirt floor that he very likely would have done if she had stayed on his knee for much longer, and *definitely* would have done had she kissed him, as she had clearly intended to do before his little speech.

But she sighed, and then stood and moved back to the stool, and the moment passed, although his erection did not, causing him to squirm uncomfortably for what seemed forever, while she told him he was right in a sad little voice, and then asked him if he thought her a harlot.

"What? No, never! Ye love me, as I love you, and I'm thinking if we had the bed and the wine and such, I wouldna give a fig for the sin of it, in truth. But I want us to remember our first time, for I think it's a powerful thing when it's done wi' love. And I want it to be a wonderful memory. I swear no' to come to my marriage bed drunken, for I want to remember every minute of it."

He drew his dirk then, and when she realised what he was about to do, she reached across and put her hand over his.

"No. Ye dinna need to swear on the iron. No' wi' me. I trust ye wi' my life, and I have done since the day I first met ye, when ye came to us even though ye could hardly walk, and all for Angus's sake. I think I've loved ye since then as well, for I'd never seen such love and loyalty as there was between you and your brother in my life until that moment. I can wait another few weeks. And I trust your word, without the swearing. I'll come to our bed sober too. And ye've the right of it," she sighed. "It'll be awfu' bonny in a bed, wi' wine and cakes, and a fire burning, and the room warm. We've waited for months, after all.

"Well then, shall we talk about the furnishings we're wanting, and see what we'll need? Susan gave me some coins, and I'm thinking if Alex is going to Glasgow, he can maybe buy us a few wee things that we canna make ourselves."

And so the conversation turned away from passion to practical matters, although their thoughts did not, and it took both of them some time to find sleep that night. In their own separate beds, at opposite ends of the settlement.

Which was just as well, because even the most sensible nineteen-year-olds only have *so* much willpower, after all.

Although Duncan would not admit it to Màiri, there was another reason why he'd been reluctant to make love to her immediately. While he knew the mechanics of sex, having seen many animals copulate, and heard many people, as was inevitable in clan life, he wanted his first experience with Màiri to be a beautiful one, not a fumbling inept farce. True, it would be wonderful to learn about each other's bodies together, for she was as virgin as he was, but he wanted to have at least *some* notion of how to make the first time perfect for her.

So it was that a couple of nights later as the three brothers lay in bed, Angus snoring softly on his mattress, Duncan was awake, his mind full of plans and thoughts. And then it suddenly came to him that there was one person who he could ask, someone he trusted implicitly who might be able to help. He listened closely for a minute, screwing up his courage, then got off his mattress and made his way silently to the box bed where Alex slept.

"Are ye asleep?" he whispered, thinking that if he got no answer he'd just do the best he could in April.

There was the sound of movement and then Alex spoke, a little drowsily.

"No. What's amiss?"

"There's nothing amiss," Duncan whispered. "I just wanted to ask ye something."

"Now?"

"Aye. I dinna want Angus to hear, or anyone to walk in on us," Duncan explained.

As rarely an hour went by without someone walking in on them or Angus not being there, because spring was coming and there was a lot to plan and do, as well as the imminent wedding feast, Alex sat up, listening, as Duncan had a moment before. Angus was definitely asleep.

"What are ye wanting to ask me?" Alex whispered.

"When ye were in France, or the other countries, did ye ever...did ye ever go wi' a woman?" Duncan asked.

"What?" Alex exclaimed, and then lowered his voice again. "Sorry, I didna expect that question! Why do ye want to ken that?"

"I thought ye might have met a harlot, as ye were in big cities for much of the time. I saw them in Edinburgh when we were there wi' Da, and in Crieff, so I thought ye might have...learnt something."

Alex was silent for a minute, then he swung his legs out of bed.

"Let's away downstairs," he murmured.

Downstairs they made up the fire a little, then sat on the *sèis*.

"Are ye wanting to know how to please Màiri on your wedding night?" Alex asked.

"Aye. I couldna ask any of the other men."

"Ye maybe could. After all, most of them were virgin on their wedding nights, I'd think. Or if no' on the actual night, on the first time they made love with their women, likely up at the shielings. It isna easy finding a willing woman in the clan to learn from, after all!"

"Aye, but I've never heard of any of them asking someone wi' experience for advice," Duncan said. "And if they did, it'd be their da they asked."

This was true. Alexander had never told any of his sons about sex, probably because they were too young before Moira died, and afterwards, even when he recovered, Alexander would not have been able to bear talking about something so intimate.

Alex rubbed his eyes to wake himself up.

"I was wi' two prostitutes," he said then. "One was a friend. She accosted me on the street in Paris when I'd just gone back from here, and we were both awfu' lonely, so I went back to her room. I didna swive her though, we just talked, and then we became friends, so I wouldna."

"Oh," Duncan said.

"But on the night before I left to go on yon 'grand tour' she tellt me she wanted to teach me how to please a woman. She was very insistent. And she was a bonny lass. And then when I was in Rome I went to an expensive whorehouse wi' some noble gomerels who treated the ladies like shite, so I didna want to do that, and tellt her so. And she taught me some more things, because she was a very different sort of whore to Jeanne."

"Was it bonny?" Duncan asked.

"God, aye. It felt wonderful. But it was a business arrangement, no' an emotional one. I would think it'll be a different thing altogether when ye do it wi' the lassie ye love. That must be a wondrous thing. I'm thinking you and Màiri will make the night memorable, even if I dinna tell ye anything of what I learnt."

"Aye, maybe, but as ye *have* learnt things, I'd like to hear them, for maybe it'll make it even more memorable, and I'll relax more too, for being the man I've to take the lead, and I havena a notion what to do," Duncan admitted.

"Aye, ye need to relax, or ye'll no' be able to do the act at all!" Alex said.

"I dinna think I'll have any problem wi' that," Duncan said. "I spend most of my time wi' her praying she'll no' see it. She's awfu' observant."

Alex laughed out loud then.

"Ye're waiting then, until the wedding night," he said.

"Aye. We're wanting to do it in a bed, wi' fresh linen and cakes and wine and suchlike. And I'm no' going to drink like I did the other night. I want to remember our first night."

"Ye might want to have one drink, just to relax ye a wee bit," Alex advised. "For though your prick's misbehaving now, it willna if you're nervous. Dinna think about trying to be an expert. Just enjoy each other."

"We will, but I'll relax more if I ken a few ways to make her feel happy and relaxed," Duncan said.

"Aye, well, I'll tell ye a few, and then we'll need to sleep, for there's a lot to do tomorrow, and the day after I'm away to Glasgow. If I think on more things I'll tell ye later, when we're alone. So, both the ladies tellt me that men usually focus on their breasts and their quim, because those are the parts that excite them. But it can make lassies feel like objects, so ye should caress *all* of their body, to show them that ye love every inch of them. And there are some parts that arouse a lassie more than others, although no' all lassies are exactly the same. Here, I'll show ye," Alex said. "It's easier than telling ye."

Angus, who had woken up just in time to hear the last sentence his brothers had whispered before going downstairs, cursed silently. He was lying at the opening of the ladder and could hear almost every word, but couldn't actually *see* his brothers. If he could see them, he'd reasoned, they'd be able to see him, which he absolutely didn't want.

But if he wanted to know more, he had to take the chance. He wriggled forward silently and very slowly until he could see them, then froze, knowing that if he stayed still he should remain unseen.

Alex had lifted Duncan's hair and was stroking his fingers down from behind his ear to his neck.

"Ye have to do it gently, and it drives some lassies mad, but it's awfu' tender too. Ye must always be gentle wi' them, the whores said. A lot of lassies like ye to kiss their ears, and suck their earlobes. I'm no' going to do that to ye though! And then a lot of lassies like to have their hair brushed too."

"What, like Ma used to do for us?" Duncan said.

"Aye. Wi' us it was comforting, and made us feel loved, cared for," Alex said, his eyes misty with memory. "I'm thinking it's maybe the same if a man does it wi' his wife, but more so, and maybe in a different way. Jeanne and Isabella both tellt me that lovemaking is about letting the lassie ken that ye love her, so ye need to take your time, and pleasure her, and then ye can teach her to pleasure you later, and she'll love ye all the more for it. She willna think ye just want to pleasure yourself, and that's the most important thing."

"What else do ye ken?" Duncan asked.

The two continued, Alex touching Duncan on various parts of his body, the pair of them alternating between being serious and giggling.

"Well, then," Alex said after a short time of this, "I'm thinking we should away to our beds. Ye've learnt enough for your first night."

They both stood and Alex leaned over to smoor the fire, while Angus shuffled back to bed, trying to calm his breathing so they wouldn't suspect he might have heard them. Just listening to them and watching them had given him an erection, which felt shameful somehow, because they were his brothers. It would be wonderful to do that to a lassie though, and feel her hands all over your body too!

He turned over and tried to think about something else as Alex and Duncan came back up the stairs and went to bed.

"I was thinking to ask Kenneth, before I thought ye might have had some experience in France," Duncan admitted softly as they settled down. "I can ask him almost anything, but I dinna ken what I'd have done if he'd shown me like ye just did!" A quickly stifled peal of laughter came from the bed, then they were both giggling like little children as they imagined Kenneth stroking their necks with his enormous hands, trying to stifle their laughter so as not to wake Angus up.

Angus lay there, wondering if it was possible to die of suppressed laughter, until his brothers finally went to sleep. And then he lay for longer, imagining what it would be like to make love to a woman, and wondering how many years he would have to wait to find out, for he did not want to have to marry a lassie he didn't love, purely because she was with child, and right now he couldn't imagine *ever* loving a lassie like Duncan loved Màiri, and wanting to spend the rest of his life with her.

He might not *ever* meet a lassie he could love. The ones in the clan were all a lot older than him, or wee bairns. He might *never* swive a lassie in his whole life!

This horrible thought kept him awake for a while longer. It was very late when he finally succumbed, but by then he felt a bit happier, because he'd had an idea.

CHAPTER THREE

"CAN I COME TO Glasgow wi' ye tomorrow?" Angus asked Alex the next evening after he'd returned from a day working with Allan.

"I thought ye wanted to spend as much time as ye could making your surprise," Duncan commented as he dished the broth out into bowls.

"Aye, well, there's a wee thing I'm wanting to get for it, if I can," Angus improvised, realising he'd now have to invent a 'wee thing' that he could use on his present. But he'd worry about that later.

"Ye can come if ye want," Alex told him. "But I'll no' be staying for long – just a day or two while I get the glass and letters and find out any news."

"Even so, I'd like to."

"Aye. I'd enjoy your company," Alex said, secretly pleased that Angus had suggested it. He was very aware that he did not feel close in the same way to Angus as he did to Duncan, because although he'd been away from his youngest brother for the same amount of time as his middle one, Duncan had already been almost a man before he left, and had changed little either in body or personality in that time. Whereas Angus had been a small boy when Alex had gone to Paris the first time, but was now teetering on the edge of manhood, his voice broken, his body rapidly maturing. Although he still had the affectionate carefree nature he'd had as a child, in the last weeks Alex had seen facets of him that had taken him by surprise; his apparent dry humour, his understanding of the grieving process. It made him realise that in many ways his brother was a stranger to him. He hated that, felt guilty about it, although it was not his fault. He loved his brothers dearly and wanted to feel equally close to both of them.

Maybe this could be an opportunity to get to know him better, without the interruption of clan affairs.

"So can ye tell me what it is ye're wanting to buy in Glasgow? I ken it's a secret, but I'll no' tell anyone," Alex asked the following morning, no more than ten minutes after they'd set off.

Ifrinn! Angus had expected to have a lot more time to think of something before Alex asked him! He thought rapidly.

"I'm making them a *sèis,*" he said after a minute or so of silence in which he hoped Alex would change the subject.

Alex whistled through his teeth.

"That's a bonny gift!" he said. "Will ye have time to finish it before the wedding?"

"Aye. Allan's helping me. We've got an awfu' fine piece of wood for the back, and I'm carving a pattern on it. But I'm wanting to add something really special to it. Allan tellt me he once saw a tray inlaid wi' mother-of-pearl, and it was truly beautiful, like someone had put wee rainbows in it."

This was true; if Alex asked Allan if he'd talked about it, then Allan would say he had.

"So ye were thinking to buy mother-of-pearl in Glasgow?" Alex asked.

"No' to buy it. Mother-of pearl is made of shells, is it no'? Glasgow isna far from the sea. I thought we could maybe collect some shells there?" Angus asked hopefully, thinking now that it actually *would* be wonderful to make such a magical piece of furniture for the brother and sister-in-law he adored. He *had* to do it!

Alex ran his fingers through his hair.

"Glasgow isna near the sea," he said.

"But I thought there were ships in Glasgow!"

"Aye, but they come down the river, the Clyde. There willna be any seashells on the riverbank. And even if there were, ye canna just scrape the mother-of-pearl off them. It's a difficult task. I'm thinking it'll be awfu' expensive to buy some – if we can find any there. And ye havena any money, have ye?"

"No," Angus said sadly. "But I made two wee quaichs. I've brought them wi' me. I thought I could sell them, or exchange them for some, if I couldna find any shells."

Alex looked across at his brother, who seemed heartbroken.

"Show me the quaichs. No' the now," he added, as Angus started to swing the pack off his shoulder. "When we get to Glasgow. I dinna ken if we'll find mother-of-pearl, but we'll maybe find something bonny to add to it."

"Like what?" Angus asked.

"I havena a notion, laddie. We'll see what there is when we're there."

When they got to Glasgow they took a room at the Dove Inn on High Street, which they shared with three other men, all of them Lowlanders and all of them much older than both Alex and Angus.

If Alex had been alone he would probably have opted to wear the breeches and frockcoat he had for when he was outside the Highlands and had no wish to attract attention, but as Angus had no such outfit he instead wore the less showy of the two *feilidhean mòra* he had for more formal occasions, this one in green, yellow and black, while Angus wore his normal one, in shades of purple and green, perfect for blending into the heather. Both of them wore spotlessly clean linen shirts and silver brooches, showing that they were respectable Highlanders, if people in Glasgow could imagine such a thing.

In case they could not, Alex was heavily armed, while Angus had his dirk and *sgian dubh,* the absolute minimum of weaponry any clansman would carry. Hopefully they would not need to use them, although Alex suspected he might, judging by the amorous glances one of the men was casting at Angus as he removed his *féileadh mór* in preparation to use it as a blanket.

When the man decided to go outside to relieve himself before settling down on his mattress, Alex seized the opportunity and followed him. He had no wish to fight with anyone in this town. Better to nip any problem in the bud. The man went out to the back of the inn, unbuttoning his breeches. Alex waited until he was in mid-flow before he spoke.

"I've noticed the way ye were looking at my wee brother," he said amiably. So amiably that the man clearly misunderstood him.

41

"He's a bonny laddie. Fair like an angel, wi' his golden hair and handsome face," the man replied, shaking the final drops off his penis. "How much—"

"He is indeed," Alex replied, his suspicions confirmed. "And if ye're wanting to piss out of that ever again," he added casually, pointing at the man's member, "or look on *anyone's* face, handsome or no', ye'll no' even *think* about coming within a league of him."

The man turned to look at him, wondering whether to make something of it, no doubt due to Alex's placid tone. Then he saw the Highlander's ice-cold expression and the razor-sharp blade he had magically produced, which glinted in the light from the inn's window, and changed his mind.

"I didna mean—" he began.

"Aye, ye did," Alex interrupted. "I'm sure ye'll have no problem finding another bed. There are taverns everywhere in the town. I'll wish ye a good night."

He turned then and disappeared back into the building, leaving the man standing in the street.

When he got back into the room Angus was already fast asleep on his mattress, tired from the long walk and the excitement of being alone with the brother he idolised and had missed so very badly over the last years.

Alex sat on his mattress, remembering Beauregard and trying to calm himself. How he hadn't carried out his threat anyway when the bastard had asked how much, he had no idea. But if he had, then they'd have had to leave, Duncan and Màiri would not get the glass for their windows, and Angus would not get the ornament he wanted to add into their *lach*. Duncan and Màiri deserved such lovely presents. And the man had not actually touched Angus.

Alex remained sitting, waiting to see if the man was stupid enough to think he could sleep here tonight, while observing his brother with different eyes, seeing the long slender limbs, just beginning to show signs that one day they would be as heavily muscled as Alex's now were, seeing the golden hair the man had lusted after, soft and glossy in the candlelight, the childish plumpness of the cheeks, the long eyelashes now resting on them. Yes, although no longer a child, his brother still carried enough traces of the angelic beauty he'd had when small to attract any pederast. It would disappear soon when his features and body became stronger, harder, but right now if outside the clan he was in danger, and needed to be aware of it.

The door opened and the man came in, pulling Alex's attention away from his slumbering brother. He shifted position, causing the man to raise his hand in a pacific gesture before picking up his small pack and leaving again.

Alex relaxed then, breathing a sigh of relief. He would maybe get some sleep tonight, after all. The other men had paid neither of them any attention, and one of them was already asleep, while the other was presumably still drinking downstairs. Even so he pulled his mattress closer to his brother's and made sure he was between Angus and the other occupants. Then he lay down, his head on his pack, his dirk underneath it, instantly reachable.

The next day they headed off to the craft area of the city, where Alex hoped to find some glass. In his *sporan* he had a couple of pieces of rope cut to the size of window pane that he wanted.

Initially interested in watching how the glass was made by spinning a bubble of hot soft glass to make a large disc, which was then cut up into small rectangles, after a while Angus grew both hot and bored, especially once Alex and the craftsman began fierce negotiating over the quality and price.

He couldn't understand why Alex wasn't sweating; it was so hot in the workshop that it was making Angus feel sick, and his shirt was wet with sweat and sticking to him. Maybe it was because he was too busy trying to get the best price to feel the heat. Or perhaps it was because when you were a chieftain you became immune to all discomfort. His da certainly had been, which was why Angus and Duncan had both been worried on that last night when he'd said he was tired and cold.

"I'll just away for a wee stroll," he suggested during a lull in the bargaining. "I'm wanting to look in the shops to see if I can find anything for the *sèis.*"

Alex turned to his brother, who was as red as a raspberry.

"Aye. I'll likely be a wee while here," he said, then reaching into his *sporan* he pulled out a few coins and handed them to Angus, who eyed them with delight. "This is for your birthday," he added. "I was going to buy ye a gift, but I'm thinking ye might want to find something yourself. Be careful. I'll meet ye back at the tavern. Dinna be too long, and mind what I tellt ye this morning."

Angus skipped off, ecstatic. He had never had money of his own to spend before! And had never been to shops which sold things either! This was the best birthday present ever! Well, it wasn't actually his birthday today, but it would be in a few days, so he could *pretend* it was today.

Alex had told him there were over two hundred shops in the city. Surely *one* of them would sell mother-of-pearl? True, that was for Duncan and Màiri, but he would get to *use* it, and then he would see the wonder on the whole clan's faces and would be praised, which would be the best birthday present in the world!

He spent some time wandering in and out of different establishments, bedazzled by the myriad exotic goods on sale; silks in every colour he could imagine, intricate jewellery set with glittering gems; and, most interesting, beautiful items made from woods he had never imagined existed. Sandalwood, which smelt wonderful, and coral-pink padouk wood. Imagine making a whole *sèis* from sandalwood! The house would smell beautiful!

After a while he realised that as interesting as it was to look at such amazing articles, he was wasting time. He didn't have the money to buy such things, and he knew Alex wanted to leave tomorrow morning, so he really should focus on finding the mother-of-pearl he wanted to buy.

And he also wanted to see if he could find a lassie who he could steal a kiss from, which had been his major reason for asking to accompany Alex to Glasgow in the first place.

He could not do that at Loch Lomond. The older women would laugh at him. Jeannie might be willing to kiss him, and she was beautiful even if she was quite old. But she was also Kenneth's wife, and would likely tell the whole clan and laugh about it. If she did that, he'd die. And the other lassies were just wee bairns. No one would want to kiss a wee bairn, or not in the way he wanted t hem to.

No, that wasn't true, it seemed. This morning over breakfast Alex had told him what had happened last night, and that there were *fir olc* who liked to swive young boys, and if any man invited him to join him for a drink, or a game, or *anything*, he must refuse and run away.

"Better to stay in public places," Alex had said, after answering the question of how men swived boys, for bulls only swived with cows, and Angus hadn't seen any other kind of sex. "No man will try to do anything to ye in a public place, for he'd be hanged if he d id."

Angus felt sick again, just thinking of it. He would keep away from any men. But a lassie...he had no idea how he was going to persuade one to kiss him, but at least he had a chance here.

And even if he didn't, it was wonderful being alone with Alex, and seeing so many exotic things!

He focussed his mind on the mother-of-pearl, but after visiting a dozen shops and finding that none of them had any, and the shop-keepers couldn't give him any ideas on where he might find some, he was starting to think that he would have to look for something else.

Maybe he could buy just a small amount of sandalwood to dec-orate the *sèis* with. Then when it was put near the fire it would grow warm and the lovely scent would fill the room anyway.

He had just turned round to go back to the shop that sold it when a feminine voice called to him from a doorway.

"Hello, laddie. Are ye lonely?" she asked.

Angus turned and was about to tell her that he wasn't, that he was having a wonderful time, when she lifted one breast out of the top of her stays, so that it hung, heavy and ripe, over her ragged dress.

He stared at it in amazement. What was she doing? It wasn't that he had never seen breasts before – Highlanders did not have the inhibitions about their bodies that city-dwellers had. The women fed their babies in public, would bathe in the loch, their shifts clinging to them as they came out, would kilt their skirts up to the thigh if they were treading the clothes to wash them. As for the men, t he *fèileadh mór* was designed for practicality, not modesty.

But the clanswomen did not pull their breasts out and then wet their finger and trace it slowly around the nipple, smiling seductively as they did. Nor did they cup their hand over their skirts where their private parts were and stroke them. She was not particularly beauti-ful, with her lank hair and dirty bare feet, but she was clearly aroused by him. Angus swallowed, feeling his penis starting to respond.

"Would ye like to suckle me, laddie? I'd like that," she said. "Ye're awfu' bonny. I'd like that a lot. Ye can suck me dry for a bawbee, if ye want."

He hesitated. Alex had told him to be careful. But there were no men about, and this would be a fine birthday present! He'd hoped to somehow kiss a lassie, but this...this would be something else altogether. He thought about what he'd overheard Alex telling Duncan two nights ago, and suddenly he was as hard as a rock. To hell with it.

"Aye," he said, moving towards her. When he was within reach she took his hand and wrapped it round her breast, pinching her own nipple until it stood erect.

"Feel the weight of it. Firm, is it no'? Shall we away inside, and ye can fill your mouth wi' it?"

He followed her into the building, up some ramshackle steps to a door, which opened onto an icy-cold room. Something skittered across the floor as they entered, but Angus hardly noticed the filthy state of the place, or the temperature. He was still holding her breast, feeling its soft warm weight, like nothing he'd ever felt before.

"Sit ye down," she told him, and when he did she leaned over him so that her breasts were level with his mouth. She pulled the second one out, but just as he dipped his head to take her rosy nipple in his mouth she gripped his chin with surprising strength.

"Ah, no. First gie me a bawbee," she said.

He reached into his *sporan*, the coins in there jingling as he selected the one he wanted by feel and handed it to her. Then he put his arm round her waist and pulled her breast into his mouth, licking and sucking at it. It was the most wonderful thing he had ever done. Her nipple was hard and pointed, and he nibbled at it, desire spiralling through his veins like liquid fire, driving away all reason.

Suddenly she moved away from him. He moaned, reaching out to pull her back, but before he could she straddled him, lifting her skirts as she did, and reaching under his *féileadh mór* to grip his penis.

To his mingled ecstasy and shame he came immediately, the touch of her fingers pushing him over the edge into climax.

"*Bàs mallaichte!*" he cursed.

"I dinna ken what that means, laddie, but dinna fash yourself. Ye'll be hard again in a minute. Feel how ready I am for ye," she said, gripping his hand and pushing it under her dress. He felt soft springy hair, and then she was guiding his fingers expertly into her. "Ye feel how

46

wet I am?" she murmured. "That's what ye do to me. Ye're driving me wild. What d'ye think if I let ye put your cock in there? Can ye imagine what that would be like?"

He could not imagine in his wildest dreams what that would be like, but all thought of mother-of-pearl, of being careful, of *anything* except having this woman now, fled from his mind. This was what Alex had done. This was what Duncan desperately wanted to do, and do well. But this woman didn't care whether he did it well or not. She wanted him so much that she would think he was wonderful anyway. He felt his penis begin to rise again as she stroked it, gently at first, and then more firmly.

He moaned.

"Ah, ye're a well-endowed laddie and no mistake," she said. "Are ye wanting to fuck me, then? Have ye a groat about ye?"

At that moment he would have given her anything. If he didn't take her now, he would die. He was certain of that. He felt in the *sporan* again, and pressed the coin into her hand.

And then she took his fingers out of her cleft and shuffling forward on his knee, replaced it with his cock. Now he needed no instruction, from Alex or anyone, because lust and instinct took over as he felt his penis slide in and out of her soft velvety warmth.

This was heaven. Never, never had he expected it would be this glorious. The filthy room, the rickety chair, everything vanished, and all that was left was the exquisite sensation of the woman's quim around his throbbing penis, moving faster and faster now as he neared his climax, every nerve in his body tingling deliciously.

And then he came again, deep inside her, feeling the glorious release, and shuddered all over as the waves of bliss washed over him.

"Oh God," he breathed. "That was amazing." He reached for her again, greedy for more, but she moved away from him now, and then s tood.

"I'm thinking that was your first time, laddie," she said now, her voice level, emotionless.

How could she be so calm? He was still on fire, although it was lessening a little and he was becoming aware of his surroundings again. There was a noise outside the door, presumably whatever had been scuttling across the room earlier.

"Aye," he said. "It was. Can we...?"

"No," she replied, looking at the door. "Ye need to leave now."

"Aye," he said, her voice and attitude bringing him fully back to himself now, although he could still feel the lassitude of afterglow and would have loved to lie down with her for a few moments. No doubt Duncan would do that with Màiri, and it would be warm, loving. But there was nothing warm and loving about the woman standing impatiently waiting for him to leave, so he stood, rearranging his kilt as he did.

"I thank ye, mistress," he said politely. "I wish ye a good day." He wanted to ask if he could come back again, but realised that he would have no time. They were leaving tomorrow, and Alex would be waiting for him at the tavern by now. Even so, he would never forget this experience, even if he lived to be a very old man.

He opened the door and walked out onto the landing, to be immediately confronted by a short but burly man, who grabbed him by his shirt and shoved him up against the wall.

"So, it's you who's been swiving my wife, ye bastard!" he shouted with mock rage into the astonished Angus's face. Any remains of lassitude or desire fled, Kenneth's training took over and instinctively Angus drove the heel of his hand up under the man's nose, causing him to screech in pain and let Angus go.

Angus turned then, intending to run down the stairs and away, as Alex had advised him, but the man moved in front of him to block his way, reaching inside his coat as he did. Angus's mind raced; Alex had told him he had not harmed the man last night as he didn't want to be arrested. Which meant that he dare not dirk the woman's husband, although the man seemed to have no such reservations about harming him as he began to pull something out of an inside pocket.

Angus saw the handle of what he assumed was a knife, and taking advantage of the ruffian's position, he grabbed the man by the shirt as he had been grabbed a moment earlier, drove his forehead into the already injured nose, and then threw him backwards with all his strength, sending him flying down the stairs.

Then he ran partway down before leaping over the rotting banister to the hallway, not wanting to come within reach of the man and be attacked again, although in truth his opponent seemed incapable of it. His face was a mask of blood, his leg twisted at a strange angle underneath him. As Angus opened the door the man moaned, which was reassuring. He hadn't killed him then. Surely you could not be hanged in the Lowlands for defending yourself?

Maybe not, but you could probably be hanged for swiving a man's wife and you *definitely* could be just for *being* a MacGregor, although Alex had used the name Drummond when he'd taken the room at the inn, so no one would know that. And Angus hadn't given his name to the woman, hadn't given her any information about himself.

He ran down the close, emerging onto Trongate Street, where he stopped for a moment to get his bearings and then made his way back to the inn. The man was in no position to come after him, and he had been alone. It was already growing late. No doubt he and Alex would have a meal – Alex had promised they would go to an ordinary and have broth and beef, and a roast with potatoes and small ale, which would set them up for the walk back tomorrow.

He relaxed now. What an adventure! And he'd had his first sexual experience with a woman, although if he'd known she was married he wouldn't have agreed to her offer. It would have been very difficult not to though, so he was glad he hadn't found out she was married until afterwards. He hadn't found anything to make the *sèis* special though, but maybe he would have time in the morning, as Alex still had to go to the Post Office and collect any letters.

Whistling, he walked into the tavern, where his brother was sitting with a tankard of ale, his eye on the door.

"Where have ye been?" Alex greeted him as he came in. "I was starting to worry about – what the hell's happened to ye?" he exclaimed as Angus drew nearer to the light from the candle on the table.

Angus looked down at himself, saw the rip in his shirt and the spatters of blood decorating it. Damn. He would have to tell Alex what had happened now, although he was partly relieved, because he was dying to tell *someone* about the best experience he'd ever had. Alex would understand. After all, he'd been with women too, and it was hardly his fault that she hadn't told him she was married.

"I'm no' hurt," he replied, sitting down opposite his brother. "Are we eating here?"

"Ye were supposed to be shopping for mother-of-pearl. We're no' doing anything until ye tell me what happened," Alex said, his voice and face hard now he realised that Angus was unharmed. In fact not only was he unharmed, he was positively glowing.

"I *did* try to buy some mother-of-pearl!" Angus answered defensively. "I went to a lot of shops and saw all manner of bonny things, but no mother-of-pearl. So I was thinking to go back to a shop where I'd seen some beautiful wood, when a woman showed me her paps..."

Alex listened with unnatural stillness as Angus told him what had happened, including his encounter with the man, and what he had done to escape him. When he'd finished Alex ran his hands over his face, then tore them through his hair. Not a good sign.

"I kept away from men!" Angus cried now. "I remembered what ye tellt me about ped...about yon unnatural men, and she didna tell me she was married! If she had I wouldna have gone wi' her, I swear it! And I didna kill the man. I maybe could have, for he was daft enough to stand at the top of the stairs so I could push him down, so he canna have been a fighter, for Kenneth tellt us never to—"

"Never mind what Kenneth tellt ye. What state was he in when ye left him?" Alex interrupted.

"Well, I'm thinking I likely broke his nose, and his leg was in a position I've never seen before, but he moaned, so he wasna dead. Ye canna die of a broken leg or nose, can ye?" Angus asked, worried now.

No, you couldn't, or it wasn't likely. But you could die of banging your head on the way down the stairs. Having said that...

"I'm sorry. I've shamed ye," Angus said in a small voice. Alex looked across the table at his brother, saw the distraught look on his face, the sadness in his blue eyes at disappointing his brother, and any anger vanished.

"Let's go to the ordinary," he said. "Ye've no' shamed me. I need to tell ye some things, but we'll eat while I do. If we dinna go now there'll be nothing left. Never mind your shirt. We canna do anything about it now."

Fifteen minutes later they were sitting in the ordinary opposite the post office, at a small table in the back of the room, waiting for their food to come.

"I'm no' disappointed wi' ye," Alex reassured Angus, who, although no longer distraught, was clearly still very uneasy. "I didna think ye'd be looking for whores yet awhile, but ye're clearly developing a wee bit earlier than I thought ye would. I wasna interested in lassies when I was twelve, or no' that I remember, but ye clearly are. Ye did, however, do a stupit thing, and it could have cost ye your life. The lassie was a whore. City women dinna do what ye just tellt me she did, any more than clanswomen do. She saw ye were raw, maybe thought ye a wee bit older than ye are, because ye're tall."

"I'm no' raw!" Angus protested.

"Aye, ye are. No' in the clan, but in the city ye are. Your clothes would have tellt her that, but also whores are experts at seeing which men will likely respond to them, and which ones they can try to rob. Remember I tellt ye this morning that although ye're changing fast now, ye've still the look of a bairn about ye."

"Aye," Angus admitted reluctantly. He didn't want to be a bairn any more. Especially now he'd had his first woman.

"Well, she'll have seen that, and likely her pimp will as well. He maybe tellt her to come out and try to lure ye in. It's a common trick. He's no' her husband, or if he is he doesna deserve the name. They'll lure an innocent laddie in, she'll find out how much coin he's likely got, and then he'll take the victim by surprise while he's weak-kneed and off guard from the swiving. He'll have expected ye to be intimidated and just give him all your money. When ye fought back, he'd have likely killed ye at that point, then taken your money anyway and disposed of your corpse later. And I had no notion what ye were doing, so I couldna have found ye, or avenged ye. I didna warn ye of such things, because I didna expect ye to be swiving lassies at twelve, for Christ's sake!"

"But ye didna tell Duncan any of this, when ye were..." Angus's voice trailed off, and he flushed scarlet. Luckily at that moment the ordinary owner arrived with the food, which took a minute or two to lay before them.

"Ye were listening then," Alex said as he drew his dirk to cut the meat. "We thought ye were asleep."

"I woke up just before ye went downstairs. Duncan said something about a harlot, so I thought I'd listen, for it sounded interesting," Angus confessed.

"It wasna a conversation for you, Angus, so after today ye'll forget ye ever heard it."

Angus shivered, recognising the shift in Alex's tone between loving brother and chieftain. He swallowed.

"I wasna going to tell ye, and I'll never tell anyone else, I swear. Duncan wouldna like it, would he?" he said.

"No. But I wouldna like it even more," Alex told him.

The food, which until a second ago had smelt and tasted delicious, suddenly became inedible. Angus put his knife down.

"I didna tell Duncan any of this because he wasna asking me about swiving a whore, ye wee gomerel," Alex continued. "He and Màiri are in love. Even if the whore hadna been intending to rob ye, she still wouldna care about ye at all. It's business to her. I realise ye thought it was wonderful, and when ye're lusting like that ye dinna see things rightly. But ye need to ken how it is, really. She didna care if ye were handsome or had a huge cock or any of the other things she might have said to ye. She wasna lonely, or desperate to feel ye in her. She wanted your money, nothing else. Now, even if she hadna intended to lure ye in so her pimp could rob ye, she could still have harmed ye. Did ye swive wi' her properly?"

"Aye. It felt awfu' good," Angus said, somewhat uncertain now.

Alex hated taking away his little brother's joy at his first sexual experience, but he had no option. Angus had clearly enjoyed it so much, he would almost certainly do it again, if he got the opportunity. Alex had wanted to, desperately, but had resisted because he was older and wiser, and because Jeanne had made him realise just how much prostitutes despised their clients.

"When ye go wi' a woman like that, ye can get the pox. D'ye ken about the pox?" Alex said.

"I've heard the word, aye. It's an illness?"

"Aye. It's a terrible illness. Ye get it from swiving. Whores swive wi' lots of men, and if one of them has the pox he can give it to her, and then she can give it to everyone. Ye can die of it, and even if ye dinna die of it, ye'll wish ye had." He went on then to explain what he knew about the French pox in graphic detail, watching as Angus paled. Good. He would think twice before he gave in to his sexual desires again. Although it would likely be a good while before he had another chance to.

"I'm sorry, laddie. I ken it was a wonderful experience for ye. But I love ye, and I willna see ye die of the pox or of some pimp's dirk because ye dinna ken the reality of it," he said finally.

"But ye tellt Duncan that ye—"

"Aye, I did. The first time I didna think of the pox, even though I wasna as innocent as you. That's what lust does to ye. It robs ye of reason. I was lucky and didna get it. Hopefully ye'll be lucky too. The next time I had a thing called a condom, that the nobleman gave me. It stops ye getting the pox. But it's awfu' expensive."

"I didna ken all that," Angus said sadly.

"Aye, well, ye do now. Ye should have tellt me ye were wanting a lassie."

"I didna intend to do that!" Angus retorted indignantly. "I was just hoping for maybe a wee kiss, no' to actually swive a whore! If ye'd tellt me all those horrible things I wouldna have done it at all!"

Alex closed his eyes and pinched the bridge of his nose between his thumb and index finger. He prayed that his brother would not get the pox, and realised that if he did, it would be partly his fault. Until this evening he had still seen Angus as a child.

The truth was, he *wanted* Angus to be a child, because he wanted to see him grow up, to be a part of it, as he had been a part of Duncan's. He could still be a part of Angus's transition into adulthood, but to do that he had to accept that adulthood was almost upon him, physically and sexually at least, not years in the future.

"I'm no' angry," he said again. "I'm disappointed, but no' wi' you. I'm disappointed that I havena seen ye grow up. Ye're no' stupit, ye just dinna ken the ways of the town, and that's no' your fault. I was two years older than you are when I went to Edinburgh and was nearly killed because I trusted two footpads, and didna realise what they were until I was alone in a dark close wi' them. I was awfu' lucky that day, as were you today. We've Kenneth to thank for that. But I learnt from my naivety, and ye must do the same. If ye do, then it's a good thing, for ye'll no' be so foolish next time."

"Ye really did that?" Angus said.

"Aye. I've done a good number of foolish things in my life. Everyone does. Just try no' to, but if ye do, learn from it. Ye canna do more. The town isna like the Highlands. It's a foreign place. I ken both now, so in future if ye're wanting to do something like that, tell me. I ken ye didna intend to do that," he added quickly as Angus opened his mouth. "But if ye'd tellt me ye wanted to kiss a lassie, I'd have maybe realised that ye're older than I thought, and have warned ye."

"I didna feel I could tell ye that. It's...embarrassing," Angus admitted.

"No, it isna. It's normal. Ye think Duncan didna feel embarrassed about asking me?"

"Aye. I suppose he did," Angus said.

"But he asked me anyway. For he kens me well enough to ken I wouldna laugh at him. He trusts me, as I trust him. Ye're my brother too. Ye must trust me, as he does. And I'll trust you too. I already trust ye no' to tell anyone what ye overheard. We've been apart too long, laddie. We love each other dearly, but we must become brothers again, and quickly. To do that we need to talk to each other, so we can fill in the years we've been apart. Can ye do that?"

Angus smiled then, a glorious smile that made his eyes sparkle. His face lit up, and all his dark, uneasy feelings vanished.

"Aye, I can do that," he said. "I'd *love* to do that!"

Angus lunged across the table to embrace his brother then, nearly setting fire to himself with the candleflame in the process.

And then, in a mood of sudden exhilaration and extravagance, Alex asked the landlord to dispose of their cold, congealing meal and bring a fresh hot one.

Suddenly he knew it would all work out. He would be as close to Angus as he was to Duncan, and together the three of them would be invincible.

"Will we have time to look for something bonny to put in the *sèis?*" Angus asked the next morning as they made their way to the Post Office to collect any mail.

"Ah! It slipped my mind last night," Alex said. "I thought ye might no' find any mother-of-pearl, so I asked the glass maker if he could think of anything else that might be suitable. Would ye be able to cut shapes in the back of the *sèis*, like wee windows?"

Angus thought for a minute.

"Well, I've carved a knotwork pattern on the arms, and I thought to replicate it on the back," he began, his gaze distant as he envisaged it. "But I could maybe cut wee shapes out of the back, and then carve the knotwork round them instead. Is that what ye mean?"

"Aye, I think so, although ye'd have to ask the glass man about it. He tellt me he's got some bonny pieces of stained glass in all manner of colours. Ye canna inlay them as ye can wi' mother-of-pearl, but ye could cut holes and put them in, like Allan will do wi' the windows. He hasna seen such a thing done, mind."

From his expression Alex could tell that his brother was running through the techniques and possibilities, envisaging what such a thing might look like, so he said no more until they were in the office waiting for their mail, when Angus suddenly emerged from his contemplation.

"Aye," he said. "That could be bonny. Is it awfu' costly? D'ye think he'd take the quaichs in payment for it?"

"I dinna ken. It'll no' be as costly as mother-of-pearl, that's certain. Will we away and see it once we've the letters? If ye like it then tell me, but dinna sound too enthusiastic."

"Like wi' the cattle dealing?" Angus asked.

"Aye, like that," Alex replied. He'd forgotten that his brother would have attended a few reiving expeditions by now, and the resulting sales in Crieff. With Duncan, but without him. He ignored the pang of regret that invoked. "If ye give me your quaichs and tell me which colours of glass ye like, then I'll bargain wi' him. Unless ye want to do it?"

"No. I've watched Da do it, and I thought it must be awfu' hard to hide what ye're feeling when ye're selling a cow for twice what it's worth. And then remembering all yon numbers...I couldna do that," Angus said.

"I felt the same way the first time I saw him do it," Alex said, smiling. "But I had to learn, for Da said when I was chieftain I'd have to do it, whether I wanted to or no'."

"And now ye will," Angus pointed out. "Can I come wi' ye when ye go reiving? Will ye go this year?"

"I dinna ken yet. I'm thinking on Duncan's wedding first," Alex told him. "When Da made me do the bargaining the first time I was so feart my legs were trembling, though I tried no' to show it, to make him proud of me."

"Ye did it well though," Angus said with such certainty it made Alex smile.

"He had to cut in and help me a few times. I havena done everything well my whole life, ye ken. Duncan remembers that. Ye're a lot younger than me, that's why ye dinna."

"Aye, and ye werena here for a lot of the time. Ye were in Edinburgh, and then Paris. So I couldna see if ye did everything well. Although ye tellt me ye didna last night, wi' the footpads."

"Aye, that's right. But ye learn by making mistakes, and ye learn by watching. So watch carefully today, and then ye'll maybe learn without making mistakes, which is always the better way, if ye can."

Angus stood, watching nervously while the glassmaker examined the quaich Alex had given him carefully. The three pieces of glass he'd chosen, in beautiful shades of ruby, gold and amethyst were lying on the bench waiting for a price to be agreed, after which the man would cut them to the shape and size Angus had still not decided on. Alex had told him not to react to anything he said, and just to observe, so he pulled his mind away from triangles, diamonds and circles so he could focus on the moment.

"Hmm," the man was saying, his tone doubtful, although his fingers were caressing the bowl of the quaich, which was beautifully carved with a similarly elaborate knotwork pattern to the one Angus was planning to use on the *sèis,* but in miniature.

"The carving's bonny, is it no'?" Alex said. "Carved by an expert in the craft. There isna another like it, nor will there ever be, for the man's long gone."

This was news to Angus, who was standing a few feet away, with another almost identical quaich in his pack. He tried to think of something neutral to keep his expression bland.

"It's old, is it?" the man asked. "It doesna seem so."

"Aye, well it's been handed down through the family, an heirloom ye might say, only used on very special occasions," Alex told him.

"Really? Handed down or stolen from?"

"I heard that King James VI himself had one very like it, likely carved by the same craftsman. Ye wouldna misuse such a thing," Alex continued, as though the man had not just insulted him and his ancestors. "My da kept it wrapped and in the kist. We used it for weddings and suchlike, nothing else. That's why it's in such bonny condition."

"So why are ye wanting to sell it for some wee bits of glass?" he asked.

"I ken the glass isna worth such a fine thing as that," Alex replied, "but in truth it's used rarely, and my brother's getting married next month. His lassie has a great fondness for the coloured glass, so we're thinking to buy her some to put in their house. Ye ken what lassies are like, always good to please them wi' a bonny gift!"

"Aye, that's true," the man said.

"Ye tellt me yesterday your daughter's marrying soon, did ye no'?"

"Aye, in June."

"I was thinking that might be a bonny gift for her and her husband. The custom is to fill it wi' a mixture of his favourite drink and hers, and then they drink from it together to show they're now one. Awfu' romantic, it is," Alex continued.

Angus looked on, watching the man's face transform as he began to want the thing. He wondered if Alex had seen it, because he wouldn't have noticed such subtle changes in expression if he hadn't been concentrating and looking for it.

"Why d'ye no' give it to your brother for his wedding then?" he asked.

"His bride isna one for such things, hasna an appreciation for such fine workmanship. She loves colours, jewels, pretty baubles and suchlike."

"Yon glass is a fine thing too," the man asserted. "It isna just painted. The colour is mixed into the glass when it's made. It's awfu' difficult to do, takes years to master. Yon glass there is stained wi' copper, manganese and antimony. It'll never fade, and the colour willna wear off."

"I'll tell her that, though I'm thinking my brother'll appreciate the making of it more. She'll just love the way the colour glows in the sunlight," Alex continued. "I'd like the quaich to go to someone who'll truly appreciate the work of a master craftsman, and the uniqueness of it. I daresay I can buy stained glass as good as that in Stirling, but ye'll never see another quaich the like of this one."

He held his hand out then, as if to take it back.

"Ye're away to Stirling directly?" the man asked, ignoring Alex's outstretched hand. A good sign, Angus realised.

"Aye. We came here to collect letters from the Post Office, but we've business in Stirling too," Alex told him. "I'm thinking we'll certainly find a buyer for this there, if we canna find another glassmaker to take it. I could have sold it here, but I was so certain ye'd jump at the chance to have such a thing in exchange for a few pieces of glass that I didna think to, and we're leaving directly. I took a liking to ye yesterday, so would have preferred another craftsman to have it than a shopkeeper.

I thought ye'd appreciate the workmanship. No matter. If ye give it back to me, we'll no' take up any more of your time."

His tone and expression were indifferent now, bored even, and Angus's heart sank, because he really wanted the glass and knew Alex had no intention of going to Stirling. With a herculean effort he managed to adopt a bored expression too, and stood away from the bench he'd been leaning against, obviously eager to be gone. Or at least he hoped that was the impression he gave.

"Wait a minute," the man said. "Can I look at it in the light?"

"Aye, of course ye can. Better ye do, for then ye'll see I'm no' exaggerating its fineness," Alex said, starting to follow the man until he realised he was going to the window, not the door. He turned his head then and nodded at Angus briefly. Then he winked, his slate-blue eyes sparkling with laughter, until the man turned away from the window, whereupon he was instantly indifferent again.

They got the three pieces of glass, which had apparently come from an ancient cathedral, cut into diamond shapes, for the price of one quaich.

"I assume ye're happy wi' your glass," Alex said as they were heading out of Glasgow an hour later, the glass very carefully wrapped and packed in his bag. He'd told Angus he wanted to walk sedately so as not to risk breaking it. His brother had no such restrictions, and skipped along merrily at his side.

"I canna believe we got the glass for just one quaich! I wish Allan was here so I could ask him what he thinks of my idea," Angus said, his face glowing. "I hope it works."

"I canna imagine why it wouldna," Alex commented. "It'll be like putting wee windows in. If Allan can put the panes I've bought in the window frames, I canna think it'll be any different to put them in the *sèis*. And dinna underestimate your ability wi' the carving. That was a bonny quaich."

"Ye almost had me believing myself that it was made for King Jamie!" Angus said laughingly. "Da didna bargain like that! I havena a notion how I didna laugh when ye tellt him all that nonsense about Màiri only being interested in pretty baubles! I willna tell her, I swear," he continued.

"Ye can tell her an ye want, after she's seen the *sèis,*" Alex told him. "She'll ken I dinna think that way about her, and why I said it."

"Did ye learn to lie like that at university?" Angus asked with absolute sincerity. Alex started laughing now.

"No. I learnt a great many interesting things, and a great many boring things. Most of them were useless for a clan chieftain. I wish t hey *had* taught me to lie well. At least I could make use of it now."

"Ye dinna need to learn it. Ye ken it already."

"Every MacGregor does. Ye did well yourself in there, didna show at all what ye were thinking when I was telling the man all that pure shite."

"I dinna think I could lie like that, though. That was awfu' impressive," Angus replied.

"So then, if we met a group of men now and they tellt us they were looking for a Highland laddie who badly injured their friend two days ago, and asked us if we'd seen them, would ye say, 'that was me,'?"

"How many men?"

"Ten," Alex said. "All well armed."

"No, I wouldna. I'd say I hadna seen any Highlanders at all," Angus admitted. When Alex didn't respond, he thought a bit more. "I'd maybe ask them what the laddie they were seeking looked like."

Alex nodded.

"Why would ye ask that?"

"So I'd ken if it *was* me they were looking for, or someone else. And then I'd tell them I hadna seen any Highlanders at all *after* that. It'd sound better, I'm thinking."

"So, ye've already got the talent for thinking on your feet, and speaking according to the situation ye're in, and no' the honest truth if it would be foolish to do so. It's in the MacGregor blood. It's one reason we've survived so long, because we can lie when we have to. But only do it when ye have to. Always tell the truth wi' those ye l ove."

"Ye didna need to tell the truth wi' yon man," Angus pointed out. "Our lives werena in danger."

"That's true. But ye wanted the glass, and I'm thinking it'll look awfu' bonny, and Duncan and Màiri will be overjoyed by your gift. The quaich *was* beautifully carved, and I didna lie about the wedding custom. He wouldna have sold it to me if I'd tellt him you carved it, for he wouldna have thought that special, though it is. So I lied, and we got what we wanted."

Angus frowned.

"But even then I wouldna have lied but for two things," Alex continued. "Firstly the man wasna poor. His clothes were good quality, even though they were working clothes, and his wig was an expensive one. And no, I didna learn that at university either. The second thing was that I blethered wi' one of his apprentices yesterday while yon mannie was talking wi' another customer, and I asked about the glass.

"He tellt me that if a church window breaks, or if the stained glass makers have waste pieces, then he goes and collects all of it, disposes of the stuff he canna use, and keeps the pieces he maybe can. And he pays almost nothing for it. The price he asked me for at the start was extortionate. So it wasna lying, more a battle, if ye like, to see who could cheat the other the most. We both won, for you got the glass ye want, which is beautiful, and he got a bonny cup, which he can tell a good tale about. Dinna ever lie to harm others unless it's to save yourself or those ye love, or in vengeance. And dinna lie for the wrong reasons. If he'd been a pauper selling yon glass on the street, I would have paid a fair price, or offered him your quaich and tellt him the truth about it."

Angus nodded.

"Aye, that makes sense. So ye dinna feel it was sinful to lie to the man, then."

"No. D'ye think it was sinful to throw yon gomerel down the stairs?"

"No!" Angus replied immediately. "He'd have killt me if I hadna!"

"Well, then. There's a time and a place for the lying, as there is for throwing men down stairs. When ye're bargaining for the silver to buy food for the clan is one of them. When ye can lie your way out of bloodshed is another. And ye need to be good at it, for it could save your life as well as any sword or dirk can.

"I'm thinking ye'll be fine at the bargaining, when ye're ready. Next time I go to Crieff, ye can come wi' me, and watch as well as ye did today, for the time after that I'll be letting ye do some of the bargaining yourself," Alex told him.

"Really? But I willna ever need to do that, will I? For you're the chieftain, and Duncan is your right-hand man. Da tellt me that."

"Did he no' tell ye ye'll be my left-hand man, when ye're grown just a wee bit more?" Alex asked.

"No! He never tellt me that!"

"Well, *I'm* telling ye that, as the chieftain. Ye'll be my left-hand man, while Duncan's to my right. And if Duncan isna there for any reason, then ye'll be in his place."

Angus stopped dead then, mouth open, an expression of utter shock on his face.

"Ye dinna mean that," he said breathlessly. "I'm just your wee brother."

"I wouldna lie to ye about such a thing," Alex said, stopping and turning to face Angus.

He reached out then, resting his hands on his brother's shoulders and making steady eye contact, for this was a serious matter, and Angus needed to know that. "Ye're no' wee any more. It's true that ye're no' quite ready yet, but I wasna when I was your age either. In a few years ye will be, so ye need to ken it now, and prepare for it. I thought Da would have tellt ye that, for ye're his son as much as I am, as Duncan is. But Da's gone now, and I'm the chieftain, and I'll be proud to have ye at my side, as soon as ye're ready."

He took his hands away now, adjusted the pack carefully on his back and walked on, Angus walking behind him, silent for a while.

"Thank ye," he said then, in a slightly strangled voice. Alex looked back and saw that Angus's eyes were full of tears, although his expression was one of absolute joy. "I'll prepare myself. I willna let ye down."

"Come here, ye wee loon," Alex said affectionately, taking him in his arms. "Ye're as precious to me as Duncan is, ye ken that, do ye no'?"

"Aye. I do now," Angus replied, his voice muffled by Alex's plaid.

"Ah, laddie," Alex said softly, momentarily cursing his father for failing his sons so very badly, and this one in particular. "Ye've been as precious to me as Duncan since the day ye were born. Duncan and I are just closer in age, so we've been companions since we were wee bairns. That doesna mean I love ye less than I love him. I love ye just as much, but in a different way, no' because ye're younger, but because ye're a different person. Duncan loves Màiri as much as he loves me and you, but in a different way, for she's his sweetheart. He doesna love us less now."

"Aye, I ken that. But Da never said...no one ever said that I'd be your left-hand man, or have any kind of an important role. I thought I'd be a clansman like all the others, wi' you and Duncan...different."

"No. Your place is waiting for ye, wi' no one else to fill it. Ye just need to be ready, then it's yours."

"I'll be ready," Angus said now, releasing himself from Alex's embrace. "I will. I'll make ye proud of me."

"I'm already proud of ye. Ye just need to learn more, have more experiences. Time will do that. Now, let's keep walking, for we canna run wi' this glass, and I'm wanting to be home before dark if we can."

They continued then, side by side. As they always would be, God willing.

CHAPTER FOUR

Duncan and Alex stood side by side, gazing across a slightly sloping piece of land a short distance from the settlement.

"I'm thinking we could start the tilling a wee bit earlier than normal, if the weather holds," Alex said. "No' the planting though, for there's likely to be more frost yet."

"Aye. That'll spread the heavy work out, and maybe more of us can go up when Kenneth's collecting the peat wi' Alasdair."

"Alasdair's still doing the peat wi' Kenneth?" Alex asked, shocked.

"Aye. He says the day he canna help wi' the peat'll be the day he'll away off and drown himself in the loch. He willna do that, but it'll break him, I think. He sees it as the last useful thing he can do for the clan," Duncan replied.

"I canna imagine how he does it. He couldna walk up to the cave when I came home three years ago," Alex said.

"He could, but it took him an awfu' long time, and he felt shamed, because the whole clan slowed for him and he kent that. That's why Da set him to watch over the settlement, so he'd still feel useful."

"That was well done. He had a fearsome pride. So how does Kenneth manage it then?"

"Kenneth has a way wi' such things. He cuts the peats smaller, for one thing, so they're no' so difficult to lift. And then when they change places he lets Alasdair cut the peats for longer while he lifts them, which is the harder work and needs more walking. Now even that isna enough, so last year some of the men went up, just to help them a wee bit. And then the women came back up when the peats were dry to help load them on the cart, and they tellt Alasdair to bring his fiddle, for the best thing he could do would be to entertain all the bairns so they didna get in the way."

Alex laughed. This was an aspect of clan life he'd missed sorely when in Paris; the care and consideration for each other, and the pains taken to avoid an elderly or infirm member feeling useless.

As they walked back he wondered if any of the English nobles were like that. Highbury certainly seemed to be, and the Harriet woman he spoke of with such fondness, but other than that the impression he'd given Alex was that they were in general a mob of ruthless cut-throats. He missed Highbury. Although he'd had no reason to expect a letter from the earl, he'd been oddly disappointed that there hadn't been one waiting for him at the Post Office.

He realised now that although he was very glad to be home, he still wanted to know what was happening in Paris; how Ashelle and Scolastica were, how the school was coming along. But they had agreed only to communicate if it was necessary, understanding the risks involved in doing so. The next time he heard from Highbury would most likely be if he had news of an imminent Stuart rising, which was unlikely to happen for years, if ever. Or if he found a way to bring him into aristocratic society as an equal, which was even less likely to happen. Alex felt a sudden pang at the realisation that he might never hear from the earl again, just as he would never know what had become of Jeanne.

"Was the trip successful then?" Duncan asked suddenly, breaking into Alex's reverie, and unknowingly reminding him that that life was in the past, and he must let it go, for this one was all he had ever wanted.

"Aye, ye saw the glass. And Angus got the wee thing he wanted, as ye ken," Alex said.

"The whole clan does, by the great effort he made to let everyone ken how secret it was," Duncan replied, laughing. "I mean did ye come closer to Angus? That's why ye took him wi' ye, is it no'?"

Alex sighed. His brother had lost none of his ability to see the depth of things then.

"Aye. He had no notion that he'd have an important role when he's a wee bit older. He thought you and I would lead the clan, and he'd be no different to the other clansfolk. It fair broke my heart. I canna believe Da didna tell him."

"Da was never quite the same, even after he came back to us," Duncan admitted then. "Angus didna ken that, for he couldna remember Da before Ma died. I think Da struggled wi' how easily Angus forgave him for how he was treated. Ye ken Angus. He isna one to hold a grudge, likely never will be. And Da felt a great weight of guilt for what he'd done. Wi' me and you it was easier to bear, for we tellt him that we couldna forget everything and trust him again, no' until he earned it, and I'm thinking he saw that as a kind of penance, and it assuaged his guilt.

"But Angus just forgave Da, ran into his arms and loved him, from the minute he recovered himself. He couldna handle that, felt he didna deserve it."

"Aye, well, he didna deserve it, in truth," Alex said.

"No. But it was a sadness, for Angus wanted his love so much, and although Da tried, there was always something between them. Angus isna as superficial as he seems to be, and he felt that, I'm thinking, although he never said it, no' even to me. It stopped Da saying a number of intimate things to him, and maybe that was one of them," Duncan finished.

"He didna tell me either. I found out by accident," Alex said.

"Well, it's good that ye did, for there's a lightness about him now. I saw it as soon as he came home," Duncan said, smiling.

"Christ, I wish ye'd been wi' me when I visited wi' Prince *Teàrlach*!" Alex said suddenly. "Ye see so much that I dinna. I'd love to have your opinion of the man who could lead us in battle one day."

"Ye really think he will?"

"It's possible. He's the fire for it, and the will. The personality too."

"Well, if he does I'll meet him when he lands here, and tell ye my view of the man then," Duncan said practically.

"I could wish ye'd see him before that day though, for I'm no' leading the clan out and risking them all for a half-hearted rising led by a weakling. I mind how angry Da was after the '19. I'm thinking if he'd kent how badly organised it was, he wouldna have gone. I tellt him about the footpads I killed in Edinburgh, how stupid I was to trust them, and how lucky I was to survive it," Alex finished.

"Ye tellt Da that?" Duncan asked.

"Ah. No. Angus. I wanted him to love me as his brother, no' worship me as a god. I dinna want there to be something between us, as ye said there was wi' him and Da."

"That was well done," Duncan reassured him. "Although ye could regret it, for he's awfu' wild and reckless at times. More so even than you were."

Alex laughed then.

"I learnt that! D'ye ken what the wee gomerel did? No' a word though, until he tells ye himself, for I'm sure he will."

For the rest of the trip back to the cottage he regaled Duncan with Angus's sexual exploits, without mentioning what had inspired them.

"Christ! I canna believe my baby brother lost his virginity before me," Duncan said as they came in sight of the cottage and saw Angus sitting outside with Màiri, his hands waving expressively about him as he explained some elaborate thing, hers quietly in her lap, head bowed, listening intently.

"I'm thinking losing yours will be a much finer experience," Alex observed, so that when Màiri looked up and saw her sweetheart coming towards her, he was beetroot-red.

"So, then," said Alex to James, as the men made their way home after a day spent tilling the fields that would hopefully provide them with oats later in the year, "how are the chickens?"

"The chickens?" James replied, automatically looking over at the patch of ground outside his cottage where the men had stopped and where a group of hens were pecking hopefully at the ground. "They're all laying still. Are ye wanting an egg? Or some to kill for the wedding?" he added, trying not to sound dismayed, for eggs were precious, but if the chieftain wanted a hen, then he couldn't refuse.

"No. I wouldna ask ye to kill a chicken, no' unless she wasna laying at all," Alex reassured him. "We'll have enough food, wi' the deer and the coneys. And the women seem to be using all the sugar and flour I bought and a fearful amount of butter to make shortbread."

"Shortbread? I canna mind the last time I ate that," Simon said. "No' wi' butter and sugar, anyway."

"Aye. I tellt Barbara that Queen Mary loved it, afore she went down to England and was murdered by Elizabeth, and so they all decided Duncan and Màiri must have it for their wedding day. I tellt them the ones wi' yeast might be more practical, but I was subjected to that look lassies give ye when preparing for battle."

"From *all* of them?" James asked.

"Aye. Well, all the ones who were there."

The men all shook their heads in horror.

"Better ye let them do as they will then," Kenneth remarked. "For even a chieftain canna fight *all* the lassies at once."

Some ribald comments followed this, after which attention returned to the chickens.

"I was thinking more about feathers," Alex said then.

"Feathers? Ye mean to make them a pillow?" James asked. "That would be a bonny gift. Catriona saves the feathers, but I dinna ken if she's enough for that."

"Er...no' exactly," Alex confessed. "I was thinking more of the foot-washing, the night before they marry."

"Ye're wanting to wash him wi' *feathers?*" Dougal asked.

"No' just wi' feathers. I was thinking of something they'd stick to," Alex said.

"Ye could use Archangel Tar," James suggested. "If it's warmed a wee bit it's awfu' runny and sticky."

"Aye, I remember ye teaching me and Duncan how to mark the cattle on our first raid," Alex said, grinning now. "That's a bonny idea!"

"Christ, Alex, he'll kill ye if ye do that to him," Gregor said.

"Duncan? No' he willna. He'll forgive me on his wedding day, when he sees all the food and drink, and when he's in his house wi' the fine glass windows," Alex said confidently.

"Màiri willna though," Gregor added. "She's been talking about her beautiful napery and how she canna wait to see it laid out on the bed for the wedding night. If he gets tar all over it, she'll be raging. And so will Barbara and Flora, for they've been weaving it for months."

There was a moment's silence while the men contemplated the ramifications of their chieftain's suggestion, and whether the fun was worth the possible consequences.

"Ye can take the tar off wi' whisky though," Angus inserted into the silence. "Ye tellt me that," he added to James.

"Aye. No' without a lot of scrubbing, though," James said.

"Can I help ye? I was too wee when Kenneth was married," Angus asked hopefully, his eyes sparkling at the thought of inflicting this torment on his brother.

"Ye'd no' have got within a league of me wi' your tar and feathers," Kenneth pointed out. He looked from Alex to Angus. With their

67

mischievous grins and matching eager expressions, they had never looked more alike than they did right now.

"Ah, well, it seems the poor laddie's doomed, whatever we say," he sighed, accepting the inevitable.

"Why are ye all standing there, staring at my hens?" Catriona called from her doorway, having noticed the group of men loitering with intent and correctly surmising that they were up to no good.

"No' a word," Alex whispered urgently. "I was thinking to make a wee present of feathers for Duncan and Màiri to use," he continued in a louder voice. "Would ye have any to spare?"

She eyed him suspiciously for a moment, noting how he elbowed Angus in the ribs when he started giggling. But she could hardly question such an innocent request, not from the chieftain. Even so...

"I dinna ken if I've enough to make a pillow. Is that what it's for?" she asked.

"Something for the wedding night, aye," Alex replied evasively.

She went back into the house, giving the men time to perfect expressions of utmost innocence, with the result that when she emerged with a bag and saw them, she was even more suspicious. She handed it over reluctantly, giving James a glare that told him he was in for an interrogation later.

"I commanded ye no' to tell anyone, for it's a wee surprise for my brother," Alex said to him, as they all prepared to go their separate ways. "If she asks ye about it, tell her that."

Alex and Angus set off for home then.

"Ye canna say a word, no' even give him a look. He's awfu' observant," Alex told his brother.

"Aye, he is. So I'm thinking he'll notice ye're carrying a bag of feathers," Angus replied dryly.

"I'll put them up at the cave wi' the others," Alex said. "And the tar, when I get it."

"Will there be enough?" Angus asked, looking doubtfully at the small bag.

"Aye, for we're no' making a pillow. We'll no' need more than a handful to cover his feet entirely. And his legs. I've more already up at the cave, for I've been collecting them for weeks, but didna have enough to do it properly until now."

They continued on their way, giggling together as they discussed how to perform the deed the day before the wedding feast.

It would all be well, Alex thought later, when the feathers were safely hidden. Duncan had a good sense of humour. It was worth it to continue his bonding with Angus, too. Duncan would understand that. All men had their feet washed with something horrible on the eve of their wedding. It was tradition, and it would put everyone in a fine mood for the next day.

Preparations continued, with food and drink made and a whistle player brought in from another branch of the MacGregors, as Alasdair could no longer play for hours at a time, and as stirring as the pipes were, it wouldn't be fair to expect Dugald to play them all night, and they were very loud were it to rain and the wedding have to be moved indoors.

Two days before the great day, Angus and James carried the finished *sèis* over to the cottage where Duncan and Màiri were making everything as perfect as possible. Much of the clan appeared as if by magic, as hadn't Angus talked of nothing else for weeks, and hadn't he gone all the way to Glasgow with the chieftain for a mysterious decoration?

By sheer good luck the sky was clear, so when Angus and James put it down outside the house and removed the blanket that was covering it, the sun shone through the diamonds of coloured glass inserted in the back, making them glow and throwing patterns of coloured light on to the ground, eliciting sounds of wonder from the MacGregors, many of whom had never seen stained glass in their lives.

"Oh, but that's *beautiful!*" Màiri said as she came out to see why everyone was congregated outside. She and Duncan had decided to be entranced regardless of what they really thought of Angus's surprise present, but the awe in her voice was unfeigned. It really *was* beautiful.

Duncan came out then, and the two of them looked at it. It was, without doubt, the finest *sèis* anyone had ever seen, beautifully made, the wood smooth and polished with beeswax, the elaborate knotwork carving on the arms and around the diamond panes on the back exquisitely done.

Màiri looked at Angus, tears in her eyes.

"I canna believe ye did all this, just for us," she said. "It's the most beautiful thing I've ever seen!"

"James did most of the construction of it," Angus said, "for I canna do the joints he can. And the smoothing and polishing, which took an awfu' long time."

"Aye, but the laddie did all the carving," James added. "And he thought of the pattern himself. He's a great eye for such things."

"It's unbelievable," Duncan said, stroking the arm with one finger, clearly loving the feel of the perfectly smooth wood and the intricacy of the carving. "This will be an heirloom, Angus, passed down to our bairns, and their bairns. I canna thank ye enough for it. I didna expect anything so fine, I'll admit."

"Aye, well, you and Alex were my ma and da for a long time, and you were both to me when Alex was away. And Màiri's been like a sister since the night Da beat ye and we both met her."

The whole clan had grown silent on hearing these words, for no one spoke of that time or of what Alexander had done, for he had been taken by a demon then. No one *wanted* to remember that time.

"And now ye're my *real* sister!" he continued, oblivious to their reaction, having never known his father before Moira died. He was so overjoyed by the obvious admiration from his brother and almost sister-in-law that the clan could probably have been struck by lightning without him noticing at that point. "I'm *so* glad ye love it," he added, almost bursting with happiness.

"Will we take it inside?" Màiri asked.

The two makers of the piece carried it in, where it was positioned firstly by the wall near to the fire, then under the window.

"For then the sun will shine through the glass," Màiri said, her face glowing with pride. "And if we're home in the daylight, we could sit there and read! Or Duncan could," she amended.

"You can read awfu' well too, now," Duncan told her, who had taught her to, and was now teaching her to write as well.

"Aye, but no' as fast as you."

"That comes wi' time," Angus said. "And ye'll learn it easily, for ye can sit still, like Duncan. I canna do that, nor Alex neither."

A burst of laughter came from the clan members who were close enough to hear it, because it summed the brothers up perfectly.

Everyone looked at it, and the consensus of opinion was that it was certainly in the best place, but could always be moved in the winter if the heat from the fire didn't reach it sufficiently.

"Oh, I wanted to give ye this as well," Angus said, taking something out of his *sporan* and handing it to them. "The glassmaker took the other one I made in payment for the glass. Alex tellt him a bonny tale about it. It seems ye share one between ye, and it signifies that ye're one now. Or will be in two days."

"We havena ever had one," Alex said, "but I was tellt that on your wedding night ye fill half the cup wi' the man's favourite drink, and half wi' the woman's, and then ye take the handles together and drink from each side by turns, and it symbolises your joining and sharing everything amicably."

"Oh, that's a bonny custom," Fiona said, to general agreement.

"Aye. Alex said the chiefs used to do it, too, when they joined together to fight, or some such," Angus continued. "To show harmony. But some of them had the bottom of the quaich made from glass, so they could see if their new friend was about to dirk them."

"Ah, that's a wise idea," Gregor said

"I dinna think you two will need a glass-bottomed quaich," Barbara observed. "I havena seen a finer match since your ma and da married, and that's the truth."

"We'll no' use it until our wedding day," Màiri said, putting it down on the table. "Only two days, now!"

The couple moved as one and sat on the *sèis,* their faces glowing with happiness, with anticipation.

The clan took the hint and left them together. It was wonderful, they agreed later, or at least the ones with happy marriages did, to see a young couple so very much in love. A rare and wondrous thing indeed. And both of them so handsome and well-made, too. They'd raise bonny bairns, one day.

Hopefully the chieftain would too, although he didn't show the slightest inclination in that way, or not yet. But surely his day would come, for he was a handsome man, and a learned one too!

But if by some unhappy chance it didn't, then at least Duncan would continue the line of the chieftains, so there would be no need for dissent when the time came to find a new one, in the far distant future, they prayed. For Alex was shaping up well, although he had not been truly tested yet. But the clansfolk had no doubt that Alexander had been right. His son would be a superb leader, and hopefully would continue so for many, many years.

Late April 1737

Duncan and Màiri sat outside their cottage on the bench, hands entwined, engaging in one of their favourite pastimes; watching the sun set over the loch and the stars appear in the evening sky. Duncan had suggested they go down to the lochside to do it, for that was their normal custom.

"No," Màiri said. "If we go down to the loch we'll likely meet others, and I'm wanting this to be our time. This is the last time we'll do this as single people. Tomorrow we'll do it as man and wife."

"I canna believe it's finally happening," he commented. "It seems like an age since I kent I wanted ye for my wife. I dinna think we'll be watching the sunset tomorrow though. We'll still be at the dancing I'm thinking, for the lassies have prepared enough food to feed an army, and the clan have talked of nothing else for weeks. We canna just away off to watch the sun go down."

"We can the day after, and we'll still be married then!" she pointed out. "But we're no' married now, and I want this last evening to be special, one we'll remember for the rest of our lives."

She rested her head against his shoulder, and he turned to kiss her hair, which was soft and smelt of lavender. They settled down, enjoying being alone together on this lovely peaceful spring evening. A blackbird serenaded them from the nearby trees, and a light breeze gently rustled through the grass and lifted their hair. Duncan breathed out softly and closed his eyes for a moment, deeply happy. Everything was perfect.

Or at least it was until half the clan suddenly appeared from the back of the cottage, taking the couple by surprise because they'd moved very stealthily indeed, as Highlanders can when preparing an ambush, but do not normally do when coming to greet friendly clan members.

"The quaich has made us all think about wedding traditions," Alex began. "And we decided to have another one, one that's done the night before the wedding, by way of a blessing on the couple, if ye like."

Angus giggled then stumbled forward as Kenneth tapped him lightly on the shoulder in warning. Duncan looked at them for a moment, seeing the men separating out to his side, the women to his sweetheart's, and comprehension dawned.

"Ah no, man, can ye no' leave us—" he began, getting no further before he was scooped up by Kenneth and Alex and spirited away, the other men following, laughing and making ribald comments.

The women watched them as they disappeared from sight.

"What are they doing to him?" Màiri asked.

"Well, the custom is a washing of the feet, and we're here to do it to you too. But I'm thinking they'll no' be using what we are to wash him," Barbara said.

"No' by the look on Angus's face, anyway," Susan added.

Màiri was then taken into her house, and although it was not the evening she'd either expected or hoped for, there was something very pleasant about having your feet washed with warm water and rose-scented soap, which ceremony was followed by ale, shortbread and plenty of advice on how to both please your man on his wedding night and then rule him for the rest of his life, while letting him believe he was the master.

By this time the sun had gone down and Catriona lit a beeswax candle, a rare treat indeed, for normally only the chieftain had such fine lighting. After a time a sweet honey scent from the candle joined that of the roses.

"They seem to be taking an awfu' long time to wash his feet," Màiri said worriedly after a while. "I was hoping to spend a wee bit of time wi' him before I came home to you."

"I'm sure he'll be back soon," Susan, who this comment was addressed to, said. "I'm so happy for ye, but I'll miss ye dearly when ye're gone from the house."

"Are ye wanting to keep MacGregor?" Màiri asked. "He's fine company, when the mood's on him."

"Ah, ye ken cats, lassie. He'll decide for himself where his home is, no' you or I," Susan told her.

Barbara was just inviting everyone to have a second piece of the wedding shortbread when the door suddenly opened and Duncan shot through it, closed it firmly behind him and then leaned on it. Feathers fluttered about in the breeze caused by his sudden appearance, and a dark and bitter smell began to fill the room, overwhelming the scent of both the beeswax candle and his rose-scented fiancée.

"Are there any men in here?" he asked urgently, a hunted look on his face.

"None excepting yourself, laddie," Barbara said. "Christ, man, what have they done to ye?"

His feet, legs and arms were liberally covered with feathers, mainly of the chicken variety, but with various others scattered among them. But it was the glue that was keeping them in place that made the women's eyes water, for it was overpowering in such a small space.

"I should have kent they were up to no good when they were all blethering outside mine, asking for chicken feathers," Catriona said then. "I thought he wanted them to make a pillow for ye. If I'd kent he was thinking to do that, I never would have given them to him, chieftain or no'."

"Will we away outside?" Susan suggested. "For ye dinna want Archangel Tar all over your clean house, I'm thinking. I'll make sure there are none of the wee gomerels waiting for ye first," she added.

While Susan was acting as scout, Màiri got the candle and brought it over to examine him a bit more closely, but not close enough to set him on fire.

"How the hell will we get it off?" she asked. "Will it wash off?"

"No. Ye'll need to get the feathers off first, or as many as ye can," Catriona told her, "and then use alcohol. When James has been marking the cows, he often comes home wi' it all over him, and I willna let him near me or my linen until he's clean, for ye canna wash it from that."

Both Màiri and Duncan instinctively looked to the boxbed which formed a partition between the room they were now in and the bedroom. In anticipation of tomorrow, the bed was already made up with beautiful snowy white linen.

"I'll get it all off," he said to her. "I swear I will. It was just a wee prank. They didna mean any harm. They did the same thing when Kenneth and Jeannie were married, ye mind."

"No' wi' Archangel Tar!" Màiri cried, her voice rising with temper. "Kenneth washed the soot off in the loch in ten minutes! Ye'll no' wash that off so easily! How long does it take James to get it off his hands wi' whisky?" she asked.

Catriona was saved having to answer this question by Susan's reappearance.

"There's no one around. I'm thinking they're all away hame, now they've had their fun. Away outside and we'll see if we can help ye remove it."

They decamped outside, Barbara popping a piece of shortbread in Duncan's mouth, as he was incapable of doing much with his tarry feathered hands at the moment.

They then spent a considerable amount of time removing feathers from Duncan's hands, reckoning that once they were clean, he'd be able to do the rest himself, with Màiri's help. Which might, in fact, be a pleasant thing, in the end. After all, tomorrow was their wedding day. No harm if they started one part of the celebrations a day early. Although judging by the look on Màiri's face, amorous adventures were the last thing on her mind right now.

"Alcohol," Màiri said, her voice tight, her face pale with anger.

"I'll away and get some," Jeannie offered.

"No. I'm needing a moment to calm myself. I'll be back directly," she said, before striding off.

"It wasna done wi' malice," Duncan called after her as she disappeared. "Christ," he murmured when she made no sign of having heard him, "I didna ken she'd take it so badly. I'm sure the others didna either."

"She's awfu' protective of ye, laddie," Susan said then, deftly removing more feathers with a pair of tweezers normally used for splinter removal. "Always has been, since the night she first saw ye."

"Aye, I ken that. But they wouldna have done it if they didna love me," Duncan said.

Susan stopped what she was doing then and sat back on her haunches.

"Màiri wasna brought up as we were. She was a virtual outcast. Well, no' her, but her parents, for her da was a brute, and her ma defended him against everyone, rejecting anyone who tried to help her. I canna imagine why they werena exiled entirely. She doesna see such rough play as love, Duncan, she sees it as hate. Has she no' tellt ye about her childhood?"

"Aye, she has. But she's lived here for so long, seen how we are. I thought she kent that we'd no' do this," he waved at his legs, "to someone if we hated them. We'd never have done this to Father Gordon, would we?"

"No, but she wasna here when he was to see what we do to people we dinna like," Jeannie pointed out. "Susan's the right of it. And ye're precious to her."

"And in truth, I canna imagine what they were thinking of, to use tar on ye," Barbara put in. "It'll take most of the night to get it off ye, and waste a lot of whisky in the process. I'd no' be happy if they'd done that to Gregor on our wedding eve."

"What did they do to him?" Jeannie asked.

"They covered him wi' shite," Barbara admitted, laughing. "It wasna Alexander's finest hour either. No' Alex's da, his grandda," she added for the younger clanswomen. "Clearly his grandson's inherited his wicked humour. But at least shite washes off. He was in the loch until he was nearly blue before I thought he was clean enough to come near me. We married in January," she explained.

"That's most of the feathers off your arms," Susan said. "Will we start on your legs while we wait for Màiri to bring the whisky back? How far up did they go?"

"Only to the knee, thank God," Duncan said. "Aye, for I'm wanting to have as much of this off me as I can before she comes back."

Alex and Angus were sitting by the fire laughing about the events of the evening and sharing a cup of whisky, when the door opened and Màiri blew in like a whirlwind. Before they had time to react she grabbed the bottle of whisky off the floor where it sat between them, pulled the cup from Alex's hand, throwing its contents in his face, then took another two bottles from the press before storming out into the night, leaving the door wide open.

The two brothers sat there in astonished silence for a moment. Alex wiped the whisky from his face with his kilt, then felt his way across to the ewer on the kist, bathing his streaming, stinging eyes with the water.

"I'm thinking Gregor was right when he said she wouldna forgive ye," Angus commented then. "She seems a wee bit fashed wi' ye."

Alex let out a snort of laughter at this vast understatement, dipping a cloth in the water before making his way back to his chair, his eyes still burning.

"I've never seen her so angry," Angus added.

"I didna see her at all, after she threw the whisky at me," Alex replied. "Likely just as well." He lifted his face to the ceiling, wringing water out of the cloth into his eyes, as Angus started laughing.

"She looked awfu' fierce," he said between giggles. "I've never seen her like that. Is she allowed to do such a thing to her chieftain?"

"I'm thinking I'll forgive her this one time," Alex said.

"It was awfu' good fun," Angus admitted. "I felt like one of you, being able to join ye like that."

"Ye are one of us, laddie," Alex said. "If there are things I dinna let ye do yet, it's only because of your age. There wasna any reason why ye couldna join in wi' the foot washing. Ye dinna ken that for there's only yourself and Fergus of a similar age. All the others are either men or wee bairns. It was different when I was your age, for there were a good number of laddies the same age as me." He laid the wet cloth across his eyes now and put his head back. Inspiration struck. "Kenneth's one of us, is he no'?" he said.

"Aye, of course he is!" Angus asserted immediately.

"Well, then, ye ask him how he felt at the '19, when Da wouldna let him go and fight, even though he was taller than all the men."

"Why would he no' let him? He's a bonny fighter," Angus asked.

"Because he wasna fifteen. He was only a few weeks from it, but Da had the rule that no laddie under fifteen went to battle. It was a good rule. I'll keep it myself. But that made Kenneth feel like you do, although it wasna true for him any more than it is for you."

Angus sat back, thinking on this for a minute.

"I'm thinking ye might be wishing ye werena one of us if Duncan canna get the tar off him tonight, though," Alex added then.

"Duncan can calm anyone," Angus said with supreme faith. "He'll make her see the funny side of it, I'm sure."

"I hope so," Alex replied, with more confidence than he felt.

"It *was* awfu' funny, was it no'? The look on his face when we tipped the feathers on him!" Angus said. He exploded into laughter, and within a minute the pair of them were giggling like small boys again.

Angus was no doubt right, Alex thought later, as they prepared to sleep. Màiri was a gentle lassie. Her good humour would be restored when she saw the feast prepared for them, and all the care taken by everyone to make sure her and Duncan's wedding day was as perfect as possible. Even the weather was looking perfect!

It was probably just as well he could not see Màiri's face at that moment, as she scrubbed at her sweetheart's legs using some old cloths that Jeannie had brought from her house. The women had all gone home now on Duncan's insistence, leaving the couple alone.

"We'll no' get any sleep at all, at this rate," she said furiously. "We'll still be trying to clean it off while the others are eating and dancing."

"No, we willna," he said. "Will ye stop a wee minute? There's only the one leg left to do now." He reached his arms out, but she moved out of reach.

"I'm no' angry wi' ye," she said. "But I'm no' sitting on your lap, for if I do, I'll smell as bad as you."

He did smell terrible, he had to admit, a mixture of smoky bitter tar and whisky, both pleasant smells at times, but not when mingled and in such concentration. He sighed, and let his arms fall.

"Susan said a thing while ye were gone that set me thinking," he told her. "I ken what they did was annoying, and we didna have the quiet evening we planned to have. But they didna ken about that, and what they did was truly from love. Susan pointed out that ye didna have that upbringing. If they'd done something like this to your da, it would have been from spite, would it no'?"

"Aye, it would," she admitted.

"We're no' like that," Duncan told her. "My da would never have let yours live in the clan at all. Ye didna ken him before Ma died, but he was a good man, and a kind one. He'd have thrown your da out and offered your ma to stay, and if she'd refused, then he'd have let her go and taken ye in, and brought ye up as one of his own. He wouldna have done this to him, for such a thing is only done from love, never from hate.

"They've spent weeks preparing a wonderful feast for us, the whole clan built the house and furnished it. Alex bought us glass for our windows, and Angus spent weeks carving the *sèis*. They love me, and they love you too. I'm thinking Alex didna realise how long it'd take to clean the tar off. He's as reckless as Angus is – ye dinna see it, for he had to grow up before his time. In truth it was good to see him laughing and so joyful tonight, for Christ knows he's had more than enough pain in his life.

"I'm no' angry wi' him, and I wouldna have ye spoil our day. I understand your anger, and love ye for the reason behind it, but it's misguided, *mo chridhe*."

She sat back then and thought for a few minutes, as was her way, and he gave her the time to do so, as was his way. He poured whisky on another cloth and worked on the leg still covered with tar.

"I canna argue wi' ye, for you're right," she said. "I only saw that they'd done a wicked thing to ye, and spoilt our last evening as single people."

"Aye, well, we wanted it to be memorable, and ye canna deny it will be," Duncan said drily.

She laughed then, the tension easing a little. Then she picked up her cloth and set to work again, but more gently this time.

It took another hour to remove all the stickiness, although his legs and arms were an interesting shade of golden brown and he stank something fearful.

"Ye said they washed your feet wi' roses?" he asked then as they shared a piece of delicious shortbread, the ground around them littered with pungent-smelling cloths.

"No' wi' roses. Wi' soap scented wi' rose petals."

"Ye smell awfu' bonny. Is there any left?"

"Aye, Susan left it wi' me, so I could wash myself wi' it before...tomorrow night," she said, blushing a little.

Duncan nodded.

"That would be lovely, but I'm thinking it might be better used if I away down the loch with it and wash myself. Hopefully it'll take away the tar smell. If ye want ye can away home to Susan's now, for it's late."

"No, I'll come down wi' ye," she said. "I'm no' tired anyway."

They made their way down to the loch armed with soap and the remaining clean cloths, where Duncan unbuckled his belt, letting his *féileadh mór* drop to the ground, then pulled his shirt over his head with his back to her, before heading into the water. She sat on the rock for a while, watching him as he bathed himself, illuminated by the almost full moon. The heavy muscles of his back and shoulders flexed as he scrubbed his arms with the cloth, stirring something deep inside her. He bent his knees suddenly, disappearing under the water for a moment before standing again and brushing his hair back with his hand so it lay over his shoulders, sleek and glossy. He was beautiful.

And then an impulse took her and she stood, untying her skirt and stays, and laying them over the rock. She stood for a moment then in her shift, watching him as he concentrated on removing all trace of the prank the clansmen had played on him, intent on calming her temper, on pleasing her. He was right, she realised; the men had done this from love of him, and he was standing in the loch at midnight, doing this from love of her.

She wanted to do something from love of him. Before she could grow nervous enough to change her mind, she pulled her shift over her head and then walked into the loch to join him.

"Let me help ye," she said softly as he turned on hearing her. She took the cloth from him, rubbed it with soap and then started washing between his fingers, not daring to look into his eyes, not because she thought to see disdain there, but because they'd promised to wait, and yet in her heart she knew that this was the right moment, this one and no other, and she thought she would die if she looked at him and saw that he felt differently.

His hand came under her chin, lifting her face to his, so that she had no choice but to look at him. And then he bent his head to hers and kissed her on the lips, very softly at first, then more firmly, wrapping his arm round her waist to pull her against him. She closed her eyes and put her arms round his neck, letting the soap and cloth fall, loving the silky feel of the cool water against her back and legs contrasting with the hard warmth of his chest against hers, the demanding pressure of his lips on hers igniting a wave of desire that burned through her.

After a while he raised his head, looking intently into her eyes for a long moment.

"Aye," he said softly then. "Ye've the right of it." He bent again and she felt his arm against her knees, and then he lifted her effortlessly into his arms and walked out of the loch to the shoreline, where he put her down. He kissed her again, more urgently now, and she returned his kiss, both of them giving in to the emotions they had held in restraint for so very long.

When he let her go this time she nearly fell, her bones like jelly. For a moment he was businesslike, as he spread his *féileadh mór* carefully on the ground, and then he sat down on it, taking her hand and pulling her onto his lap. He stroked his fingers gently down her side, brushing them lightly across her breast, then rested his hand heavily on her hip. She shivered, but not from cold, as it was an unseasonably warm night, and in any case she was on fire, every nerve in her body tingling.

She pressed her lips against his chest, and then reaching up kissed the strong column of his throat, lifting her hands to run them through his wet hair. She felt the stirrings of his arousal against her thighs, and then she threw her head back and laughed from the pure joy of this glorious, perfect moment.

She looked at him then, eyes sparkling, and saw her emotions reflected in his, and then she pressed herself against him, running her hands down his spine, feeling the strong muscles of his back and knowing that he would always love her, always protect her. She was safe with him as she had never been in childhood, and always would be. Her children would be safe with him too, would be loved, so very much.

"I want to make a bairn wi' ye," she whispered her thought aloud.

"Now? Are ye sure?"

"Aye, right now," she replied. "I've never been more sure of anything in my life," she added, smiling.

She shifted her body then so that she was still sitting on his knee but with her legs around his back, her intention being to make it easier to kiss him, but then it occurred to them both at the same minute that this was a perfect position for other things, especially as they were not in a bed, but on the ground. They giggled in unison, and then she shifted position again, putting her arms across his shoulders and touching her forehead to his.

"I dinna ken exactly what to do," she admitted.

"Nor do I," he said, not telling her that Alex had given him advice based on his experience with a prostitute. It was glaringly clear to Duncan now that this was a very different thing to what his brother had described. "But I'm thinking we're doing fine right now, anyway."

"More than fine," she agreed.

They kissed some more, adjusted position again, and then he was inside her, moving very slowly for fear of hurting her, stopping when he felt a slight obstruction, excruciatingly aware of every glorious second of this moment he had dreamed of for so long.

And then she tightened her legs around his back, pulling him into her, and winced with the sudden pain as she lost her virginity. He froze then, his face a mask of concern.

"Did I hurt ye?" he asked.

"No. Susan tellt me it would hurt a wee bit, when...I'm no' a virgin any more," she said, then laughed, loving the feel of him inside her. Nothing could be more intimate than this. Nothing could be more wonderful. "Let's see if we can make a wee bairn now."

He smiled, and continued moving inside her, gently at first, and then more quickly as his desire built.

And then she realised, both of them realised that it could indeed be more wonderful, as they climaxed together in a storm of unbearably delicious sensation, the glory of which they could never, never have imagined.

They lay silently for a while together afterwards, listening to the soft susurration of the loch against the shore, gazing up at the stars sprinkled across the velvet sky, both of them happier than they thought it was possible to be. And then she laughed quietly and he turned his head to look at her.

"We almost made it, but no' quite," she said.

"I'm thinking this was the perfect moment after all," he agreed.

"Aye. We've the rest of our lives to do it in a bed, wi' our fine linen and wine. This is our special place," she added, glancing across to the rock they'd spent so many hours sitting on, together or alone, looking across the loch, watching the sunset, the sunrise, the moon and the stars.

They both looked up to the heavens again, and lay a few minutes longer.

"We'll remember this night for the rest of our lives anyway now," Duncan said. "I will, at least."

"God, aye," she replied. "When I'm dying, this is the night I want to remember as I say goodbye to the world."

"Me too. But no' for many, many years yet," he said.

She sighed then.

"It's awfu' late. Will we sleep in our cottage tonight?"

"No. I'm thinking you should sleep at Susan's, for she'll be expecting ye, and it doesna seem right for me to wake up next to ye on the morning of our wedding, somehow. That's something we can look forward to doing tomorrow."

He was right. There would be a different intimacy in sleeping next to the man you loved, all night. That would be a new experience, a different one, and not one you could do lying at the side of the loch, where half the clan would come down to wash or collect water in a few hours.

They stood then and helped each other dress, after which they walked hand-in-hand through the sleeping settlement. When they reached Susan's they stopped, and he wrapped his arms around her then, kissing her once more.

"*Chun a-màireach, mo chridhe*," he said softly and then turning, melted away into the trees, leaving her standing alone, suddenly unaccountably lonely.

She shook her head then at her own silliness. She would never be lonely again. And then she smiled, and opening the door went in to sleep her last night in her aunt's house.

CHAPTER FIVE

THE NEXT DAY DAWNED warm and sunny, and to look at the couple as they pledged their wedding vows to each other, no one would have known that neither of them had slept at all on the previous night.

In fact no one *did* know, with the exception of Susan, who had woken on hearing her niece creep into the house late in the night, go briefly to bed, then get up again, having given up on any idea of sleep. She had got up as well then, and the two of them had sat together chatting until the sky lightened and then grew pink. Although Susan had neither asked about nor been told what had happened after all the women had gone home from the foot washing ceremony, Màiri was glowing with happiness, far more so than she had been earlier, which had told Susan all she needed to know.

Now, watching them as they kissed and the clan roared their approval at the match, she was not the only woman whose eyes filled with tears. A good number of the men were clearly emotional too, Highlanders not feeling the need to hide their gentler emotions as many men did.

They were a handsome, radiant couple. Màiri wore a beautiful heather-purple gown, her dark hair flowing loose to her hips and a wreath of wood anemones circling her head. If Duncan's legs and arms were both darker and more hairless than normal, no one commented on that, not at this point in the proceedings at any rate, preferring to focus on his fine *féileadh mór* of red, black and green, and on his blue bonnet, which sported the pine sprig of his clan along with a single eagle feather denoting his relationship to the chieftain.

After the vows had been exchanged Susan, standing in place of the bride's mother, broke the bridecake over Màiri's head, the resulting mass of small crumbs that showered her eliciting another roar of approval, as the cake breaking into tiny pieces was a good omen, indicating that the marriage would be a fruitful one.

This done, Duncan then produced the quaich.

"As ye all ken," he announced to everyone, "as well as the *sèis,* Angus made us a quaich, so we thought to start a new custom, well, new for us at least, and drink a wee toast to all of ye who have put so much work into making this the happiest day of our lives."

The quaich was duly filled with their preferred drinks, Duncan's side with whisky and Màiri's with wine, after which the couple drained it between them, somewhat clumsily and with much laughter, as it took them a few mouthfuls to become coordinated in tipping the cup between them.

Angus looked almost as radiant as the bride and groom, overwhelmed by them making his gift a centrepiece of their vows, and also by being given an eagle feather for his bonnet, which only the chieftain's brothers were allowed to wear, and which confirmed that Alex had meant what he'd said when he'd told him he would have an important role in the clan one day. He watched his brother and sister-in-law laughing as they tried not to pour alcohol all over themselves, and thought that even they could not be happier than he was right now.

This done the celebrations started, and the clansfolk began the onerous task of eating and drinking part of the enormous amount of food that had been prepared, after which they would sing, dance, have good-humoured if sometimes rough games, tell stories, and then repeat the whole process until either dawn broke or everyone was too drunk and tired to continue.

The MacGregors set to this task with great enthusiasm, and several hours later, although many of the children had succumbed and were now sleeping in Gregor and Barbara's house, the rest of the clan showed no signs of tiring, although a good many were unsteady on their feet and their clothing was not quite as pristine as it had been earlier.

As a result of this, the reels they were dancing to the accompaniment of Dugald's pipes, Alasdair's fiddle, and Brian's whistle, although still being performed with exuberance, were growing increasingly uncoordinated. Alex had had to leap forward more than once to prevent people falling into the fire which had been lit in the centre of the clearing, as the temperature had plummeted once it grew dark.

In spite of Duncan and Màiri declaring they were not going to drink on the day, they both appeared almost as intoxicated as many of the other MacGregors were. The quaich ceremony seemed to have abolished that resolution.

Alex looked around, and saw that one group of men seemed about to engage in a highly inebriated dirk-throwing contest, while another group within earshot were discussing who would be the fastest to swim across the loch. He was thankful now that he had moderated his drinking, wanting to ensure that the wedding was perfect from start to finish. It was perhaps time for a short break. He made his way over to the musicians and a moment later the music stopped.

"I'm thinking it's maybe time for a wee rest," he called, once everyone had realised that the music suddenly stopping, combined with the chieftain standing in the middle of the clearing might signify something. "After all, ye've been dancing for hours, and it's customary to tell a few tales on such a night. Even if ye dinna need a break, Dugald, Alasdair and Brian surely do, and it would be an insult to the bride and groom should they no' be able to play them to their bed at dawn."

He did not look at the bride and groom as he said this, because he was very aware that he was not Màiri's favourite MacGregor at the moment, after last night. This comment would do nothing to restore him to her favour either, as neither her nor Duncan were lovers of noisy gatherings, and would normally have quietly disappeared by now. They could hardly do that at their own wedding though, and seemed to be thoroughly enjoying themselves. Both of them had danced almost continuously, accepting invitations from everyone who asked them, and showed no signs of wanting to leave. Maybe they *would* stay till dawn.

But whether they would or not, Alex was not a lover of drowned or dirked clansmen, and a break would stop the contests without him having to lay down the law, so a few minutes later the clan was sitting round the fire, while he told them how he'd managed to convince the glassmaker to exchange Angus's quaich for the beautiful stained glass.

"Was the man a Sasannach?" Kenneth asked, after everyone had stopped laughing at his account, added to by Angus.

"No. He was a Lowlander though," Alex said by way of justification for his outrageous lies.

"Ah, well, no' much difference in many cases," Simon added.

"There is a difference," Alasdair commented. "Grandda always says ye can sell anything to a Sasannach if ye've an outrageous enough tale, and anything to a Lowlander if ye make it seem that ye dinna ken the true value of what ye're selling."

"Aye, for Highlanders are awfu' brutish and dull-witted, and ken only about fighting. They have no understanding of the finer things," Kenneth agreed.

"I'm glad yon mannie thought so, for it got me the lovely glass for a couple of hours work," Angus said happily.

"I'm looking forward to your first cattle sale at Crieff now," Alasdair said. "An awfu' lot of the dealers are Sasannachs and Lowlanders. Ye'll be selling them cows as unicorns, I'm thinking."

"Aye. If ye stick horns on their foreheads wi' Archangel Tar, they'll no' come off until they're halfway home and we'll be long gone by then," James added.

This was greeted by a great roar of laughter, followed by assorted comments about the rose-scented, smooth-skinned groom.

"Ye'll be thinking ye're bedding wi' a lassie the night, Màiri, once ye blow out the candle," Simon remarked, eliciting another shout of laughter.

"No I willna, for it's no' his legs and arms I'll be stroking, once we're alone together," Màiri shot back. "If he smells like a lassie that's your doing, ye wee gomerels, and if ye carry on I'll maybe be borrowing my husband's dirk and making some of ye *true* lassies before the night's over."

The women roared approval at this response, while the men all shrank back in mock horror.

"She would too," Angus affirmed. "She's an awfu' temper on her. I thought she'd blinded Alex last night!"

All attention switched to Alex then, who told them what had happened, complete with exaggerated actions, even mimicking Màiri's voice with remarkable accuracy. After this, and before any more ribald comments could be offered to make him even more unpopular with his sister-in-law, Alex said maybe they'd better finish the food now, and then there'd be time for more dancing, if the musicians were happy to play.

They were, and a few minutes later everyone was up again, while Alex sat by the fire for a few minutes, apparently enjoying a piece of shortbread and a drink, while actually watching to make sure none of the clansmen remembered the ridiculous contests they'd been about to perform earlier.

"I didna really blind ye, did I?" a female voice came from behind him. He looked round to see a worried-looking Màiri. He patted the bench next to him, and she sat down.

"No, although I couldna see anything for a while, for my eyes were streaming and burning, and they're still a wee bit prickly. But I can see as well as ever. And I'm thinking I deserved it. How long did it take to wash it off? Duncan didna come home at all."

"No, he slept in our cottage last night," she said, her mouth curving upwards at the joy of realising that it was now truly *their* cottage, and later they'd sleep there together for the first time. "I went back to Susan's, but it was awfu' late. We went down to the loch to wash it all off wi' the soap Susan gave me. It took half the night, though." She blushed furiously then as she remembered what the other half of the night had been spent doing, but luckily Alex missed it, as he was still casting glances round at the clansfolk.

"Aye, well, I'm sorry. Duncan tellt us ye'd wanted a quiet evening together, watching the sun set. He didna tell us that until after we'd feathered him though," Alex told her.

"Would ye have stopped if he'd told ye before?" she asked.

He looked directly at her then, and grinned.

"No, I wouldna! He's my brother! I had to do something particularly evil to him. I'll do the same to Angus when his turn comes. Maybe no' wi' Archangel Tar though."

"I'm thinking they'll likely do the same for you too, when you marry. If they do, I'll be asking to be one of the party," she told him.

He laughed then.

"When I get married, I'll give ye permission to join them," he promised. "Am I forgiven for spoiling your wedding eve, then?"

She considered for a minute.

"Aye. Ye didna spoil it, in the end. It was just memorable in a different way," she admitted. This time he caught the blush as it flooded her face, but before he could say anything she stood, patted him on the shoulder and went back to the dancing.

He sat for a minute longer then, smiling to himself, happy that his brother was so well married, and wondering if he would ever find someone as suitable for him, someone he could love and be loved by, as much as Duncan and Màiri did. He doubted it, as there was no one in the clan he liked in that way, and he could not imagine having the time to get to know a lassie well enough during his future brief visits to other clans. It seemed likely to him that he'd remain single, or marry mainly to have bairns, as so many people did. But only time would tell. Right now he needed to become the best chieftain possible. His clan deserved that.

And then Jeannie came and asked him to dance with her, and he allowed himself to be swept back into the music, not wanting any silly thoughts to mar this perfect night.

The bride and groom did stay well into the night, finally leaving just a couple of hours before sunrise. Thankfully Alex had either forgotten his promise that Dugald should pipe them home or had changed his mind, because in the end they walked, or rather reeled back to their cottage to the sound of the clan still laughing and dancing, the pipes fading as they drew closer to the home they would share for the rest of their lives.

"I canna believe we stayed so long," Màiri commented as they entered to find a peat fire burning in the main room, which meant that the house was pleasantly warm instead of freezing as they'd expected. "That'll be Susan," she added, smiling.

Aye, well, we'll only marry the once, so it was worth enjoying all of it. Almost all of it," Duncan said, as when they'd left the clan had shown no signs of finishing. He yawned. "We can sleep late the morrow, for I'm thinking no one will be up and about much before noon!"

"Barbara tellt me that the women have all arranged that we'll no' be disturbed by *anyone* until we want to be. No' just until noon, but for as long as we like," Màiri told him, her cheeks reddening.

They both stood in the middle of the room feeling suddenly awkward, and then he smiled, took her hand and said, "Will we away to our bed, then? In truth if we dinna go soon I'll likely fall on the ground and sleep there, I'm so tired!"

"Did ye no' sleep at all?" she asked.

"No. Did you?"

She shook her head.

"I'm thinking we were right to have our wedding night last night, then," he said. "For tonight we can just sleep, unless ye're wanting to—"

"I *am* wanting to," she admitted. "But I think I'd rather just sleep tonight. For we can stay in bed as long as we want to, and there isna a law that says ye can only make love at night, is there?"

"If there was, I wouldna pay heed to it. The law doesna apply to MacGregors, after all," he said laughingly.

They made their way into the bedroom, to find the floor liberally sprinkled with dried lavender and lemon balm which released a lovely scent as they walked on it. A kist had been drawn up to the side of the bed, and on it was a beeswax candle, a bottle of wine, two glasses and a plate of cakes. Màiri exclaimed with delight, because this was exactly what she had dreamed of, what they'd both wanted on their wedding night.

"*This* isna Susan, but Alex," Duncan said then. "I tellt him this is what we wanted on our wedding night, when..." His voice trailed off.

"When what?" Màiri asked when it was clear he wasn't going to continue.

"When I...er...when I asked for his advice about how to please a lassie. For I hadna ever...and when he was in Paris, he tellt me he'd been wi'...er...and she'd shown him how to please a lady."

Màiri, who had been lighting the candle, stopped and looked up at him, then started laughing, because her strong fearless husband and protector looked remarkably like a small child at that moment, biting his lip and looking down at the ground.

"Ye're telling me ye asked your brother about his experiences wi' a harlot?" she said.

"Aye," he admitted, reassured by her obvious humour. "I didna want it to be clumsy...wanted it to be a beautiful experience."

She nodded.

"But I didna do any of the things he said, in the end," Duncan hurried on. "For everything just happened, and it wouldna have felt right, somehow, anyway, to do any of those things to ye."

She came into his arms then, and embraced him.

"I ken ye dinna think of me as a harlot, ye loon," she said into his shoulder, "but I'm glad ye were just natural last night, for it was perfect. Shall we go to bed? We can have a wee cake and some wine then."

They undressed quickly, just letting their clothes fall to the floor, and then climbed between the crisp, clean sheets, before instinctively curling up against each other, his chest to her back, her head resting on one arm, while he wrapped the other one protectively around her waist.

And then, both exhausted, and both very, very happy, they fell instantly asleep.

Duncan woke first in the morning, although the light coming through the window told him that it was more likely afternoon. He smiled, realising that it didn't matter. They could spend the whole day in bed if they wanted. His wife slumbered on next to him, so he did not stretch as he normally would but just lay still, loving the feel of her body against his, so much smaller than his, so trusting.

A great surge of protectiveness pulsed through him, taking him by surprise, and he knew in that moment that if anyone ever tried to hurt her, he would kill them without hesitation. He breathed deeply for a few minutes, letting the overwhelming emotion pass. No one would hurt her now. Those days were over. Her father and mother were dead, and everyone in the clan loved her, would protect her exactly as he would, although maybe not with the same intensity of feeling.

He kissed her hair softly, then just lay there and let her sleep, taking in everything; the bedroom with its herb-strewn floor, the way the light fell through the panes, the kist with the cakes and wine still untouched on it, the candle burned to nothing. The smell and feel of her hair against his face, the weight of her head on his shoulder, the softness of her skin, and the sweet smell of roses, enhanced by their shared bodily warmth, along with the slight underlying bitterness of the tar.

He smiled to himself, knowing that he would never forget this moment, just as he would never forget the moments down by the loch, or the touch of her lips against his as they had sealed their wedding vows.

So many moments to cherish already, and so many more to come. Thousands of them.

And then she moaned softly and stirred, and they began the first day of the rest of their lives together.

France, June 1737

The Earl of Highbury was about to eat his last meal in Paris, in a tavern where he ate regularly, close to the apartments he had rented for the last four months. He had said his farewells to Ashelle and Scolastica on the previous day, which he had dreaded doing.

He had grown very close to them in the last months, visiting them regularly, sometimes on business, but more often for pleasure. They had worked wonders with the house he had purchased for them, and their school was now running properly, with most if not all of the teething troubles dealt with. Any problems that arose from now on would hopefully be minor ones, which he was confident the two ladies could deal with without his help at this point.

Having compared their generally humble attitude when dealing with tradesmen to the more imperious ones of various ladies of his acquaintance at home, he had offered to give them lessons in how to deal with people as the gentry or lower nobility would.

"You must remember that you are no longer poor, and stop feeling that tradesmen and officials are doing you a favour by selling you things or performing a necessary duty for you," he had told them. "It is the other way round – if you were not using their services, then they would not have work. It might be hard to do at first, but until it becomes second nature, you must pretend – be an actress, like the ladies we have seen at plays!"

After he had watched their happiness when they'd attended the play Alex had performed in, he had managed to acquire a box for the season, and the three of them attended regularly. He enjoyed the performances immensely, but his pleasure was always tinged with sadness, because he was reminded of Alex, and of the fact that he would almost certainly never see him again.

The resultant lessons he had given to Ashelle and Scolastica had been alternately frustrating and great fun, but they were quick learners and now, as he prepared to leave them to continue running their school and living their lives without him, he felt a lot more confident that they would not be abused or cheated. Last night he had told them that they must not hesitate to write to him if they encountered any problems, or even needed any advice, as it would be no hardship to him to return to Paris if necessary. Indeed he would relish an excuse to.

Then they had embraced each other, and many tears had been shed.

He would miss them terribly, he realised now, as he waited for his food to arrive. As he missed Alex, and wondered often how he was, if he had adapted to life as the chieftain of his clan, if he ever thought of Paris and his friend William.

He probably did not, Highbury thought gloomily. Leading a clan in dangerous and challenging conditions, the likes of which Highbury could not imagine, must surely leave little time to reminisce about the past. And Alex had promised never to reveal the earl's identity, so perhaps he'd found it easier to dismiss him from his mind completely.

To his surprise Highbury felt extraordinarily distressed by this. *You are being ridiculous,* he told himself. *You have no idea whether he has forgotten you or not. And really, it doesn't matter, as you aren't likely to meet again.*

He looked around the room, trying to pull himself out of this low mood he'd thought himself into. The tavern was very busy today. In fact it was full. He was very pleased that he had taken a whole table for himself, as he did every time he came here. He was not in the mood for small talk with strangers, even though he felt suddenly lonely, sitting alone in the midst of conviviality. Perhaps he should have invited Ashelle and Scolastica to come and dine with him.

He watched as a middle-aged lady entered with three younger females, who were almost certainly her daughters as they all bore a remarkable resemblance to each other, and to her. Although Highbury was too far away to hear what the landlord was saying to her, the man's gallic hand gestures made it clear that he was telling her there was no room.

He would miss the expressive gestures of the French, he realised. He would miss so much, in fact. He would return, he decided. After all, he could do whatever he wanted. He did not have to wait for Ashelle or Scolastica to need him.

The woman was now responding to the landlord as expressively, so was certainly French herself. She looked round the room impatiently, and then pointed directly at Highbury's table. Their eyes met briefly, and in that moment the earl realised that in spite of spending a year in Europe, he was still indisputably an English gentleman, incapable of ignoring her plight now she knew he had seen her. It would be unspeakably rude not to invite her and her daughters to join him.

Sighing inwardly he stood and gestured to the landlord, who came across to him, an expression of the utmost relief on his face, as it was clear the lady was somewhat of a force of nature, and within a few minutes they were seated together at the table, and had ordered their own food, Highbury asking for his to be brought at the same time as theirs, although he had ordered earlier.

Perhaps tonight small talk would distract him from his gloom, Highbury, who normally enjoyed it as much as Harriet did, told himself fiercely.

"I cannot tell you how grateful I am, we are to you, for offering to share your table with us, for I will admit we are all most fatigued," the lady began in perfect English, to his surprise.

"Then I am gratified to be of assistance. Lord William," he added, his instincts telling him not to divulge his title, although there was no reason why he shouldn't.

"Delighted to meet you, my lord," she replied. "I am Lady Peters, relict of Sir John Peters, and these are my daughters, Anna, Caroline and Beatrice."

"Enchanted," Highbury replied. "I'm delighted to have such charming company. You must allow me to buy you dinner. It is the very least I can do. Have you only just arrived in Paris?"

"Yes. We are staying here for a few days, then travelling on to Geneva. And yourself?"

"I have been in Paris for some time, dealing with business," he said vaguely. "I leave tomorrow."

"Oh! Such a pity!" Lady Peters cried. "For in truth we know no one in the city, and some respectable company would be delightful! It is hard, my lord, to be alone in the world, at my age."

From the corner of his eye Highbury saw the two older daughters exchange a glance, one rolling her eyes to heaven.

"But surely your daughters must be excellent company for you, my lady," he responded, wondering how quickly he could dispose of his food and make an excuse to leave.

"Oh, yes, of course," she said, as though she'd forgotten they were there until that moment. "I mean of course without a gentleman. I miss my dear husband so very much!"

"I am very sorry for your loss," he replied automatically. "Are you recently bereaved?"

"Papa died in 1719, my lord," the eldest daughter Anna interposed coolly, earning a spiteful look from her mother.

"Yes, and left us destitute!" her mama cried, as though this had happened yesterday rather than eighteen years ago. "Such a blow! So many years alone."

Highbury swallowed the standard polite observation that surely such a handsome woman must not be short of suitors, as he wished to avoid saying anything that might encourage her. He now knew why he had not introduced himself as the Earl of Highbury.

At this point the food arrived, and he seized the opportunity to change the subject.

"Are you then travelling to visit friends in Geneva, my lady?" he asked, once the waiter had gone. "I believe it is a delightful place," he added, having no idea what sort of place it was. "I am sure you will have many wonderful stories to tell your friends when you return to England."

"We will never return to England," Anna said, before her mother could finish chewing her mouthful of food and reply. "When Papa died, he left nothing but gambling debts, so Mama had to sell the house in Cheshire to pay off his debts, and we have been travelling ever since. I have only the vaguest memories of England."

"Oh really, my dear, you exaggerate!" her mama cried, having swallowed hastily. "It is true that Sir John was a little careless with his money, but he was a good man at heart! I admit, though, that we are in much reduced circumstances. Are your estates in Cheshire, my lord?" she asked eagerly.

"No," Highbury replied. "So what takes you to Geneva?"

"Our grandparents," the second daughter Caroline told him. "Mama is going to take care of them, as they are quite elderly now."

"Oh, how kind of you!" the earl said. "I'm sure they will be most grateful to you for travelling all that way to care for them."

Lady Peters smiled, and reaching across the table, actually patted his hand. Appalled, he stiffened, but managed to resist the urge to snatch it away.

"You are so generous! It is not actually *in* Geneva. Indeed I think it would not be safe to travel to the city as there is great unrest there at the moment. We are going to a small village in the hills surrounding the lake, which my parents assure me is untouched by the riots," the lady said. "I have resisted until now, as I was hoping to find husbands for my daughters before I buried myself in a tiny village and sacrificed myself to my parents' needs. Not that I care about myself, of course, but I fear my daughters may never find suitable matches! Are you married yourself, my lord?"

Dear God! The woman was insufferable! Her poor daughters would never be married, if she had anything to do with it.

"If you will excuse me for one moment, ladies," he said, gesturing to the waiter to bring more wine. He stood, and bowing politely made his way outside, as though needing to answer a call of nature.

Once there he leaned against the wall, closed his eyes and took some deep breaths. He would give his soul to have Harriet appear now! He stood there for a minute or two, imagining what she would say and wishing he had the courage to do as she would. He wanted nothing more than to run away, eat a quiet meal at his apartment, alone. After all, he was leaving in the morning, so there was no chance that they would meet again if he did.

He could not do that. Every ounce of his upbringing would not allow him to. Nor could he tell her exactly what he thought of her, as Harriet, and possibly Alex would. He opened his eyes, braced himself, and had just turned to go back into the tavern when the door opened and Anna Peters appeared.

"Oh good, I was right, then. You came outside to escape my mama," she said bluntly. "I wanted to speak with you. I'm sure you think she is quite outrageous, and indeed she is, but she is harmless too. As long as you do not propose marriage to her or us, you're in no danger, I assure you.

"No, no," she added, when he made a gesture to deny this. "You must save all your lies for when you are back in the tavern. In truth she is lonely, my lord. Her life has not been easy. I was only four when

Papa died, but even then I knew he was a selfish fool who cared for no one but himself. After he died Mama left the country with the four of us, to escape the shame of being penniless, I think. She was not then as she is now. The difficult years have made her that."

"The four of you," Highbury said.

"Yes. We had a brother, Anthony. He was six when Papa died, and Mama put all her hopes in him. He inherited Papa's title and she thought that if she could raise him well, one day he would redeem the whole family from penury. So we moved to her friend's chateau in Blois. But both her friend and Anthony died the following year, and she has never been the same since then. She loved her friend dearly, and my brother too, of course.

"Since then we have travelled from one place to another, staying with various distant cousins, but of course penniless widows with young families are never welcome, so we have had to move many times. She *has* resisted going to our grandparents, for in truth she will be treated like a slave there. I think it is desperation that makes her so bold with you, my lord.

"I wished to tell you that, for I think you are a kind man, but you clearly wanted to escape as quickly as possible, which I do not blame you for! I will say this; if you are kind to her you will be in no danger, other than to have your hand patted and to have to pretend interest in tedious topics. But I think you are accustomed to that, are you not? All the nobility are. If you can bear to do this, you will make her happy, and raise her spirits for a few days. I would like to see that, for she is very unhappy."

"I think you love your mama very much," he said then. "What you have told me took courage."

"Yes, I do love her. Well, not always, but most of the time. Life has been hard for her, but she has always taken care of us. That is worth much, I think."

"It is. Thank you," he replied, feeling ashamed of himself for judging Lady Peters so harshly. "I will gladly spend the rest of the evening in your company."

"Are you really leaving tomorrow?" Anna asked, but in a natural way that raised no alarms.

"Yes. I leave for Calais tomorrow, and then home," he replied.

"Then I will be grateful if you can spend your last evening giving my mama a memory to cherish when she is buried in a hillside village," Anna told him, smiling.

"Will you be safe there, if there is rioting?" Highbury asked.

"Yes, I am sure we will be. It is many miles from Geneva, and an insignificant village. Chardonne," Anna replied. "I believe there is nothing there worth fighting about. In any case, we have little choice, for our funds are almost gone."

They turned to walk back in together, but just at the door, she stopped.

"Oh! Do not mention my brother!"

"I was not going to mention that we have spoken at all," Highbury said.

"Yes, perhaps that is better. But Mama never speaks of him, not to anybody, not even to us. I think it was the only way she could deal with her grief when he died, to pretend he never existed, until she could almost believe it herself."

In the end he spent the whole evening with the tragic Peters family, paying for their meal, and then on impulse asking them if they would care to visit the theatre with him, for he had a box and it would be pleasant to spend his last night in Paris in such excellent company.

"The performance tonight is *Hypolite et Aricie,*" he told them as his carriage took them to the theatre. "Do you like Rameau?"

"We have never seen his works, my lord," Anna leapt in, before her mother either invented an inane opinion or had to admit that they had not been to the theatre for years, "but we have heard of the controversy surrounding his opera. It will be interesting to see it for ourselves, and form our own opinion. We have seen Lully's *Proserpine* and *Roland* many years ago."

"Indeed," Highbury said, noting that Anna's main role in the family seemed to be as her mother's protectress. "I think Rameau brought a freshness to the *tragèdie en musique*, but it will be interesting to hear your opinions, once you have seen the performance."

At the theatre he had bought them a small posy of flowers each, ordered champagne and cakes to be served in the interval, and in general took as much effort to make their evening as pleasant and memorable as possible, as he had with Ashelle and Scolastica, although Lady Peters' overblown compliments on his appearance, his generosity and his kindness, along with assorted amatory hints made him uncomfortable at times. He hoped that Anna had been right when she'd said he was in no danger, as he could not imagine what he would do if she *did* make some sort of romantic proposal.

In the end she did not, to his utter relief, and as he assisted them down from his carriage, having taken them home after the performance, he realised that on the whole it had been a very pleasant last night in Paris. They had held a surprisingly lively and interesting debate in the interval as to the merits of Rameau and Lully, and which aspects of each they preferred or disliked, and Highbury found himself indeed feeling dreadfully sorry for the widow and her daughters. They did not deserve to be shut up in a tiny village nursing elderly parents who it seemed had done nothing to help them when they'd needed it.

The three ladies descended from the coach and after fond farewells and other pleasantries, made their way into the rooms they had taken. Highbury frowned as he watched them go into the building. This was not the safest part of town for unaccompanied ladies to stay in.

And then one figure broke away and rushed back to him.

"Thank you, my lord," Anna said breathlessly. "Truly, I did not expect you to do that. I am indebted to you! My mama will talk about this night for years!" She reached up impulsively and kissed him on the cheek. "So will I! I wish you a safe journey home. Goodnight!"

Before he could reply she ran away, up the steps into the house, and was gone. He stood thoughtfully for a moment, still feeling her kiss on his cheek, and then got back into the carriage.

The next morning as the carriage clattered out of Paris, Highbury smiled to himself, in spite of his sadness at leaving the city he had come to love, a city that had taught him so much, about himself and about aspects of life he could never have imagined. Life as a Highlander, as a slave, as a poor person. How the poor viewed the aristocracy, which was something he imagined very few of his peers would ever know, as they had no intimate dealings with anyone outside their tiny group. It had been fascinating.

And he had learnt how naïve he was, how privileged, how little he knew about anything outside his own circle. And how much he had been missing of life as a result. He had learnt that he got great joy out of making other people happy, of giving them the opportunity to make the most of their skills, and he resolved to continue doing that when he returned home.

He had made a good start this morning, by paying for an extra month in the luxurious apartments he had stayed in for several months, and by withdrawing a generous amount of cash from his lawyer and leaving it on the table with a note. Then he had sent his trustworthy coachman to the house where Lady Peters and her daughters were staying, describing them to Jean, and telling him that if the ladies were out he must wait for them to return, even if it meant they were to leave Paris late, or even the next day.

In the end Jean had returned no more than two hours later to the café Highbury had retired to to have breakfast and wait.

"They were overjoyed, Monsieur le Comte," the man said, sitting down when invited to, used to the familiarity the earl now treated him with. Highbury raised his hand to call a waiter. "The older lady is very effusive, as you said. I waited for them to pack their things, and then assisted them with the baggage. Lady Peters burst into tears and fainted when she saw the money you had left for them! I think they hoped to see you, but I told them you had already left, as you wished to make an early start. As you told me to, Monsieur le Comte."

Yes, that had been a good thing to do. He had not left them enough money to change their lives; he did not have ready access to such a sum. But it *was* enough to allow them to spend a month in Paris making more memories if they chose, or to live more modestly somewhere else for a longer time, hopefully until the riots in Geneva were over. Maybe the girls would find suitors, and they would not have to go to Geneva at all. At least they had a choice, for a short while.

They had left the city behind now. Highbury looked out of the window at the French countryside, both looking forward to and dreading going home.

It would be wonderful to see Harriet, Melanie and Philippa again. He had missed them terribly. He had communicated with his steward, and the man was very capable, but even so there would be a lot to do when he got home. At least he would be too busy to become melancholy.

But right now he was not too busy. He had nothing to do for the next days but stare out of windows and endure the rigours of travel. And think of how to deal with Daniel. It had been impossible not to compare his own son with the man he had come to love as a son in the last year. Only three years separated them in age, and yet Alex MacGregor was a man, in the best possible sense of the word, while Daniel Barrington was a child, in the worst possible sense of the word. How could he transform him into even half the man the Highlander was?

Highbury realised that he had no idea, none at all, how to work such a miracle. He should have done that when Daniel was a child, listened to Harriet's warnings, instead of assuming his son was like him, and would one day magically become him. Daniel, most definitely, was not like his father. Anything he did now would only be damage limitation.

Gently but firmly, melancholy descended.

CHAPTER SIX

ONCE THE WEDDING WAS over, life went back to normal for the MacGregors. In May the shielings on the hillsides were repaired and the clan carried up dairy equipment, pots, basic furniture, heather mattresses and blankets, after which the cattle were driven up to feed on the mountain grass until late summer, cared for mainly by the women and girls, who spent their days making the butter and cheese that the clan would depend on for survival through the winter.

Some of the women and the men stayed down in the settlements, where crops were sown, peats cut and other tasks done. In the evenings the young men would often make their way up to the shielings to visit their sweethearts. It was, generally, a simple, happy time. Songs were sung, stories told, romantic relationships blossomed, while everyone enjoyed the long, warm summer days.

Duncan spent his days down in the settlement, helping Alex in his first year as chieftain to make sure that everything possible was done to ensure a good winter, no matter the weather. Every evening would find him, along with a number of other young men, making his way up the track to the mountain, where he would spend the night with his wife, exchanging small news of the day, discussing hopes and dreams for the future, and planning for the more realisable ideas.

And they would make love, partly because it was such a glorious, perfect way for them to show their love for each other, and partly because they were young and blissfully happy, and very much wanted to start a family. In the evenings they would sit outside, listening to the cattle lowing, looking at the grass bending in the wind, the bees in the heather, and, later and later as summer wore on, the sun setting over the mountains and the loch below.

Some of the young women shared a hut, several of them sleeping in the one room, but Duncan had made sure that Màiri had her own hut, so that he could visit and be alone with her. It suited both of them, as they both needed more time alone than most members of the clan did, and, being newly wed and so very much in love, everyone thought it was lovely. Many of the younger girls hoped one day to have such a devoted husband as Màiri had. And some of the young men hoped one day to have such a bonny wife as Duncan had.

Down in the settlement Alex was also very happy, although all thoughts of bonny wives were far from his mind. Everything was going very well so far. The peats were cut, the oats were growing, and the bere could soon be cut and would be used for making beer, whisky and bannocks.

The weather had been perfect and the cattle were healthy and growing fatter. Many of them had calved this year, too. Alex had decided to go to Crieff in the autumn and sell some of them, maybe acquiring a few more along the way if possible. Then he would buy more food supplies for the winter, and hopefully some luxuries as well.

He very much wanted his first year as chieftain to be a good one, a year of plenty and peace, to instil confidence in his abilities with the clansfolk. It would be a good omen, and people would remember it as one of happiness, one where they all emerged from their huts the following spring well-fed, or at least adequately fed, and happy. Once he'd had a year of learning every aspect of managing the routine life, he thought, he would be ready to deal with the more unusual, unwanted events that occurred from time to time.

So far, so good.

September 1737

In the end the weather was so good, a perfect mixture of rain and sunshine that a bumper harvest was brought in, and some of the women went down from the shielings to the settlement to help to thresh, winnow and grind the grain, leaving fewer to look after the cattle and make the butter and cheese.

Because of that Màiri, who stayed on the mountain, was working harder in the daytime, both milking the cows and churning the butter, and was usually tired by the time Duncan made his way up to her. He would bring her small treats; some of Barbara's honey, a ribbon he'd bought on a trip to Glasgow to fetch the mail, along with the news that they'd gathered. Sometimes she would fall asleep wrapped in his arms, sitting outside on the grass, and would wake refreshed. Then they would go into the hut and make love long into the night.

One evening they sat outside on the grass eating bannocks with honey, and enjoying a glorious sunset that turned the sky succeeding shades of pink, red, gold and purple. It was so spectacular that others had come out of their huts to watch it too. The low murmur of their conversations punctuated with sudden laughter drifted across to the couple.

"Susan came up today," Màiri said quietly, once the vibrant colours had started to diminish and the first stars twinkled in the darkening skies. "I was glad of it, for I wanted to ask her something."

Duncan waited. If it was something she wanted to share with him, she would. There was no need for him to ask; she knew he was interested in everything about her, as she was in everything about him.

"My courses are a wee bit late," she said after a pause. "Only a few days, but I'm normally so regular. So I wanted to ask her how late they have to be before ye ken ye're with child." She looked at him then, saw the sudden comprehension on his face and his instant look of absolute joy, and her heart felt as though it would burst from love of him.

"How late do they have to be?" he asked eagerly.

"Later than they are," she admitted. "I wasna going to tell ye until I was sure, for Susan said many things can cause a lassie to be late, so we mustna get our hopes up yet. But I couldna bear to keep it to myself. It didna seem right."

He leaned into her then and kissed her, tenderly, lovingly.

"Ye did right," he said. "For if ye are wi' child, then we should share the joy from the start, and if ye find ye're no', we should share the disappointment. D'ye feel any different?" He looked at her stomach as though hoping to see some evidence, and she laughed.

"No. She said I might feel sick, and more tired. I *am* more tired, but that's wi' all the extra work in the last few weeks. All of us are, and no' all the lassies are wi' child. In truth I dinna ken. As soon as I do I'll tell ye – or if my courses start."

"Oh, but it'd be bonny if ye are," Duncan said, putting his arm round her waist and pulling her into his side. "Are ye happy?"

"Aye, of course I am! I canna wait to have a wee bairn. I'm wanting more than one though. It's lonely being an only child."

"Our bairn wouldna have your parents, though," Duncan pointed out reasonably. "He or she will never ken a minute without love. But we can have as many as ye're wanting!"

He kissed her again then, more passionately now, and she responded with all her heart.

"Can we still...?" he asked, as she prepared to stand and go into the hut.

"Aye, of course we can!" she said, laughing. "We dinna even ken if there's a bairn there yet! Come on, ye loon," she added affectionately.

He went.

Màiri stood outside the hut in the early afternoon sun, rotating her shoulders in an attempt to release the overworked muscles. She had more butter to churn today, so could not stop yet. She turned her neck from left to right and stretched, grimaced, then glanced at the hut on the far side of the clearing. No sign of life there.

She looked across the mountain at the cattle, all chewing the grass peacefully, and felt the overwhelming urge to lie down and close her eyes, just for a few minutes. She shook her head to banish the thought.

Peigi and Janet had admitted yesterday that they all often had a sleep when the sun was at its strongest.

"Then we can work into the evening, when it's cooler," Peigi had told her. "It isna shirking. We do the same work as you do, just at a different time. We havena got the same incentive to finish early as you have."

The other women had all giggled at this, for it was well known that Màiri worked like a demon all day so that her evenings were completely free to spend with her husband.

They were probably all asleep now. Maybe she *should* join them, Màiri thought. After all, Duncan would understand. He'd told her he would be late tonight as he had a lot to do, so she could probably have a nap and still be finished before he appeared. He would help her, if she was still churning when he arrived.

In a few days they would head back down to the settlement anyway, and then she could spend every evening with him, and parts of the days too, when the weather grew colder and the agricultural work was done.

She would just have a few minutes. She went into the hut, lay down on the heather mattress and was asleep before she knew it.

At the top of the mountain, concealed behind boulders, and well camouflaged by their green and brown *fèilidhean mòra*, a group of youths were watching the cattle and the huts with great interest.

"I dinna think we should do it," one of them murmured.

"Why? There's just a few lassies, and that's three days now they've been away to their beds at this time. Excepting the one, but she's gone too today. We'll be half way home before they wake up," another said. There were several nods of agreement to this statement.

They had indeed been watching the shielings for three days now, and most of them were eager for action, wanting a reward for their patience. They were young, and keen to prove themselves to their chief, who thought them reckless and stupid.

"They're MacGregor cattle. If they find out we've taken them, they'll be awfu' fashed. MacIain'll no' take kindly to that," the cautious one said.

"The MacGregors willna ken we've taken them!" another remarked. "That's why we've spent three days being eaten alive by wee beasties. We can tell MacIain we dinna ken which clan owns them. He'll just be happy to have such bonny cattle!"

"It's a way to prove ourselves. If we do, then he'll maybe let us go on the next wee stramash," a dark-haired youth named Andrew said.

The cautious one, whose name was Niall, was still not convinced.

"Everyone does it," Jamie pointed out. "The MacGregors willna be *very* angry."

"I've heard the MacGregors are angry about everything," Niall retorted.

"They're fearsome fighters. But they dinna kill wi' no reason," Andrew replied. He honestly had no idea whether this was true or not, but was sick of hiding in the rocks doing nothing.

"And ye think stealing their cattle isna a reason?"

"No' if they dinna ken who's taken them. We'll no' prove our bravery and readiness to fight to MacIain if we away hame wi' only midge bites to show for our time away," Jamie said scathingly. "I vote we do it. Yon lassie, the one that doesna usually sleep, was yawning for an hour. She'll sleep through the whole thing."

Aye. We're wasting time. We need to act now."

Everyone agreed to this, and as Niall was clearly alone in his reluctance, he gave in.

"What if we take the cattle that are the furthest from the shielings, then?" he suggested.

"Aye, let's do that. But let's *do* it!" Andrew cried.

Decided now, they readied themselves, then crept down the mountainside, spreading out to drive the cattle to the right of the shielings away from the huts, after which they'd take them over the summit and be gone.

In the hut Màiri woke suddenly out of a deep sleep, and for a few moments had no idea where she was. Then she remembered; she was having a wee nap. She settled down again, her eyes heavy, and was drifting off when she suddenly realised that the cattle were lowing in a way they only did if they were disturbed.

Instantly awake she shot out of bed and ran to the door, looking across the mountain to where the cows were heading away from the pasture for no good reason. She rubbed the sleep out of her eyes, and then she saw the movement of a figure in the grass, and then another, and realised what was happening.

She watched for another moment or two, ascertaining how many reivers there were, for the men would want to know that. Ten...no, eleven. There was no point in waking the other women, she realised; that would waste time, and there were too many men for them to fight off. Better to alert the clansmen.

Màiri took off, running down the mountainside like the wind, hoping the reivers were concentrating too hard on the cattle to notice her. As soon as she was within earshot of the settlement she would start screaming to attract attention.

She made it partway down before a figure suddenly ran into her from the side, knocking her down and winding her. Before she could recover he had grabbed her, pinning her arms to her sides with one arm and putting his hand over her mouth to stop her shouting for help. She fought like a wildcat, kicking and trying to twist out of his grip, at one point almost succeeding. Then he pinched her nostrils closed with his thumb and index finger and suddenly she couldn't breathe.

She fought even more desperately for a few more moments, convinced he was going to kill her, and then he whispered fiercely into her ear.

"Will ye wheesht, lassie? I dinna want to hurt ye. If ye'll stop fighting I'll let ye breathe."

Having no choice, for he was far stronger than her, after a moment she stopped struggling, and true to his word he released his grip on her nostrils, although he still kept his hand over her mouth to prevent her from calling for help.

He dragged her up the mountain, while she hindered him as best she could, this time by being limp and stumbling over every heather root or rock, hoping to hold him up for as long as possible. If the other women came out of their hut it would be over, because they would run in all directions and the reivers would not be able to catch them all. Belatedly she realised that she would have been better to wake them after all. But it was too late now.

Once over the summit she saw the group of young men, who had now herded the cattle into a group and were waiting for their friend to join them.

"*Bàs mallaichte!*" Jamie cried when he saw what Andrew had brought with him.

The youths all looked at the cattle. They'd taken about thirty of them, and were over the mountain, so there was no chance of them being seen by the clansmen. All they had to do now was to keep driving them, making sure to take them out of the way and over water, maybe drive them along a river for a while, to stop the MacGregors tracking them. They would be home in three, maybe four days, and MacIain would be overjoyed to have thirty fat healthy cows, including several calves.

Except for the lassie, who was glaring at them over Andrew's hand.

"I tellt ye we shouldna have done it!" Niall said angrily. "Now what do we do?"

The youths all moved away out of earshot, while Andrew sat down on the ground, taking Màiri with him. Tentatively he removed his hand from her mouth, but she knew he would replace it if she made any noise. There was no point in doing so anyway. No one would hear her now.

"I'm sorry," he said again. "Ye should have stayed in the shieling, then this wouldna have happened."

"They'll kill ye when they find out what ye've done," she spat fiercely.

"No, they willna," he replied reasonably. "For ye dinna ken what clan we're from, or even if we're broken men, do ye?"

She did not reply to this, because she did indeed have no idea what clan they were from, although she was sure they were not broken men. They were all dressed in the same colours, for one thing, and were not ragged and filthy as broken men generally were. She thought rapidly. It was clear he had no wish to hurt her. If he did he would have killed her immediately. Whether the others felt the same way or not she had no idea, but none of them had suggested that, and one had clearly been unwilling to take the cows at all.

She could not escape them, so she would wait and see what they decided to do. Maybe they would just release the cattle and her and run away. That would be the most sensible thing to do, after all.

They did not decide to do that. Their chief was a good judge of character. When he had told them they acted like wee bairns and didna have one decent brain between them, he had not been insulting them so much as making an accurate observation.

Instead they decided to take her with them, heading in the wrong direction until they were too far away for the MacGregors to have any chance of catching up with them. They would let her go when they were near a river, after which they would drive the cattle along the river for a while before changing direction and heading to Glencoe. When she did reach home she would tell the clan they were heading toward Drummond lands, which would take anyone following them the wrong way entirely. They would just have to be careful to make no mention of anything that would reveal they were MacDonalds.

They promised her they would let her go as soon as they were in their own territory, and as she knew she had little to no chance of escaping them, she decided that the best thing to do was to hinder them as much as possible. If the other women didn't notice she was gone or count the cattle, Duncan certainly would when he came up later. And he would still come up, no matter how late. He was very observant, would surely notice that cows were missing, and then he would raise the clan. The reivers could not move as quickly herding cattle and trying to cover their tracks as the MacGregors could. All might yet be well.

In fairness they were very kind to her, sharing their food and water with her, and accepting her oath, sworn on iron, that she would not run away. She kept the oath, instead looking for ways to slow them down.

She did not get many opportunities to do this. Pretending to have a bad stomach which necessitated her going behind a rock regularly only held them up for a few minutes at a time, but anything that might allow her clansmen to catch them was worth trying. Other than that there wasn't much she could really do. As reckless as they were, they certainly knew how to drive cattle, and these were all of one herd so were quite happy to be driven together.

In the end it was the cows themselves slowing due to fatigue and hunger that made the youths take a short break, but not until the middle of the night. When they did they tied Màiri's feet together and her hands behind her back, looping the rope round a rock so she couldn't crawl away, and then all sat down a short distance away from her to relax themselves.

After a short while Niall came over to her, carrying his *féileadh mór*, which he wrapped round her.

"I thought ye might be cold," he said. "There's a chill in the air tonight."

It was a kind gesture, so she didn't tell him that she was too angry and worried to think about the temperature.

"Thank you," she said instead, and he sat down near her.

"Are ye hungry?" he asked, offering her half of a somewhat stale bannock.

"I am. But I canna eat wi' my hands tied," she told him.

He looked at the others for a moment, and then coming to a decision took out his dirk and cut the rope.

"Ye swore no' to run," he reminded her.

"I did, and I'll keep my word," she said, accepting the food and then the leather flask of water he offered. "Ye didna want to take the cattle, did ye?" she said once she'd eaten and drank.

"No," he admitted. "But I canna change that now."

"Can ye no' persuade them to at least let me go?" she asked him. "If the MacGregors catch ye, they'll no' kill ye unless ye force them to it. In fact if it's only the cows ye've got, they might give up, for ye've covered your tracks well, and it'd likely be easier to reive more, than spend days trying to find ye. But they'll never stop hunting ye if ye've got me, whether ye're on your clan lands or no'. And when they catch ye they'll certainly kill ye."

He bit his lip then, looking deeply troubled. He was still a child really, she realised. All of them were not much older than Angus.

"I'd like to, but I canna," he said. "All the others voted to do it. But we'll no' hurt ye, and we'll let ye go tomorrow, I'm thinking."

"If ye let me go now, I swear I'll tell them ye were respectful of me. I dinna ken your clan, and I dinna want to. I'm wife to the chieftain's brother," she told him. Duncan would be beside himself when he found she was gone. By now he certainly would have done. "They ken this land well and they're fast, and will be faster because ye've taken me. If they find ye they'll no' be asking questions, and they'll no' be feeling merciful. If ye let me go now I could be a good way home by morning, and I'll likely meet them on the way. I can stop them following ye."

"Why would ye do that?" he asked.

"Ye're young, and ye've made a mistake. I'm thinking ye're wanting to prove yourselves. The chieftain will understand that. They all will, for they've felt the same way when they were younger. Abducting his sister-in-law isna the way to do it though. I'm thinking ye ken that?"

Niall swore very softly but very feelingly, then stood and walked back to the others. They all argued together for a while in low but fierce voices, and then Niall came back over to her.

"I'm sorry," he said. "If it was my decision I'd let ye go, and I'd even take ye home to make sure no harm befell ye. They said they'll let ye go tomorrow, and when they do I'll go a part of the way back wi' ye, until ye ken where ye are, for it isna right to leave a lassie wandering the hills alone, and I'm thinking our chief would feel the same. I canna do more."

She gave in then.

"Aye. When I get home, I'll tell them ye're a good man," she said.

She would have to find another opportunity to stop them moving. If Duncan and Alex did intercept them, she'd do her best to stop them killing this young man, at least. All of them, really. They were just bairns who'd bitten off more than they could chew.

In the end it was early the next morning before she found an opportunity. Apart from the short break they had travelled through the night, anxious to put as much distance between them and the MacGregors as they could, but by mid-morning the cattle needed milking and were tired and hungry again, and so harder to keep moving. The youths were currently trying to stop the cows eating and keep them going, at least to the next river, when they had decided to allow the cows to feed for an hour or two. Then they would let Màiri go, change direction and go home as quickly as possible.

The cows who had calves kept stopping to let their babies feed, and it was at that point that Màiri saw an opportunity to stop them altogether. She hated having to do it, but knew that if she stopped the calves moving, the mothers would refuse flatly to go any further. The clan would certainly be after them by now. The moment day broke and they could see to track them, they would have set off, although the reivers had taken the herd along three rivers up to now, zigzagging to put the pursuers off.

She gritted her teeth, drew her knife out of her pocket and swiftly hamstrung three of the calves, apologising quietly to them as she did. She would rather cows were injured than MacGregors while attempting to replace the stolen cattle on the way to Crieff. Then she moved as far away from them as she could without attracting attention.

The result was absolute chaos, as she'd expected. Although she hated to break her oath not to run away, she reasoned that they'd thank her if she retraced their steps, as if she did she'd certainly meet her clansmen, who'd be so relieved to see her that they'd surely not kill the idiotic youths when they caught up with them. And she would then be able to lead them at least back to here.

She stood quietly, awaiting her opportunity as the young men stopped the cattle, herding them together before trying to find out what all the noise was about. They were too close for her to attempt to run at the moment.

It was while they were examining the injured calves and discussing whether to leave them and their mothers behind or try somehow to keep going with all of them that Andrew looked up the mountain to the side of them, a sudden flash of blue having caught his eye. He scrutinised the landscape briefly, then suddenly leapt to his feet, drawing his sword as he did and cursing.

The others all followed his gaze, including Màiri, and then the hillside erupted in blue, green and yellow as a band of Highlanders, realising they'd been seen, stood and charged headlong down the mountain, drawing their pistols as they ran.

The cows and Màiri forgotten, the MacDonalds drew their own pistols, slinging their targes from their shoulders as they did, preparing to fight. Oath or no oath, there was no way she was waiting around to see who won this fight, although it seemed almost certain the attackers would, as not only did they have the advantage of running downhill, but at a glance there seemed to be more of them. She had no idea if they would be as respectful of her as these youths had been. She stood, then scurried backwards, and after glancing back to make sure no one had seen her, took off running up the hill on the opposite side of the track, as the first pistol fired. Once out of sight of them she would get her bearings, she decided.

In the end the attackers did not win, although it was a hard and bloody fight. The MacDonalds might have been inept at planning cattle raids, but they were good fighters. When the surviving attackers retreated, a number of them wounded, three of their men and two of the MacDonalds lay dead in the grass, and the cattle were scattered all over the hillside.

The MacDonald youths sheathed their swords, checked their clansmen and on realising nothing could be done for them, sat down, exhausted and wishing very much that they had just stayed at home.

"*Ifrinn,*" Andrew cursed. "What do we do now?"

"We canna worry about the cattle now," Jamie said. "I'm thinking we need to take Alasdair and Robbie home directly. I wish we hadna done this."

"Do ye think God's cursed us because we disobeyed MacIain, and then took the lassie?" Rory asked fearfully.

"I hope no', for I'm thinking that when MacIain finds out what we've done, he'll likely send us to the Lord directly," Andrew commented gloomily.

"Where is the lassie?" Niall asked then, breaking into their pessimistic thoughts. They all looked round, but there was no sign of her.

"She'll have run. I would, an I were her," one of the other youths said. "Forget her. Let's think about what to tell MacIain."

Niall stood up.

"I tellt her I'd see her safely on her way, go wi' her until she kens where she is," he said. "It's the least I can do for her. I'll away and see if I can find her."

Logic told him she'd have headed in the opposite direction to the fight, so without waiting for his clansmen's approval he started up the hill that she'd run up earlier. He was about half way up before he saw her, sprawled face down in the heather to the right of him. He crossed himself and made his way across to her, dropping to his knees when he reached her, praying she'd just fallen and knocked herself unconscious somehow.

Very gently he turned her over, saw the blood, so much blood that the grass and earth under her were soaked with it, as was the bodice of her dress. He closed his eyes for a moment, silently uttering a heartfelt prayer, then he tenderly brushed her hair back off her face, shuddering as he saw her staring at him accusingly.

She was not staring at him accusingly. She was not staring at him at all. Her eyes were expressionless, vacant. He closed them gently, then, sitting next to her, he burst into tears, for nothing could make this right. Nothing would ever make this right.

"Have ye run daft, man?" Andrew said. "Ye canna do that! They'll kill ye if ye do!"

"I'll deserve it if they do, for I said I'd protect her and I didna. We all said that," Niall countered.

"Ye couldna protect her! None of us could! We didna ken the MacFarlanes were going to attack us!" Andrew shouted, losing his temper. "We didna kill her!"

"In truth we dinna ken who killed her," Niall said, remaining preternaturally calm. His outburst of emotion on the hillside as he'd sat next to a beautiful young woman who would never see another day, and knew that he was at least partly to blame for her death, had passed. Now he felt cold, emotionless. Drained.

"It would have been the MacFarlanes," Jamie said reasonably. The attackers' clan had been established by the sprigs of cranberry in the bonnets of the three dead men. "For they were shooting in her direction. We were shooting the opposite way."

"It doesna signify," Niall said tiredly. "We swore to protect her, and we didna. If we hadna taken her she'd still be alive. This is on us."

"I think we should do what Charles suggested," Patrick said. Charles' suggestion had been to bury her with the three MacFarlanes and then take their own dead home, and just tell the chief they'd been attacked and got the best of the encounter. There was a general murmur of assent to this suggestion.

Niall bestowed a look of such utter contempt on Patrick that he looked away.

"Ye can do as ye like," he said. "If ye want to be kent as cowards for the rest of your lives, that's up to you."

"No one'll ken, if we all stick together!" Patrick said.

"*We* will. I'm already deeply ashamed of what I've done here. I should never have even left Glencoe wi' ye. I'm no' leaving a man never knowing what happened to his wife, and burying her far from her clan, so I can claim glory for being a brave fighter who beat the MacFarlanes!" Niall said, his voice rising now as his temper broke. "I'm no' discussing it. Ye do as ye want. I'm taking the lassie home, and if the MacGregor kills me then it's what I deserve. If he doesna, then I'll come home and tell MacIain the truth of what happened here myself. If ye're wanting to kill me as well, do it now."

They all watched in shock and disbelief as he knelt down, lifted Màiri gently in his arms, and then set off southward, wondering if at any minute he would feel a bullet hit his back, as the young woman he carried had. Right now he didn't care if he lived or died. He was just determined to do the right thing, no matter the consequences.

He had reached the top of the hill and was starting down the other side, when he heard someone coming up behind him. If they had decided to kill him he could not stop them, so he kept walking. After a minute Andrew caught up, moving in front of him to stop him. Niall stood silently, waiting to see what he would do.

"Ye've the right of it," Andrew said then, red-faced, looking at the ground. "We'll come wi' ye. Patrick and Charles will take Robbie and Alasdair home. And they'll tell MacIain the truth of what happened. We'll help ye carry the lassie home. Will ye wait while we round up as many of the cattle as we can? For we'll take them back, too."

Niall nodded then, suddenly unutterably relieved that he wouldn't have to face the MacGregor chieftain alone. He sat with his precious burden and waited for the others, praying that her soul was now with God, and that he would be forgiven for his part in killing her.

After a time they joined him, driving fifteen of the cattle, which was all they could find, and the party, very much wiser, headed directly south to Loch Lomond.

When Duncan made his way up to the shielings in the evening and found Màiri was not at the hut waiting for him, he sat and waited for a while, thinking that maybe she was collecting herbs for Susan, which she would sometimes do in her spare time.

When the gloaming came and there was still no sign of her, he felt the first stirrings of worry. She would not be looking for herbs in the failing light. He'd gone over to the other huts then, where the rest of the women were, to see if she was there.

"No, we havena seen her. We're all working awfu' hard at the minute to get the last of the butter and cheeses made, so we wouldna notice if she'd gone looking for plants," Peigi told him.

"She was tired earlier," Janet said. "I tellt her to have a wee nap, for that's what we do when the sun's hot. She doesna normally do it, because she wants to finish her work before ye come, but she kent ye'd be late tonight. When we woke up and she wasna outside we just assumed she took our advice. I havena seen her since."

"Since when?" Duncan asked.

"This morning. Late this morning," Janet said. "Are ye thinking she's maybe fallen and hurt herself looking for the wee plants?"

Duncan ran his hand through his hair and without answering, ran out of the door. The women, along with Simon and Alasdair who had come up the mountain earlier, looked at each other, and then went after him.

When they got to him Duncan was in her hut, trying to work out what she might be doing. Màiri's arisaid was hanging on a nail on the back of the door, the blanket thrown roughly back from the heather mattress on the floor.

"Màiri's awfu' neat," he said to the others as they arrived. "She wouldna leave her blanket trailing on the floor. And if she'd gone to pick plants, she'd have taken her arisaid to carry them in, if no' to wear." The first stirrings of panic fluttered in his stomach and he quelled them.

"We need to look for her," Simon said then. "See if we can find which way she went before the light fails completely."

They all set off in different directions immediately, aware that they only had a short time before it became too dark to follow her trail, if they could find it at all. As they searched they shouted her name, stopping to listen, hoping to hear her call back, heading for the places where there were sudden drops, although she knew the hillside as well as any of them, and it was unlikely she'd have wandered off the edge of a ridge.

It was about half an hour before Alasdair suddenly let out a piercing whistle that echoed across the mountain, and which brought all of them running to him.

"Where is she?" Duncan asked as he arrived.

"She isna here, but look," Alasdair said, pointing to the obvious signs of a number of cattle all heading towards the top of the mountain together. "They wouldna do that unless they were driven."

"D'ye think someone's taken cattle, and Màiri too?" Janet said fearfully.

"*Cac!*" Duncan said, fighting the urge to follow the tracks immediately. He could not just run off over the mountain alone, or even with Alasdair and Simon. It was already almost dark, the moon was new so would give no help, and it would be impossible to follow tracks at night without light.

"I'm thinking she maybe heard them, and that's why she didna fold her blanket, or take her arisaid," Duncan said. "We need lanterns if we're to follow the tracks by night."

"We didna hear her shout, or we'd have come out," Peigi said. "D'ye think the reivers maybe--" She stopped suddenly as Duncan shot her a look of such ferocious denial it froze the words on her tongue.

"No," he said. "No. I would ken if...no. Lassies, can ye stay here so we dinna waste time finding the tracks when we come back?"

They agreed instantly and seconds later Duncan, Alasdair and Simon were running headlong back to the settlement to collect lanterns, weapons and other men to start the search.

Alex stood at the edge of the settlement, staring up the mountain where the shielings were, praying to see Duncan and the other clansmen come over the ridge with Màiri unharmed, and hopefully the cattle too, although as long as Màiri was unhurt he would be happy. Cattle could be replaced; she could not.

After a short time of seeing nothing but grass and heather, he directed his gaze along the track by the side of the loch, and then into the trees, from where an attack might come. He tore his hand through his hair, wishing for the hundredth time that he'd gone with his brother after all.

"Ye did the right thing," Barbara's voice came from behind him. She came to stand next to him. "Ye were right. It's no' normal for cattle that are being watched to be taken in the middle of the day. That's what the night time is for."

When Duncan, Alasdair and Simon had told Alex what seemed to have happened the previous night, his first impulse had been to collect all the men and lanterns and head off after the reivers. But then he had thought for a minute about the likely motives for such a brazen raid conducted in broad daylight, a raid that anyone standing where he was now could have seen. And why had they taken Màiri? They could have tied her up, knocked her out, if she'd seen them. Was it a decoy, designed to lure all the men from the settlement so a larger party could swoop down and attack while they were away?

It had seemed likely that this might be the case, especially as anyone would know that abducting a clanswoman was a serious matter and would incite an emotional and possibly reckless response, so Alex had opted to stay with half the men and the women, while the others had armed themselves and set off over the mountain. Now, with no sign of imminent attack, he was wondering if he'd done the right thing.

"Maybe they *were* going to attack, but havena because ye didna fall for their plan," Barbara added, squinting up the mountain.

"Aye, but it's awfu' hard no' doing anything," Alex admitted.

"Anyone can track cattle, but we'd need the chieftain to defend us against an attack," Barbara pointed out. "And Duncan wouldna have stayed here to act in your place. Come and have something to eat. Ye'll need it if there *is* an attack."

When he got back to his house the remaining clan members were assembled outside, all fully armed. Some of the women had gone up to the cave with the children, while the others were sitting on the grass outside his house, eating. He sat down and joined them, for although he wasn't hungry Barbara was right.

They had been sitting there morosely for a few minutes when Robbie came running down the track as fast as his seven-year-old legs could carry him. Everyone shot to their feet instantly, the men picking up their targes and drawing their swords.

"There're men!" Robbie shouted, gasping for breath. "Six men!"

"Only six?" Alex said urgently.

"Aye, and cows...but...they've got Màiri," Robbie wheezed.

Then everyone looked to the track, because coming into sight through the trees were the cattle, followed by the six men Robbie had just announced, and they did, indeed, have Màiri.

Barbara made an instinctive move forward when she saw who the leader of the group was carrying, but Alex put a hand on her arm to stop her, just in case.

"There's no one else, Robbie?" he asked the child, who he'd pushed behind him for protection.

"There's no one else," the youth holding Màiri said as the small group came to a halt. "We're needing to speak wi' the chieftain." He looked around, and Alex realised in that moment that whichever clan these youths were from, they had not heard of his father's death. Not a close one then.

He nodded, and Barbara and Janet ran forward, taking Màiri from the young man's arms and laying her on the ground to see what they could do.

"I...we're sorry," Niall said inadequately, white-faced. The others huddled behind him, clearly terrified, as anyone with sense would be if faced with a number of heavily armed men staring at them with intense hostility.

Barbara sat back, crossing herself, and shook her head at Alex.

He was the chieftain. He could not do what he wanted to do right now, what all of them clearly wanted to do. He closed his eyes momentarily, fought down the rage, then addressed the fair-haired youth.

"I'm the chieftain," he said. "Alexander died this year. Are ye the leader of these...?" he waved his hand contemptuously at the terrified group.

"No," Niall said, his voice trembling. "We dinna have a leader. We do things by a vote. I wish we hadna," he added softly to himself, but Alex heard him.

"Gregor, will ye take Màiri to her house? Will ye take care of her, Barbara?" Alex asked.

"Aye. Will we fetch Susan?" she asked.

"God, no. She canna see her niece like this," Alex said.

"We'll do it," Janet said, moving forward.

A tense silence fell on the group as the young woman was gently lifted and taken away. It was not until she was completely out of sight that Alex turned his icy blue stare on the group of youths again, who looked as though they were about to die of terror.

"What clan are ye?" he asked.

All the youths except the fair-haired one looked down.

"MacDonald," Niall answered. "Glencoe MacDonald."

Alex nodded.

"Ye'll be telling me why ye killed my sister, then. Your clan is a friend to us. *Was* a friend to us," he said, causing the youths to look even more terrified.

"We didna kill her!" Andrew cried then.

"Ye didna? But she's dead, and I'm thinking ye took her, wi' the cattle?"

A series of nods came from the boys. The absolute stillness of all the clansmen coupled with the icy expression of the chieftain was clearly making all of them wish they had never come here.

"So I'm thinking ye killed her. Ye'll tell us what happened then," Alex commanded.

They stood, shaking like leaves, and told him what had happened, although in truth it was mainly Niall who spoke. By the time they'd finished Alex was not the only MacGregor who wore a look of utter disbelief.

"So ye're telling me she was killed by accident, most likely by MacFarlanes, but ye brought her back to us? If ye're wanting to die, there are easier ways to do it," Alex said bluntly.

"We...we dinna want to die," Niall said, his voice breaking on the last word. He swallowed, and pulled himself together with a herculean effort. "But we couldna leave her, and your brother never knowing what happened to her." The others looked horrified at this, for they hadn't known that she was the MacGregor chieftain's sister-in-law until this minute. "We promised to protect her, and we didna. I'll never forgive myself for that," he cried out suddenly, tears brimming in his eyes and pouring down his cheeks unheeded. "I dinna want to die. But I couldna live unless I faced what I'd done, either."

Alex stared at him. There was no doubt that he at least was speaking the absolute truth. And whatever the others huddling behind him would have done without this youth's moral courage, they *had* come with him, to face whatever brutal punishment Alex ordered.

And in that moment, as much as he wanted to, he knew that he could not order the brutal execution of these stupid, reckless, brave and honourable MacDonald fools. Not when Angus, no more than two or three years younger than them and potentially every bit as reckless, was standing next to him, mouth open with shock.

They had made a mistake, a terrible, terrible mistake, and Màiri was dead as a result. Alex shook his head, feeling the red mist rising again and brutally quelling it. Killing these youths would not bring her back. Nothing would bring her back. They had not murdered her. It had been a terrible accident and they had owned up to it, risking their lives to do so.

He had never killed anyone who did not deserve it, and he could not do it now.

"Wait," he said brusquely. Then he turned away from his clansmen, from all of them, and went down to the loch. Angus made to follow him, but Kenneth gripped his arm, then knelt down next to him.

"No' the now, laddie," he said softly. "He's your chieftain now, no' your brother, and he's deciding what to do. He needs to be alone."

"Will he kill them?" Angus whispered, wide-eyed.

"I dinna ken. That's for him to decide. That's what the chieftain does."

Everyone stood there in hostile silence for a time, the MacDonald youths deathly white and trembling, until Alex finally returned from the lochside, his expression hard, determined.

"Ye tellt me the others have gone back to MacIain wi' your dead," he said to the youths.

"Aye. And they swore to tell him the truth of what happened," Niall replied.

"Have they the honour you have?" Alex asked. "Or will they lie?"

The uncertain looks on the faces of the boys gave him his answer.

"I canna let this go unpunished," he said then. "And if ye'd all run away and left her, when we'd found her, and we would have, for there's men out following your tracks now, your clan would have made enemies of the MacGregors. I'm thinking MacIain would likely kill ye if that happened, for he willna want a war with us, any more than we do wi' him."

"That's true," Niall answered.

"So, if I allow ye to go home, will ye tell your chief what happened here this day?"

"I will."

"Niall said he was going to anyway," Andrew admitted.

"Aye, well, ye've shown courage today. Tell MacIain I'll be paying him a visit before the winter, to make sure ye've kept your promise. Kenneth," he said then. "I'll be needing your help. Hold them," he said to the others, drawing his dirk.

A few minutes later the six youths, all of them deathly pale and lacking the little finger from their right hands, were heading away from the settlement, accompanied by a group of MacGregor clansmen, who Alex had ordered to stay with them until they were a good distance away.

He bent to the bloody stone near his house, took out a handkerchief and wrapped the six fingers in it. Then, for the first time since the youths had appeared on the path he showed emotion, sitting on the bench outside his house and covering his face with his hands.

Angus, who had watched as Alex coldly amputated the fingers of the MacDonalds while Kenneth held them down, ran to his brother, sure that now he could give him comfort.

"Christ, how will I tell him?" Alex murmured to himself as Angus neared him.

"I'll tell him, if ye canna do it," Angus offered, desperate to do *something.*

Alex lifted his head and looked at his brother.

"Ah, laddie, no, I wouldna ask ye to do that," he said then, and pulling his brother into an almost painful embrace the tears spilled down his cheeks and he buried his head in his brother's hair, wondering if he'd done the right thing after all in being so merciful. *Duncan will understand, when I explain to him,* he told himself fiercely, clutching Angus even more tightly.

After a few moments he lifted his head and became aware of the remaining clan members standing there, clearly wanting to do *something* as well, but not sure what that something should be.

"Find Duncan," he said to them, his voice choked with tears.

Silently but rapidly the clansfolk dispersed, leaving Alex and Angus to grieve together.

CHAPTER SEVEN

DUNCAN LOOKED AT THE five fingers lying on the bloody handkerchief on Alex's table, and then back at Alex.

"So ye're thinking these make everything all right?" he asked his brother. His voice was quiet, calm; he might well have been giving his opinion on what they were going to eat for dinner rather than on his brother's punishment of the MacDonalds for the death of his wife.

"Christ, no! Nothing can make that right!" Alex said, thoroughly unnerved by his brother's demeanour. "Duncan, I—"

"Yon laddies murdered my wife, and ye consider that sufficient payment for them. Ye must, or ye wouldna have let them go afterwards," Duncan continued, as though Alex hadn't spoken. His gaze was cool, level, and intensely unnerving because of that.

"If they'd murdered her, I'd have killed them, ye must ken that?" Alex replied, his voice conveying all the emotion Duncan's did not. "It wasna murder. It was an accident. And they brought her back. They didna have to do that. It took courage."

Duncan closed his eyes for a moment, then braced his arms on the table.

"They didna need to take her. If they hadna taken her, she'd still be alive. They had a duty to take care of her, and they didna do it," he said patiently, as though explaining something to a small child. "They killed her. By their actions they killed her. And ye let them go."

"It was their right hand finger," Angus said from the corner of the room. He'd watched as Alex had told Duncan what had happened, had watched Duncan's preternaturally calm response to it, and was desperate to help Alex, who was as unnerved as he was by their brother's attitude. "Kenneth tell me never to underestimate the importance of that wee finger, for it gives your hand its strength. So they'll likely die anyway, next time they fight."

"They should be dead NOW!" Duncan roared suddenly, making his brothers jump violently. He stood straight again then, and cast Alex a look of utter contempt. "Where is she?" he asked, his voice calm again.

"She's at your house. The women are taking care of her, and—" Alex began.

Duncan turned abruptly and walked out of the door, leaving it wide open.

Alex and Angus stood for a moment, staring at the door as though expecting Duncan to come back through it at any moment. Then Alex sank down into a chair and tore his fingers through his hair.

"Christ," he said, with great feeling.

Angus closed the door and came over to the table, sitting down opposite.

"I havena ever seen him like that before," he said nervously. "Should we go to him?"

"Neither have I, and I dinna ken," Alex replied truthfully. "No, I'm thinking we should leave him be for a wee while. He doesna—"

He bit back the words he'd been about to say, realising how badly Angus would take it if he said that it seemed Duncan hated them, or at least him, at the moment.

"When Da died I didna want to go in and see him, because I kent that when I did, I couldna pretend he wasna dead. D'ye think that's why Duncan was so...normal? Well, no' normal...so calm? Because he doesna believe she's dead?" Angus asked.

"Maybe...maybe he kens it here," Alex pointed to his head, "but no' here," pointing to his heart. "Truly, I dinna ken, Angus. I didna expect him to react like that."

"How did ye think he'd react?" Angus asked with genuine interest.

Alex pondered for a minute, then realised he'd assumed Duncan would react as *he* would, which was silly, because Duncan was nothing like him. And in truth, he didn't *know* how he'd react to such news; he just *thought* he did.

"I dinna ken. More emotional." He reached across the table then and wrapped the severed fingers, unsure what to do with them now. He didn't know what Duncan would want to do with them, either. He didn't know anything, it seemed.

He stood then and went out, heading toward Duncan and Màiri's house, followed by Angus, although he had no idea what he was going to do when he got there. He just wanted to be nearby in case his brother needed comfort when he saw Màiri and the truth of it hit him.

Standing outside the firmly closed door of the cottage were Susan, Barbara and Janet.

"What was he like?" he asked them.

"He just looked at her, and then tellt us to get out," Janet said.

"I tellt him we'd have a respectful wake for her, and she wouldna be left alone," Barbara added. "But he said, 'there'll be no wake. I'll be with her,' and closed the door in our faces. Should we come back in a wee while?"

Alex looked at the closed door. Both Duncan and Màiri had treasured their alone times. And Duncan had told him how hard it had been for him to be social at their da's wake. Maybe he could make amends by doing the right thing now, as it seemed he'd done the wrong thing with the MacDonald youths, in Duncan's eyes at least.

"No," he said. "I'm thinking he'll want to spend all his time wi' her, alone, until the burial tomorrow. We'll give him that, at least. Thank ye for what ye've done."

"She looks bonny," Janet said, her voice trembling. "As bonny as she can," she added.

"Away home and rest," he said to them. "Susan," he added as they all turned to leave.

She turned back.

"Come home with us," he said simply, taking her arm, seeing that she was about to collapse and giving her no alternative but to go with him. He had done the wrong thing with her too, he realised suddenly, despairingly.

Once in the house he sat her on the *sèis,* and pulling a chair over sat opposite her, close enough to take her hands. She looked dreadful. Her face was almost grey with grief, and she seemed to have aged several years in less than a day.

"I'm so sorry," he said then. "I should have taken more thought of ye."

"Ye had to think of your brother. Ye were right," she said.

"No. She's your niece. Ye've kent her her whole life. And ye're grieving dreadful, I can see that. Ye must stay here with us tonight. Ye canna be alone," he added when she made to object. "No' tonight."

"Aye," she said very softly. She looked at his hands holding hers so tenderly, then closed her eyes suddenly, screwing her whole face up in an attempt to hold back the flood of tears, and succeeding for just a moment before letting out a wail of utter grief, and collapsing forward into his arms.

They stayed like that for a while, him lifting her onto his knee and holding her while she sobbed and wailed, the torrent of grief overwhelming her completely. Angus poured three cups of whisky, tears pouring down his own face, although he said nothing, and Alex stroked Susan's back, muttering endearments and words of comfort until finally she fell silent, exhausted by the flood of grief that had demolished her.

"Dinna say ye're sorry," he told her softly as she finally attempted to do just that. "Ye've nothing to be sorry for."

She took the drink that Angus offered her then, and moved from Alex's knee back to the *sèis,* wiping her face with her arisaid and pulling herself together, although she still looked dreadful.

"What was he like when he saw her?" Alex asked, after the three of them had finished their whisky and Angus was pouring another.

"Quiet," she said. "Very quiet. But very firm. He was...dangerous," she added thoughtfully. "I dinna ken what he'd have done if we'd refused to go."

"Aye, that's how he was with us," Alex agreed, realising she'd summed Duncan up perfectly. Quiet. Dangerous. "He'll be needing time, I'm thinking. Time alone. I need to be wi' people. Duncan needs to be alone. He's always been so."

"I hope so," Susan said, a little uncertainly. "I dinna need to stay—"

"Aye, ye do. For we want ye to, and I can see ye're no' wanting to be alone tonight," Alex interrupted, hoping he was right, but no longer sure he was.

She gave a watery smile then, and accepted the second cup of whisky Angus offered her.

"I will then, for ye're right. When she first married I missed her dreadfully, but I became used to her no' being there. I kent that if I wanted to see her I could, and if I asked her to stay for a night, she would. So I never needed to. But now there's a great dark space where she was. I canna imagine what Duncan must be feeling. Well, I can, a wee bit, for I loved Rob as he loves Màiri. But Rob died naturally, no' like...well, ye ken."

Alex did ken. But he had thought Duncan would understand why he could not exact a brutal revenge on the youths, had thought he would understand it had been an accident, would have admired their bravery in bringing her back.

He would, he told himself fiercely for the rest of the evening. Given a little time, maybe a few days, Duncan would understand why he had acted as he had.

The funeral was held the next day, Duncan having opened the door mid-morning to the clansfolk assembled outside after ignoring several knocks, and allowing Kenneth to help him carry her down to the boat that would take her across to Inchcailloch Island.

It was a silent, sombre ceremony, in part because of her youth and the terrible manner of her death, and in part because of Duncan's demeanour. All of the mourners later agreed that although he had always been more introspective than the rest of them, as he stood by Màiri's grave it had seemed that he was completely alone there, the rest of the clanspeople non-existent to him. He had said nothing, acknowledged no one, shown no obvious emotion.

With one exception, although only the recipient was aware of it. As they'd got out of the boat on the island, Duncan had reached out his hand to assist Susan out of it. Once she was on land he had locked eyes with her, his gaze deep, penetrating. And then he had nodded once and squeezed her hand, before releasing it and turning to help take his wife to her last resting place.

Susan had stood for a moment watching him as he moved into the trees with the others, and then Angus was with her, asking her if she needed his help to walk up the steep path to the grave site. She had not needed it but recognised that he wanted to feel helpful, because it was clear Duncan would accept nothing from anyone.

"He's grieving, laddie," she said softly as she accepted his arm. "He's grieving terrible."

"Is he?" Angus said uncertainly. "He seems...as though he isna there any more, somehow."

"Aye, he's there. He isna like your da. He'll come back, and soon. Ye must be patient, and leave him to do it in his own time," she said, not knowing if this was true, but needing to reassure the youth.

That he was grieving she *did* know, because as he had looked at her she had seen his agony, his despair. He had shown it to her because she felt the same, and had nodded in acknowledgement of that. Then he had blinked, and in that moment had hidden his pain, his gaze becoming indifferent as he turned away from her and went up the hill.

Afterwards the others headed back to the boats, leaving Duncan standing by the mound of earth. The closest mourners often stayed for longer after a death. Kenneth, Gregor, Barbara and Flora had after Alpin's burial, and Alexander, Moira and the boys had stayed after Morag's, so no one was surprised that Duncan would. Susan had thought about it, but it had been so clear to her that he was not ready to talk and wanted to say his last goodbyes to Màiri alone, that she went with the others. They left a boat for him so that he could row himself back later.

Alex and Angus stood back from the grave, watching their brother, matching expressions of worry on their faces.

"Ye away back wi' everyone else," Alex said softly to Angus then, "Look after Susan for me. I'll stay wi' Duncan for a wee while."

When Angus was gone, Alex sat down silently, watching for what seemed like an age as Duncan stood there, as still as a statue. He almost prayed for Duncan to drop to his knees, to sob, scream, show *any* kind of emotion that would allow him to comfort him, to break through the ice that he had encased himself in.

Finally Duncan turned round and saw Alex sitting there.

"Ye shouldna have stayed, you of all people. I dinna want ye here," he said icily.

"I couldna just leave ye here alone," Alex said.

"I *am* alone," Duncan replied. "I'll always be alone, now." He turned back to the grave then, dismissing him.

"What can I do to make it right?" Alex asked helplessly, the pain of his brother's rejection of him almost physical. "I didna ken ye'd—"

"Ye canna bring her back. No one could have done that," Duncan cut in. "But ye could have avenged her, showed her respect, that her life had some value to ye. But ye didna."

"Duncan, they didna kill her. It was an accident," Alex said.

129

"Aye. But she's dead and they're alive. If I kill every MacDonald in Scotland it'll no' bring her back," Duncan told him. "But when I go to her, she'll ken I loved her enough to avenge her, which is more than you do. Chieftain? Ye're pathetic. Away hame. I dinna want ye here. Ye dinna deserve to be here."

These last words were uttered with such contempt that Alex actually flinched as though they were blades, which in a sense they were.

He walked away abruptly, crashing through the trees, hardly aware of where he was going, just knowing he could not stay there another moment. When he came back to himself he realised that he had gone in the wrong direction entirely, and was heading the opposite way to the boat. In no mood to go home and face the others he kept walking until he reached the tip of the island, where he sat, staring at the breathtaking view without seeing it and wondering if he had lost his brother forever, and if he had, how he would continue.

When he finally pulled himself together and made his way back to the tiny bay the boat was gone, which told him Duncan had gone home. He swam back to shore, meeting Gregor as he walked along the track to the settlement.

"Where's Duncan?" he asked, before Gregor could enquire as to why he was dripping wet.

"He came back a wee while ago, and went into his house," Gregor said.

"Is he still there?"

"Aye, I think so. Barbara's making him some food, hoping he'll eat. Why?" Gregor asked.

"When she takes it, will ye go wi' her? If he's there, then I want ye to guard the door, and no' let him out. Or stay wi' him if he comes out. Ask Kenneth to stay with ye. Will ye do that?"

"Aye, if ye want me to. What's amiss?" Gregor asked.

"He said...he said a lot of things, but he might be intending to take revenge against the MacDonalds. I'm thinking it's the grief talking, so I dinna want him to go while he's no' thinking straight. Just a couple of days should do it. He's always been the sensible, calm one. He'll come round by then," Alex finished, somewhat desperately.

Gregor looked at him for a moment, as though about to say something, and then changed his mind.

"Aye. I'll away now, before Barbara finishes the food," he said, and turning, ran back along the track, leaving Alex to follow.

Duncan *would* come back to himself, Alex told himself firmly. It was the grief talking. Grief made people do strange things. Look at his da! Duncan was not like their da though. He saw the depth of a thing. He would see that Alex had done the right thing in punishing but not killing the youths, that they had been guilty of stupidity, but not of Màiri's death. He would understand that Alex's punishment of them had been just, maybe even more than they'd deserved, for Angus had been right when he'd said that the little finger gave the grip its strength.

It would all be well. He just had to wait.

Glencoe

MacIain sat in a chair, eyeing the six clansmen standing in front of him, each of them with an improvised bloody bandage wrapped round their right hands, torn from the bottom of their shirts. None of them could meet his eye, he noticed with some satisfaction.

After watching them grow increasingly uncomfortable by his silence for a while, he spoke suddenly, making them all jump.

"In truth I'm surprised to see ye at all," he said. "Patrick and Charlie tellt me what happened. I'd have expected Alexander to take a lot more than a finger."

"It wasna Alexander," Niall said finally, after realising that none of the others were going to speak. "Alexander's dead. His son is the chieftain now. It was he who ordered this. We deserved it," he added quietly.

"Aye, ye did. D'ye ken that by your disobedience ye could have caused a blood feud between our two clans? No, ye didna think of it, did ye, ye wee gomerels? He should have killed ye, for he'd have saved me a job."

He saw their eyes widen, their sudden pallor. Good.

"No, I havena killed your two friends," he said then. "I punished them for their disobedience to me, then waited to see what the Mac-Gregor did to ye for causing the death of his clanswoman. Bring them in," he said to the corner of the room. A number of MacDonalds left quietly.

Another minute or two of silence passed, and then Patrick and Charles came into the room, walking stiffly, their faces lighting up when they saw their friends.

"Well, then," said MacIain, giving the fools no time to greet each other. "This is what the MacGregor ordered as punishment for your offence against him. Unwrap your hands," he ordered the six youths.

They did, revealing their bloodied stumps. Andrew's appeared to be going bad, MacIain noticed with indifference.

"Ye'll have the same. And this is what I ordered as punishment for your offence against me. Take off your shirts," he said to Patrick and Charles.

They did, revealing their backs to be a bloody mess of criss-crossed wounds from the flogging they'd received. All eight youths closed their eyes, knowing what was coming next.

"Ye'll have the same," he said coldly. "Take them away. Wait," he added as men came forward to take them and administer the punishments. "The MacGregor has been merciful, it seems. Maybe because of your youth, I dinna ken. I'm doing likewise. But I willna again. Ye disobey me once more and ye die. Remember that. Go."

When they were gone he sat back in his chair, thinking.

So the Lomond MacGregors had a new chieftain. And a soft-hearted one, it seemed.

A soft-hearted MacGregor chieftain. That would be interesting.

Loch Lomond

In the next days everyone went about the business of preparing for the winter to come, although instead of singing and chatting as they worked, they were, except for necessary conversation, mostly quiet. This was partly from respect and grief for young Màiri's death, for she had been very popular with everyone, and partly because everyone was aware of the deep rift between the chieftain and his right-hand man. If they forgot it for a moment, they only had to look at Duncan's house, at its closed door, smokeless chimney, and at the two men standing outside, waiting for its occupant to appear.

Every day Barbara took food for him, which was left outside and ignored. Every day Angus knocked on the door, which was not opened, after which he would tap on the window and ask if he could do anything. Then he would come back to Alex and say that Duncan had just told him to go away, he would come out when he was ready.

On the third day Duncan finally opened the door, blinking for a moment in the autumn sunshine until his eyes adjusted. Then ignoring Allan and Dugald, who had replaced Gregor and Kenneth on guard and who followed him, he went directly to his brother's house and without knocking walked in.

Alex and Susan, who were sitting by the fire discussing how long Alex should wait before breaking the door down, stopped in mid-sentence, staring at him in shock for a moment. Then Alex leapt to his feet, an uncertain smile lifting his mouth.

"Duncan!" he said. "Will ye sit down and have some *brochan*?"

"Aye," Duncan replied after a slight hesitation, moving forward a little, but not sitting. Susan filled a bowl with the porridge and handed it to him. He thanked her and stood to eat it, swallowing it as though it was full of broken glass.

"How are ye feeling?" Alex asked awkwardly, his heart aching as he realised he had no idea what to say to the brother who had been the other half of him for as long as he could remember, aware that now was not the time to let his impatience to make it right spoil everything.

Duncan finished the food, shaking his head when Susan offered him more.

"I'm feeling that I need to be alone for a wee while," he said. "I need to think, and I canna do that wi' all her...all the things around me."

"Susan's staying here for a few days," Alex said. "Are ye wanting to stay at hers? Ye wouldna mind, would ye, Susan?" he asked belatedly.

"No. Ye'd be welcome. And it's on the edge of the settlement, so ye'd no' be hearing the others, if it's silence ye're wanting," Susan said.

"No. I need…" He looked into the distance for a moment, "I need to be away, really away. I canna think clearly. I need to think clearly. I'll come back when I'm myself again."

Alex thought rapidly. He didn't want Duncan to go where he couldn't watch him. But he couldn't force him to stay. Well, he could, but he knew that would likely increase the rift between them, which he so desperately wanted to mend. Duncan was sensible. He was the peacemaker.

He was honest.

"Duncan, do ye swear no' to go hunting for the laddies who took Màiri, to kill them?" he said. "Ye tellt me ye wanted revenge."

Duncan looked directly at him then, for the first time.

"I'll no' go hunting for the laddies who took Màiri," he said woodenly.

A moment passed in which Alex tried to find a plausible reason to refuse this reasonable request, but couldn't.

"Aye, then. But will ye go to Barbara's and get some food to take wi' ye, at least?"

"Aye. I'll need food," Duncan replied. "Thank ye," he said. Then he put the bowl down on the table, turned and left, closing the door quietly behind him.

Susan and Alex sat there for a minute.

"He seemed calmer than when he spoke to me last," Alex said. "He was angry then, hated me. He didna seem to hate me just now, did he?" he added uncertainly.

She looked at him, saw the despair in his eyes. The years fell away and in that moment he was a small boy again, desperate for reassurance, wanting to make everything right, and having no idea how to do it. She swallowed back the words she'd been thinking to say, replacing them with what he needed to hear.

"I dinna think he hates ye, Alex," she said. "He's grieving, and people dinna think rightly when they're grieving. He's angry wi' everyone for taking his happiness away from him. He took it out on you because ye're his brother, the closest person to him."

"Ye really think that?" he said.

"Aye, I do."

She did. But she also thought a lot of other things, among them that Duncan was too calm. And still dangerous. But Alex could not stop him, if he wanted to go away for a time, to think.

Susan sent up a silent prayer that that was indeed all Duncan wanted to do.

It was a busy time of year, as the nights were lengthening now and there was a lot to do before the weather turned, which it could at any time from October onwards, although this year had been remarkably mild and continued to be so.

Even so it was good to have a lot to occupy everyone, routine chores that needed no leadership. Alex was in no state of mind to have to make decisions. Any further talk of a trip to the market at Crieff had been shelved, partly because no one wanted to bring up the subject of cattle with the chieftain, and partly because it was clear that he would not even consider going away until his brother returned. If anyone asked Alex a question he would be silent for a moment and then seem to return from a long way away before answering them.

Every morning and evening Angus would head off down the track Duncan had disappeared along on the day he'd left, returning later looking unhappy. If people were reminded of when he'd run up and down the track eagerly looking for Alex three years ago, no one mentioned it. It did not seem the time to mention anything light-hearted, somehow.

In the evenings they would sit in their cottages, eating, nursing their children, preparing for bed, and would exchange opinions of what had happened in the last days. But nobody spoke those opinions to the chieftain, even the ones who really wanted to and maybe could have. It was not their place, and he seemed not in the mood to listen to them. And even if he did, what could he do? Nothing until Duncan returned.

Nobody spoke of what might happen if Duncan didn't return at all, but as the days passed with no sign of him, more and more of them would stop working from time to time and stare along the track, praying to see him coming home, to see him meet their eye, return a greeting. To be Duncan again.

When he finally returned, nine days after he'd left, no one saw him coming along the track, because he arrived after sunset, when everyone had finished work for the day and were either in their homes or down by the loch washing off the dirt and sweat of the day.

He limped through the settlement, leaning heavily on a branch he'd cut from a tree a couple of days previously, hesitated outside his own house for a minute, and then changing his mind continued on to his brothers', where the curl of smoke coming from the chimney told him that at least one of them was home.

He hesitated outside there as well for a minute, and then, bracing himself, he opened the door and limped in.

Angus saw him first and let out a cry of joy which brought Alex out of the bedroom, where he'd been putting all the clean dry washing away, the women having made the most of possibly the last few warm days of the year to wash and dry everything.

"I'm back," Duncan said unnecessarily, before collapsing gracelessly on to the floor in a heap.

It was three days before he recovered consciousness, the fever rendering him delirious, so that when he spoke most of what he said consisted of incoherent mumbling, while the odd coherent sentence was nonsense.

During those days Susan, Alex and Angus fought to save him. Susan had washed the sword wound in his side with wine, had cut away infected tissue, then stitched and bound it, after which they had taken it in turns to bathe him in cold water when he was burning, and wrap him in every blanket they had when he was shivering. In line with her husband's views, Susan did not bleed him as most physicians would, saying he had certainly lost a great deal of blood from the wound, judging by the state of his blood-drenched shirt and kilt.

136

Other members of the clan called in with broth for the patient and more substantial food for the carers, Kenneth lifting Duncan from the mattress while the women replaced his sweat-soaked sheets with clean dry ones.

It was a huge relief to everyone when on the third night the fever broke and he slept long and deep, waking at noon the following day and looking round the room with understanding.

"I'm alive, then," he said, as though it was a matter of indifference to him.

"Aye, ye are, although for a time we thought we'd lose ye," Susan, who was sitting by his bedside said coolly, although she wanted to dance a reel round the room. "Your brothers are sleeping, for they've been awake most of the last days. I'll away and wake them."

"No," Duncan said, reaching out to grip her arm and stop her, although his grip was so weak she could easily have broken it. She sat back down. "Give me a while to accept I'm alive again, for they'll drown me wi' questions when they ken I'm awake."

She nodded.

"I'll make ye a drink. D'ye think ye can eat, just a wee bit? Ye really need to," she asked.

"Aye," he said. She went then, pottering about near the fire while he lay staring at the roof, listening to the sounds of clan life outside, wondering how he would continue. Wondering why God had not taken him, as he so wanted to be taken. Then wondering why he had made his way home if he wanted to die, which he would surely have done had he just laid down with the others and waited.

He felt tired again then, but Susan had returned with a bowl of thin porridge, putting it down to help him sit up enough to eat it. He owed it to her to at least try to eat. Her of all people.

"I'm sorry, Susan," he said once he was propped up with pillows, as she lifted the bowl and stirred the porridge with a spoon.

"Sorry? It wasna your fault ye were fevered. I'm just glad we could save ye," she said.

"Aye, it was my fault. But that's no' what I meant. I didna consider ye, and ye're the only other one who's grieving as much as I am, I'm thinking," he said, then opened his mouth dutifully as she brought a spoonful of the mixture to it.

She did not answer, instead letting him eat, and it was only when the bowl was empty that she finally spoke.

"Aye, I'm missing her fearful," she admitted. "But I'm no' the only one. Everyone loved her, and your brothers have been distracted, trying to deal wi' her loss and yours too. No, dinna argue, for I'm stronger than you right now," she said, smiling to soften the current truth of this. "It isna for me to question your brother's decision, for he's the chieftain," she continued. "Ye can do that, an ye wish. But he didna do as he did through lack of love for Màiri. I can see that ye thought that, for ye were raging wi' grief. But ye werena thinking right."

"Aye, well, it doesna matter now, for I've avenged her myself. No' as much as I wanted to, due to this," he waved a hand at his side, "but enough, I'm thinking."

"Ye're awake then," came Alex's voice from the doorway. He came in, dressed in his shirt, yawning.

"He's eaten a wee bowl of porridge, and he's cool," Susan said. "I'll look at the wound later, but I'm hopeful he'll heal, wi' care. He's awfu' weak though."

Alex smiled then, but hesitantly, clearly unsure of the reception he'd get from his brother. Then he pulled a stool over and sat at the bedside.

"I'll away and get some sleep," Susan said, although she was not tired. "I'll come back in a while."

"Thank you," Duncan said, before Alex could. "Ye're a good woman. I'm sorry I worried ye. Ye've enough care on ye already."

"It kept me busy," she replied. "I need that."

Alex didn't speak for a minute after she'd gone, and Duncan closed his eyes, apparently waiting patiently, which Alex hoped was a good sign.

"I'm sorry," he said finally. "I should have thought about how ye'd feel. But it—"

"Dinna tell me it was an accident again," Duncan interrupted. "It doesna signify why ye let them go any more. It was my place to avenge her, as ye didna, and I have."

Alex stared at him in horror for a moment, fighting the emotions this sentence evoked.

"What have ye done?" he asked then, his voice unnaturally quiet.

"I killed five of the bastards," Duncan said coldly. "The last one did this, or I'd likely have killed more. But five will suffice."

"Ye swore to me that ye wouldna hunt the laddies who took her," Alex said, outraged at the betrayal from the one person he trusted above everyone. His temper rose.

"I didna break my vow. I didna hunt the laddies who took her. I didna ken what they looked like, and wasna of a mind to examine all their hands for missing fingers. I killed five Glencoe MacDonalds. That will warn them no' to treat our women lightly, and will tell her, when I go to join her, that I love her. It seems I'll no' go as quickly as I hoped, though," he said matter-of-factly. "Ye should ken I wouldna break an oath."

"I dinna ken ye at all, right now," Alex replied hotly. "Ye're the one who looks at a whole situation, who stays calm and sees all the options before acting. It's me and Angus who act impulsively, no' you!"

"I lost my wife!" Duncan shouted. "And ye thought more of the bastards who took her than of her, or me! Ye're no' the only one wi' strong feelings! The least ye could have done was keep them until I returned, and let me decide what should be done!"

"But I'm the—" Alex began.

"The chieftain. Aye, I ken. But I'm your right-hand man, or so ye said. Ye've asked for my thoughts on a number of decisions since ye've been back. No' all, but I dinna expect that. But *this* one...Christ, Alex, *this* one was mine to make. Ye showed me no respect, nor Màiri neither. So I made my own choice. I'll accept your punishment, whatever it is. But I'm no' sorry for doing what you should have done."

He lay down then, exhausted by the effort this had cost his weakened body, and Alex choked back his response, seeing his brother's sudden pallor and realising that he was not out of danger yet. Instead he sat silently, watching as Duncan's eyes closed, as he slid back into sleep. Only then did he take his brother's hand, which was lying on top of the blankets, intending to tuck his arm in but instead keeping hold of it, needing to feel its warmth, to feel the life pulsing through it.

He bent his head then and prayed. And then he sat and let the despair and grief take him, but silently, so as not to disturb the man whose hand he held so tenderly between his. He sat like that until Susan returned and Angus woke up, and then, leaving Duncan in their care, he put on his *féileadh mór* and went down to the loch.

He needed to think.

Alex had been sitting there for over an hour, pondering two things.

Firstly he was trying to think of a way to make Duncan see that his decision had been the right one, the only one he could have made and lived with himself afterwards. It had been an accident, surely everyone could see that? No one had said anything against it when he'd made the decision to let them go after maiming them.

Secondly, how was he going to stop MacIain making a blood feud of this? He would be within his right if he did, because the killing of the five MacDonalds by Duncan had been no accident. If they happened to be five of the youths who'd taken Màiri, then perhaps it would be considered as just retribution. But the chances of that being the case were negligible. And Glencoe had four times the men he did and a vast amount of experience in leading them.

He stared across the loch, trying, as he had so many times, to see the depth of the thing, because his brother seemed incapable of doing so at the moment. Maybe Duncan would come to see his point of view when his grief for Màiri lessened. But the second problem would not go away by waiting. He needed to act, and act quickly, before the MacDonalds did.

He wiped his hand through his hair and then heard footsteps behind him, and knew before the man spoke who it was. Kenneth. No one else would disturb the chieftain when he was sitting here alone. He smiled sadly to himself.

"Are ye wanting to be alone, or will company help ye?" the giant asked.

"I've been here alone for a time now, and I'm no wiser," Alex replied.

Taking that as a yes Kenneth moved forward, offering his chieftain a bannock spread with honey. Alex accepted it and took a bite. Kenneth sat down on the ground opposite him.

"Ma gave me some to take to Duncan. She tellt me he's awake again. I didna go in, for Susan's wi' him, and she tellt me ye'd come here to think. I wondered if ye needed someone to think with."

In spite of his misery Alex laughed at that, because it was exactly what he needed, although he hadn't realised it until that moment.

"I've been trying to find a way to convince Duncan that I made the right decision, and that it's the only one I could have made," Alex began, once he'd swallowed his mouthful. "And trying to think of what to do next, for I dinna want a war wi' the MacDonalds. Glencoe's got four times our men."

"It isna for him to question your decisions," Kenneth said after a minute. "It isna anyone's right to do that. Ye're the chieftain. We'll abide by what ye decide."

"Aye, but he's my right-hand man. He's the one I'd normally be asking about what to do next. He's the one who sees the depth. Da tellt me that and he was right. But he canna do it at the minute. He said some awfu' cruel things to me," he added sadly, then flushed, for he hadn't meant to say that last sentence.

He looked up then to see Kenneth's pale blue gaze, full of sympathy, and for a moment he was a child again.

"He tellt me I could have avenged her, that her life didna mean anything to me," he blurted out. "That I should have let him make the decision. That I was pathetic as a chieftain, I showed him and Màiri no respect, and that at least the MacDonalds will ken no' to abuse our women now!" He stopped then, and actually put his hand over his mouth as though to stop the flood of emotion. He looked away across the loch and swallowed hard, fighting to be a man again, whatever that was.

When he finally looked back, Kenneth was still observing him. There was no sign of contempt on his face at the outburst, but Kenneth was good at hiding what he was thinking.

"How do I convince him I did the right thing, Kenneth? And what do I do to stop the Glencoe MacDonalds if they want to make a fight of this?"

"Ye canna convince him ye did the right thing," Kenneth said carefully.

"Aye, because he's grieving. I ken that. D'ye think he'll see why I did it, when he's no' so emotional?"

"Ah, laddie, dinna ask me that," Kenneth said then. "For I canna answer ye. Ye're maybe thinking about it the wrong way, is all I can say."

Alex heard the reluctance in his companion's voice then, and he pushed aside his hurt and grief, realising that there was something Kenneth wasn't saying, which he probably needed to hear.

"Kenneth," he said earnestly, leaning forward. "Whatever it is ye're no' wanting to say, say it, for if you willna no one will, and I need to ken it, I'm thinking. Forget I'm the chieftain," he added, when Kenneth still seemed doubtful. "Whatever ye say, I'll listen, and I'll no' hate ye for it. I'm needing some help right now, for I have to act and I havena a notion of what to do."

Kenneth sighed then, looking over Alex's shoulder into the trees for such a long time that Alex was about to turn and see who was coming down to the loch. Then he suddenly spoke.

"Ye said Duncan sees the depth of a thing, and ye're right. He shouldna have killed the MacDonalds as he did, for he acted against your wishes. He did it from grief, as I killed the men who took Alpin's life from grief. I can understand that in a way ye maybe canna, for ye havena felt that rage. I'd feel the same if someone hurt Jeannie. One day ye likely will too, when ye love a lassie."

Kenneth had never spoken of the day he found Alpin before, which made Alex pay even more attention to his words.

"But ye killed the laddies who murdered him," he said. "The MacDonalds didna murder Màiri."

"The laddie I killed last didna murder Alpin," Kenneth said. "He was unconscious the whole time. And your da had to talk to me for a time before I'd allow the priest to bless Alpin."

"Aye, but the laddie was a part of it. And ye wouldna have killed Father Gordon. Would ye?"

"Aye, I likely would have then, for I was wild wi' grief."

"Maybe ye should have," Alex commented dryly, making Kenneth laugh.

"But that's no' what I mean," he said. "The things he said to ye, they were coming from the grief of losing someone who ye canna imagine living without. So he didna say the words in the right way. He took revenge, but didna do that in the right way either. I'm thinking ye need to be asking a different question than the one ye are," Kenneth said then, throwing caution to the wind.

A minute passed, and then another, while Alex gazed across the loch, his face expressionless, his mind racing. Then his focus suddenly snapped back to Kenneth, comprehension dawning.

"It's no' just Duncan," he said then, in a low voice. "You think I made the wrong decision too. Do *all* of ye think that?"

"I dinna ken what everyone thinks, but there's many who didna think ye should have let them go, aye. But as I said, it isna—"

"--for you to question the chieftain," Alex interrupted impatiently. "So what's the question I should be asking, then?"

"Duncan's still seeing the depth of it," Kenneth said. "He canna do otherwise. It's who he is. The grief is making him cruel, reckless, which is why he said those things to ye, why he killed some MacDonalds who were nothing to do wi' what happened. He wouldna normally act that way, just as I'd never hurt anyone before Alpin. But he didna act only from grief. He saw what ye didna see, what ye still canna see."

"Because I'm asking the wrong question," Alex said.

"Aye."

The two of them sat there in silence for another few minutes.

"Thank ye, Kenneth," Alex said finally. "I see it now."

Kenneth stood then, squeezing Alex's shoulder gently as he passed to make his way home.

Alex sat there for a good while longer, and when the sun was over the loch and starting its descent, he made his decision. Then he stood and made his way back through the settlement, calling at Gregor and Barbara's on the way.

"Gregor, will ye ask everyone to come up to the cave?" he said. "No' Duncan. Dinna go to my house. Everyone else."

And then he went up the hill, sat on the rock at the edge of the bowl-shaped depression outside the cave, and waited.

When everyone arrived he waited again, until they were all settled. Then he stood.

"There's a lot of ye who'll remember when Kenneth threw me in the loch, deservedly so. I stood in the cave then, when I apologised to ye and tellt ye I didna deserve to be chieftain," he began.

There was a murmur of acknowledgment at this and a few smiles from those who remembered well. Normally there would have been jocular comments, but everyone was now aware of what Duncan had done and why, and they knew that Alex would not call them all away from their work in the middle of the day to reminisce about something that had happened in the distant past.

"I dinna feel so different now to how I felt then," he continued, "and I've Kenneth to thank again for helping me see what I couldna. So the first thing I'm wanting to do is apologise to ye all, for I see now that my decision a few days ago to let the MacDonald laddies go has put us all in danger. So I intend to remedy that, hopefully."

They all listened intently as he told them exactly what he intended to do to hopefully avert a blood feud between themselves and the Glencoe MacDonalds. When he'd finished there was silence. Complete and utter silence, which unnerved him. Had he made yet another terrible decision? He looked to Kenneth for approval, and saw acceptance. Grudging acceptance, but acceptance, which reassured him a little.

"This was the first big decision I've had to make since I became chieftain, and it seems that many of ye thought it was wrong when I made it. And now I'm of a mind to agree wi' ye. I ken a chieftain's decision is final, and ye have to abide by it, whatever it is. That's the way of clan life. But I also remember when Da wasna himself, and the terrible decisions he made that put all of ye at risk for little or no gain. None of ye could tell him he was wrong. I dinna ever want to be like that.

"So I'll say this now, and I mean it no' just for this situation, but for everything going forward. If I make a decision, and ye dinna agree wi' it, and have a good reason for it, then tell me. I ken ye couldna have done that when the MacDonalds were standing there, for ye needed to stand behind me then. But when there's no one here but us, then I want ye to give me your views, and I'll listen to them. For I dinna ever want to become a tyrant, as Da did for a time. I'll still make the decision, and I'll expect ye to abide by it, but maybe it'll help me make better ones, and that will benefit all of us."

Everyone looked at each other then, absorbing this new idea, but no one spoke up. Alex waited for a minute until it became clear that no one wanted to be first to speak.

"Can we start now, then? Why did ye think I was wrong to let the MacDonalds go? Did ye think I was disrespecting Màiri?"

"I didna think ye were disrespecting Màiri," a voice came from the back of the group, and everyone looked back to see Susan standing there, having just made her way up the hill. "Angus is wi' Duncan in the house," she added. "I ken ye loved her, everyone did. And I ken ye saw it as an accident, a stupid misfortune that could have happened to anyone, even yourself when ye were their age, and that they were brave to bring her back. That was all understandable. But ye needed to think beyond that. Ye needed to think how Duncan would feel, for she was his life mate, as your ma was your da's. Ye needed to think whether ye would have taken cattle by daylight as they did, and if ye'd have abducted a young lassie to do it."

A lot of heads nodded at this statement, and there were murmurs of agreement.

"And ye needed to think what the MacDonald chief would think of a MacGregor chieftain who thought it was acceptable for his men to take one of his clanswomen at all, and even worse, no' to protect her."

"Aye, Susan's the right of it," Allan said, and others agreed.

Alex stood there for a moment, stunned, because he hadn't thought for one minute that anyone would believe he found it acceptable that Màiri had been abducted and killed. On his return from Paris he had been worried about feeling the cold, about losing his fighting skills. It hadn't occurred to him for one minute that he would forget what it was to be a Highlander. In spite of killing Beauregard and maiming Joseph in the duel, he had forgotten how ruthless Highlanders had to be when the situation called for it.

And this situation had called for it.

He brushed his hand through his hair and sighed.

"So am I right in thinking that ye believe MacIain may have been planning to attack us even before Duncan killed his men?" he asked.

"No' necessarily," Gregor said then. "But he wouldna be afeart to do so, for he'll ken now we've a new chieftain, and that...well, what Susan said. What he'll think of one of your clansmen deciding to take matters into his own hands is another thing. If he kens it was the lassie's husband, he'll maybe understand. But it gives the wrong message about ye."

"He'll think I'm no' fit to lead the clan. And that puts all of ye at risk," Alex said then.

"Aye. But we were at risk anyway, before Duncan did what he did," Gregor said.

"At least he'll ken there's a MacGregor who doesna think what they did was right," Jeannie put in somewhat waspishly.

"We dinna think ye thought it right," Kenneth jumped in, frowning at his wife, "but MacIain likely will. I'm no' sure what I think of your idea to solve it though."

"I'm thinking Duncan should be the one to challenge him, for he killed the Glencoe men. Likely that's what'll make MacIain come, for a blood feud is a matter of vengeance. He canna ignore that," Dugald commented.

"Aye, that's true," James agreed. "Ye maybe should have killed the laddies who took Màiri, but it's Duncan who should fight MacIain, no' yourself. I'm thinking MacIain would understand that."

"From what ye've all tellt me, if I go then it should at least tell him I'm no' a coward," Alex said. He felt terrible. This was a lot more truth than he'd expected to hear. "I canna pretend I'm happy wi' what ye've tellt me, but I needed to hear it, if I'm to be the chieftain ye deserve. For ye're in the right. I see that now. I *was* asking the wrong question," he said this last sentence softly, but those closest to him heard it, Kenneth among them.

"Ye'll no' be any kind of chieftain to us if ye're dead," Barbara said. "I dinna think ye should go."

"What d'ye think I should do, then? Duncan isna fit to go, and willna be for a while yet. And in truth, I'm thinking it's my place to go, no' his. He wouldna have done what he did if I'd done the right thing in the first place. If I wait and MacIain comes here wi' all his men and maybe others too, then many of ye'll die due to my bad decision. And it seems he may well do, for either vengeance or opportunity. If I die, then Duncan can lead ye. He'll be a bonny chieftain. And Kenneth could be his right-hand man until Angus is old enough, for he's led me well over the years. If ye ken another way than waiting for Glencoe to come down the track, then tell me."

He waited, but no one could think of a sensible alternative other than Duncan going, and Alex could not accept that.

"So, I've made my decision then," Alex said. "Alasdair, Dugald and Allan, will ye come wi' me? Only to witness and to tell the clan what happened, if I canna. We'll leave in the morning."

The clansfolk stood then, preparing to leave, as it was clear the meeting was over.

"I just want to say thank ye," Alex added. "I ken it's no' the normal way, and hopefully one day ye'll have no objections to my decisions, for they'll all be good ones. But until then I'm needing to learn, and today ye've helped me do that. I'll no' make that mistake again."

"No," said Duncan, when Alex told him what he was going to do. "Ye canna do that. If anyone challenges MacIain it should be myself, for I'm the one who killed his men, no' you."

He was still in bed, for the fever, along with the blood loss and lack of food for over a week had weakened him badly. But he was sitting up and was no longer pasty-faced, which was a good sign.

"Aye, well, that's the issue," Alex replied. "For I should have killed the laddies who took Màiri. I realise that now."

"Ye do?" Duncan said softly. "Truly?"

"Aye. I owe ye an apology, for now I see how ye felt, and it was understandable. I loved Màiri, and I miss her terribly, ye must believe that, and I see now I should have avenged her, or given ye the opportunity to. I wasna thinking right. I just saw…" he glanced at Angus, who was sitting by the fireside with Susan, quietly listening to the exchange.

"Ye saw that they were only a wee bit older than him, and thought of the things we did at that age," Duncan finished.

"Aye. But even though we disobeyed Da then, we wouldna have done what they did - taken a lassie against her will. We endangered ourselves, no one else. I should have avenged her, for you, for her, and for the clan. For now MacIain will likely think me a weakling, which puts us all at risk. And that's my doing, no' yours."

"It was me who killed his men, though," Duncan pointed out.

"It was. But he'd likely come anyway, if he thinks I'm weak, whether ye'd killed his men or no'. He'll just come quicker now."

"Even so, ye're the chieftain and the clan needs ye," Duncan said.

"Aye, and because of that it's myself that needs to go. He'll think me more of a weakling if I send you in my place."

"Ye willna be sending me. I'll go anyway," Duncan persisted.

"No, ye willna. For ye're no' even strong enough to get out of your bed, and I need to act quickly. Ye're no' going, and that's final. If I die, then ye'll be chieftain, and ye'll make a good one, I'm sure of that. I've tellt the clan that Kenneth can advise ye until Angus is old enough to."

"So ye're expecting to die then," Duncan said brutally, causing Angus to cry out, although he'd promised to say nothing.

"No, I'm no' expecting to die!" Alex said. "But I ken it's a possibility. I'm expecting to stop a blood feud that could kill a lot of people, and even bring in other MacDonalds and MacGregors. I'm the cause of it, and I'm the chieftain, so I'll end it!" he said, his voice rising as he saw Duncan was still not convinced.

"I'll be well enough to go in a few days," Duncan insisted. "He'll no' come that quickly I'm thinking, and if he does I'll go out and meet him. It doesna matter that ye didna avenge her, for I killed men that had nothing to do wi' the matter. He'll accept that I've come to acknowledge that, as yon laddies did to you. He willna think you weak."

"What?" Alex shouted. "No ye willna! Ye're no' offering to fight him at all, are ye? Ye're wanting to sacrifice yourself for my stupidity! No."

"Alex," Duncan said then, softly, so that Angus wouldn't hear. "Ye've everything to live for. I havena anything, no' now. I dinna want to go on. Please, let me go."

"No," Alex said. This was grief talking, as it had talked to their father. He would recover in time, learn to live without her, as he had lived before he'd fallen in love with her. "No. That's an end of it. Ye're no' going." He started to get up from the stool he was sitting on then, but Duncan reached out and gripped his arm desperately.

"If ye willna let me go, I'll go anyway. It's for me to resolve, for she was my wife, and I killed the men. I canna let ye do this," he said, his tone stubborn, determined.

Alex looked at him. It was clear that he *would* go, as soon as he was capable of walking at all. And there were some who would likely help him to, for both Dugald and James thought it should be Duncan not him who went, and others had seemed to agree with this.

If they thought he could fight. They would not let him go if he was incapable, which he clearly was. But he was also very persuasive, and determined enough to appear to be better than he actually was.

He tore his arm from Duncan's grasp then, and standing, went over to the hearth.

"Angus," he said, "will ye fetch Kenneth for me?"

He went outside then, sat on the bench under the window, and closed his eyes. He would learn from this, he told himself. The next time he was thinking to be merciful, he would consider the likely consequences first.

After a few minutes Angus returned with Kenneth. Alex stood, and the three of them went into the house.

"Kenneth, I need ye to hold Duncan's arm for me. His hand, and his forearm," Alex said.

"There isna anything the matter wi' my arm," Duncan said, puzzled.

Kenneth looked between them.

"Just do it," Alex said, the uncertain boy by the loch earlier a million miles away, his voice clearly that of the chieftain now.

Kenneth did as he was told, and before Duncan could react to this Alex drew his dirk and brought the hilt down hard on his brother's wrist. There was an audible crack, and Duncan let out a cry of agony.

"Ye can let him go now," he said to the giant. "Gently though." He turned to Susan. "Will ye do what ye do for a broken bone?" he said coolly. He looked back at Duncan then, who was staring at him, his face white with pain and shock.

"Ye're no' going, and that's final. Ye'll no' be able to fight for a good while, so there's no reason for ye to go. I'll be back long before ye're healed. Right, I'm away to my bed, for it's been a long day, and I'm wanting to leave early in the morning. Kenneth, I'll need to speak wi' ye."

He sheathed his dirk, and climbed up the steps to the loft area where he was sleeping while Duncan was needing the bed, leaving his two brothers, Kenneth and Susan staring after him, wearing matching expressions of absolute shock.

Then Susan shot to her feet and went to her patient, breaking the spell. Angus followed her to see if he could help, and Kenneth followed Alex up to the loft area, as requested.

It seemed the MacGregor chieftain could be ruthless, after all.

CHAPTER EIGHT

THE FOUR MACGREGORS SET off the following morning, the clan coming out to watch them silently, worriedly, as they disappeared through the trees. Angus stood at the door of the chieftain's house, white-faced, Duncan, Kenneth and Susan with him.

Once the group vanished through the trees they went back indoors, leaving the rest of the clan with a multitude of unanswered questions, although one at least had certainly been answered, due to the fact that Duncan's right arm was splinted and in a sling. Alex *had* broken his brother's arm then! Would this make the rift between them even deeper, when Alex came back?

If Alex came back.

After a short period of futile waiting in the hope that Duncan, or maybe Kenneth would re-emerge with some news, the clan went about their tasks, sending up silent prayers that Alex would succeed in his endeavour.

In the house Angus poured ale into cups, Duncan lay on the bed so that Susan could check his wound, and Kenneth sat on a stool watching the proceedings. He had slept there the previous night, Alex having spent part of it outlining his temporary duties until he returned from Glencoe. Neither of them had talked about what would happen if Alex didn't return, as both Angus and Duncan had been within hearing.

"If he doesna come back I'll never forgive myself," Duncan said now, heedless of Angus's feelings in his despair. "I did this. It should be myself to go, no' him." He winced as Susan pressed at the edges of the wound.

"It's healing well now," she told him. "He's the chieftain, Duncan. It's his task to do, no' yours. If he'd let ye go it would have emasculated him. Ye were in no condition to fight anyway. If ye'd obeyed him he wouldna have needed to do that." She waved a hand at his arm.

"So ye agree wi' him," Kenneth said.

"I do. What option did he have? I dinna want him to go either. But in truth he had no choice, if he's to keep the MacDonalds from descending on us."

"Do ye really think they would?" Angus asked, coming forward with the cups.

"They'd be daft if they didna, laddie," Kenneth replied. "For they've just cause, *and* cause to believe the chieftain's weak. What would we do in that case?"

"He isna weak!" Angus protested, handing Kenneth his cup. He put Duncan's and Susan's down on the floor for when they were ready.

"I ken that, we all do," Kenneth said, although he suspected a number of the clansfolk had doubted it until Alex had walked out of the settlement this morning. "But the MacDonalds dinna. Alex has gone to show them they're wrong. He's the right of it."

Susan had replaced the dressing on her patient's wound, and handed him his drink before sitting down herself.

"I wish he'd taken me wi' him," Angus said sadly.

"Ye're needed here more," Susan said. "For Duncan canna help me wi' heavy things, and Kenneth has his own home to go to."

Kenneth grinned. Susan always knew the right thing to say to Angus. She no doubt already had a vast multitude of tasks in mind to occupy him with for the next days. Now he needed to find some of his own, because he could not imagine Alex not coming home, and if he didn't, not being able to avenge him.

But he would not be able to, none of them would. For if MacIain accepted the challenge Alex intended to give, then the loser's clan could make no retaliation.

"And we all need to pray that Our Lord brings him safely back to us," Kenneth added.

Until they knew if He would, they just had to wait.

151

Glencoe, late September 1737

Just before they entered MacDonald territory, Alex and his companions changed from their everyday outfits into their formal *fèilidhean mòra* of scarlet and black tartan. They all wore a blue bonnet with the pine sprig that showed they were MacGregors tucked into it, Alex adding the two eagle feathers that denoted his status as chieftain. Then he knelt, closed his eyes and offered up a silent prayer that he would survive this day. He crossed himself and stood, and then eyed his clansmen.

"Good," he said approvingly. "MacIain'll no doubt ken we're on our way once we cross into his territory, but even so when I give the word ye play us in, Dugald."

Dugald prepared his pipes so that he could start as soon as he was told to.

"Are ye sure ye're wanting to do this?" Allan asked.

"I've never been more certain of anything," Alex replied. While it was not true that he actually *wanted* to do what he was about to do, he was sure this was the only practical way to avoid massive bloodshed. "If I'm killed they willna touch ye, and ye *mustna* retaliate. For it'll be a matter of honour, and ye'll shame my memory if ye do. Instead ye'll leave wi' dignity, having obtained MacIain's word that the blood debt is paid, and leave together. Once ye're outside their lands ye can run on, Allan, for ye're still the fastest of us, and take the news to my brothers. Now, let's do it."

When they arrived MacIain, who had in fact been amply warned that four MacGregors, including the chieftain were on their way to see him, presumably in peace as they were announcing their presence, was sitting in his wood-panelled hall in the presence of a number of his clansmen and the eight fools who'd started all this.

When they entered he stood as a courtesy to the MacGregor chieftain, and both men bowed to each other.

"Am I right that ye've come peacefully, to discuss the situation between us?" he asked.

"Aye, I have," Alex replied.

MacIain waved his hand and a chair was brought for the chieftain, after which brandy was offered to all the men, and both chiefs sat,

Alasdair, Allan and Dugald standing just behind theirs, while the MacDonalds stood around the room, watching intently.

"Ye dinna seem surprised, so I'm thinking ye ken the whole reason why I'm here," Alex began.

"The most of it. My clansmen acted against my orders, and took it upon themselves to raid your cattle."

"They acted against your orders?" Alex asked.

"They did. They tellt me they were trying to prove themselves, and they succeeded in proving what a liability they are to me, which wasna their intention. I've added my own punishment to yours. The only reason any of them are alive to witness today is because ye decided no' to kill them. I'm truly sorry about your clanswoman. They deserved to die for it." He glanced across at the youths, who appeared to be trying to melt into the wall.

Alex turned then and gave them a look of such animosity that they flinched. It seemed the kind-hearted chieftain who'd let them go was a thing of the past.

"They did. I see that now," Alex admitted. "I made a wrong decision. I willna do that again. But it's done, and it's because of that I'm here."

"Because your clansman killed five of my men, and wounded another," MacIain said.

"Aye. He acted against *my* orders. I havena punished him, for he's my brother and the husband of the lassie whose death your men caused. He's been punished enough, for they were only married six months and he tellt me she was maybe wi' child."

The three MacGregors behind him gasped at that, for it was the first time they'd heard that she was expecting a baby.

"Ah, Christ," MacIain said. "I'm even more sorry now. I understand why he killed my men, then. If he'd come to me instead, I'd have let him kill those fools, and end this."

"I wish he had too, but he wasna thinking rightly. I'm sure the men he killed had families too, and ye'll be wanting to avenge them. And that's why I'm here. My brother wanted to come in my place but he's wounded, and it's myself who's the chieftain in any case. I'm here wi' a proposition to end any blood feud today, if ye're in agreement."

"Let me hear it," MacIain said.

"I'm proposing a single combat between us, or between myself and a man of your choosing," Alex said. "Your clansmen started this, but mine killed five of yours. I'm asking ye to end all blood debt between us, whichever of us dies. My clan will abide by this, if yours does."

MacIain sat back for a moment, sipping his brandy and considering. He looked at the young man sitting opposite him. He was tall, strongly built, clearly a warrior, and very earnest. A man of honour, and a brave one too, to come to his enemy's house and propose such a thing. Not at all the kind of man he'd expected the MacGregor chieftain to be after his judgement of the cattle raiders. He reassessed his opinion. This was not a man to have as an enemy, but as a friend, MacIain thought.

If he fought him, would he win? He was a good twenty years older than the man sitting opposite, but was still in full strength, with years of battle experience behind him. But he had no knowledge of his opponent's ability or experience. Even so, if he agreed it would be an interesting contest, and would indeed end the feud between them.

Alex sat, also sipping his brandy, waiting patiently and apparently coolly for the Glencoe chief's response to this proposal.

MacIain finished his drink and handed the glass to a man behind him. Then he nodded to Alex.

"I canna let my clansmen's deaths go unavenged. But I'm thinking this is a fair way to end our dispute," he began.

"Ye canna be thinking to agree to this ridiculous offer," came a scathing voice from the background. "He isna worth risking your life for. He's a MacGregor! Ye could kill all four of the vermin and no one would act against ye!"

A gasp of horror ran round the room, and the three men behind Alex stiffened, their hands automatically going to their sword hilts.

Alex held up a hand warning his men not to act, then turned, locating the speaker in the shadows of the room.

"The other vermin would," he said, with icy contempt. "*All* of them."

Christ! MacIain thought. This was getting worse, for the MacGregor had just made a declaration to potentially involve all the MacGregors, not just the Lomond men. And there was no doubt now in MacIain's mind that this man had the ability to raise them, and lead them. Indeed he doubted they'd need much raising, if they were to hear this insult against them.

"Malcolm!" MacIain said. "Will ye step forward?"

As it was apparent from the tone of voice that this was not a request but an order, the man came forward, reluctantly.

"Ye tellt me that ye'd accept a man of my choosing should I desire it, wi' no loss of honour to yourself?" he said to Alex.

"I did," came the reply.

"Would ye be willing to fight this man in my place? It wouldna be beneath ye to do so, for he's a cousin to me by my father's sister," MacIain asked.

Alex assessed the man, who was clearly now wishing he'd kept his mouth shut.

"I would be delighted to," he replied, turning back to the chief, his eyes sparkling.

"And I would be delighted for ye to do so," MacIain replied. The two men exchanged a look of perfect understanding. "Malcolm. Ye have half an hour to prepare yourself to meet the MacGregor. Alasdair, William, ye'll accompany him to make sure he doesna forget his way back." A ripple of laughter ran round the hall. This Malcolm was clearly not popular, then.

Go," he commanded when his white-faced cousin began to object. He waited until Malcolm and his guards had left the room, then turned back to his guests, smiling.

"It's generous of ye to accept my substitute. I havena been in the best of health lately, so I'm thinking Malcolm will be a more fitting opponent than myself," he said.

"Aye, I'm thinking that too," Alex agreed.

While we wait, can I offer ye some food, or would ye prefer to wait until afterwards?"

"For myself I'll wait, for I've eaten today and I'm no' wanting to fight on a full stomach," Alex replied. "But my men may wish to accept your offer."

They said they would also wait, all three of them looking more relaxed than they had at the thought of their chieftain fighting MacIain. True, this Malcolm was a tall and strong-looking man, closer in age to Alex, but such a fool and a braggart would surely be no match for their chieftain. Whether Alex felt that way or not they had no idea, for he'd seemed perfectly relaxed since he'd stepped onto MacDonald territory, although he'd been visibly tense until then.

Half an hour later Malcolm returned, armed with sword, dirk and targe, his silver-blond hair tied back. He went to his chief and bowed, then stepped in and whispered something urgently to him.

"I'm thinking it's a wee bit late for that," MacIain replied. "But it isna me ye insulted, but these men. Will ye accept Malcolm's apology for his earlier remark?"

"I will not," Alex replied instantly, "For he didna just insult me, but all my clan, and unforgivably. It's a matter of honour."

"It certainly is. We'll go outside then," MacIain said.

They went outside, assembling on a meadow near MacIain's house, much of the MacDonald clan, who were eager to see such an unusual event, assembling behind Malcolm, although MacIain waved them all back when they threatened to come too close.

"Ye may watch, if MacGregor agrees," he called. "But if he does, ye willna crowd in, and ye willna make a sound no matter what happens. For there are only three of them to support their leader and many of you to support Malcolm, and I wouldna have it said that this wasna a fair combat in every sense possible. The field is flat," he continued, speaking to Alex now. "There are no boggy parts, no stones or holes to trip ye. I tell ye this for ye're a stranger here, and havena had time to observe the land. Do ye accept my word regarding it?"

"I do," Alex replied, his respect for the Glencoe chief growing as he realised the man was doing his utmost to make it as even a fight as possible. He doubted that MacIain was not feeling well, but he did not doubt that whichever man died, he would not lose. For it was clear that this Malcolm was a troublemaker and generally unpopular from what he could see of the MacDonalds' expressions.

Finally the two men stood facing each other, each armed with their own broadsword, dirk and targe.

Their eyes met, and Alex smiled as Malcolm's cornflower-blue gaze failed to hold his. He felt a sudden surge of elation and swallowed it back, knowing that overconfidence could get him killed.

"This is a fight to the death," MacIain called. "Whoever wins, the blood feud between our clans will be at an end, all animosities will be forgotten, and we will move forward from this day as friends.

Furthermore the MacDonalds of Glencoe will not raid cattle from the Lomond MacGregors for as long as I live, and, I hope, longer."

"And I vow the same for myself, and hold my brother, who will replace me should I fail today, to uphold it." Alex replied.

Allan, Alasdair and Dugald agreed to take the message, all three of them praying they would not need to, and then MacIain gave the signal for the fight to begin, and everything except the wish for Alex to be victorious flew from their minds.

The two men locked gazes, the onlookers, the chief, everything fading away as they gauged each other. Malcolm licked his lips nervously, and advanced forward and left, bringing his sword downwards in an attempt to cut Alex's forward leg, then retreating rapidly as Alex brought his targe down with lightning speed to block it, looking for an opportunity to penetrate his foe's defence.

This continued for a few minutes as the two men aimed to cut the body and legs of each other, primarily trying to assess the other's ability while hoping for a lucky strike that would end it. Then they both paused, Alex noting with satisfaction that Malcolm's breathing was fast and there was sweat on his brow, although he himself was still breathing normally. The MacDonald was not as fit as he was then, but fast when he struck, and strong.

Alex considered, his mind working rapidly. Malcolm was unpopular. He needed to impress his chief, his clan, by winning quickly and impressively. If he was forced to work hard to no avail, he would be more likely to grow impatient and make a mistake in his attempt to win. Whereas Alex had no such motive. He was not here to put on a show; he just wanted to kill this man by any means, impressive or not, end the feud and go home to his clan.

The best way to beat him, Alex decided, was to make him work until he weakened and then attack, hard and fast. With that he adapted his technique, keeping out of reach of his opponent, forcing Malcolm to do all the work and come to him. When the man attacked Alex defended himself, but made few attacking moves himself, mainly moving backwards or sideways, so the two of them circled each other.

After a few minutes of this the MacDonalds who had clearly been hoping for a dramatic and spectacular fight started to vocalise their disappointment, stopping only when MacIain raised his hand imperiously. But Malcolm had heard them. His mouth twisted in frustration and he lunged harder, hoping to get through Alex's defences before he could employ his targe or leap athletically out of the way.

Another few minutes passed, at the end of which, although both men were breathing more heavily now, Malcolm's shirt was soaked with sweat, whereas Alex had only a slight beading of sweat on his forehead. He did have a minor cut on his thigh from a lucky blow and could feel the blood trickling down the inside of his leg, but it was nothing that concerned him. *Now,* he thought.

He stood normally, just for a moment, then smiled mockingly at his opponent, watching with satisfaction as the man's mouth twisted with rage. And then Malcolm lunged at Alex, bringing his sword high and then down, aiming for his head. Alex raised his left arm, felt the shock as the sword hit his targe, and then drove forward, slashing the man across the side.

He leapt back again, observing with satisfaction the speed with which the red stain spread across his opponent's shirt, and then Malcolm ran forward, blocking Alex's sword with his targe, while Alex, with no time to retreat, did the same, the result being that they came in so hard and fast both men's weapons were rendered temporarily useless.

When Malcolm started to pull back, clearly expecting Alex to do the same, as he had spent almost his whole time until now retreating, instead Alex wrapped his arms around his foe's back then hooked his right leg round Malcolm's knees, bringing him down to the ground hard, a classic Kenneth move, one he taught all his pupils.

Before the man could leap up Alex brought his sword down with all his might, driving it first through the man's neck and then through his chest, thus bringing the fight to an abrupt end.

He stood, watching coldly as Malcolm convulsed for a moment and then stilled. Then he turned to MacIain and bowed to him, while the audience stood in stunned silence.

"Are we agreed that all animosity between us is now ended?" he asked.

"We are indeed," MacIain replied. "And very glad I am of it, for our clans have always been allies and friends." This was not *completely* true, but neither man was going to bring up the distant past now. "Let us move forward once more as friends and allies!"

MacIain put his arm around Alex's shoulder in a gesture of comradeship.

"In truth, I'm awfu' glad ye won, but I'm thinking ye ken that," he said jovially.

"I do, and I'm awfu' glad I won too, and disposed of a troublesome clansman for ye."

"I'm obliged to ye. Will you and your men accept my hospitality for this night?" MacIain asked.

"We will, and gladly," Alex replied, a great flood of relief washing through him as it sunk in that he had ended the feud with honour and had proved, both to the MacDonalds and the MacGregors, that he was not a weak chieftain.

After this he never would be, he decided. Once he learnt something he never forgot it. And this would be etched in his mind forever.

The evening went well, all the more so because MacIain had carefully selected the guests who were to enjoy the feast celebrating the alliance between the two clans. Alex sat next to the chief and was served by his wife Isabel, as befitted his rank. The other three MacGregors all sat at the same table, the rest of the invited MacDonalds at side tables.

It was an excellent meal, Alex had to admit, better than anything his clan could provide without warning, and MacIain's house was far grander than his, which was really not much different to his clansmen's. But then the Glencoe men were more numerous than the Lomond men, and, which was more important, they were not only legal, but a branch of the huge MacDonald clan.

It had been worth risking his life, he thought, to end a feud with such a clan. And such a leader too. From his behaviour today Alex had already decided the chief was a fair man, and during the evening nothing happened to change his mind.

"Ye said your brother was wounded," MacIain said, as everyone laughed and chatted over their food. "Will he recover?"

"Aye, I'm thinking so. We have a powerful healer wi' us. He had a fever but it broke the day before I left, and the wound is healing well. It isna in his nature to behave as he did normally," Alex said.

"Aye, well, grief can do terrible things to a man. Can I ask ye, why did ye let the wee gomerels go?"

Alex thought for a moment of how much to say. As much as he respected MacIain and they had vowed to be allies, alliances were fluid amongst the clans and he had no desire to reveal anything he would not want an enemy to know, should they become so at some point.

"I remembered some of the stupid things I did at their age, although in truth I would never have abducted a lassie. And yon Niall laddie. It was himself who insisted that they bring Màiri back, even though he kent they could have just buried her where she fell and we wouldna have been any the wiser. He kent he could well be killed, but he did it anyway. I'm thinking he'll be a mighty clansman to ye in time. I thought maiming them was enough. As I said, I made a mistake, but I'm thinking I would still have let him at least go, for I admired his courage and fairness."

"Ye're right. I'd dismissed him as one of the band of fools, for they are, but I'll think again about him. Maybe keep him away from them now and give him a chance to prove himself," MacIain said.

"Ye said yon Malcolm was your cousin?" Alex said then. "I'm taking it he's no' blood kin to ye, but through marriage, for there's no one else here tonight who looks like him. In fact I havena seen anyone wi' such a colour of hair before."

"Aye. I've kept his direct blood kin away, which is why ye'll no' see anyone else wi' his colouring. But they're a story in their own right. There's a tale that the first of the lassies to be born wi' silver hair and such blue eyes was a changeling, but I dinna believe that.

"There are a number of them now, though no' all of them have the same hair and eye colour. But all the ones that do are stubborn, hot-tempered and can be reckless, though they're no' all idiots like yon Malcolm was. He was a troublemaker, has caused me many problems over the years. This was a perfect way to remove him without killing him myself, and no one can complain about it." He grinned then and accepted another glass of claret from his wife, who filled Alex's glass too.

"Will they no' do so anyway, if they're as ye say?" Alex asked.

"Aye, they may do. But they canna say I wasna fair in view of his insult to ye, or that he didna deserve it. Their matriarch has come home recently. She's had a great many experiences, and although she's an old woman now she rules them wi' a rod of iron. It's a blessing. She came back to die in her native land, but shows no sign of doing so for a good while yet, thank God!"

They stayed the night, leaving the next morning with enough food to keep them going for a far longer journey than they had before them, all four of them in high spirits if a little physically sluggish, the former induced by the result of the combat, the latter by the amount of excellent food and drink they'd consumed the night before.

"I'm thinking ye made the right decision there," Allan said, once they were well away from MacDonald territory.

"Aye, but if I'd made the right decision at the start, I wouldna have needed to do this," Alex admitted. "I'll no' put ye all at risk again. I'm hoping Duncan will accept this now."

"He'll have to, will he no'?" Dugald said.

"Aye, if I tell him to. But I mean accept it in his heart," Alex explained.

The others fell silent for a minute then, realising that Alex was by no means sure Duncan would reconcile with him, even now. They hoped he would, because the bond between the two of them was uncanny. It was, as Alexander had said when they were boys, as though they were two parts of a whole, and since they'd argued so badly the difference in them had been astonishing. The whole clan had seen how diminished they both were, and had also observed how utterly devastated Angus was by this, which neither brother seemed to have appreciated yet, so intent were they on their personal feud.

But that was not something any of them felt they could say to their chieftain, and certainly not now, when there was so much cause for celebration. The winter should be peaceful, the MacDonalds were friends once more, and the chieftain was very much wiser as a result.

So instead they chatted and laughed, and in the evening they made a fire and cooked some of the food they'd been given. Allan did not run ahead, for Alex said he'd only wanted that if the worst had happened. Now they could all arrive together, and although they could not have a ceilidh with music and dancing they would certainly have a meeting, where he would tell them what had happened, and the result of it.

But first he needed to speak with his brother, and as Alex got closer to home he started to feel apprehensive. For if Duncan did not forgive him now, he could think of nothing else he could do to make him do so.

If he had to command his brother to accept the alliance he would, but that would be a last resort. Now the threat of attack was over and

Màiri avenged, his whole being was focussed on reconciling with his brother by any means possible.

When they arrived at the start of the rough track that led to the Mac-Gregor settlement Angus was there, sitting on a rock in the pouring rain, his back against a tree. As soon as he saw them he leapt up, and running to them launched himself at Alex, as he had three years before.

"You're back!" he cried ecstatically, then burst into tears.

This time Alex succeeded in keeping his balance and hugged his little brother back, smiling down at the dripping blond head buried in his chest. *God, but he's growing quickly,* he thought.

"Ye thought MacIain would kill me, then? Ye havena much faith in my fighting skills," he replied with mock severity.

Angus lifted his head then, his brimming slate-blue eyes meeting his brother's anxiously, before realising he was joking. He smiled and made a visible effort to pull himself together.

"I kent ye'd beat MacIain," he said with absolute conviction, "but I didna ken if the MacDonalds would kill ye for doing it, and ye couldna fight them all!"

"Have ye been sitting here the whole week, laddie?" Dugald asked.

"No. I just came down twice a day for a wee while, hoping to see ye coming back. Like I did when Duncan was gone," Angus said, brightening now. "Will I run ahead and tell everyone ye're back?"

"No, we're nearly there now. Walk wi' us. I've missed ye," Alex said, realising at that moment that he had. He'd been so obsessed with the MacDonald problem and his estrangement from Duncan he'd hardly thought about his other brother for ages.

I need to do better than this, he told himself.

They walked the rest of the way together, Angus skipping with happiness that his brother was safe, Alex smiling at his childlike carefree attitude to life, and comparing it with when he was thirteen.

When he was thirteen he'd been in Edinburgh, he realised, killing two footpads and vowing to become a man as quickly as possible so that he could replace his incompetent father as chieftain. Would he have been like Angus, if circumstances had been different?

Aye, likely I would, he thought, for everyone said Angus was like him in many ways, not just in looks but in personality. *Never will I force him to make that choice,* Alex vowed then. *Long may he continue so carefree, as long as he can fight well and defend himself.* And he could. Kenneth had said that Angus was becoming a bonny fighter. He could not imagine ever being estranged from his youngest brother, which was a relief.

Duncan had always been more intense, did not wear his heart on his sleeve as Angus did. Alex realised now that he should not have been surprised by the intensity of Duncan's feelings when Màiri had been killed. Even if he couldn't understand it from personal experience, he should have realised what such a catastrophic event would do to his brother, and have acted accordingly.

He would never make such a mistake again, that was certain. Now he could only hope that his brother would be satisfied by his actions, and would forgive him for his insensitivity.

When they reached the settlement Angus, unable to restrain himself any more, ran ahead, telling everyone he met that they were all home, and all well, with the result that when Alex arrived at his house Duncan was standing at the door, his arm splinted but no longer in a sling, still looking tired, but with good colour. He was *definitely* on the mend now.

Alex stopped and the two of them eyed each other for a minute, while the rest of the clan, who had begun to gather, fell silent.

"So ye killed the MacIain, then," Duncan said matter-of-factly.

"No' the MacIain. He appointed a champion for me to fight, which I agreed to. He's dead, and the blood feud is ended between us," Alex replied.

Duncan nodded.

"Ye were wounded, though," he said, glancing at Alex's leg. "Ye're favouring the right."

Trust Duncan to notice what no one else had, not even his companions on the way home.

"Aye. Nothing serious, but I'll have Susan look at it."

"Will ye away in, then? She's still here," Duncan said, as though it was his house rather than Alex's. He moved to the side of the door and Alex went in, followed by Angus.

The rest of the clan stood outside for a minute, wondering if Alex would come back out to give an account of what had happened.

"On the way back he tellt us he'd hold a meeting when he was home, to tell ye what happened," Allan offered when everyone looked to him, Dugald and Alasdair. "I'm thinking he'll do that, when he's sorted out what's between him and his brother."

Reluctantly they dispersed, hoping Allan was right. Alex coming home told them that any feud with the MacDonalds was over. That was the most important thing. Everything else could wait.

Inside the cottage Susan was examining Alex's wound on the inside of the thigh, which, while indeed not serious, was still several inches long.

"Ye were fortunate he didna cut deeper," she said while she was cleaning it, checking to make sure it wasn't going bad. "There's an artery there. If he'd caught that there'd have been no saving ye."

"That's likely what he was hoping for. I leapt away before he could," Alex said. "I was forcing him to do all the work so he'd tire and maybe make a mistake."

"But ye made one instead," Duncan commented.

"Aye, I did. I brought my targe up to block him, and he slid his sword down it and caught me. He was a bonny fighter."

"No' bonny enough, though. I'm glad of that," Duncan said then, watching as Susan pressed at the partially healed edges of the cut.

"Are ye really?" Alex blurted out, and then flushed. "Forget I said—"

"Of course I am," Duncan interrupted. "If ye'd been killed I'd never have forgiven myself for it, for it was my actions that caused ye to go."

"Aye, well, it was my actions that caused *you* to go in the first place," Alex replied, then sucked in a sharp breath as Susan hit a tender spot.

"It isna too bad," she said then, studiously ignoring the conversation the two brothers were having. "I'll just put some comfrey on it and bind it for a few days, to be safe." She went into the bedroom then, where her medicines were, leaving the brothers alone. Angus stood near the doorway silently, not wanting to disturb this crucial moment.

"MacIain said if ye'd gone to him, he'd have let ye kill the youths who took Màiri," Alex added, oblivious to Susan and Angus, all his attention on Duncan.

"Would he? Aye, I'd have been wiser to do that, for if he'd killed me for it, it would have been a blessing," Duncan replied. "And I'd have killed those I wanted to and no' some that hadna done anything to me. I wasna thinking rightly. I regret that now I've had time to consider."

"Is it healing well?"

"Aye. It's still painful, and Susan said I need to keep the splint on a wee while longer if I dinna want my arm to be weak for life. But it's healing, she thinks. It isna as swollen now."

"Christ, I'm sorry I did that to ye," Alex said. "I couldna think of any other way to stop ye."

"There wasna any other way to stop me," Duncan admitted. "Ye did right. Or at least now ye're home safely ye did right. If yon laddie had killed ye, I'd have thought differently."

"I'm glad I did it whatever the cost," Alex said, "for I loved Màiri, and I'm mourning her too. I should have avenged her. Maybe I deserve to lose ye, but I'm hoping ye'll find a way to forgive me."

"Aye, well, Susan's a hard woman, wouldna let me use the hand at all, so I've had a lot of time to think while ye were away," Duncan said. "Ye canna bring my wife back, no one can do that, but I dinna want to lose my brother too. I've been beside myself these last days, thinking I might have done just that. Màiri wouldna want it either."

"So do ye love each other again now?" Angus asked hopefully from the doorway, the yearning in his voice unmistakeable.

Slate-blue eyes met grey, and then Duncan nodded.

"Aye," he said.

"We do," Alex replied.

For the second time that day Angus burst into tears.

"Ah, laddie," Alex said a few minutes later, when Angus, with great effort, had pulled himself together but was still wrapped in the embrace of both his older brothers. "We've loved each other the whole time. We just lost our way for a wee while, that's all."

"It didna seem that way," Angus said in a watery voice. "I thought ye'd hate each other forever. I tried and tried to think of what I could do. I wanted to go to Glencoe myself, but I'm no' strong enough to fight MacIain yet, and I couldna think of anything else to make ye love each other again. It was worse than Da," he added, "for I didna remember him before as ye did. I just thought he'd never loved us. But we werena like that before."

Over his youngest brother's head, Alex closed his eyes for a moment. Why hadn't he thought about his brother's childhood, realised how deeply he would feel the rift between him and Duncan? He hadn't even considered it, he realised. He opened his eyes then and saw that Duncan was feeling exactly the same way.

"Angus," Duncan said then, pulling back a little so he could look his youngest brother in the face. "Alex and I will always love each other, as we'll love you, no matter what happens. I ken we've just had maybe the worst fight of our lives, and I'm hoping we'll never have another like it, but we still loved each other, even if we didna think we did. Or at least I didna think I did," he added with brutal honesty.

"So it's really over now?" Angus asked.

"Aye, it's really over. But it's no' over wi' Màiri for me," Duncan said. "Alex has avenged her but no one can bring her back to me, and I'll need a lot of time to find a way forward. Sometimes I'll need to be alone, but it isna because I dinna love ye, or Alex. It's because the missing her is too much for me to be wi' anyone at all."

"Like Da wi' Ma," Angus said.

"Aye, but Duncan isna Da, and neither am I," Alex said. "We should have realised how much this was hurting ye too."

"That doesna signify if ye love each other again now," Angus said happily. "I'll stop hurting if ye do."

"We do," Alex said, suddenly feeling like an old man, although he was only nine years older than his brother. How long was it since he'd been able to swing from misery to happiness in a moment as Angus was now doing?

"Since Da died," Duncan said, reading his mind, and clearly feeling the same way.

And then Alex knew for certain that he had won his brother back. The sun came out from behind the black cloud he'd been living under for the last weeks, and he did indeed swing from misery to happiness, in a moment.

He was more like Angus than he'd thought he was.

CHAPTER NINE

Late March 1738

AFTER WHAT SEEMED LIKE hours of tossing and turning in her bed, Susan finally gave up any hope of falling asleep and instead decided to get up. Maybe doing something useful would take her mind off the dark thoughts that were keeping her awake, that had kept her awake on many nights since the terrible events of the previous year.

She lit a candle, made up the fire and sat beside it, wondering what she could do until day broke. It seemed to be earlier than she'd thought when lying in bed. In a minute she'd go down to the loch to fetch water, then would make some chamomile tea to help her sleep. Otherwise she would waste the daylight hours by being too tired to function properly.

She was managing well during the daylight hours, generally, although she was very happy that the days were now lengthening, which meant she could keep herself occupied for longer, and so keep the grief at bay a little.

The rest of the clan had been wonderful during the winter, realising that she was grieving terribly for Màiri and would probably not want to be alone as much as she normally did. Consequently she'd been invited to a different house almost every night, and had a standing invitation from the chieftain to visit or stay at his house whenever she wanted to. Initially she had taken him up on that, finding it impossible at first to countenance being alone for any length of time, but as the months had passed she had realised that she would never recover from the death of her niece unless she faced up to it, and she could only do that by resuming the normal pattern of her life. She could not impose on the clansfolk forever.

Duncan had not imposed on the clansfolk at all, but then no one had expected him to. Although always approachable and good-natured, he had never been one to pay unnecessary visits to people, and the death of his wife had not changed that. He did spend more time with Alex and Angus than he had when married, and occasionally called on her, but other than that spent a good deal of time alone, once he'd physically healed enough to do so. He seemed to be coping with Màiri's loss, although it was impossible to be sure with Duncan.

One thing he had done which had surprised her was to tell her that she was welcome to call on him any time she wanted to, day or night.

"For I'm thinking ye'll be needing company at times, but maybe no' conversation," he'd told her. "And I'll likely feel the same way. There's no' many in the clan who understand that, but I ken you do. We can help each other, I think, when the grieving is too fierce."

He had meant what he said, so at times she had called on him, although she had not abused his offer. It would be easier when the weather improved, she told herself. Only a few more weeks and the ploughing and planting would start, and then there would be so much work to do that there'd be no time to mope.

She stood suddenly, aware she was in danger now of doing just that, and wrapping her arisaid around her shoulders she picked up a jug and left the cottage. By the time she got back the fire would be hot enough to boil water.

She had filled her jug and was just making her way back through the trees when she thought she heard voices. She froze, listening intently. The voices had come from the north, and she couldn't imagine why any MacGregors would be further north along the loch than her cottage, which was at the top of the settlement. No one was out hunting, and anyone on watch would be silent.

She had been standing stock still for a few minutes before she heard it again; a masculine voice speaking softly, and then another answering, after which someone laughed quietly. They were a short distance away, she surmised, and certainly hadn't seen her. She crouched down, spreading mud across the bottom of her clean white shift and along her legs. Then she put the jug down, pulled the top of the arisaid over her head before knotting it round her waist, and carefully, silently, made her way through the trees in the direction of the voices.

When she was close enough to hear part of what they were saying she knelt down in the bracken, listening. They had stopped moving for the moment, and from the sounds she could hear seemed to be settling down where they were. She estimated there were a good few men, but the only way she could find out how many would be to risk being seen, so she opted for listening instead, hoping she could find out why they were there, and where they were heading.

"What do we do now, then?" one man said after a few minutes of clanking and shuffling as the group attempted to make themselves comfortable by the side of the loch.

"We wait for the rest to row across and join us," came the reply.

"I canna see anyone," another man muttered.

"Aye, well, that's because Conall's taking them north in a loop, so none of the MacGregors'll see them coming across, if anyone should be on watch," the first man explained.

"I didna think they had laddies on watch. They didna last year," another said.

"They had a lassie on watch then, did they no'? Just the one, guarding all the cows too," the second man commented.

"She willna be watching tonight!" someone giggled.

"It seems she was the fiercest of the Lomond MacGregors, from what I hear."

"Didna help her, for she's dead now, poor lassie," the first man said.

"Had more courage than the new chieftain, Conall says," another said.

"Aye, well he'll die dunghill tonight," another retorted, which hope was followed by a spontaneous cheer.

"*Ist!*" the first man muttered fiercely. "Coward or no', we dinna want him, or any of them to hear us before the others arrive. Get some sleep if ye can. They'll be here before too long."

Even if the men hadn't fallen silent at that point, Susan had heard enough. Very slowly she backed away on her hands and knees, taking great care not to disturb the bracken, although if she did they'd likely think it was some wild animal, disturbed by their scent. Even so, better if they suspected nothing.

After what seemed like an age she judged herself far enough away from them that she would be neither seen nor heard if she stood upright. Then she ran as fast as she could through the trees and into the settlement, stopping outside the chieftain's house for a moment to catch her breath, before opening the door quietly and slipping in.

Alex was already awake and out of bed before she reached the bottom of the steps that led up to the area where he and Angus slept.

"It's me," she said, hearing his movement and not wanting to be dirked before she could tell him her news.

A moment later he appeared dressed only in his shirt, and ran quickly down the steps.

"What's amiss?" he asked, making no effort to be quiet, for he knew Susan would not come to the house in the middle of the night at all, let alone in her shift with her hair tangled on her shoulders unless it was an urgent matter. Whatever it was, Angus would need to wake up.

"There are men by the loch, north of my house. They're waiting for others to row across, then they mean to attack us."

"Did ye see the boats on the loch?" he asked.

"No. One of them said Conall was taking them north in a loop so we wouldna see them. He tellt the others to try to sleep, but I'm thinking they intend to attack before dawn," she told him.

"MacLarens," Alex said softly. "Are ye sure they're intending to attack us, and no' someone else?"

"I am. They said..." she hesitated then, not wanting to upset him.

"What did they say?" he asked, already heading to the kist in the corner where weapons were kept. Angus came down the steps, rubbing his eyes and yawning.

"They said Màiri was the fiercest of the MacGregors, and that ye'd die dunghill tonight," she admitted.

"Did they now?" Alex said quietly. "Angus, dress yourself quickly and away to the others and wake them. Tell the men to bring their arms and come here, quickly. But quietly. Ye said they're beyond your cottage?"

"Aye. Down by the lochside," Susan said. "I can show ye, when ye're ready."

"Sit down a wee minute," Alex told her, pulling assorted weapons out of the kist. Angus had disappeared back upstairs, but reappeared a couple of minutes later, dressed and wide-awake now.

"Can I fight too?" he asked excitedly.

"I dinna ken yet, laddie. Away and wake the clan. If ye do that without noise, I'll think on it."

Angus shot out of the door like a rocket, but closed it silently behind him, causing both Susan and Alex to smile, in spite of the seriousness of the situation.

"Ye were right," Alex said then, deftly folding his *féileadh mór* round him, and buckling his sword belt. "Ye said MacIain would think less of me for letting the laddies go."

"But ye went to him, proved yourself," Susan protested.

"Aye, to MacIain. But no' to the other clans. It seems the MacLarens are hoping to do to us what we did to them nearly two hundred years ago," Alex said. "Well, I dinna think it was the Lomond men, but certainly MacGregors."

"What was that?" Susan asked.

"It was when the Campbells drove us off our lands. One band of MacGregors went to Balquhiddir, which was MacLaren land, in the middle of the night and killed everyone, then took their homes and land over."

"Everyone?" Susan said, her eyes widening.

"Aye. Everyone. Men, women, bairns. It wasna our finest hour. But I'll no' remind the others about that, for it'll no' inspire them to anger if they ken the MacLarens have good reason to hate us. Many clans have reason to hate us."

Before Susan could respond to this the door opened and Dugald and Dougal came in.

"I've sent Fergus to help Angus wake the others. Silently," Dugald said. "I didna bring the pipes, for I'm thinking ye dinna want to announce our arrival to whoever's wanting to attack us?"

"Ye've the right of it. Sit down. I need to think before everyone else arrives," Alex said. "Susan, when we go, will ye head back to your house, so if anyone's wounded we can bring them to ye?"

"Aye of course I will, but ye'll be wanting me to lead ye to them," she said.

"I will. But after that. I dinna want ye caught in any fighting. Ye must leave the minute we ken where the MacLarens are."

"MacLarens?" Dougal asked.

"Aye. Susan heard them say Conall was bringing more men across the loch. That's MacLaren's brother. But let me think a minute now before everyone else arrives."

He did not speak again then until the cottage was crammed with grim heavily armed men and a good number of women too.

"I'm sorry to wake ye in the night," he said then, "but Susan couldna sleep so went for a walk and saw a group of MacLarens by the loch, north of here. She heard enough to tell me they're waiting for others to come across the loch in boats and join them, after which they mean to attack us directly."

"So will we away and take them before the others arrive in their boats?" Simon asked.

"No. For I'm thinking if we do that, there's a chance the rest willna come ashore."

"Will they no' come to help their own?"

"Aye, they might. But they might no'."

"Would that no' be a good thing?" Allan asked.

"It would be, aye, but for one thing. Susan heard them say I'd die dunghill tonight. So I'm thinking ye were right and word has spread that ye've accepted a coward for your chieftain, so ye're ripe for the killing," Alex told them. "It's only March. If we dinna send a message far and wide now, then we'll be plagued wi' clans wanting to prove themselves all summer."

"But ye challenged MacIain!" Janet said. "That proved ye're no' a coward."

"Maybe the message hasna spread. It was the start of winter. Or maybe they think I'm a fool as well as a coward to do that," Alex said. "It doesna signify. It's nearly spring now. I'm wanting to send a message no one can ignore, and the MacLarens are about to give us a perfect chance to do that. For even when their men on the loch join them, we've still more fighters than they have. Conall kens that. That's why he intends a surprise attack."

"What do ye mean to do?" Kenneth asked.

"I mean to go past them, wait until the boats are landing, then attack from behind, from the north. They'll no' be expecting that. If the men have rowed in a great loop, then their arms'll be a wee bit tired, and they'll no' be ready for us. If they've sent a scout out to watch, they'll send him south. I'll leave a few men in the trees just south of where they are. When ye hear us attack, ye head to the loch and kill anyone running towards the settlement. That way we attack them from the front and the back. Susan said they've settled down to sleep a while, so if we move quickly but quietly we'll be in place before the boats land. And then we kill everyone. No quarter given."

"Everyone?" Susan asked.

"Aye. No, wait. If there's any young laddies who surrender, then take them prisoner if ye can. I'll pick one or two to spread the word that if ye attack the Lomond MacGregors, ye die. The rest I'll kill. No mercy. That should get the message across. If ye've any opinions, speak now, for we havena time for a long discussion."

Silence followed this statement for a moment which, along with many of the men nodding their heads, told Alex they agreed with his plan.

"I agree, but I'd add something to that, for ye willna be able to when we're there," Duncan said from the back of the room.

"Aye, of course," Alex replied.

"It'll no' be easy to move fifty men past another group of High-landers, unless we travel a long way to the side of them. It seems we've time to do that, but ye need an alternative if they *do* hear us."

"And ye have one?" Alex asked.

"Aye. If we're heard, then we attack immediately, and kill all except one. If the MacLarens in the boats see and turn back, then we send the one to tell them that if they think to try again, then we'll no' stop at killing the men, but will go to their homesteads as they intended to come to ours, kill everyone, and burn the place to the ground."

There was a gasp at this, but no one objected to it, although a number of the clansfolk turned to look at Duncan, clearly not expecting such a brutal statement from the peacemaker of the chief-tain's family.

"*Ein doe and spair nocht.* Remind them of our clan motto. Aye, that's a bonny idea," Alex agreed. "Right then. Susan will come with us at first, to show us where the enemy is. Then she'll away hame. Peigi, Barbara, Janet, will ye go to her house now? Anyone wounded can either go there, or we can carry them there once we've finished it. The other women, collect the bairns and away up to the cave, just as a precaution, although I dinna expect anyone to be bothering ye. Right, let's go and show the MacLarens and every other gomerel who thinks to challenge us that we're MacGregors for a reason!"

An enthusiastic but muted cheer followed this statement, as everyone was already mentally preparing to move so silently that even other Highlanders wouldn't hear them.

"Can I go too?" Angus asked eagerly. "Ye said ye'd think on it if I was quiet waking everyone up!"

Alex looked at him, standing so proud, already wearing his sword and dirk, his targe slung over his shoulder. Alexander had always stated that no one under fifteen could go to battle, and Alex intended to keep to that. But this was not a battle. In truth it was more likely to be a rout. Angus was nearly fourteen, the same age Prince Charles had been when he'd seen battle at Gaeta.

"I'll watch him, if ye let him come," Kenneth said then, no doubt remembering his own feelings so many years ago when he'd been left behind as the clan had marched out to fight.

"I canna allow that," Alex said. "For ye're worth ten men when ye fight, and I dinna want ye distracted."

"I'll watch him," Gregor put in then. "I'm no' the fighter I was in my youth, and it'll be a privilege to show the laddie his first real fight."

"Aye then, ye can come," Alex said. "But ye do *exactly* what Gregor tells ye. If he tells ye to hide ye hide, to run away ye run away, ye hear?"

"I will! I swear it!" Angus said, his face lighting up like the sun.

Alex lifted his hand, intending to ruffle his brother's hair, then realising that he would almost certainly embarrass Angus if he did, he ran his fingers through his own hair instead, then picked up his targe.

"Right, let's away then, and turn the MacLarens' wee dreams into a nightmare they'll no' forget for a long time," he said.

Quietly everyone left the house, the men melting silently into the trees, the women heading equally silently back to their homes, to wake sleeping children, gather up essential items and head up to the cave.

Once the men got to Susan's house they stopped for a moment. A soft yellow light came through the window, showing that Janet, Peigi and Barbara had wasted no time in getting there.

"Put something over the window when ye go in," Alex said softly. "We dinna want any scout to ken anyone's awake."

"I will. So, I took my jug and went through the trees there," Susan murmured, pointing to a faint track through the woods. "I heard voices, but a good way off. So I came back into the trees, then to the end of the copse and through the bracken, for maybe a hundred steps. Then I could hear them well enough to make out the words."

"And they were settling to sleep there, ye say," Alex whispered back.

"Aye."

"Good. Ye dinna need to come further. Away in now," he said.

She nodded and went to the door, watching as he used hand signals to direct some men to head to the loch, and others to follow him, before heading east, slowly, but very quietly, the clansmen making almost no sound in spite of their numbers.

When they had gone she went in. The three women had made the fire up properly now, and were sitting round it, clearly reluctant to rummage through her belongings until she returned.

"We'll need water," Barbara said then. "For drinks and for cleaning wounds."

"Aye. Hopefully just for drinks," Susan said, taking off her arisaid and hanging it over the window to block the light.

"I'll away down the loch, but no' until I reach the settlement," Barbara said.

"Are ye wanting me to go?" Susan asked.

"No, lassie. I've been walking this land for over fifty years. I ken every blade of grass. Ye'll be needed more than I will if there are any wounded," Barbara said. "I'll no' be long."

Before anyone could object she picked up a pail by the side of the door and headed out, as quietly as any of the men.

"Do ye think there will be casualties?" Janet asked.

"I havena a notion," Susan replied. "The men dinna seem to think so, but they never do. We'll prepare as though there will be, then hope there are none."

They all set to work then, preparing cloths, salves and herbs, and once Barbara came back with the water they put it to boil, ready to wash Susan's instruments, for they all knew by now she had this strange notion that wounds had to be cleaned, and that everything that might touch one should be washed in boiling water, learnt from her husband, the city physician.

Then they made themselves a drink and sat down again, quietly, ears straining for the first sounds of battle.

After the men had headed east for a while, Alex stopped them and told them that they'd now go north and then curve back towards the loch.

"We should be a good way behind them now," he said. "Allan, ye're still the fastest of us. I'm wanting ye to head straight to the loch now, find exactly where they are and if they're asleep, if ye can do it wi' no danger to yourself, then head north along the lochside, until ye're maybe two or three minutes away from them. Then wait for us. That way we'll ken the exact place to stop."

"What do we do then?" Alasdair asked.

"Then we wait until we hear or see the boats landing before we do a Highland charge and put the fear of God into the bastards," Alex replied.

Muffled giggling greeted this statement, and then they carried on, Allan breaking away from the group to head west.

Much quicker than they expected, the MacGregors, having curved back towards the loch, met Allan, running lightly along the track to them.

"Ye need to stop now," he murmured. "They're maybe three minutes' walk away, no more. Most of them are asleep, but no' all. I couldna make an exact count, but there's no more than thirty."

"Ah, that's bonny work," Alex said.

"Why d'ye think some of them are coming in boats?" Angus asked in a whisper.

"Because they're expecting to surprise us in our sleep. Likely they'd send two or three to each hut, kill everyone inside, then take whatever they want. They'll take the plunder away on the boats, and the thirty walking will take our cattle," Gregor said, having had more experience of battles than anyone except Alasdair, who had stayed at home, declaring that he would be a liability rather than an asset if he came along.

"And that's why I'm intending to kill everyone tonight, laddie," Alex whispered. "For if I dinna send a clear message, others will try the same. Ye'll learn a hard lesson this night, but a necessary one."

As I have, he thought, but did not say. No one would ever say again that he was a coward. No one would even *think* it, if this night went as he intended.

The MacGregors settled down to wait silently, every ear listening for the soft splash of the oars. An hour passed, but no one, not even the restless excited Angus, made a sound.

And then they heard what they'd been waiting for and started to rise, but Alex waved them back down and whispered to Allan, after which he shuffled off through the trees like a snake, heading to the lochside and returning a couple of minutes later.

"Four boats," he said. "Just two men in each boat."

No more than thirty-eight, then. And he had the advantage of surprise. Excellent.

He motioned his men then, and in absolute silence they stood, and following his signal began to make their way toward the unsuspecting enemy, until they could hear the two men on guard duty talking softly together, and the sound of wood on pebbles as the boats came in to shore.

They stood then, motionless, every eye on Alex, waiting for his signal. He felt the adrenaline surge through his veins, wiping out all fatigue, all uncertainty. He focussed on the fact that these bastards intended to kill everyone, even the bairns, and felt the killing rage take him, as he intended.

"*Àrd choille!*" he roared then, and as one the MacGregors charged, no longer children of the mist, but killing machines.

At least ten men were killed before they were able to unroll themselves fully from the plaids they'd been sleeping in, and then the fight began in earnest. A few more were killed while the remaining MacLarens gathered their wits and weapons, and then they began to fight back desperately, aware that they were being attacked from the north *and* south, the path back to the boats was now blocked by ferocious MacGregors and that attempting to swim across the loch would result in almost certain death and absolutely certain contempt from their chieftain if he heard of it.

Alex and Duncan were in the thick of the fighting, wielding their broadswords with devastating effect, but Angus, though desperate to be with his brothers, was held back by Gregor.

"No, laddie," he said. "Now's a time for watching and learning, and one day ye'll be as bonnie a fighter as they are. And Kenneth," he added, as his son dirked one man through the throat and then threw him at another two, before finishing them off, one with his sword, another with the deadly spike on the central boss of his targe.

Then suddenly Gregor made a strange keening noise, his hand falling away from Angus's shoulder where it had been resting until then. Angus spun round, driving his sword forward instinctively as he did and raising his targe to parry any attempt to kill him. From the corner of his eye he saw Gregor fall to the ground, but had no time to do anything about that as his opponent's sword smashed into his targe with enough force to make him stagger backwards.

He crouched low, driving his sword forward below the targe, an unconventional but successful move, as he managed to slice deep into the man's shins, cutting through muscle and into bone, bringing him to his knees. Angus brought his targe up then, smashing it into the MacLaren's face with such ferocity that he stunned him. Then Angus leapt to his feet and drove his sword down and through his semi-conscious enemy's chest, killing him instantly, although that last move had been a lucky blow. He'd had no time to aim carefully.

He stood for a second then, astonished and exhilarated by what he'd done, then remembering Gregor, looked quickly around to make sure that no other enemies were about to attack him, before bending over the older man.

"Are ye alive?" he asked fearfully, deeply relieved when Gregor laughed throatily.

"Aye. I'm no' killed so easily laddie," he said, his voice laced with pain. Angus made to kneel down to see what he could do, but Gregor waved him back.

"Dinna think of me now. Never think of the wounded while the fighting's still going on. It's the quickest way to be killed, and ye'll be no use to anyone if ye're dead. Ye did well there. I'm proud of ye."

"The fighting's nearly over now. I think they're all dead," Angus said, stopping as one man let out an unearthly howl as Allan hacked at him with his broadsword. "Nearly all dead," he amended.

They were. Another few minutes passed, during which time Angus stayed by Gregor's side, although instead of looking to see how badly wounded the man was, he instead watched for signs of anyone else attempting to attack them. He knew nothing about treating wounds, but it seemed he did know something about fighting. In spite of everything he laughed joyfully and then immediately felt ashamed, for surely it was wrong to feel so happy when your clansmen were fighting for their lives, when the man you were standing over could be mortally wounded.

The fighting all but over, Kenneth came across to his father and Angus, his arms covered in his enemies' blood.

"Are ye all right, laddie?" he asked.

"Your da's wounded," Angus replied.

"Dinna fash yourself," Gregor responded immediately. "I'm no' dead. The bastard caught me in the back, I'm thinking. The laddie killed the man who did it though."

"Ye did?" Kenneth said, clapping his hand on Angus's shoulder, making him stagger and wince. "Ah, ye're the chieftain's brother, right enough. Ye can go to your brothers now. Tell Alex I'm taking Da to Susan's."

The fighting really *was* over now, the MacGregors checking to see if anyone was feigning death as the sky lightened in the east, dirking anyone who moved, as the chieftain had said no mercy and so none was given.

On the shore three youths, none of them older than Angus, were sitting, Duncan standing over them, stern-faced, sword drawn. Not seeing Alex, Angus went across to him instead.

"Are ye hurt?" he asked.

Duncan shook his head.

"Are you?" he asked, seeing with alarm the blood spatters on his youngest brother's face.

"No. I killed a man!" he announced, then flushed. He hadn't meant to say that, had meant to tell Duncan and Alex later, matter-of-factly, not brag about it like a wee bairn.

"Dinna be embarrassed, laddie. It's a thing to be proud of, if ye do it to an enemy in battle. Was he trying to kill ye?"

"Aye. He wounded Gregor. Kenneth tellt me to say he's taking him to Susan's."

"Ah. Is he sore wounded?" Duncan asked, frowning.

"I dinna ken, in truth. When I'd killed the man, he tellt me no' to look to him, but to watch for anyone else trying to attack."

"Aye, that was good advice. Ye did well. Alex'll be awfu' proud of ye, as am I," Duncan said, making Angus's heart swell with pride.

"Will Alex kill these laddies too?" he asked then.

"I dinna ken yet. That's for him to decide," Duncan replied, his voice expressionless.

The youths were looking up at Angus now, their eyes huge, terrified, and in that moment he thought that he never wanted to be chieftain. Because he might be able to kill someone who was attacking him or those he loved, but he could never kill these terrified boys.

"Dinna pity them. They'd have killed you, had they had the chance," Duncan commented, reading Angus's mind as he had a habit of doing.

And then Alex was standing next to him, putting his arm round Angus's shoulder and embracing him quickly but fiercely, before observing the three youths at his feet.

"Stand up," he said coldly.

They scrambled to their feet and stood in front of him, trembling visibly.

"Is it just women and bairns left in your village?" he asked. "If ye dinna tell me I'll away over the loch myself to find out, and if I do I'll leave none to tell the tale," he added when no one answered.

"Aye," one boy said hoarsely, then cleared his throat. "And some old men."

The rest of the MacGregors had finished the gruesome task of killing survivors now and were gathering round their chieftain, curious to see what he would do.

Alex nodded, then looked at them for a moment, considering.

"Ye'll take one boat back across the loch," he said then. "And ye'll tell your women and bairns, and your old men, and anyone else ye see, that the next time anyone attacks the Lomond MacGregors, we'll no' just kill all the menfolk as we have today, but when we have, we'll come to their village and kill everyone else. *Everyone* else. D'ye understand?"

The three boys nodded.

"Good. Tell me what ye'll tell your clansfolk, and any other Highlanders ye meet."

"That ye'll kill anyone who attacks the Lomond MacGregors, and then come to the village and kill everyone else," the boys stammered.

"Good. Again."

When they'd repeated it three times, he nodded.

"Take a boat," he said then, "and row directly home. If your womenfolk want to row back and take their men home to bury, tell them to do it before nightfall, and we willna harm them. We'll leave the other boats here for them to use. If they dinna, we'll bury them as best we can and say a prayer over them, for we're godly men. Go."

They needed no second telling, and in seconds were in the nearest boat, fumbling with the oars then rowing clumsily away.

Alex passed one hand over his face, suddenly looking unutterably weary, and then he sighed, and turning, addressed his men, his expression warm now, approving.

"Ye've done a bonny job here today. I'm thinking when word gets round, we'll likely be left in peace now. Is anyone wounded, apart from Gregor?"

James, Alasdair Og and Dugald all had what they called minor wounds, so he sent them off to Susan, telling Angus to go with them and check on Gregor. He told the men to check the corpses once more to make absolutely sure that all of them were dead, after which he asked for volunteers to stay back in the woodland and wait to see if the women came to take their men.

Then he told the rest of the men to go home and get some well-earned food and rest, and said that tomorrow, when the volunteers were back and had rested, they would have a ceilidh to celebrate their victory.

Finally, accompanied by Duncan, he went to Susan's, to see how badly wounded Gregor was.

They entered Susan's to discover that Gregor seemed to be engaged in teaching the occupants every Gaelic curse he'd ever learnt in his fifty-eight years on earth.

"Ye canna be too badly wounded then, if ye can remember that many curses," Alex commented.

"Susan's just washed it wi' wine," Angus said unnecessarily.

"It's a nasty wound," she said. "It seems that his ribs took the worst of it though. If the sword had gone through them he'd likely be dead. He's lucky."

"I dinna feel lucky at the minute," Gregor said. "I didna imagine ye healing it would hurt that bad. I wasna expecting it to."

"It does when she cleans it," Alex told him, remembering the pain he'd suffered when she'd washed his leg wound the previous year. "It burns something fierce. It'll no' last long though."

"Ye're going to hurt for a good while though," Susan said brutally. "I'm thinking your ribs are broken. I'll stitch the wound and bind it, but ye willna be weaving cloth for a while yet."

"Ye can teach Flora," Kenneth cut in, seeing Gregor opening his mouth to object. "It's time she started to learn the weaving proper, as she doesna look likely ever to marry. Ye're no' getting any younger, Da, and ye've a fine skill to teach."

"I'm obliged to ye for your comforting words, son," Gregor shot back. "But aye, ye're right. Angus saved my life," he added then to the chieftain. "He was awfu' fierce. A bonny piece of fighting, that was."

Angus, helping Janet to cut cloth to bind wounds, flushed scarlet at this, but his eyes were shining with pride.

"It seems I was right to let ye come then," Alex said. "I'm awfu' proud of ye. No' just for killing an enemy, but for looking out for Gregor too. That was honourably done. Ye did a man's job there."

If he lived to be a hundred Alex would never forget the look of absolute joy that lit up his youngest brother's face at that moment. And it truly hit him then that Angus needed his approval in exactly the same way as *he* had needed Alexander's. In that moment Alex vowed that he would never crush Angus as his own father had crushed him.

At nightfall the other men returned from the loch with the news that the rest of the MacLarens had come across in the afternoon to take their dead home for burial. It had been a terrible thing to witness, Simon told them, for their grieving was fierce.

"We didna let them see us, for it seemed a private thing, something they wouldna want their enemy to witness," James added.

"Aye, well, I'm sorry for their grief, but it was a necessary thing to do," Alex said. "Better they're grieving than us. And hopefully any other clans that hear of it will think again before they decide to attack us. With luck we'll be left in peace now, although I'll post extra guards for a while, just in case."

He really hoped that would be the case. He had had enough difficult decisions to make in the last months, and although he had learnt a lot from the experiences he wanted a year or two at least of peace, to allow him to settle properly into his role as chieftain. He wanted to fully heal his damaged relationship with Duncan, watch his youngest brother grow to manhood, maybe even see if he could find a lassie who would one day make a good wife, although there was no rush for that.

But first he had a victory ceilidh to plan. Once everyone had had a good night's sleep.

It seemed that word did spread, for although extra guards were posted all year and everyone kept their weapons as sharp as razors, no one came anywhere near the part of Loch Lomond that the MacGregors lived on that year, nor the next, not even to try and reive cattle. For which Alex was deeply grateful.

CHAPTER TEN

London, March 1740

WHEN CAROLINE HAD CALLED on her Aunt Harriet three weeks previously to announce her intention of holding a 'rehearsal dinner', she had expressed the intention of it only being a small affair.

"It's just that in April we're having a very important dinner party. Most of the senior cabinet members are coming, so we want to have a rehearsal. Just for you," she'd said, smiling at Harriet, Melanie and Highbury. "And Philippa of course. But I want us to do everything formally, and for you to tell us if there's anything we can improve on. We need to make a very good impression, to help Edwin's career."

"You're coming along well, I hear," Highbury commented.

"Thank you. Yes, I seem to be," Edwin replied, smiling. "And I really love the work."

"But you all know how it is," Caroline continued. "One tiny mistake and you're the laughing stock of the Commons. We want to make sure that won't happen."

"Formal dinners are very different to debates in the house. I don't want to unintentionally offend anyone," Edwin added, who still struggled at times with the complex system of noble etiquette, in spite of having had numerous lessons from both his wife and Highbury.

"I can't see any way you'll make a mistake with place settings, menus and suchlike," Harriet had commented. "Been attending such nonsense events since you were a child, Caroline. Need to pay more attention to the guests. Tiresome things, guests. They behave in unpredictable ways. If you can deal with them, then everything else will be easy."

"So are you going to behave in a tiresome way for them, then?" Melanie asked her sister.

"Me? God, no. Invite a load of tiresome guests. You know plenty of them who'll be honoured to accept an invitation from you. Winters, Cunninghams, that sort of fool. Should be plenty of practice for you in dealing with problems there."

"I'm not sure they'll be honoured if I invite them," Caroline pointed out. "They've mainly avoided us since I married Edwin."

"There, just the sort of bloody fools you want," Harriet said. "Won't refuse your invitation if *I* go though, will they, even though they hate me? Bring Highbury too. Marchioness and an earl. Too tempting. Won't make any suggestions for improvements until they've gone home, unless it's urgent, in which case I'll go to the privy and you can follow me."

"I thought once seated you weren't supposed to go to the privy until dessert," Edwin said uncertainly.

"Yes. Bloody ridiculous notion. Need to piss, have to go, don't you? Won't matter if I do it though, as everyone knows I'm mad. As long as *you* know not to do it, eh? You are coming, William?" she added, looking at Highbury.

"Of course" he'd said, grinning. "I wouldn't miss the opportunity of seeing you behave impeccably for the world, Harriet."

And so here he was, sitting next to Caroline and opposite Harriet, enjoying an evening of excellent food and mainly tedious company. For all the 'tiresome guests' Harriet had suggested had accepted the invitation and were now seated around the table, eating from the enormous variety of dishes placed upon it, which included roasted hare, pheasant, stewed mushrooms, pureed carrots and assorted other delicacies.

So far the conversation had been innocuous, mainly consisting of effusive comments from the ladies on the beautiful floral arrangements and a somewhat pompous account from Lord Winter about his latest evening at the Society of Dilettanti, but as the wine flowed and the company relaxed, so the opportunities for Edwin in particular to deal with a challenge began to present themselves.

Caroline had already succeeded admirably in politely preventing Lord Winter from elaborating tediously about some artefact he had recently purchased, and had then interrupted Lord Edward as he'd taken advantage of a momentary silence to talk about his hounds, which he was known to drone on endlessly about, given the chance.

"I really admire your shoes, Charlotte," Caroline had enthused. "I noticed them the moment you entered the room. The beading is quite enchanting!"

Charlotte, probably the most timid of the Cunningham sisters, which was really saying something, blushed profusely at this compliment.

"Oh thank you, my lady," she replied. "They were very costly, you know. My dear Frederick is so generous!" she added.

"As a man should be with his wife, if he appreciates her," Highbury said, joining in this game of witless small talk which he hated, but which every aristocrat worth his or her salt was adept at.

Lord Edward was now sulking a little, which everyone pretended to be unaware of with the exception of his sister Isabella, who wore a distressed expression. She often wore a distressed expression when at any function with her older brother.

"Ridiculous things. As well as the extortionate cost of them, I now have to call the carriage for even the shortest journey, in case a drop of rain or speck of mud falls on them," Lord Stanton huffed.

"That's only to be expected, surely? Such exquisite beadwork must be treated gently. How considerate of Charlotte to treasure your gift so. Surely you would not wish them to be ruined before everyone had an opportunity to realise what a generous husband you are to your dear wife?" Caroline said sweetly.

"Well, no, of course not. You mistake my meaning," he replied.

Edwin looked up, caught Harriet's eye and swallowed back the words of defence he'd been about to utter. Caroline was an expert at knowing when to rise to a challenge, when to deflect one, and when to ignore it completely; he was learning. This was an opportunity.

"The design is beautiful," Caroline continued smoothly, turning her shoulder away from Lord Stanton to address his wife, which was a pointed snub. "You really must let me examine them more closely before you leave. I would very much like such a pair of shoes, for when I attend Court."

"*You* will be attending Court?" Lady Winter said somewhat incredulously.

"Why would she not?" Harriet put in crisply. "I am sure that being of the lowest rank in the peerage you would have little occasion to make use of such an expensive pair of shoes, but the daughter of a duke and niece of a marchioness is quite a different matter. She attends Court regularly, as do all the Ashleighs."

This is going to be a very long evening, Highbury thought despairingly, as Lady Winter paled and her husband flushed, but neither of them dared to respond.

The second course was now removed and the company waited for the dessert dishes to be brought in. Wine glasses were refilled. Edwin hunted for and failed to find a suitable topic of conversation to fill the silence, resolving to memorise a list of topics before next week.

"Tedious time, the season," Lord Edward stated. "Looking forward to July immensely, returning to the country."

"Ah, yes. The season has its entertainments, but at the end of a busy parliamentary session I confess I'm always ready to spend a little time in the country," Edwin replied, smiling. "There's nothing like a brisk walk in fresh country air."

"Never mind walks, man," the lord stated. "Hunting, I'm talking about! Can't wait to try out the new hounds, see how they are in the field!"

"Nothing like a good hunt," Lord Stanton agreed. "There's excellent riding on my estate, and a good number of foxes. You can be sure of a kill or two, maybe more every day. Nephew to be blooded this year, too," he added. "His first hunt. Looking forward to it immensely, he is."

"I prefer to spend the spring and summer in the country," Melanie said. "It's ideal for painting. Flowers, landscapes. Nothing can match painting outside all day in fine weather."

"How old's your nephew, Stanton?" Edward asked, ignoring Melanie completely.

"Eight."

"Ah. Perfect age to make your first kill. It'll be a great day for him."

"Lady Hereford," Philippa said formally. "Am I right in believing that it is common politeness at a dinner to choose topics of conversation that are not offensive to anyone present?"

"You are indeed, Philippa," Harriet replied.

"Thank you. My lords, as riveting as you find this conversation, I find that it removes all my appetite for dessert, which I was until this moment anticipating with relish," Philippa continued.

"Surely you are not offended by such an innocuous subject?" Lord Edward said, reluctant to relinquish his favourite topic now it had been reintroduced.

"Lady Philippa has just stated that she is, most clearly, my lord," Caroline replied icily. "Are you doubting her honesty?"

"Ah. Er...no, of course not," Lord Edward replied, glancing nervously at Harriet.

"Excellent. Then perhaps we might focus on the entertainments of the season, instead," she said as the servants re-entered, carrying numerous plates full of sweetmeats. "The entertainments that *anyone* might enjoy."

"I'm sure your abilities to hold a polite conversation have not deserted you entirely, my lords," Melanie added. "If they have, now is an excellent time to refresh your skills."

"Privy," Harriet announced suddenly, leaping to her feet. The men all stood immediately, as politeness dictated. "No need to bob up and down," she said before exiting the room.

"If you will excuse me for a moment as well," Caroline added, making no objection to the men, who had just sat down, standing again.

When both ladies were out of the room the men resumed their seats, Lords Edward, Winter and Stanton now all looking deeply offended. Edwin sighed. As amusing as it was, the purpose of the dinner had been to *avoid* uncomfortable atmospheres. Both Charlotte *and* Isabella Cunningham looked distressed now. He tried to think of a neutral topic.

"I...I read today in the Gazette of a most tragic affair," Isabella ventured timidly before Edwin could come up with anything.

"You did? What was that?" Melanie asked.

"It seems that poor Lady Peters and all her children have died, within days of each other, swept away by the smallpox!" Isabella said a little more confidently, now that someone had expressed an interest.

"Tragic indeed," Melanie replied. "Was the lady an acquaintance of yours?"

"Oh no! In fact I hadn't heard of her until I read it. It seems the whole story is tragic. Her husband was a baron or a baronet, but died insolvent, leaving her penniless with four young children. She was living in Geneva, the Gazette stated, taking care of her elderly parents, when the contagion took them all!"

"What, the parents too?" Highbury asked. "And all four children?"

"I believe so. No, three children, daughters. They had a son too, it seems, but it appears he was not there. The article stated that he may now attempt to claim his father's estate, so I don't think he can have died," Isabella said.

"I can't imagine why he'd come back, a child alone," Lady Winter said. "If his father left them penniless, there'll be nothing left. I'm sure the boy will be taken in by someone. This is why I had the inoculation, once the king declared it safe by having his own children treated. It is said to prevent one contracting the disease at all!"

"Do you believe it works, my lady?" Edwin asked.

"I believe so. After all I have never had the illness, and nor have any of the princes and princesses! It was most painful though."

"But surely less painful than smallpox," Melanie remarked.

"Indeed. Did not the marquis die of smallpox?" Lord Winter asked.

"Yes, he did. It changed my sister's life completely," Melanie replied neutrally.

"How dreadful for the poor lady!" Charlotte cried somewhat dramatically.

The conversation continued in this dull but non-contentious manner while dessert was eaten and Edwin wondered when Caroline and Harriet would return. He must speak with her later, ask how she managed to deal with fools so masterfully, if she had any suggestions. She was so adept at it.

Thinking of that, she had been out of the room for some time. What could Harriet have observed that needed to be urgently addressed, and why was it taking this long to address it?

Caroline had been wondering the same thing when she left the room, until she had entered the dressing room Harriet had gone into to find her convulsed with laughter.

"I take it there is no urgent faux pas you need to discuss with me immediately, then?" Caroline said on seeing this.

"What? Oh God, I'd forgotten that," Harriet said. "No. I just needed a moment. Most entertaining dinner I've been to in a while. Sorry. Broke my promise, didn't I? Promised to behave impeccably."

"In fairness, you did. By your usual standards, at least. And you were not alone. I think the Ashleigh ladies have surpassed themselves today."

"Ha! We are magnificent. Still my fault though."

"Why? You're not responsible for their boorish conversation," Caroline said.

"No. But I suggested you invite the Winters *and* the Cunninghams. A dinner can only stand so many fools, unless diluted by a very large number of intelligent people. The men are so used to riding roughshod over the women they do it to everyone unless they're regularly squashed. And the women are stupid. I'm sure you won't have that problem next week. Or I hope not. Guests next week run the damn country, should have more sense than tonight's crowd. I can't believe Charlotte managed to find an even more obnoxious man to marry than her brother is. That took some effort. If there's anything I can't stand more than a pompous fool it's a pompous lazy fool, which Stanton is. Waste of time, the whole family."

"Isabella's harmless enough," Caroline said. "I wonder what she'd have been like if she hadn't been bullied by her brother for so many years."

"And her father before him. Another obnoxious man. Couldn't look at him without wanting to call him out."

"I never met her papa. But she's like many spinsters, she has no choice. If she displeases him he could throw her out, and then she'd be destitute. She knows that."

"You're right," Harriet said. "Need to be more charitable. Wouldn't be destitute though. I'd take her in, if she ever did have the courage to stand up for herself."

"Would you really? You can't stand her!"

"If she stood up for herself, I'd change my mind. She won't. But if she does, yes. Take any woman in who stands up for herself against a bully or a fool. Pelham at the dinner next week, is he?"

"What?" asked Caroline, momentarily confused by her aunt's sudden change of subject. "Oh, yes. Why?"

"Tell Edwin to keep close to him as well as Walpole."

"Edwin holds Walpole in high regard, I know that," Caroline said. "It's due to him we've had peace for so long."

"That's true. But he's in decline now. Watch out for Pelham. Man of integrity, which is rare. Prefers peace, like Walpole. Bit inept at leadership though. His brother Newcastle's important too. Together they'll make more of themselves when Walpole falls. Edwin needs to know that."

"Really? How do *you* know that?" Caroline asked.

"Know lots of things. I know that if Edwin survives tonight's affair, then next week's will be child's play. Better get back, in case he needs rescuing, eh? Bloody Edward talking about hunting. Only does it because he knows Edwin doesn't hunt."

Edwin did not need rescuing, although he was relieved to see his wife and aunt by marriage return. The conversation was rumbling on, still mainly about horrible illnesses and who of their acquaintance had succumbed to them, and dessert was nearly over.

"Do you know the Peters family, Harriet?" Highbury asked once Harriet and Caroline were seated.

"Peters? No. Why?"

"Isabella was telling us about an article she read in the Gazette," Melanie clarified for her. "A whole family wiped out by smallpox. Except for a son, it seems. There is speculation that he might return to England. They were living in France."

"Yes. The father was a baron or baronet, it seems. The son is called Anthony, I remember now," Isabella said.

"No barons called Peters," Harriet said. "But there are so many baronets, I only learn of them if they come to my notice for some reason. Could be a baronet."

"I thought you knew everything about every member of the nobility," Lord Edward remarked coldly.

"Indeed I do," Harriet replied, giving him a pointed look. "At least everyone who is a peer. But a baronet is not a peer, as you should know."

"You said they were in Geneva, did you not, Isabella?" Highbury said, to avoid more hostilities breaking out.

"Isn't that part of France?" Philippa asked.

"No, it's a republic of its own, I believe."

"Did you visit it on your travels?" Edwin asked.

"No. I believe there was rioting there at the time, although that is over now. I had no reason to go. I have been told it's an interesting city though. Maybe I will visit one day."

"You feel the need to travel more, after the lengthy tour you made a few years ago, my lord?" Lady Winter asked.

"Perhaps. I enjoyed myself enormously, and met a number of interesting people while I was there," the earl replied. "Perhaps I will visit them, and Geneva too, one day."

"Dear God," said Caroline, throwing herself down in a chair after seeing her annoying guests out several hours later, following a musical recital. "I hope it's a long time before I have to do that again. I'd forgotten how unbearable they are."

"We're doing it next week," Edwin pointed out gently. "Isn't that the reason we endured tonight?"

"Said to Caroline earlier, it'll be child's play now, Edwin," Harriet said, sipping a brandy, which Caroline had poured for all the desirable guests, who were staying the night.

"Maybe," Edwin said doubtfully. "I was thinking, I need a list of suitable topics of conversation. Maybe if I memorise them I won't be at a loss, as I confess I was many times tonight."

"Excellent plan!" Harriet said. "Weather always a good one. State of the roads."

"Problems with servants," Highbury suggested. "Stewards, gardeners etc for the men, cooks and maids for the ladies."

"We don't have any problems with our servants," Edwin commented.

"No, because you treat and pay them well," Melanie said. "But you can either invent a problem, or ask them if they know of any excellent under-gardeners or some such, as you may soon have to hire one. That will keep the conversation going for hours."

"Gossip. Read a few interesting articles about foreign nobles. Criminal conversation particularly. Well, not with pathetic people like the Cunningham women. Although they might faint away, which would be diverting," Philippa said.

"You may be better with innocuous gossip, topics such as the one Isabella introduced," Caroline commented.

"I met them," Highbury said suddenly.

"Met who?" Harriet asked.

"Lady Peters and her daughters. On my last night in Paris."

"Why didn't you say so at dinner?" Melanie asked.

"I don't know. Maybe because Wilhelmina would have pestered me for details, with that disgusting eagerness she has about such things. She doesn't care about the people at all, just about how to impress someone by knowing an extra piece of information that's not in the periodicals.

"It made me sad to know they all died. They were quite a tragic family. And they were all dreading going to her parents. It seems they were horrible people. But they had no choice," Highbury explained. "I had hoped they would find a way not to go, or that the parents would die quickly and leave them well provided for."

"Let's all make a list of possible conversation topics tomorrow shall we?" Harriet suggested. "We can meet up at breakfast maybe and give you a copious list, Edwin."

"Oh, that would be helpful!" Edwin said.

If he didn't attend another dinner all season, tonight's would have been enough, Highbury thought later, as he lay in bed unable to sleep. God, that had been exhausting!

Interesting, though. It was sad that the two eldest daughters in particular had died, for they had showed such promise, and had been beautiful, considerate girls. He had indeed felt quite choked when Isabella had announced their tragic end.

But now, lying in bed, he began to have another thought. It seemed the papers were speculating as to whether the son Anthony would return to England. Lady Winter had assumed he was a child, but Highbury knew he would be twenty-five, and fully capable of travelling to England and setting up home, if he wished to.

Had he not died when he was six.

It seemed the periodical didn't know that fact. Neither did Harriet, who knew most things about the peerage, although, as she said, a baronet, while being noble, was not of the peerage. And there were indeed a lot of them.

Anna had said her mother never spoke of her brother. If that was true...but maybe she *had* spoken of him when she was in the little hillside village. Or maybe there was an engraved gravestone in the cemetery in Blois where the boy had died. Or maybe everyone in the area of Cheshire the dissolute Sir John Peters had lived knew exactly what had happened to the son.

In the end Highbury abandoned any idea of sleeping. Instead he put on his banyan, lit a lamp and wrote a list of every suitable topic of conversation he could think of, surprising himself by how many ideas he had.

Then he sat for a while longer, until he heard the maids moving about the house, preparing fires, getting the house ready for Caroline, Edwin and their guests to rise. By the time the house was ready he had made another list, but this one was only in his head. And he had also made a decision.

It was time he checked on his estate in Cheshire. And on Ashelle and Scolastica in Paris. Spring was the perfect time to travel. Perhaps he would spend a little time in Blois too. It was on the way to Geneva, after all, so would be an ideal place to rest from the rigours of travel for a few days.

He called for his valet to help him dress, then went down to breakfast, wide awake in spite of his lack of sleep. Suddenly the summer held promise. Hopefully a lot of promise.

Chardonne, May 1740

"So here is where they were buried, Monsieur," the curé said, pointing to a mound of earth on the slope beneath the hillside church, marked only by a wooden cross. "It was indeed, a most sad event. A whole family taken in less than a month!"

Highbury took off his hat, which was in danger of being blown away by the stiff breeze, and looked at the mound, on which grass was already starting to grow. Soon there would be no sign that anyone had ever been buried here. Maybe that would be better, if his idea bore fruit.

"You were a friend of the family, Monsieur?" the curé asked.

"No, not a friend. I met the lady and her daughters last year, when they were in Paris. We enjoyed a meal, then attended the theatre together. I read of their deaths in a London periodical and wanted to pay my respects. It is very sad. They were an enchanting family."

"In truth they did not socialise with the village," the curé replied. "I would not normally speak ill of the dead, but Lady Peters' parents were most ungodly people. I do not say that because they were not of the Roman faith, Monsieur, I assure you. Everybody in Chardonne would say the same. They were very unpopular, with good reason. When Anna married Sir John, they disowned her entirely. It was most unnatural."

"The family did tell me that he gambled his whole estate away," Highbury said, realising the priest wanted to chat. It was unlikely that he met many strangers, after all.

"That is true. But they did not disapprove because of that. He was not known as a profligate man. He was very handsome, wealthy and respectable. He was a great catch, for Anna was not noble, but although her parents were wealthy they refused to give her a dowry. But he still married her. They disapproved because they wanted her to be an unpaid servant for them. In spite of their wealth they had no other servants, no other children in fact.

"Everyone was happy for her when she left, and very sad when she returned with her daughters three years ago. For we know she would not have done, had she had any other option. The parents are buried over there," he added, waving to a distant spot, which, although it also had a mound, appeared not to be marked even with a wooden cross. "We thought the lady and her daughters would not have wished to be buried with the people who made their lives such a hell."

"Has her son Anthony visited the grave?" Highbury asked.

"Son? She had a son?" the curé asked, astonished.

"Yes. The periodical said she had a son, Anthony."

"Ah. Anthony was Sir John's other name," the curé said. "No, he has not visited at all. If he had, someone would have known. And they tell me everything, of course."

"Perhaps he doesn't know of his mother and sisters' deaths," Highbury said.

"Do you know where he is, Monsieur?"

"No. If I did, I would of course tell him, as gently as I could," Highbury replied. It was true that he did not know *exactly* where Sir Anthony was, but even so he felt guilty for lying to a man of God.

I will have to grow accustomed to lying, if I am to pursue this insane plan, he told himself.

"Thank you, Father," he continued, knowing from Alex that this was how you addressed a Roman priest. He reached into his pocket and produced a gold coin. "Please, take this for your trouble. I appreciate you coming to show me their burial place on such an inclement day."

"The wind is normal in this part of the world, Monsieur, but thank you. You are very kind. Would you like to see the church record of their deaths and have some refreshment before you continue on your journey?"

"Oh, that is very kind!" Highbury said. "I would be delighted!"

The earl sat in the rooms he had taken in the village, drinking a glass of excellent burgundy and looking moodily out of the window. *Alex would love this view,* he thought.

It was, indeed, an incredible view. The village was situated halfway up a mountain overlooking Lake Geneva, an enormous lake surrounded by blue-hazed mountains. He wondered idly if this was what Loch Lomond looked like. He thought it might be; it seemed very close to the misty-eyed description Alex had given of his home, when he had been missing it so badly.

How was Alex coping with being the chieftain of his clan? Highbury wondered. He had been chieftain for over three years now. Certainly he would be doing a wonderful job. It was, after all, what he wanted to do, what he had been brought up to do. If he could make such a fine job of all the things he had *not* really wanted to do when he was in Europe, surely he would be a perfect chieftain!

Highbury sighed. He had wanted to write to his MacGregor friend so many times. He had even started a letter on more than one occasion, before abandoning the idea and throwing the paper on the fire. It was too risky, he knew that. And they had promised only to correspond with each other if there was a reason to, and then word any letter carefully.

Alex had insisted on that. Not because he didn't want to keep in contact, he had explained, but because if there *was* another rising for the Stuarts in the future, it would be likely to start in Scotland, and would therefore put the earl at risk if he was found to have been in regular correspondence with a Highlander, particularly if he was to be suspected of Jacobite sympathies, or have enemies who wanted to cast suspicion on him.

Highbury, touched by the Scot's concern for him, had realised that as young as Alex was, he had lived a lifetime of risk, whereas he had lived a lifetime of luxury and relative naivety. So he had agreed, and had kept his promise.

Until now.

Because he had spent two intensely busy weeks on his estate in Cheshire, not that there were any problems with the estate, for his steward was second-to-none, but because he had been finding out as much as possible about Sir John Anthony Peters.

He had discovered that the man had not been an habitual gambler, although he had had a lot of debts. But so did many members of the gentry and nobility. So why he had suddenly decided to join a gambling club and spend much of his time there was unknown. But he had, and had indeed run up an enormous amount of gambling debt, which had resulted in him losing his estate. He'd died of an apoplexy shortly afterwards, leaving his wife and children homeless, although with enough independent income to live comfortably for a few years.

Nobody knew anything about where his widow had gone after she left the area; only that she had taken her children to visit a friend somewhere in France. Nobody knew that Anthony had died. In fact nobody had heard anything about him at all. Ever.

After that Highbury had travelled to Paris, and spent a pleasant two weeks staying with Ashelle and Scolastica. They had delighted in showing him how happy they were, and how the school was progressing. It had lifted his spirits hugely to know that at least a part of his money was being spent on such a wonderful cause.

For not only was it making his two friends very happy, but also their pupils. The pupils he'd met not only seemed happy, but also much more healthy than other pauper children he had seen. This was no doubt due to the food that Ashelle fed them when they were in school. He was sure their families were also healthier, for the ladies had told him that they always sent a parcel of food home with the pupils. They had known that the food would be shared with the family rather than just eaten by the pupils, but they were happy that it was. As was Highbury, which he had told them, then had gone on to raise their yearly allowance, so that they could increase the amount of food they gave away.

They had talked about Alex too, reminiscing about the happy times they had spent together, and wondering how he was doing now. But they had not talked about what else Highbury was doing, or where he was travelling to next. He had told them he wanted to see how the school was coming along, and how they were, and they had assumed that was his only reason for visiting France. For he was wealthy and the cost of such a trip would be nothing for him.

Next he had gone to Blois, which, to his dismay, was an enormous town. He had spent a miserable two weeks there, first visiting every church and cemetery he could find and talking to as many priests and churchwardens as possible, but no one had ever heard of the Peters' family, nor of the death of an English child, nor did they care. It was so long ago. Many people had died since then.

After a week he had stopped searching for the grave, realising that it seemed highly unlikely that anyone would *ever* find out what had happened to the child. As numerous people had said once they realised he was not a close relative, the natural death of a boy twenty years ago was not something *anyone* outside the family would remember.

They might, however, remember an inquisitive and persistent Englishman who asked a lot of questions about the boy, and tell anyone enquiring in future years about him. He could do nothing about that, Highbury realised, but he could stop his fruitless search now, and so minimise any further issues.

Because it was clear to him now that what he had been hoping for, but had never for one moment believed would happen, had in fact occurred.

Against all the odds he had found an identity, one that no one could disprove, or not without an enormous amount of work, with which he could introduce Alex MacGregor into English society.

He turned away from the window and refilled his glass. The question now was, did he still want to do this? Had he ever really wanted to do this, or had he just embraced the idea of supporting the Stuarts by introducing a spy into the midst of the Hanoverians *because* it was so unlikely to ever be possible?

Although he still believed the Stuart cause to be a just one, and had for many years, he had never seriously anticipated acting on his belief, until he had met the extraordinary phenomenon that was Alex MacGregor. Highbury had never met anyone like him, knew it was unlikely he ever would, and had been completely captivated by him.

And still was, he realised now. He would give anything for his son to be half the man Alex was. His capacity for absorbing information was extraordinary, as was his ability to adapt his knowledge to almost any situation. He was disarmingly honest about his weaknesses and flaws. He was trustworthy, loyal, and honourable. Any doubts Highbury was having now were not because he believed Alex would betray him if things went badly. He knew, with absolute certainty, that the young Scot would never betray him. He could not say that about his own son, he thought sadly, nor about much of his acquaintance, with the exception of Harriet and Melanie.

Even so, there were many ways for him to be betrayed, other than from Alex confessing. So, was he willing to risk everything to support the Jacobite cause? He had a comfortable, pleasant life, and had already done some good things for other people. He had made Ashelle and Scolastica very happy, and through them had hopefully improved the lives of their pupils; he had given a sizeable donation to the new Foundling Hospital, which would soon be built; and had contributed to many other ventures, which he did not talk about in public, but which made him feel more fulfilled.

Did he really need to do this?

He sat for a while thinking, during which time a servant came in, lit the candles, drew the curtains, and asked Highbury if he was in need of anything else. Highbury ordered some food to be brought to his rooms, waited for it, and when it arrived ate it without really tasting it.

By then he had made up his mind.

Yes, he did still need to do this. If he did, he could be partly responsible for the rightful king sitting on the British throne, instead of a German usurper who cared nothing for the island, who saw it and its people only as a source of funds and men to protect his beloved Hanover from its many enemies. And he could be partly responsible for the lifting of the unfair, barbaric proscription of the MacGregor clan, who he now felt a profound interest in, because of the man he had loved, still loved, like a son.

If I do not do this, he thought, *I will always wonder if I should have done. On my deathbed, as I hand everything to my son, who will fritter it all away and leave the best man I have ever met an outlaw, I will regret it from the bottom of my heart. Better to risk everything and fail, than to risk nothing and fail anyway, in the end.*

He stood then, suddenly decided, and, taking his wine with him, walked across to the writing desk, which was in the corner of the room. He took out a sheet of paper, pots of sand and ink, and trimmed a quill. Then he sat for a moment thinking, before dipping the quill in the ink, and starting,

Geneva, May 15th.

Mr Drummond,

I have been informed by a former master of yours that you are seeking employment as a valet. You have been highly recommended to me by him as a trustworthy and experienced man. As I now find myself in need of such a person at my address in Durham, and would prefer to employ someone who has been recommended to me rather than trust to an agency, I beg you to advise me at your earliest convenience as to whether you are still seeking such a position. If you are, we can arrange an appointment at an appropriate date once I return to England, which I intend to do imminently.

Please address your reply to me to the Post Office at Durham.

Yours, &c

William Barton Esq

Now he would return home, or rather to Durham, where he did in fact own property, and find out if Alex MacGregor still wanted to engage in such a foolhardy adventure.

Loch Lomond, late May 1740

Kenneth and Alex sat side-by-side on the ground, eating bannocks with cheese, sharing a leather flask of water and staring with satisfaction at the work they had done so far.

"Aye, I'm thinking another cartload of peats after this one, and we'll be finished," Alex commented. He sat up straight and rotated his shoulders, reaching back to massage the right one with his fingers.

"Ye'll no' be wanting to practice the fighting wi' Angus and me later then," Kenneth said after observing this.

Alex looked at his companion, trying to ascertain if he was joking.

"Ye didna really agree to fight wi' Angus after a whole day of taking the peat down to the settlement?" Alex asked incredulously.

Kenneth sighed.

"Aye, I did," he admitted, "and I canna let the laddie down now. Ye ken what he's like. Ever since he turned fifteen he's been obsessed wi' being the best fighter in the clan. Excepting yourself, of course. *He* believes ye must be the best fighter, because ye're the chieftain."

"Does that mean ye dinna believe it then?" Alex asked, noting Kenneth's emphasis on 'he'.

"I'm sure ye could be, an ye practised more. But ye've neglected it sadly, these months past."

"Aye, ye've the right of it. I've been awfu' busy though, wi' all the chieftainly things I have to do. Da made it look so easy," Alex said.

"He wasna as intense as you are," Kenneth replied. "If he couldna do something in one day, he didna waste an hour being angry wi' himself about it. He just did it as soon as he could. He didna feel the need to be perfect, as ye do. Angus is the same, but wi' the fighting. He wants to prove himself when he fights his first battle by killing every enemy before anyone else has time to draw their sword."

Alex laughed at this, because Kenneth had summed Angus up perfectly. Come to that, he'd summed him up perfectly too.

"I'll be coming to ye for some fighting practice, then," he said after a minute. "No today though. And I'm hoping Angus willna have to meet anyone in battle for a good while yet."

"Aye, well, your trick wi' the MacLarens seems to have worked," Kenneth said. "No' a soul has come anywhere near us since. No' even a peddler."

"That's why I havena had time to practice wi' the sword. I've been travelling about buying things and hearing what news there is instead," Alex said, laughing. "Normally the peddlers bring news wi' their goods. But I'd rather have no peddlers than every clan in the area coming down the lochside to fight the cowardly chieftain."

"Ye did well there. Saved a lot of killing. No' that the MacLarens would agree wi' that, mind."

"I think your da might no' agree wi' it either," Alex said sadly. Although Gregor had seemed to recover rapidly from the wound he'd sustained in the battle, he still had spasms of pain in his back so severe that they rendered him incapable of moving, sometimes for minutes, sometimes for hours.

"Aye, he would. He does," Kenneth said. "We all ken the risks of fighting, and we all accept them. He's alive, and he's thankful for that." He finished his bannock, brushed the crumbs from his kilt, then stood. "Come on then, let's finish, then I can rest for a wee while before Angus."

Alex took another mouthful of water, then joined him. One more cartload of peat, and that was it for another year.

"Aye, I remember," Kenneth said when Angus came running up to them as they finished unloading the last cartload of dried peat. "I'll away hame and get some food and sit down a wee minute first. And only a short session, for I've had a heavy day's work."

"Kenneth's getting old now, Angus," Alex commented. "He's needing to rest his weary limbs."

"I'll remember ye said that tomorrow," Kenneth said ominously.

"Ye're going to fight tomorrow?" Angus asked. "Can I watch?"

"No. Ye can help to harrow the land, for most of the lassies are up at the shielings now, so they canna do it," Alex told him.

"Ah. I tellt Allan I'd help him mend some of the tools as well. Maybe next time. Oh, and Alasdair Og's back from Glasgow wi' the mail. There's letters for Susan, and there's one for yourself, too. Will ye open it?"

"Will ye give me a minute to wash myself, and think?" Alex said good-humouredly.

In the end he did not open the letter until Angus had left to fight with Kenneth. For he had recognised the handwriting on the address, and had known that whatever information this letter contained, it would be better for him to read it when he was alone and had time to think.

When he finally did break the seal, which was stamped with a small acorn, he read the letter twice and then sat for a time, deep in thought. Then he left his house, taking the letter with him, and went to his brother's.

"Why did ye no' tell me before?" Duncan asked, once he'd read the letter and Alex had explained the possible meaning behind it.

"I did. I tellt ye I'd met a nobleman, and we travelled round Europe together, that he taught me how to behave as a nobleman would."

"Ye did. But ye didna tell me that he was a Jacobite and wanted to help ye become a spy!"

"Aye, well, there was a lot going on at the time, if ye remember," Alex said defensively. "And in truth I thought it was just wild speculation, for we couldna imagine a way I could *ever* become part of the nobility. I still canna imagine it. It would be like a Campbell coming here and telling us he was Da's cousin. We'd ken instantly he wasna. The nobility's like a clan in that way. Ye could maybe be accepted to the first event, but then they'd investigate and find out ye were an impostor."

"The letter's awfu' vague," Duncan said. "Do ye think he *has* found a way, or it's about another matter entirely?"

"I dinna ken. I canna think what else it could be, though ye're right."

"So are ye going to apply for this position?" Duncan asked.

"I'm curious to see what he has to say, aye," Alex replied. "I'll no' be away for more than a few days. Durham's in the north of England after all."

"Who is the laddie?"

"Ah. I canna tell ye that, for I said I would never tell anyone the man's name. He has a lot to lose if it's discovered he's a Jacobite," Alex said.

"Ye swore an oath on it?"

"No' on the iron, for the aristocrats dinna understand that, but aye, I did. I'd tell ye otherwise, for I trust ye wi' my life."

Duncan nodded.

"Ye've a lot to lose too," he observed.

"It isna a secret that the MacGregors support the Stuarts," Alex said.

"No, although ye're in a lot less danger surrounded by your clan than ye would be in London, alone. I didna mean just that though. I mean ye wouldna be living here, wi' your people, as ye should be, leading them, which is what ye were made for. The whole clan kens that. Ye're a great chieftain."

"I wasna at the start," Alex said.

"Ye were learning. Now ye are a great one. And ye're happy, I can see that. Would ye be happy alone in London, among the enemy?"

Alex fell silent then, thinking.

"I can tell ye're decided on going," Duncan said after a minute. "I wouldna try to stop ye, even if I could. I'd ask ye to promise me one thing though."

"What's that?"

"That if this noble laddie *has* found a way for ye to be a spy for the Stuarts, ye dinna agree immediately. Come home and talk wi' me first, wi' Angus, and maybe Kenneth too. For we've all a different way of seeing things, and this isna a decision ye should make alone."

Alex smiled then, suddenly feeling less burdened by knowing that whatever Highbury had to say, his brothers would be beside him when he decided what he wanted to do about it.

"Aye, I can promise that, and gladly," he said. "I'll tell Angus tonight, but no' anyone else, no' until I'm leaving. Then I'll tell the clan I'm visiting wi' a friend I met in Paris. For it may well come to no more than that."

"Aye. Let's hope it does," said Duncan, who had never agreed with their father placing the burden of raising the clan's proscription on Alex's shoulders. His comment made it clear his opinion on the matter hadn't changed.

Alex wrote a letter that evening, telling Mr Barton that he would be at his convenience, as soon as the gentleman returned from his travels. Once it was on its way he determined to put it to the back of his mind, until the earl wrote back to say he was home. There were, after all, plenty of things available with which to occupy his mind.

Not least ensuring that Angus did *not* become a better fighter than the chieftain.

CHAPTER ELEVEN

Durham, June 1740

"Ah! I have been expecting him. Send him in," the Earl of Highbury said, when his much-awaited visitor was announced.

"You find me still at breakfast, Mr Drummond," he continued when the young man had been announced, had entered and bowed to the earl.

"I will be pleased to wait outside until your lordship has finished his meal," Mr Drummond suggested in a soft Scottish accent.

"Nonsense! You must be hungry after such a lengthy journey. Take a seat, then choose some food for yourself. Cook always makes far more than I can eat. John, will you fetch Mr Drummond some ale. Or would you prefer chocolate?" he asked.

"No, ale would be excellent. You are most kind, Lord Highbury."

"Ale it is."

The footman disappeared, and the visitor selected some rolls, butter and meat from the dishes on the sideboard, then sat a respectable distance away from the earl.

"We must continue to speak in this vein until the ale arrives," Highbury said softly. "So, Mr Drummond," he continued in his normal voice, "you come most highly recommended to me by your previous employer. If you are suitable, the duties you will perform for me will be very much as they were for him, although I will probably be asking you to travel with me from time to time. This house, unlike my main country estate, has only a few necessary servants, as I am seldom here. I have a permanent valet at my home in Hertfordshire, who travels

206

with me to London in the season. You will be expected to travel with me when I visit my other houses, and may be asked to undertake a few additional tasks as needed. Ah, John! That was very speedy. If you place the jug on the sideboard. Thank you, that will be all."

Mr Drummond nodded his head in thanks to the footman, who then left, closing the door firmly behind him.

"What duties would those be, my lord?" Alex asked, glancing at the door. He stood, moving over to the sideboard to get himself a tankard of ale.

There was a moment's silence as the earl considered this question. And then he stood, smiling broadly, and moving across to Alex, took him in a brief but fierce embrace.

"By God, but it's good to see you," he said.

He pulled back then, keeping his hands on his friend's shoulders as he looked at him.

"You've grown," he said. "Not in height, but in breadth. And you look...sterner."

"Aye, well, I can thank Kenneth for the muscle, and three years as chieftain for the sternness. I'm thinking by sterner ye mean older," Alex replied in his normal accent now.

"Is it what you thought it would be?" Highbury asked.

"Aye, but much more difficult. I made some mistakes at first, but I learnt from them. It's a good life."

"Better than being an English gentleman?"

"Aye, much better. But I daresay ye'd find being an English gentleman better than being a clan chieftain, for it's what ye were brought up to be. I take it ye've no' brought me here to ask me about being a chieftain though?"

"No," Highbury agreed. "Although I've thought about you on numerous occasions, have even started a few letters. But I didn't send any of them until last month. Let us finish breakfast, then I will take you to my rooms before we talk of more treasonous matters, which will be perfectly acceptable if you are to be my valet."

They both sat down again.

"I chose the position of valet because it's ideal for our purpose – our possible purpose. I'm hoping you'll stay for a day or two, and if you do you won't have to associate with any of the servants, and it'll be acceptable for you to sleep in a room adjoining mine. Which will

207

give us plenty of time to talk without attracting suspicion from the staff," Highbury continued.

Alex laughed then, suddenly looking like the exuberant youth the earl remembered from Paris.

"Ye're thinking like a spy already," he said.

"I'll need to, if we do go ahead with this venture," the earl replied.

"Ye've found someone then."

"You must be the judge of that. But yes, I think I have."

An hour later they were upstairs in Highbury's private rooms, which were expensively and tastefully decorated in blue and silver, the windows and doors securely closed to ensure they could not be overheard.

"So ye're certain there's no chance of anyone discovering that the wee laddie's dead then?" Alex said after the earl had told him of his chance meeting with Lady Peters and her daughters, of Isabella's gossip at the dinner and his subsequent investigative travels around Europe.

"I'm not absolutely certain, no. But I think it would need some very intense study in order to find *anything* out. I was particularly diligent in Cheshire, because I know that if anyone *does* suspect you of being a fraud, it is there that they will search first. The only thing that can put you in danger, if you *do* take on his identity, is if they find out he died. And I found absolutely nothing in over four weeks of constant searching.

"Sir Anthony died in Blois, and nobody there remembers anything of him at all. After a week I stopped making intense enquiries for the reasons I've just stated, but in the second week I did visit every other churchyard in the city, and read every gravestone. There was nothing. In truth I cannot imagine how anyone could find out that he died in Blois at all. Everyone who knew seems to be dead."

"But they might find out he'd died somewhere," Alex replied.

"If they do hear that, you could dismiss it as gossip, I would think."

"Or I could say that I had indeed been very ill at some point, but most certainly hadna died," Alex agreed.

"You could. There is one way I could find out for certain, but I'm very reluctant to do that," Highbury added after a moment of silence. "My friend Harriet, who I told you about. She knows everything about the members of the peerage. Baronets are nobility, but not of the peerage. However, if I asked her to find out about Sir Anthony she would. She makes it her business to know everything that will help her to live the life she chooses, which is not a conventional one. She has the money and resources to find out anything. She is quite remarkable. If she cannot find Sir Anthony no one will."

"But ye dinna trust her?" Alex said.

"I trust her implicitly. But I will not reveal your identity to *anyone*. And if you *do* take on his identity I will never tell anybody that I know you to be anyone other than Sir Anthony. I take it that you trust your brothers."

"Aye, I do."

"Have you told them who I am?"

"No. I swore that I wouldna. But if I do decide to become this baronet, I'll tell them what I'm doing, and why. In fact I promised Duncan I wouldna make a decision without hearing his viewpoint."

"Duncan is the one who sees deeply?"

"He is. He doesna want me to do this, but he willna let that stop him telling me the truth."

"Do *you* want to do this?" Highbury asked then.

That was the burning question. The one that Alex had thought about for all of his journey here. And he still wasn't sure.

"In truth, no. It was my da who always thought I could raise our proscription by mixing wi' nobles and persuading them that we're no' savages. When I was a bairn I believed I could too. Now I realise that it isna possible, no' for me to do it in the way *he* imagined. He didna ken as much about the nobility as I now do. The only way to lift the proscription is for the MacGregors to do something that the king will be grateful to us for.

"No matter how good my German is, I'll never get close enough to the usurper to speak wi' him as a MacGregor, no matter how aristocratic I appear. However, I've already been close enough wi' the rightful heir to the throne, and as a MacGregor, to make a good impression. The only way I could ever help to lift the proscription is to act as a spy for him, and help him win the throne back for his da. I'm thinking he'd be awfu' grateful if I did that."

"I think he would be too," Highbury agreed. "But you still don't want to do it?"

"Not if I think only of myself, no. But if I've a chance to help the Stuarts regain the throne *and* lift the proscription, then aye, I want to do it. But do you want to do it? Ye'd be risking everything, wi' no gain, but much to lose."

"I've thought about that a lot, because you're right. I have everything I need, except a son worthy to carry on my name. And restoring the Stuarts won't change that. But it would be good to know that if I couldn't rear a worthy son, then at least I've helped a worthy cause."

"Good enough to risk your life and your fortune for?"

"My fortune will be dissipated when I die anyway. In a hundred years no one will remember the name Highbury, or if they do it will be with disdain. But if I restore James to his rightful place, then my name will go down in history, and that is worth much to me. My life will have had meaning. And if we fail, then at least I will have tried. The worst failure is never trying at all."

Alex nodded.

"Then there's only one thing left to do, before I make my decision," Alex said.

"Talk with your brother."

"Ah. Two things then. Talk wi' Duncan, and visit Charles, to see if he's still worthy of us risking our lives for. The last time we saw the laddie he was fifteen and a boy. He's nineteen now, and a man. If he isna worthy now, then I'll return and tell ye. If he *is* worthy, then I'll find out if he still needs a spy. For he may already have one operating in the German lairdie's court. If he doesna, then I'll return and tell ye that. And then we'll need to find a way to achieve this. But there isna any worth in wasting time wi' details until we ken if it's worthwhile to do it at all."

"You're right. Shall I come with you to Rome?" Highbury asked.

"No. It's better that the prince doesna see us together again. That way, if I ever *am* discovered, in the unlikely event that people remember ye took me on a grand tour, ye can say ye had no idea I was Sir Anthony. Ye'll no' be able to do that if we visit the prince together again."

"You're not even going to tell Charles I'm your sponsor, are you?" Highbury said then.

"No' until he wins the throne back, no. Then I'll tell him and wi' pleasure. If we do this, it will be a dangerous thing. I'll no' put ye at risk for no reason. I care too much for ye to do that. And there would be no purpose to it," Alex said earnestly. "But first let me go to the prince, and find out if there's any purpose in either of us risking ourselves."

He looked at the earl then, whose eyes had filled with tears at this declaration.

"I'm sorry, man," he said then. "I didna mean to upset ye. But I canna decide yet. I—"

"No, you're right. That's not why I'm upset, really it isn't. Will you stay tonight, and we can talk? I want to hear what you've done in the last three years."

"And I want to hear what you've done too," Alex said. "I'll gladly stay, of course."

"Excellent!" Highbury said, wiping his tears away and blowing his nose. "Tomorrow I'll tell you that I'm unsure if you will be suitable or not, and that I need a little more time and discussion with the person who recommended you before I decide. If you *do* say yes, then acting as my valet will be a perfect way for you to spend a lot of time alone with me, and for us to travel, while we perfect your persona as the baronet. Then we can travel to London together, leaving here as my valet, and arriving as Sir Anthony."

"You have already thought it through then," Alex said, smiling.

"Only this far. I will not think on it again until I know it's worth doing, as you so rightly said," Highbury replied.

He would, however, whether Alex accepted or not, think that he was the finest young man he had ever met, and probably would ever meet.

"So then," said Alex, sitting back and relaxing now that the business part of the visit was over, "this is a 'small' house, is it? How many rooms does it have?"

Highbury smiled.

"It has six bedrooms, a dining room, breakfast room, library, study, solar...and others. A kitchen, stables...and servants' quarters, of course. But nevertheless it *is* small from an aristocratic viewpoint, as you'll find out if you do become Sir Anthony, for I will rent a similar house in London for you for the season. The garden here is small and it has no other lands, no tenants. Am I right in assuming from your expression that it's larger than your house in Loch Lomond?"

"This room is about the same size as my house," Alex informed him.

Highbury looked round.

"Really? You are not making a joke?"

"No' I'm no' jesting wi' ye. There are chiefs who live in grand castles, but they're no' MacGregors. I wouldna want to live in a grand castle, although if I could, I would have to, probably for the same reasons you have this pointless house that ye rarely visit, and an enormous one in Hertfordshire."

"To show your wealth and power," Highbury said.

"Aye, although it's our fighting men who are our power. But living in a cold draughty castle announces it to the world, rather than ye having to call all your clansmen together to prove it. Why did ye buy this one, if ye never use it?"

"I didn't buy it. My grandfather did, but I have no notion why. However, I'm glad he did, because it will be a wonderful place to perfect Sir Anthony before we launch him on the world. If we go ahead with it. It's far away from London, and absolutely no one of my acquaintance has a house here, so we are not likely to meet anyone I know, or have them call unexpectedly. I have few servants, and no visitors, so they have no chance to gossip with other households. And we will be circumspect. I am a very considerate man, and allow my servants a free day every week when I am here. If Sir Anthony is going to call on me, he can arrive on that day."

"Ye *have* thought a lot about it. Ye really do want to do this," Alex said then.

"I do. But I agree that there is no purpose to it unless the likely gains are worth the risks. If they are not, I'm sure I'll find something else that will be fulfilling. I would really like to visit your home, in that case, meet Duncan and Angus. And Kenneth."

Alex laughed.

"If we dinna go ahead wi' this crazy venture, then I'll gladly take ye to Loch Lomond. I canna imagine what ye'll make of Kenneth though, or he of you," he said.

He couldn't imagine what Highbury would make of the clan in general, or their way of living. Francis Ogilvy had struggled, and he was a pauper next to the man sitting opposite him now. It would be like visiting another world entirely.

As it would be for him, if he *did* end up becoming a spy for Prince Charles. It was one thing to imitate a noble for a short period of time. Actually living constantly as one would be a completely different matter.

Loch Lomond

"I'll come if ye want me to go wi' ye, but I canna see the point to it," Duncan said when Alex put the question to him, a week later.

"Do ye no' want to see the prince?" Angus asked incredulously. "I'll come if he doesna want to. In fact I'll come if he does! Can I?"

"No, laddie, ye canna. I'm wanting Duncan to come because he sees things and people in a way I canna, in a way ye canna either," Alex said. "And if he does come, then ye need to stay here to help Kenneth, for I mean to ask him to act as chieftain while I'm away. It'll be good for ye to have more responsibility, for soon ye'll be chieftain if we canna be for any reason."

"Ah," Angus replied. "But I'd love to meet the prince too."

"I'm hoping ye will one day," Alex told him.

"Will Kenneth want to be the chieftain?" Angus asked.

"No. But he'll do it if I ask him. And he'll be a good one, I'm thinking. He just needs to grow in confidence. Ye can help him wi' that."

"It'll be costly for the both of us to go to Rome," Duncan said. "And ye're a good judge of character now. Ye've just assessed Kenneth perfectly. I'm sure ye can do the same wi' the prince."

"I maybe can. But it's too important for a maybe. The clan's future will depend on it. I'll be a lot happier if ye think he's worthy too."

"And if I dinna?" Duncan asked.

"Then I'll rethink the whole idea," Alex said. "And I'll no' tell anyone where we're going or why, except for Kenneth. So ye must keep this secret, Angus."

"I will," Angus promised.

He would. Impetuous and reckless as he still was, Angus was utterly trustworthy. *I'm blessed in my brothers,* Alex thought, *and in my clan.* No matter how rich Highbury was, he couldn't trust his worthless son. Some things no amount of money could buy.

On the evening of the day Alex had told the clan that he and Duncan were going away for a few weeks, that at the moment he couldn't tell them where or why, but would when he came back, Susan came to Alex's, where he was sitting with Duncan, Angus and Kenneth, making final preparations to leave.

"The whole clan is talking about where ye might be going and why," she said once she'd been invited in. "I'm thinking ye might have been better to invent a place ye were going to, than leave everyone so curious."

"I willna lie to them," Alex said. "But I canna tell them the truth, no' yet. No' until I ken what happens next."

"Aye, well, you're the chieftain," she replied. "I'm no' wanting ye to tell me, I'm just wondering if ye're going to Edinburgh, or that way?"

"Why do ye ask?" Alex said.

"If ye are, I wanted to know if I could come wi' ye as far as Edinburgh."

"What's amiss?" Duncan asked then. "Ye said ye wouldna go back there. Ye like towns as much as I do!"

"No, laddie, ye hate them far more than me," she said, smiling now. "I dinna think ye could live in a town as I did, no' even for someone ye loved."

Duncan thought for a minute.

"I could have lived there for Màiri, if I'd had to. But ye're right, I couldna have been happy there. I dinna ken if I could have loved someone who *wanted* to live in a town though."

"Are ye wanting to visit Dr Ogilvy?" Angus asked.

"Aye, I am. I've had a letter, and I'm a wee bit worried about him."

"What did he write? Is he ill?" Alex asked, instantly concerned.

"He wrote what he usually does, about the small happenings of the city, as I write about the small happenings here. It isna that. Mrs Ferguson wrote to me. She tellt me that Francis isna well, and hasna been for some time. He doesna see patients any more. I ken she doesna approve of me. She's awfu' protective of him, like a mother more than a housekeeper. She wouldna write to ask me to come without good reason. She's loyal to him and will see her letter as betraying him, for she'll no doubt ken, or suspect at least, that he hasna told me about his health in his letters," Susan explained.

"We can go through Edinburgh, can we no'?" Duncan asked Alex.

"Aye, of course we can," Alex agreed immediately, although they had intended to travel more directly south, not across to the other side of the country. "Maybe we can stay there for a night, and take...never mind," he said, realising that if he finished his sentence he'd be telling her his own secret.

Susan let out a sudden breath and relaxed then.

"Thank ye," she said. "I didna want to go alone, but I would have done if ye werena going that way."

"Ye're very worried about him," Duncan said.

"Aye. Mrs Ferguson doesna ken about medicine, but she kens Francis. I'll away and pack some things I might need then. Ye leave in two days, ye said?"

"Aye, we do. If we're going to Francis, we can take a garron, if ye're wanting to take a number of things," Alex suggested. "Francis will take care of it, and we can collect it on the way back. It will be good to see him again, in truth. He's been a good friend to me."

By the time they rang the brass bell outside Francis Ogilvy's house, which both Alex and Duncan remembered from that desperate night after their father had learned of their mother's illness, Susan looked almost as worried as Alexander had that night, although not as belligerent.

After a minute the door was opened by Mrs Ferguson herself, who, initially alarmed at seeing two Highlanders on the doorstep, relaxed when she saw the woman they were flanking.

"Ah, Mistress MacIntyre," she said. "Ye came, then."

"Aye, of course I did. What's amiss wi' Francis?" Susan asked, her lack of any customary greeting betraying her worry.

Mrs Ferguson stood to one side to allow them to pass her, then took them into the library, which was empty.

"He's in his bed," she said when the visitors looked round the room, clearly expecting Francis to be sitting there. "I didn't tell him you were coming, in case you couldn't, and in any case..."

"He'll no' be pleased ye've written to me," Susan finished.

"No. But I'm awful glad you're here, and I'm thinking he will be too. I'm wanting to talk to you for a minute before I tell him you're here. Mr MacGregor, I'm sorry I didn't greet you. You've grown so, I hardly recognised you!"

"This is my brother, Duncan," Alex told her. "Ye only saw him the once and he was a bairn then."

"Hello. Aye, I remember you now. You had a ferocious stare!"

"Did I?" Duncan said. "I'm sorry if I frightened ye, mistress."

"No, you were just a wee laddie then," she replied, smiling. "I never saw such a young one glare like that though, and for so long!"

They sat down, and she explained to them that Francis had been ill for some time and slowly deteriorating, but had only agreed to see a physician recently, after her begging him to for some time.

"He started with being tired and a wee bit breathless. We thought he'd just caught a chill or some such thing, and he treated himself but he didn't recover. In recent months he's lost his appetite, and it's awful hard to persuade him to eat more than a few bites of anything. He's tired all the time too, after the slightest exertion. And he's had a cough now, for months.

"He insisted it was nothing, and that he'd be well soon, but when he stopped taking patients, I really started to worry. I asked him if he wanted you to come, because I knew you would if he asked you, but he said no, you were happy in your new life, and he didn't want to inconvenience you."

Susan rolled her eyes to heaven at that, and shook her head.

"Aye, that's what I believed you'd think," Mrs Ferguson continued. "But I didn't think it was my place to write then. He's a physician, after all, and knows a lot more about medicine than almost anyone. But now he's sleeping more and more, and his legs swell from time to time at night."

"Morag's legs used to swell sometimes," Alex said softly. Mrs Ferguson looked at him. "Our sister," he added, but did not elaborate any further.

"Aye, they did. There was something wrong wi' her heart," Susan said. "But I talked wi' your ma and da, and when they tellt me she'd always been ill, then I kent that it was a thing she was born wi', and when it is, there isna any curing of it. But Francis has never had any symptoms of a heart problem. Nor is he a very heavy drinker, which is another cause. I'm thinking it might be a dropsy. A dropsy can be caused by other illnesses, like jaundice or a consumption of the lungs."

"Can ye do something if it is?" Mrs Ferguson asked.

"Maybe, to help him at least. Rob tellt me he'd heard of a medicine that the healing women brew wi' foxgloves, but he said although it's said to help some, he'd seen people die when they were given it, so it seemed that it wasna a thing ye could be sure would work, even if ye kent the recipe for it. It was one of the things he was wanting to research more, but he never did."

"What can ye do to help him?" Mrs Ferguson asked.

"Well, the first thing I can do is see him," Susan said, businesslike now. "If ye want, ye can tell him that we've just arrived unexpectedly, for Alex and Duncan are on their way somewhere else, and I thought to come wi' them, to visit. If he doesna want to see me then I'll go directly back, but I was thinking to stay until the laddies come back and go home wi' them, for it isna safe to travel alone. They'll likely be a couple of weeks, maybe more."

Mrs Ferguson laughed then, and clapped her hands.

"That's awful kind of you," she said.

"If he doesna ken ye wrote to me, then ye can do it again, should anything else happen, and he'll no' be suspecting ye," Susan pointed out.

"I'm thinking if I tell him what you've just said, he'll be wanting to come down to see you," Mrs Ferguson replied. "Will I ask the cook to prepare some victuals for you, while you're waiting?"

"Aye, for the laddies have to travel on if they canna stay the night, and if I'm to go directly home, I'll need something too. If he says he'll come down, then let him, for taking moderate exercise is a good thing. Lying in bed all the time isna."

Mrs Ferguson stood, and made her way to the door, then turned back.

"You know it was never yourself that I didn't like," she said then. "It's true I thought you didn't always behave as a lady should, assisting your husband as you did. But I was younger then, and had a narrower view of things, I realise. I liked you for yourself, but not the effect you had on him. But that wasn't your fault. I know that now, have done for a long time."

"Thank you, Elspeth," Susan said then, smiling.

Mrs Ferguson smiled back, and then left the room.

As Susan had expected, when Francis knew who his visitors were, he did indeed say he would come down to see them, and that he wouldn't hear of Alex and Duncan going on their way without staying for at least one night.

They sat in the library, eating the food that was brought to them there and waiting for the master of the house to arrive.

When he finally did, he had obviously made a great effort to appear well, but even so it was clear that he was not. He was breathless, for one thing, although he hadn't rushed down the stairs. And his ankles and calves under his pristine white stockings were very swollen, although he did not seem to have gained weight anywhere else.

Alex and Duncan stood immediately and bowed as he entered.

"Hello!" he said brightly, his eyes sparkling. "What a wonderful surprise! Sit down, please! You have no need to stand on ceremony with me. Susan, you are of course welcome to stay as long as you want. Mrs Ferguson tells me you are travelling onwards?" he said to Alex and Duncan.

"We are, Francis. We will stay for the night though, of course. It's awfu' good to see ye too," Alex told him.

"My God, but you have grown!" he said. "Both of you. You are truly men now. And finally chieftain of the clan! I'm very glad that you did not have to fight your father after all, although I was grieved to hear of his death." He sat down then on a chaise longue near to the fire, and abandoning the remnants of the food the others joined him, sitting in nearby chairs.

"Susan tells me that you're a very fine chieftain, Alex," Francis continued.

"I've made some mistakes, but I'm learning now, and Duncan is a wonderful help to me," Alex said.

"Where are you going from here?" Francis asked, jumping in before Alex could say anything about him, or ask any questions.

"I canna talk about that. It's something ye dinna want to ken."

"Ah," Francis replied.

"He hasna told the clan either, so it isna that he doesna trust ye," Susan added.

"No, that's very wise. The best way to keep a secret is to tell nobody about it," Francis said, smiling.

"And how are you?" Alex said quickly. "Dinna tell me ye're in perfect health, for I can see ye're nothing of the kind."

"I'll admit I have an annoying cough at times," Francis said. "Sometimes I cannot sleep at night due to it, which is why you found me abed in the daytime now."

"There's no purpose in lying to them, sir," Mrs Ferguson said, who was just opening the door and had heard the last sentence. "For when they arrived I told them you haven't been well for many months now. And Mistress MacIntyre is a healer, I'm sure you cannot fool her."

"No, ye canna, Francis. How long have your ankles been so swollen?" Susan asked.

Francis sighed, defeated.

"For a short while. It's usually better in the morning, but then gets worse as the day goes on," he said.

Susan nodded.

"Is it the dropsy?"

For a moment he looked so utterly dejected that she wanted to take him in her arms like a child, and comfort him. But it was neither the time nor the place for such a thing, and maybe never would be.

"Are the bedrooms being prepared?" he asked his housekeeper then.

"Aye sir, that's what I came to tell you," Mrs Ferguson said. "The maid has lit fires in the rooms, and the sheets are airing. Will I ask cook to prepare a hot meal for you all?"

Francis looked at the others.

"No, we—" Alex began.

"Yes, if she would be so kind," Susan interrupted him. "But no' immediately, and anything will suffice. It will be lovely to eat together tonight, before Alex and Duncan go on their way."

"I'm sure it will be no trouble at all," Mrs Ferguson said, understanding Susan's reasons. "I'll tell her now."

Francis waited until the door was closed before he continued.

"Yes," he said. "I believe it is a dropsy. I have reduced the amount of liquid I drink a little, and the swelling is only in my legs at present. But it is only a matter of time, I think. There's no cure for this. I don't want Elspeth to know that, though. She is very fond of me."

"We're all very fond of ye, man," Alex said. "Is there anything that can delay the inevitable, and bring ye relief?"

"The fatigue is the worst," Francis admitted. "It's difficult to fight that, when you just want to sleep all the time."

"But ye must, Francis. For exercise is a very good thing for a dropsy, if it's moderate," Susan said.

"I know, but it's hard to feel motivated, when...it's just hard. I have been giving in to it. You're right."

"Aye, well, I'm here now, and I'll stay a while, if ye want me to," Susan said. "I'll see if I can motivate ye a wee bit."

Francis brightened immediately.

"You would do that for me? I don't want to be a trouble to you," he said.

"It's no' a trouble. I was thinking to visit you anyway. It will do me some good too, I think."

He leaned forward then and took her hands in his, regardless of propriety.

"Thank you," he said, tears sparkling in his eyes. "Oh, it is so good to see all of you. I don't have many visitors! Are you sure you can only stay the one night?" he asked the brothers.

"Aye, for we need to go to the continent, and it will take us some time, as we'll either have to walk or take coaches," Alex said.

"If you ride it will be much faster, even having to rest your horses," Francis suggested. "You are welcome to borrow horses from me, if you wish. I rarely ride now, and I know you will take good care of them."

"That would be a bonny idea, but Duncan is as I was before I was taught to ride well. He walks for the most part, and has only ridden a garron before, and that seldom," Alex told him.

"Ah. That is a pity. It would be much speedier otherwise. Where are you riding to? Or can you not tell me?"

"No, but we have to ride a long way, and for many days."

"Would it be quicker for Francis to teach Duncan to ride while ye're here, than to take the coaches?" Susan asked. "Ye'd be willing to do that, would ye no', Francis?" she continued. "Ye wouldna have to run around. Ye could even sit and instruct him."

Alex opened his mouth to say something, then changed his mind.

"I'll be happy to try if ye think ye can teach me, Mr Ogilvy," Duncan said. "Unless Alex thinks it will take longer for me to learn than to take the coaches."

"It maybe wouldna, for ye can already ride a garron, and ye dinna need to ride like a nobleman, which is what I was learning. How long d'ye think it would take him to learn, Francis?" Alex asked.

"Well, I don't know, in truth. If he was very determined and willing to spend hours in the saddle each day, maybe two weeks?" Francis said uncertainly. "Although he will certainly ache a lot!"

Alex thought rapidly. Charles didn't know they were coming to see him. The only reason he felt rushed was his own impatience, and reluctance to be away from the clan for any longer than was necessary. But if he *did* take this job on, he would be away from the clan anyway. Duncan would need to learn to ride, if he had to be able to get to London quickly. And it would give Francis, who loved helping people, motivation, which had clearly been Susan's thought in suggesting it.

"Oh, that would be *so* helpful, if ye're willing to do it," Alex said then. "It would likely save us a lot of time."

"Well, I could certainly try," Francis replied, a little hesitantly.

"I'd be awfu' obliged to ye, sir," Duncan added, joining in the plot.

"Then of course I will do it," Francis agreed, having been backed into a corner. "But please, call me Francis. It would be tiresome to be addressed formally for two weeks."

"Then thank ye, Francis," Duncan replied, winking at Susan, who smiled.

If Duncan had been a willing conspirator at the start, three days later he was changing his mind. He tried really hard to hide his discomfort, and although he thought he'd made a good job of it so far, the looks on both Susan's and Francis's faces when he walked into the dining room for supper told him he was wrong.

"It isna too bad, just a wee bit uncomfortable," he replied when Susan asked him where it was hurting.

"Ye're walking as though ye've soiled yourself, Duncan," Susan told him. "Ye wouldna be doing that if it was 'a wee bit uncomfortable'."

"Is it the muscles?" Francis asked. "If so, you'll feel better in a few days, once you become accustomed to it. You are sitting a little stiffly, and clenching with your knees, but that's a common fault. Once you're more adept you'll relax."

Duncan sat down very carefully, trying not to wince, as he knew that every eye was now firmly on him.

"Aye, I'm sure I will," he said.

"It isna your muscles, is it?" Alex asked. "When I learnt, my muscles were a wee bit stiff, but no' enough to cause me to walk like that. And that was when I hadna been living in the clan for years. We're both used to fighting and labouring every day now. Is it your arse?"

Duncan flushed scarlet.

"Aye," he admitted. "Partly that."

"Right, let me look at it," Susan said. "I've some salve that might help."

The flush darkened by a couple of shades.

"I'm no' exposing my...parts to ye over supper," he said. "I'll heal. If ye give me the salve I can apply it myself. Thank ye."

The footmen came in then with the food, which halted talk for a minute, as Francis was the only one who was accustomed to servants and could continue a conversation in front of them without feeling awkward.

"That will likely be partly from your inexperience too," Francis said, once the servants had gone and they were all eating. "Tomorrow we'll focus on you relaxing your legs more. Once you learn to move with the horse's motion, it will become very much more enjoyable."

"Aye, I'll try that," Duncan said, relieved and worried in equal measure, as although it would be good to learn the art of riding, the thought of riding for hours tomorrow was not a pleasant one, when he was actually trying to hover above the dining chair at the moment, rather than sitting on it.

"But you really should allow Susan, or myself if you prefer, to examine you, for I have seen saddle sores become...it really would be advisable," he finished, leaving Duncan far more worried than he'd been a moment before. He was about to insist that he was fine, then glanced at Alex, whose expression told him that he would *not* be impressed if they had to delay their departure for Rome because he was being an idiot. He gave in.

Two minutes later he was standing in Francis's study in his shirt, while Susan and Francis examined him.

"Christ, laddie, why did ye no' tell us it was this bad?" Susan said. "Ye look as though ye've been burnt!"

He did indeed. His buttocks and the inside of his legs were raw and bleeding.

"I just thought it was a part of learning the riding, wi' a saddle and on such a big horse," Duncan said.

"I wasna that bad," Alex, who was standing in the corner, said. "I'm thinking ye need to start wearing breeches. Ye'll have to wear them where we're going, in any case."

"A tailor is coming tomorrow to measure you," Francis said. "He cannot wear your clothes, Alex. I assume you're heading on important business, and need to make a good impression?"

"Aye, ye could say that," Alex admitted.

"Well, then. I don't wish to know any more, but you will both need clothes that fit you properly. Your clothes are too tight now, Alex, the frockcoats at least, for you've put on muscle in your arms and shoulders. And they will not fit your brother at all. I insist," he added, anticipating the brothers' objections to him spending money on them. "You escorted Susan here, ensuring her safety, and your visit is already benefitting me enormously. Oh, I have just thought of something!" he said.

"He's the right of it," Susan said, when Francis had left the room to fetch whatever it was he'd thought of. "He's already looking better, and Elspeth tells me he has more energy than he's had in months. Let him do this."

"Will ye stay wi' him?" Alex asked.

"Aye. I tellt ye that already."

"No, I mean for longer than just the time we're on the continent."

"Ah. In truth, I dinna ken. I canna leave him until he...until I've done all I can for him. He's a good man," she said.

"I'm thinking he might be doing something for you, too," Duncan commented. "I think ye needed to be away from home for a time, from the memories. It'll maybe be good for me too. Is that the real reason why ye wanted me to come wi' ye?" he asked his brother.

"What? No! I tellt ye the real reason," Alex told him. "But if it'll help ye, both of ye, to recover from Màiri, then I'm happy. I thought ye to be over the grief, or the worst of it, anyway."

Susan and Duncan exchanged a look of pure understanding.

"I daresay I'll recover, in time, though I'll always miss her," Susan said. "Duncan likely never will, just as Flora willna from Alpin, and I willna from Rob. It's a different kind of grief, when ye've found your love match."

"Susan's right. Ye canna understand it unless ye have, I'm thinking," Duncan said then. "I hope one day ye find someone ye love as much as I loved Màiri, but if ye do then I hope whenever ye die, ye die together. For I wouldna wish this on anyone. It's growing easier wi' time, but it's always there."

"Maybe ye'll find someone else, in time," Susan said. "It's different for me, I think, because I was much older when Rob died. Maybe years from now. Màiri would want ye to move on wi' your life."

"Aye, I ken that," Duncan said. "But I canna imagine it happening. It hasna for Flora."

"Flora hardly goes out of Gregor and Barbara's cottage," Susan said. "It isna healthy for her. I've tried to tell her that, to get her to come collecting plants wi' me, to go *anywhere,* but she willna. Dinna ever be like that, Duncan."

"No, I wouldna. Màiri would hate that for me. And I canna anyway, for my damn brother's dragging me across Europe!" Duncan said, laughing.

They took the hint, and would have changed the subject if at that moment Francis hadn't reappeared and done it for them.

"Here we are!" he said, holding up a pair of pale yellow breeches that had clearly seen considerable wear, and a pair of thin linen ones. "I will certainly ask the tailor to arrange for some to be made for you both, but in the meantime I think these will do very well. I haven't worn them in years. They're made especially for riding," he explained. "See, they have no inside seam, and are made of deerskin. They should help enormously with the chafing. And if you wear these drawers underneath, then the skin should not chafe at all!"

Duncan looked at them dubiously.

"Ye need to be able to wear breeches as though ye're accustomed to them," Alex said.

"And I'll give ye the salve to help wi' the chafing ye've got now," Susan added. "If ye put that on for a few days, ye should be healing well."

"I have several pairs of drawers, and they're very inexpensive to buy," Francis commented. "So you do not need to worry about the salve staining them."

Duncan held his hands up in surrender.

By the time ten days had passed Duncan's legs and buttocks were healing well, and although he did not ride with elegance, as Alex now did, there was no need for him to. He could stay on a horse, control it well, and ride for hours. All that was needed now was practice, which he would get plenty of, riding through England, then across Europe to Rome. In a couple of days the suits of clothes Francis had ordered for them would arrive, and then there was no reason for them to stay any longer.

"I ken ye're wanting to be on your way," Susan said, having knocked on the door of the bedroom the brothers shared, the night before the tailor was due to arrive.

"I am," Alex agreed. "But if ye think we're still helping Francis, then we can find a reason to stay for a few more days."

"No. Your whole future depends on what happens in the next weeks, I'm thinking," Susan said. "Ye'll be impatient to find out what that will be, as will Kenneth and Angus. I talked at length wi' Francis this evening, and he's agreed to start seeing some patients again soon, wi' me to assist him. Only two afternoons a week, to start."

"Oh, that's bonny news!" Alex cried. "D'ye think he's ready for it? For his legs are still swollen by the evening. Has he reduced his drinking more, as ye said he should?"

"He has. I think it will raise his spirits to receive patients, as it has to teach ye to ride, Duncan. He loves to help people, and at the least it will take his mind off his illness, which canna do him harm. I'll be there to make sure he doesna tire himself."

"Ye're no' anticipating being here for a long time, though," Duncan said. Susan looked at him with alarm.

"How do ye ken that?" she asked.

"Duncan sees everything, ye ken that, Susan," Alex said. "I wouldna. Ye dinna seem very worried to me. Or ye didna until this minute."

"In truth, if he was a young man, then I'd have hope for him," Susan admitted. "But he isna. And the cough worries me, for although it isna bothering him a great deal, it's persistent. Which means he may have water in his lungs as well. But I might be wrong, and even if I'm no' he could live for a good while, especially if he doesna give in and lie in bed all day."

"Which ye willna let him do," Alex said.

"No. Ye've no reason to stay, once your outfits arrive. But ye *must* tell me what happens on your journey, for I canna relax until I find out."

Three days later the brothers set off on the first stage of their journey to Rome, carrying enough food to keep them going for days, courtesy of Mrs Ferguson, and several new outfits, including one for each of them that must have been very expensive, as they would certainly ensure that if they were refused admittance to the *palazzetta*, it would not be because they were shabbily dressed.

CHAPTER TWELVE

Rome, early July 1740

THE TWO MACGREGORS, RESPLENDENT in full formal highland dress, stood outside the *Basilica del Santa Apostoli.* The taller of the two, dressed in a red and black *fëileadh mór,* with a beautifully tailored black jacket, a silver brooch set with garnets pinning the top part of the plaid to his left shoulder, was clearly telling an anecdote about the basilica to his slightly smaller companion, who was equally gloriously attired, the only difference being that his tartan included a dark green stripe. Even if they hadn't been so fetchingly dressed they would have attracted attention, particularly from passing females, who eyed the handsome, powerfully built Scots with admiring gazes.

The two men, intent on the importance of the task they were about to attempt, hardly noticed the passers-by at all; all their attention was on preparing themselves to meet the man who they prayed would one day soon succeed in gaining the throne for his father, and legality for their clan. If the attendants would let them in.

"So this is where we met the prince, after Mass," Alex was saying. "He lived in the *palazzetta,* there," he pointed to their left, "and I'm hoping he still does. I dinna want to wait five days to see if we can meet him in the basilica this time."

"Ye dinna want to wait five minutes," Duncan said, an amused smile on his face. "Ye look ready to explode. Come on, let's do it. Ye're sure wearing this is better than yon silk clothes Francis bought for us?"

"I'm no' sure, but I'm thinking we'll at least make a more memorable impression than we will wi' conventional outfits, no matter how fine. And I feel more like myself wearing this, too," Alex admitted.

"Aye, I agree wi' ye on that. Come on then, let's do it. Ye can tell me more about your last time in Rome later."

"Is His Royal Highness expecting you?" the attendant asked in heavily accented English.

"He is not," Alex admitted, his accent unmistakably Scottish, but much softer than normal. "But I'm certain he will see me, if you tell him who I am, and that my purpose for calling is to continue the discussion we had regarding the opera *Artaserse* which we attended together some time ago."

"*Artaserse*," the attendant said, scanning them from head to foot with a sceptical gaze. "If you wait here, I will enquire further."

"Well, he certainly noticed our outfits. D'ye think he'll talk wi' the prince, or wi' his superior?" Duncan asked as they stood in the street waiting for the result of Alex's request.

"I'm hoping he'll talk wi' the prince. That's why I tellt him we attended the opera together. If he doesna, maybe his superior will go to Charles, for he willna ken if we're good friends or good liars, but hopefully willna want to take the risk that he might be turning away someone the prince would want to see," Alex said.

They waited for what seemed an interminable length of time, during which even Duncan became impatient. Alex was on the point of knocking again when the door suddenly opened, and the attendant firstly bowed to them, then asked them to follow him, his attitude now deferent, which surely had to be a good sign.

Then they were shown into the same room that Alex and Highbury had been admitted to nearly four years previously, which was still beautifully furnished and decorated in the same blue silk as it had been then, although there was no fire burning in the hearth now.

And then the young man who had been sitting in a chair next to it stood, moving forward to greet his visitors, and Alex saw that although the room had not changed in four years, Prince Charles certainly had.

He was much taller and broader, of course, of slender but athletic build, and was now growing into a very handsome young man, his features regular, his brown eyes lively and intelligent.

"Your Royal Highness," Alex said, bowing deeply, Duncan following suit, Alex having spent half of yesterday helping him to perfect a bow to royalty.

"Mr MacGregor," Prince Charles said, his eyes sparkling. "What a pleasure to see you again." He looked to Duncan then.

"This is my brother, Your Highness. He accompanied me this time, and very much wished to meet you," Alex explained.

"I'm very pleased to meet the brother of such a fine and loyal subject," Charles replied. "But please, be seated. I think we have much to talk about. Or I hope we do." He waved to a sofa and the two Highlanders sat.

"Giovanni, will you arrange for refreshments?" Charles asked the attendant, who was awaiting any further instructions. The footman bowed, and made to depart.

"Oh, wait. How does your sister? Is she recovered?" the prince asked, speaking Italian.

"It is kind of you to remember her. She is still very unwell, Your Highness," Giovanni replied. "The apothecary gave her a cordial, but it does not seem to be helping. We are all very worried about her."

"I'm sure you are. Such a young woman, too. She has been unwell for too long. I will send my physician to her. You must tell me where she lives."

"Oh! That is...I have no words...but I think the physician will not come, for it is not a...not the safest part of town for such a great man to attend," the footman said.

"Of course he will, if I order him to," said Charles. "Have no worry about that. Give her address to my secretary, and I will arrange it as soon as my visitors have departed."

The footman left, clearly in a state of shock, and Charles came across to his visitors, sitting down again.

"Poor woman," he explained, in English this time. "Her husband died only a few months ago, leaving her with four children, and now she has fallen ill. Giovanni is a good servant. I hope my physician can save her. If not, perhaps the children can be employed here in some capacity. I must ask him how old they are.

"But I will think of that later. It is wonderful to see you both, and so finely attired! I too have a complete Highland dress, you know! It was gifted to me recently, by the Duke of Perth and his brother, although it has breeches rather than the kilt you wear so well. The tartan is similar to yours, Alex, but with a gold stripe. It is very fine, and I am proud to wear it. Had I known you were to visit me today, I would certainly have worn it in your honour."

"I am sorry I didna write to ye, Your Highness," Alex said then. "But in view of the matter to be discussed, I thought it better to speak of it in person."

"Ah, a matter to do with *Artaserse,*" Charles replied, smiling then glancing at Duncan. "I still possess the book whose contents we discussed."

"As do I. I trust my brother wi' my life. We can speak freely in front of him," Alex said. "Although I havena tellt anyone the identity of my companion the last time we met, for his safety."

"I understand entirely," the prince said. "I have forgotten his name myself, and indeed everything about him. Then am I right in assuming that you are now in a position to perhaps learn of things that might be useful to our cause?" he continued, coming straight to the point.

"Maybe. I believe I may soon be in a position to adopt the identity of a nobleman who has unfortunately died," Alex replied.

"Really? How could that be possible?" Charles asked, clearly intrigued.

"He died many years ago as an infant, but as the family were...travelling at the time, and never returned to their homeland, his death isna kent to the English aristocracy. It was discovered by chance, but has since been investigated. His whole family are deceased, and it's wondered if he will now return to England. I havena investigated the practicalities of adopting his identity yet, because I saw no point to it until I had discussed it with yourself, Your Highness."

"I see. Who is this nobleman?"

"I would prefer to say as little as possible to *anybody* about either his identity or how I would accomplish his entrance into noble society, no' because I dinna trust ye of course, but because the best way to keep a secret is to tell *nobody,* except those who need to ken," Alex told him.

Charles nodded, not at all offended as Alex had feared he might be.

"There is sense in that. But will I not need to know, if I am to receive correspondence from him?"

"No, for I would write in another name, which we can agree on. If you believe that I can be of use to you in such a capacity, for although I would gladly risk my life for you, I would prefer no' to do it needlessly. And others inevitably would be at risk as well. So I came partly to ask if you still require the services of a spy at the Elector's court, or are there others already performing that service for you and your father?" Alex asked, hoping that the prince would indeed tell him that numerous others had already infiltrated English society and that he would be far more useful as chieftain of a fighting clan, when the time came.

"I do indeed not only need, but would greatly welcome such a person!" Charles cried immediately, quashing all Alex's hopes. "There are others in England, of course, who send information from time to time, but in truth none of them can be relied upon. Much of the information is either already known or irrelevant, and of that which is not, we cannot be sure how much of it is true and how much the invention of the sender, in the hope that we will continue to pay them. And then of course we can never be sure as to whether they are in fact informing for both sides, as it were.

"An excessive amount of money is being spent on such information, in the hope that something crucial will be provided at some point. I would much rather that was spent on a true believer in my father's cause! I'm sure he would, too. How much would you ask, if you are able to accomplish such an undertaking?"

"I would ask nothing, Your Highness!" Alex replied, affronted. "If I do this, I do it for loyalty, no' for monetary gain. My father fought for the House of Stuart, and his father before him, and if I do this I'll do it for the same reason they did. I would only hope that when you are successful in regaining the crown from the usurper, that you would consider raising the proscription of the MacGregor clan, in thanks for no' just my loyalty, but theirs, throughout the years."

"You are extraordinary. Information from such a moral and trustworthy man would be truly valuable. I cannot tell you how important that would be," Charles enthused. "But as for your reward, I...my father would of course raise the proscription on your clan anyway! It is most unfair. There must be something else I can do to repay such a gift? For I think that to do it you will be putting yourself in great danger."

"I will gladly do that if it helps restore your father to the throne, Your Highness," Alex said. "It will be an honour to help."

"Then I know my father will accept your offer, as do I, with gratitude! Thank you! This is a good day! When do you think you could start providing information?" Charles asked, virtually fizzing with excitement.

"It willna be for some time yet, Your Highness, for I must ensure the clan is well provided for if I am to be away, and I have to proceed wi' great caution if I'm no' to make a fatal error and be discovered. It will take a considerable amount of planning," Alex told the prince.

"You plan for your...er...friend to introduce you into society?" Charles asked.

"Initially, but I want to separate myself from him as soon as possible, for his safety. Once the initial introductions are made I need to be able to insinuate myself into as many places as possible where I might hear useful information. Gentlemen's clubs, soirees, balls...and, if possible, the Court," Alex said.

"St James's? That is ambitious! I'm told the usurper is a boorish man who does not entertain," Charles said.

"It seems he doesna, Your Highness, but if I can succeed in being introduced to the man, I have an advantage."

"Which is?"

"I can speak German."

Charles started laughing.

"You have really prepared for this! Or did you learn German for another purpose?"

"No, I learnt it in the hope of gaining an introduction. But if I'm to be successful in this and no' be discovered, I will need to think about the role I'll have to play, the character," Alex said.

"Most of our informants are, or seem to be insipid, colourless people," Charles said, thoughtfully. "It seems to be a successful stratagem. But I do not think that would work in your case – you are one of the most memorable, compelling men I have met in a long time. I am interested to know how you intend to play your role."

"I'll need to give that a good deal of thought. I canna tell you now, for I havena a notion at the minute. That will be a large part of the planning, I think!"

"If you are to do it, you say. So you have not yet decided. I understand entirely. It would be a great and dangerous undertaking. I will not try to persuade you – you must decide for yourself.

"Now, will you dine with me today? Perhaps I can show you some of the sights of this great city? Or would you care to see an opera perhaps, as you did last time? Or a play?"

"We could dine with ye, Your Highness," Alex replied, "but I'm thinking it wouldna be prudent for us to be seen in public with ye, in view of the prospective undertaking."

"Oh of course! How remiss of me," Charles said. "But you can and will dine here with me. You can tell me of life in Scotland! I would love to hear about that."

He shot off then to arrange for a meal for his guests. Alex threw Duncan a questioning look.

"No' the now," Duncan murmured. "Later."

Over a very substantial dinner, served in Charles' private chambers to ensure secrecy, the prince bombarded the brothers with questions about their country, clan life, the duties of a chieftain, how the Highlanders viewed the Stuarts, and how the rest of the country did. He gave Alex and Duncan time to answer each question, listening intently and with genuine interest, often asking them to elaborate on small points that most people would find completely uninteresting.

"Forgive me," he said, after about an hour of this interrogation, "but this is information I cannot find out from reading, or from the exiled Scots who visit, for many of them have not seen their homeland for years. Those who support the cause and visit tell me that the whole of Scotland would rise for me in a moment if I appeared, but you tell me that is probably not the case?"

"In truth I dinna ken how many of the clans would rise for ye," Alex said. "I doubt much of the Lowlands would, for the Presbyterian faith is strong there. Your support would come in the main from Episcopalians, and Roman Catholics, although there are no' so many of those. But they would have much to lose should another rising fail, so I believe the only way to be sure of sufficient numbers fighting for ye would be if ye come wi' an army yourself."

Charles sighed.

"Last year I was prepared to travel to Madrid, in the hope of encouraging the Spanish to fight for us, which they seemed eager to do, but then Papa discovered that the Court was not sincere, so there was no more talk of me going, which saddened me. And then of course there is the issue with the Pope, or rather the lack of one, which concerns my father greatly. I think he will not make any great decision until he knows who is to succeed Clement XII, for the choice will of course be of great importance to us, living here as we do," Charles told them.

"I think the English wouldna welcome a Spanish army, Your Highness," Alex commented. "There is no love for Spain in England at the moment."

"There is no love for France, either, I believe," Charles said.

"No' in England. But there has been an alliance between Scotland and France for many years. There isna the same animosity there. Only uncertainty regarding faith. But the Spanish are Catholic too."

"That is true. And really France has always been our hope, for she has supported us, and has the ability to provide a considerable army. I think my father now seeks a bride for me, in the hope of cementing relations between the Stuarts and a country who could help us to regain the throne," Charles confided.

"A French bride?" Alex asked.

"Yes. Or maybe a Spanish one, a princess. But I think a French princess would be preferable. We shall see."

"Will ye be happy wi' such a thing?" Duncan asked.

"In truth I have no eagerness to marry. All my thoughts, all my endeavours are on regaining the throne for my father. But if a marriage were to advance that, then of course I would do my duty. Even if I wished to I could not refuse, for I have not yet reached my majority. But I would gladly marry if it enabled me to sail for your fair land and release your people from tyranny! But let us speak no more of such heavy matters. Let us speak of lighter things now and enjoy the rest of the evening!"

They enjoyed the rest of the evening, and by the time the two Highlanders left the *palazzetta,* armed with enough information about places to visit in Rome to keep them occupied for a month if they wished, it was dark.

"Holy Mother of God," Duncan murmured as they walked past the basilica, heading for the very pleasant rooms they had taken, which had been paid for by Highbury.

"Ye felt it then," Alex said.

"I'd have had to be dead no' to feel it," Duncan replied. "I'm thinking he could persuade yon German lairdie himself to give up the throne, if he could just have a wee blether wi' him. No. Dinna ask me what I think of him yet, for I'm needing time to recover from the charm of the man before I can see what's underneath it. Did ye understand what he was talking to the footman about?"

"Aye, or part of it. It was as he said. The man's sister is very ill, nothing is helping her, so Charles is going to send his physician to her. The footman said the physician might refuse to go to such a part of town, and Charles said he *would* go."

Duncan laughed.

"Aye, I'm sure he will. Give me a wee while."

They walked back to their rooms in silence, where a fire had been lit for them and candles were burning, in anticipation of their return.

It was not until they had undressed and were climbing into bed that Duncan finally spoke.

"Did ye refuse the opera invitation because ye found it so tedious last time?" he asked.

"No," Alex replied, a note of impatience in his voice. "I tellt the truth. But I think ye'd hate opera too. It's nothing like *The Gentle Shepherd*."

"Ah, but that was a bonny play," Duncan said. "I would like to see such a play as that again, one day."

"Aye, maybe we can," Alex replied curtly, the impatience obvious now. "Ye were awfu' quiet for much of the time. What do ye think of him?"

Duncan sighed.

"He's young," he said then, "and impatient. Reckless maybe, a wee bit like Angus. But he was genuinely interested in what we had to say about home, wasna just being polite. He seems truly to care no' just about becoming king one day, but about the people. I'm thinking that's a rare thing. He seems to care about Britain, and, when he's a wee bit older, would make a good king, or at least a better one than that bastard on the throne now."

"That isna saying much though. I'd make a better king than Georgie," Alex said.

"Aye. But he's regal too. He's a natural way about him, that commands respect. He's got an air of authority, as have you when ye're being chieftain and no' my brother," Duncan continued. "But he can talk to anyone, like the footman, and seemed to really care about the man's sister. He listened to your advice, and appeared to take it, but I'm wondering if he'll take advice that doesna agree wi' what he wants to do. He's headstrong. Everything about him is focusing on one thing."

"Is that a fault?" Alex asked. "He'll need to be single-minded if he does come to Scotland."

"He will. But he'll need to listen to men wi' more experience than he's got too. And he'll need to ken when to retreat if the time isna right, and do it."

"Do ye think he willna?"

"I dinna ken, Alex. I can see a lot, but I havena the sight! He seems to be trustworthy – I liked what he said about the nobleman who'll be supporting ye. And he clearly wasna going to say anything in front of me, until ye reassured him that I was trustworthy. I liked him. I think it would be almost impossible for anyone who met him for any length of time *no'* to like him. That's a great strength, I'm thinking, and it's natural to him."

"Aye, I agree wi' ye there," Alex said, smiling.

"It could be his weakness too, though," Duncan added. "For I'm wondering how he'd deal wi' a man who had the same determination he did, but in a different direction, and who was immune to his charm. If he had to work wi' him."

"Ye mean another clan chief?"

"Aye. Or a whole lot of them. Will he be able to give way if it's necessary, even though he doesna want to?"

"We canna ken that until he's in Scotland, wi' the clans around him and a French army at his back," Alex said.

"No, that's true," Duncan agreed.

"Ye havena said anything bad about him, apart from that he's reckless. Maybe he'll grow out of that soon."

"Aye, maybe he will. So then, he seems compelling, trustworthy, enthusiastic, and genuine. And reckless. And there's some antipathy between him and the king."

"What? Why d'ye say that?" Alex asked, astonished.

"The way he talked about him. He was almost dismissive of Jamie's concerns about the papal election. And he seemed to think that if he'd been allowed to go to Spain he could have persuaded them to support him, even though his da couldna. I'd say he feels his da's holding him back, maybe even doesna want the crown any more. It wasna just what he said, but his expression. I was watching him closely. That's what ye asked me to do, after all."

"Aye, it was. I didna see that at all. So ye think if he does win the throne back, his da willna want it, and it'll all be for nothing?"

"No, I think if he wins it back then James will take it. Few men wouldna, given the opportunity. But whether James will abide by his son's promises or no' is another matter. And if he doesna, then there could be another war. Did ye no' say the Elector's eldest laddie hates his da, and does everything he can to thwart him?"

"So I've been tellt," Alex said, frowning. "D'ye think Charles is worth fighting for?"

"If he comes wi' an army, aye, I do, absolutely," Duncan said then. "For I agree wi' what Da said; James hasna the personality or the determination to lead another rising. Yon laddie there definitely does. I would fight at your side for him wi' no hesitation.

"But that doesna mean I think ye should leave your homeland, go to London and live a lie every day. Ye'd be lonely, and I'm thinking ye'd find that unbearable, for ye need people," Duncan added then.

"I wouldna be lonely. I'd be surrounded by people," Alex protested. "I'd have to be, or I wouldna find out anything useful!"

"That isna what I mean, as ye ken well," Duncan shot back. "Being alone and lonely are no' the same thing. Being lonely when ye're wi' a lot of other people is the worst loneliness there is. I ken that well. Being alone is far better than that."

"I havena really experienced that, no' as you have," Alex said.

"Maybe no', for ye make yourself at home wherever ye are. For a short while. But ye tellt me ye longed for home when ye were in Paris."

"Aye, I did."

"Well, this will be far worse. For ye'll be homesick, and in danger every minute of the day, wi' no clansmen to fight wi' ye, and ye'll have to pretend to be someone ye're no', think of every move ye make, every word ye say," Duncan continued passionately.

"Ye make it sound terrible," Alex said.

"That's because I think it will be." He sighed again, deeply. "Alex, if ye do this, then I'll support ye in every way I can. No matter what ye need of me, I'll give it, and gladly. But I canna pretend I'm happy for ye to do it, because I'm no'. I think ye'll be desperately unhappy, and there isna a prince in the world worth that."

"I'd no' be doing it for the prince," Alex said.

"Aye, well, there isna a da in the world worth doing it for either," Duncan added, and seeing Alex flinch at that, knew he'd hit the nail on the head. "He's dead, Alex. Follow your own path, no' his."

Duncan lay down then, and pulled the covers over him. He watched Alex as he sat on the edge of his bed, staring at the floor, deep in thought, and said nothing more, for there was nothing more he could say, nothing that could make any difference, in any case.

Alex sat like that for so long that the candle was guttering by the time he came back to the present. He looked up, to find Duncan still watching him, his eyes full of concern, full of love.

"Thank ye," he said then. "I need to think about what ye've said. Everything ye've said. I ken it cost ye to say it, but I needed to hear it. I canna imagine no' having ye by my side."

"Ye'll never need to, while I live," Duncan reassured him. "But I canna do this with ye, no matter how much I might want to."

"No, I ken that. I didna mean that. I meant—"

"I ken what ye meant. I'll always be there for ye, Alex. I always have been, and always will be, as ye've been there for me. Angus too. He's just younger. But he's growing, and fast."

"He is. But the bond is different between us."

"Aye, it is. Da was right in that at least. Go to sleep. It's been a hard day, a tiring one. Ye dinna need to make your decision now. Take the time ye need."

Alex nodded, and licking his fingers reached out and snuffed out the candle.

Duncan lay awake in the dark for what seemed like hours, wondering if he'd done the right thing in telling the truth. Should he have lied, said that he'd thought the prince to be superficial, careless, that there was nothing worthy underneath the surface glamour? If he had, would Alex have believed him, or would he have realised that he was lying, trying to stop him doing this?

As tempted as he'd been to lie, he could not have done. He would have been betraying not only his brother but his own principles if he had. Even so, it did not make him feel much better to know that by staying true to his principles he had possibly tipped the balance.

Alex would take on this ridiculous, monumental task. Duncan knew that, even if Alex didn't yet. He would take it on for his clan, for his prince, and, above all, for his father.

Duncan had forgiven his father for his behaviour after their mother's death, especially since he had discovered first-hand just how soul-destroying such grief could be, how it could twist your heart, turn you into a person you never thought yourself capable of being, a hateful, bitter person. But he still could not forgive him, probably never would forgive him for the terrible lonely burden he had placed on Alex's shoulders. It was a cruel and unreasonable thing to do, not something you should do to your child, to anyone.

Having closely watched Charles throughout the evening as he had increasingly relaxed from being a royal prince to being a young man with friends, Duncan had realised that James had almost certainly done the same thing to *his* eldest son, charged him with restoring the House of Stuart to the throne of Great Britain, as Alexander had charged Alex with restoring the MacGregor name.

And as he watched them, not taking much part himself in the conversation that flowed as they ate the sumptuous meal that had been laid out for them, he saw that even though they were unaware of it, some part of them recognised that the other bore the same almost unbearable burden of feeling bound to live up to their fathers' expectations, whatever the cost.

And that subconscious recognition drew them together, made Charles truly relax with Alex as he probably would not with anyone else, as he certainly had not with Duncan, although he would not have noticed that had he not been observing the prince so very closely.

Da, why did ye do this to him? Why could ye no' have let him just live the life he wanted, the life you lived? he silently asked.

Alex's breathing deepened as he gave in to sleep, but Duncan lay awake, alternating between cursing his father and praying for forgiveness for doing so. All he could do now, as he had promised Alex he would, was support him in any way possible, and be there to console him and help him to move on and find meaning in life if either or both of the young men failed in their almost impossible task.

That he would do, with every fibre of his being.

Late July 1740, Durham

"So you have actually decided to do it?" Highbury said in a tone of such astonishment that Alex stopped pouring the brandy from the decanter into two crystal glasses and instead looked at his friend. They were sitting in the drawing room together, all servants having been told they could go to bed, as the earl had everything he needed and his potential new valet would help him to undress tonight.

"Ye really believed I wouldna, then?" Alex asked.

"In truth I doubted you would, yes," the earl confessed, accepting the glass that Alex offered him. "It is such a huge undertaking, after all. When I was with you, both in Paris and Rome, and then here, it seemed eminently possible. But once you left I started thinking, for there is nothing else for me to do here, and the more I thought, the more ridiculous and impossible it seemed."

"Ye stayed here the whole time I was away?" Alex asked, throwing himself down opposite Highbury. As they would not be disturbed now, he had removed his shoes, frockcoat, waistcoat and stock and now stretched out on the chaise longue, flexing his toes blissfully.

"I assume those shoes are not as comfortable as the *bròggan*, then," the earl commented on seeing this.

"No. The toes pinch a wee bit. Dinna change the subject."

Highbury sighed, delayed having to reply by taking a mouthful of brandy and then removed his own stock and waistcoat, during which time he worked out how much to tell Alex.

"I was thinking to go home, but then my steward wrote to tell me that my son had returned from Kent unexpectedly."

"To London?"

"No, to Hertfordshire, which means he wanted to see me. He would not have gone there unless he was impecunious and hoping to persuade me to advance his allowance. I did not wish to travel all that way to engage in combat with Daniel, only to have to return here anyway once you came back. So I stayed."

He also could not bear the thought of seeing Daniel at his very worst, petulant, sulky, demanding, and then throwing a tantrum when his father refused his demands for money, which he intended to do. It would be bad enough normally, but after just spending time with the young man now sitting opposite him, the comparison would have been unbearable. True, Daniel could never have had the life experiences that had forged Alex into the man he was, but he *could* have been a cultured, responsible, capable young man, but for his parents' failings.

He did not want to discuss that now, though.

"You could not have come to Hertfordshire, not at this point," Highbury continued. "I think it better for you not to go to any place where you might encounter the nobility until you have perfected the character of Sir Anthony. Are you sure you wish to do it?"

"I dinna exactly *wish* to do it, as ye ken. But my brother agreed wi' me about Charles's potential. He's still got the same fire and passion, and the same compelling personality. But he's a man now. A fine-looking man, tall and athletic. I'm thinking he's the best chance we have both of restoring the Stuarts to the throne, and of raising the proscription of the MacGregors. If I dinna do it, I'll always wonder what would have happened if I had. So aye, for that reason I wish to do it. Are ye still of the same mind though?"

"I am, for the same reasons I stated at our last meeting. I think it will arouse no suspicion if I facilitate your introduction into society. As I said, I have been thinking. A number of the Ashleighs already know that I met Lady Peters and her daughters when I was travelling. I can say that I also met you by chance somewhere, and thought it too remarkable a coincidence to ignore, and so I took you under my wing. It is the kind of thing people would expect of me."

"It's the kind of man ye are," Alex commented. "Ye *did* take me under your wing, in Paris."

"No, I did not. It was an agreement which brought mutual benefit. In fact, I think I got a great deal more from the experience than you did, in many ways," the earl replied.

"Aye, well, I could give ye an argument on that. Ye definitely willna get more from this experience though, even if we're successful. So if ye change your mind before we start, ye must tell me, and I'll understand. In the meantime, I tellt Charles that if I do this I canna begin immediately, for I have to learn to become this Anthony laddie. But I also have to go home until the autumn, for there's a lot to do at this time of year, and I need to be sure the clan is secure for the winter, wi' enough food to survive, and everything possible done."

"When will you come back?" Highbury asked.

"I'm thinking likely October, maybe November," Alex said. "Will that suit?"

"Yes. I can return here then, and we can spend the winter perfecting Sir Anthony. I have your measurements, so I can have some outfits made for you suitable for various occasions, and then when we go to London, we can order more, as needed."

"I've been thinking I canna go into society looking like myself," Alex said. "Even if yon Clarence man doesna remember me from Versailles, I'm sure Joseph and his friends will. Ye dinna tend to forget someone who cut your hand off. It was a memorable meeting," he added wryly.

Highbury frowned.

"You are right, of course. Perhaps you could dye your hair a different colour? Grow a beard?" he suggested.

Alex started laughing.

"I canna imagine I'll be accepted into noble society if I look like a savage! In all my time in Paris I didna see one aristocrat wi' a beard. I canna think England is so different."

"Your family all died of smallpox," Highbury pointed out. "You could say you've grown a beard to hide the scarring from your own illness. That might be acceptable."

"No. I have an idea," Alex continued, swinging his legs off the chaise longue and sitting up. "I've been pondering it ever since I left Rome. Ye remember when I was in yon play that ye came to see me in, wi' Ashelle and Scolastica?"

"*The Relapse.* Yes, of course I do! You were superb!"

"Aye, but ye watched the whole play and ye didna recognise me until my wig fell off at the end."

"No, but...my God, you cannot mean you intend Sir Anthony to become Lord Foppington? He's a figure of ridicule!" Highbury cried.

"Aye. But Sir Anthony has lived in France, and in Geneva, where France has an influence. If he's an effeminate fop no one in England will be surprised – they'll just think it the corrupt influence of the immoral French nobility with whom I've been mixing. It should keep any lassies away from me, and any mistakes I make in etiquette I can blame on French ways, or the ways of Geneva, which most people havena ever visited. If the three of ye didna recognise me, yon wee gomerels willna."

Highbury sat up too, now, thinking.

"I cannot imagine it. You will be mocked. People will not accept you, or at least not enough to confide in you, which you will need if you're to collect information."

"I dinna intend to be *exactly* like Foppington," Alex said. "But when I *was* him, I found it easy to stay in the role, because Foppington is the absolute opposite of me. And if Sir Anthony is completely different to me, then if it ever *is* discovered that he died when he was six, if I can escape before I'm apprehended, then ye could invite me to dinner the next night as the laddie ye met in Paris, and no one would suspect I was Sir Anthony. I wouldna do that," he added quickly, seeing the earl's look of horror, "but it would mean I could disappear, and *no one* except yourself would ever ken my true identity. It would protect both you and me, and my clan, should that happen. I'm thinking it's worth finding a way to make that work, even if only for that reason."

Highbury stood suddenly, and picking the two glasses up from the table refilled them, and then sat down again.

"I think I need this," he said, taking a large mouthful. "It seems a crazy idea to me."

"Aye, it did to me at first. But I've had days of riding across Europe to think about it. We'll need to find a personality for the laddie, one that isna Foppington, but that suits Anthony's physical appearance. I can say I wear the paint to hide the scars – as ye said about a beard. Or maybe people will assume that. It doesna matter if they mock me, as long as they let me stay in their company. You'll help wi' that, for ye're an earl. If you accept me, they likely will. And if they do, they'll talk in front of me, if no' *to* me. I can feign complete ignorance of British affairs and politics. I'm sure there are any number of men who'd be wanting to show off their importance and knowledge to the ignorant frenchified laddie."

Highbury started laughing.

"I must introduce you to Bartholomew and Edward," he said. "I'll tell you about them later. Yes, you are right. There are many such men, who are likely to be indiscreet as well in their attempt to show off their importance, especially if they think you're a fool and easy to impress. But it would also be a great advantage to you if you could win the ladies round," he added, entering into the spirit of it now. "For many ladies know a great deal about politics, and about court gossip, which could also be of interest to you.

"I can introduce you to the gentlemen's clubs and suchlike, but if you can win the hearts of the ladies, then you'll be invited to all manner of soirees and balls. I find people are more likely to speak indiscreetly at such events than in their clubs, for they're more relaxed, especially as the evening goes on. Also, men behave differently when ladies are around, because they want to make a good impression on them, show their superiority, and so on."

"Ye're an astute observer of people," Alex remarked.

"If I am it's because I dislike large gatherings, with all the artificiality, the strutting and simpering that goes on. If I have to attend them, then I am usually more of an observer than a participator. I realise that if we do this, I will have to attend a lot more events, maybe even spend the season in London. But it will be worth it, I think. Especially if you are going to be a version of Foppington!" Highbury said laughingly.

Silence fell for a few minutes as both men pondered how a Foppington figure could win over the females of the nobility.

"If I'm something like Foppington, none of the husbands will see me as a rival, will they?" Alex said finally.

"Absolutely not," Highbury agreed, grinning.

"So if I have an interest that the ladies have and the men dinna generally share, and I'm no' a threat, would that work?" Alex asked, yawning suddenly.

"I suppose so. If you can think of one," the earl said. "Let us sleep on it, for it's very late, and you've been travelling all day. I wish your brother could have stayed tonight."

"I would like ye to meet him. Perhaps ye will one day, but the fewer people ken who my sponsor is, the better. It puts him at risk if he kens and it goes wrong," Alex said. "I wouldna have that."

And on that very jolly note, the two men finished their brandies and made their way to bed.

"Fashion," Alex said suddenly over breakfast the following morning.

"Fashion?" the earl asked.

"Yes," Alex said, using his English 'valet' accent, as servants were around now and wandering in and out of the room from time to time. "Something the ladies would be interested in, but not the men. And something a foppish young fool might be obsessed with."

"A lot of men are interested in fashion," Highbury commented.

"Really? Why?"

"Because the clothes a man wears are a very important part of the impression he makes in society, just as a lady's are. You remember how carefully I chose your outfits in Paris, surely? I certainly remember how bored you were!"

"Ah. Aye...yes, I remember that, but the aristocratic ladies I eavesdropped on talked about it a lot, and could discuss the trimmings on a hat or a sleeve for *hours.* The men never did that. If they talked about it, it was far more general," Alex said.

"Ah, I see what you mean. Yes, I daresay that is true. I think I spend too much time with Harriet and her family, who don't care about such things at all," Highbury said. "But that would mean you would have to learn all about such things. I cannot imagine you being interested in them!"

"I've had to learn an enormous amount of things I'm not interested in over the years," Alex pointed out. "If I learn this though, it will help me to suggest the perfect outfit for every occasion for you, and in the latest style, my lord, which will be invaluable, I think. If that pleases you, of course."

"Wha—" Highbury began, a puzzled look on his face, then saw Alex glance quickly over his shoulder, then back to him. "What a splendid idea," he amended. "That is indeed a most valuable attribute for a valet to have. I have neither the time nor the interest to learn about such matters."

"Then it will be my pleasure to do so," Alex replied, smiling ingratiatingly.

They continued speaking in this manner until the footman retreated, his arms full of dishes.

"My God, you're good," Highbury said, after the door had closed. "Everything about you changed in an instant; your posture, demeanour, even your expression."

"Yes, well, when I heard the footman opening the door I thought of myself as your valet. I did the same thing the first night you saw me, in *L'Accueil Chaleureux*. I was impersonating a fop and the Elector. I had to change from one to the other instantaneously."

"How do you do it?" the earl asked.

Alex thought for a moment.

"I spend a little time beforehand thinking about what such a character would be like. Sometimes I copy a person I've observed, making a few changes. That's what I did with the fop. Sometimes I have to invent them from just a few things I've heard or read – as I did with George. The most difficult is when I have to invent them completely, but those characters are the most fun to portray, because I can make them anything I want.

"When I've decided what the character will be like, his voice, how he walks, his mannerisms etc, then if I have time I will sit and close my eyes, and let him become...absorbed into me. It's awfu'...awfully difficult to explain. But once I have him, then I can bring him to mind and just be him whenever I want. This is harder."

"What is?" Highbury asked, absolutely fascinated.

"To be myself, but with a character's voice and accent. That's why I've used Scottish words sometimes today, because I'm thinking as me, not your valet. But if I speak Scottish any servant approaching the door will hear the different cadence, even before they can hear the actual words I'm saying."

"You are incredible," Highbury said.

"All actors do it on stage," Alex said, shrugging his shoulders. "It's just something you have to learn."

"Maybe. But when the performance is over, they can be themselves again. If you become Sir Anthony you will not be able to do that," the earl pointed out.

"Yes, I will. You said you'll rent a house in London for me," Alex said. "When I'm there I'll be able to be myself."

"No, you won't, because you will need to have servants. Maybe not as many as I do, unless you are to entertain, but you absolutely will need them, to clean, prepare meals, to open the door to visitors. You will need a coachman too, gardeners, footmen...I'm sorry," Highbury finished, seeing his friend's look of absolute horror as he realised the truth of this.

Alex tore his fingers through his hair.

"*Bàs mallaichte,*" he said softly. "I hadna...hadn't thought of that. I need to think more about this, because I absolutely cannot be Sir

Anthony, to be *anyone* else all the time. It would be unbearable. I must find a way around this, or I won't be able to do it."

"*We* must find a way around it," Highbury said. "If we go ahead with this we will do it together, discuss and deal with any difficulties together. And I must learn how to think as quickly as you just did, to change conversation at a moment's notice. And, when I am talking to Sir Anthony, to *believe* in him, and not to see Alex at all when I do. I think you need to teach me how to form a person in my head and believe in him, if I am to be able to forget you when I need to, and to accept Sir Anthony completely as whatever you make him."

"You're right," Alex said. "I need to talk with my brother about this in more depth. He might have good ideas. By the time I come back from home in October, I should have an idea of who Sir Anthony is. It will be easier then, I think. Can you stay here for the whole winter then?"

"I can do whatever I wish," Highbury told him. "My steward is excellent. Daniel will not come here, especially in the winter. He thinks the north is a barren wasteland. And I see no one I know in Durham in the summer, although there is always the danger that someone might decide to visit me. There will be no such danger in the winter, when the roads are impassable. Impassable to coaches," he added, seeing Alex smile. "Not to Highlanders, I'm sure."

"No. I'll be able to get here," Alex agreed. "And once we have Anthony, then we can practice together. I can be him for a whole day or evening, and I'm sure you'll soon learn to just see him. It just takes practice, and a little imagination. When you go to the theatre to see a play, for that time you don't see the actor, but the character he's playing, and believe in him, yes?"

"Yes, if he's a good actor," Highbury agreed.

"It's the same thing. Except you'll have more incentive to believe in me than in an actor in a play. Because our lives will depend on it," Alex said.

Which was a sobering thought, but true, nonetheless.

The following day Highbury arranged for a tailor to call and to bring cloth samples with him, and also for a wigmaker to visit.

"You will take the head measurements of my valet," he told the man, "and will then make two copies of a head for me. You will need one to make him some wigs, which must be of the finest quality. And I will also need one, in the event that I should decide to purchase another for him whilst we are out of town, of course."

This last was not a usual request, but if the earl had said he wanted a wig made from unicorn hair the wigmaker would have found a way to do it. He was very nervous. You did not see many aristocrats in this part of the world, and such a customer could be very lucrative, not only monetarily, but in the enhancement of his reputation, if he did a good job.

It was true that many aristocrats were also very difficult customers, not only in their exactitude, but in their reluctance to settle bills. But the Earl of Highbury was known for settling bills promptly, which caused the wigmaker to be even more nervous.

"Yes, of course, Lord Highbury," he said.

"Excellent. He will require a bob-wig for travelling, a queue wig, and a bag wig should he need to accompany me on more formal occasions."

After the wigmaker had taken detailed measurements of Alex's head and Highbury had stressed that his valet would *not* be shaving his head to accommodate the wig, the man left, and the tailor was called in to take measurements and show samples of various materials, in a rainbow of colours.

This took almost the whole afternoon, not least because Alex, who had struggled to maintain an interest in the details when his suits for Paris had been made, now showed an interest in almost *everything*, although he did not ask anywhere near the number of questions he wished to ask, as he was acutely aware he was playing the part of a valet, who would already know a great deal about gentlemen's clothing.

In the evening they both determined not to talk about the insane project they were about to embark on, once they had agreed the wording of the letter Alex would send to say he was ready to take up his valet's duties if the earl still wanted him. In the morning he would leave, and would walk home, refusing the earl's offer to allow him to take a horse, as it would not only be of no use in the Highlands, but would attract both suspicion and thieves.

In the end they had a very pleasant evening, exchanging anecdotes and talking of small events that only close friends would be interested in hearing about. Because they were, indeed, as they both acknowledged, close friends.

Which, as they also both acknowledged, was wonderful and probably unique, given their differences in background, age, nationality...in almost everything, in fact.

Except in their wish to see James Stuart back in his rightful place, as King James VIII and III, monarch of Great Britain and Ireland. And to see the proscription on Clan Gregor abolished, once and for all.

CHAPTER THIRTEEN

ALEX SET OFF FOR home the following day, travelling via Edinburgh so he could visit Francis Ogilvy, return the borrowed horses, collect the garron that had been left with him, and see if Susan was ready to go home, in which case she could come with him.

He had been very concerned about Francis when he'd left for Rome with Duncan. He didn't know much about illnesses, being more familiar with wounds of one sort or another, but he remembered his sister's illness, and how suddenly she had died. As he drew closer to the house he prayed that Francis was still alive, and that Susan's care had led to an improvement in his condition.

She really was quite remarkable in her ability to heal people, and was willing to try almost anything that had been proven to help, rather than relying on bloodletting and purges as most physicians did, at least in Alex's very limited experience.

It seemed that his prayers had been answered, because on arriving, somewhat dishevelled and muddy, he was shown into the drawing room by a very welcoming Mrs Ferguson to find Francis sitting at a table poring over a chessboard, looking much better than he had three months ago.

"Alex!" he cried on seeing his visitor. "It's wonderful to see you! How were your travels?"

"Very successful," Alex replied.

"You must tell me all about them! Or as much as you feel you can, anyway," Francis amended. "But first I think you should rest. You look tired."

Francis, Alex noted with relief, did *not* look tired. Or at least not as tired as he had the last time he'd seen him. His colour was good and his eyes clear. Alex smiled.

"I'm no' tired," he said automatically. "Well, maybe a wee bit," he amended, seeing Francis's sceptical expression. "We travelled as quickly as we could, so didna waste too much time sleeping. Duncan went straight home, but I thought I'd stay here for two or three nights, if that's acceptable?"

"You can stay for as long as you like! I'm sure you know you're always welcome here, and always will be. I will have the maid prepare a room for you, but in the meantime you must use my room to wash yourself and change your clothes, and if you wish to lie down for a time, then food will be ready for you when you emerge. Susan will be so pleased to see you!" Francis added. "She has gone to the market to buy some provisions, but should return soon."

"She seems to be taking good care of you," Alex observed as they mounted the stairs, noting that Francis was slightly breathless on reaching the top. Slightly. Surely that was not a bad sign?

"Oh, she is a miracle worker! She's been very strict with me, and I will admit I am not a good patient at times, which is unforgivable of me, because I know her advice is sound," Francis said, opening the door to his room and beckoning Alex to go in. "In truth I think that I'd given up a little, and had accepted that I was going to die."

"We're all going to die, Francis," Alex pointed out.

"That's true. But I'm going to die sooner than I maybe would have done if I did not have this illness," Francis said matter-of-factly. "Please don't look so unhappy. I have accepted that. But Susan's insistence that I walk every day, eat more vegetables, stop drinking alcohol and other things, mean that day is hopefully very much further away than it would have been if I had continued as I was. Now, there is water in the ewer and soap here, and towels in the drawer there. Do you have dry clothes? If not you can wear one of my shirts and a banyan and we will ensure your clothes are laundered. I will leave you to recover a little. Do not rush. I'm practising for a game with a friend tonight. He is calling later, and is an excellent opponent. If I had known you were coming, of course, I would have rearranged the game."

"No, it will be pleasant to watch ye. It's awfu' good to see ye looking so healthy, Francis," Alex admitted. "I was worried about ye."

Francis smiled.

"You rest. I can see you're very tired, in spite of claiming you're not. You don't have to be the clan chieftain here! I will wake you before supper, if you do sleep."

He went out then, closing the door quietly behind him. Alex smiled. His friend's legs were still swollen, he'd noticed, but not as much as they had been, and his love of life had clearly returned.

"God bless ye, Susan," he murmured to himself, only now realising by the wave of joy that lifted his spirits, just *how* worried he had been. Francis was very dear to him, had been like a father to him when his own father had rejected him. The bond that time had engendered was a lifetime one. Hopefully death would not break it for many years.

He stripped off his dirty clothes, washed himself as thoroughly as he could, combed his hair with his fingers, realised the spare clothes in his pack were also wet, and so donned the shirt and banyan Francis had offered, then decided to lie down on the top of the bed for just a few minutes, and rest his weary limbs.

It would be nice to spend two or three days here, he thought. It was true that he was eager to return home and see how Kenneth and Angus had coped with acting as chieftain, but Duncan would already be home by now, and Alex knew the clan was in good hands with him. He should be able to spend another night here when he headed south again in October or November, but after that he had no idea when or if he would see Francis again. That would depend on how this ridiculous mission went.

He lay down, stretched out luxuriously, closed his eyes and fell almost immediately into a deep sleep.

When the knock came on the door he leapt instantly off the bed, reaching instinctively for a dirk that was not there. Then he remembered where he was, that his dirk was on the table by the ewer and bowl, and relaxed, sitting back down on the edge of the bed.

"Good evening," he called to whoever was rousing him, having ascertained by the light coming through the window that he must have slept for hours. He stretched, and then the door opened and Susan's face appeared round it.

"Ye're dressed then," she said, coming into the room.

"Aye. Well, no' by Edinburgh standards perhaps, but I'm a wee bit overdressed for the clan," Alex replied, then standing, he opened his arms.

She walked into them. He wrapped his arms around her, and she laid her head against his shoulder.

"Ah, it's good to see ye, laddie," she said.

"And good to see ye too. Ye've worked a miracle wi' Francis, it seems," Alex replied.

She lifted her head, but made no move to pull back from his embrace. *Maybe no' a miracle then,* he thought.

"He's better than he was," she said, "but I canna cure him. Only God could do that. I've reduced his liquid intake, so at the moment only his legs are swelling. But at some point his abdomen will start to swell too."

"He seems to accept that this illness will shorten his life," Alex told her.

"Aye, he does. I havena tried sweating him yet, for I dinna think it necessary, and it's very uncomfortable. Or tapping him. I really dinna want to do that, for I've seen such wounds become infected and kill the patient anyway."

"Ye've worked a wonder anyway, Susan," Alex reassured her. "He's very much better than he was when you arrived. Ye've given him a reason to live."

She frowned then, and blushed a little.

"I ken that," she said. "And it's why I canna come back wi' ye. Unless ye need me to."

He released her then and held her at arm's length, looking her over.

"No," he said. "Want ye to, aye, for I love ye, ye ken that. The whole clan does. I think ye should stay too, and no' just for Francis, although I think ye're right about him. If ye leave he'll die much quicker than if ye dinna, and no' just because of your treatments. I ken ye hate the town, but ye're looking much happier than ye have since Màiri died. I'm thinking ye're still grieving for her, no' as badly as Duncan, but still sore."

"I am," she admitted. "I thought I'd stay wi' the clan forever. It's still my home, but something died in me when Màiri was killed. I canna get that back, but I was reminded of her every day there. She was such a huge part of my life, more than any other person since Rob."

253

"And ye're no' reminded of her the same way here," Alex said. "For ye were never here wi' her."

"No. She never came to Edinburgh at all. I still think of her a lot, but it's different. No' as painful."

"Then stay," Alex said. "If ye ever want to come back, to visit or to live, then we'll all be delighted. Ye dinna need my permission to stay, but I give it anyway."

She embraced him again then.

"Thank ye. I needed that," she mumbled into the green silk of the banyan, and when she released him her eyes were moist. "I'll stay here at least until…"

"D'ye ken how long that might be?"

She shook her head.

"It could be years. I hope so. He's looking to start taking patients again next week. Just two afternoons a week at first. But enough of me and Francis. I'm being selfish! Was your trip successful?"

"Aye," Alex said.

"Ye dinna sound certain it was," Susan commented.

Alex thought rapidly. He wanted to tell her *so* much. And Francis, for that matter. He trusted them both, implicitly. He would be telling the clan, after all, and Susan was part of the clan. But it wasn't only about trust, he told himself. It was about keeping as many of those he loved as safe as he could.

If he was discovered and his true identity revealed, then he could do nothing to protect the clan, except say that none of them had known what he was doing. And if he *was* arrested, then Highbury would warn them somehow, and they would scatter. He made a mental note to arrange that with Highbury, and to tell the clan. But if Susan and Francis's connection with him became known, then they would certainly be questioned, very carefully, and the only way they could be proved innocent was if it was very clear they were. Neither of them were good liars. The only way to protect them was to tell them nothing.

"No, it really did go well. I want to tell ye, Susan, but I canna." She nodded.

"Well then, are ye coming down for supper?" she asked.

"I havena anything I can wear," he said, looking at the corner where his pack was. "All my clothes are either dirty or soaking wet."

"Ye'll be fine as ye are," she told him, going over to the pack and picking it up, along with the dirty clothes he'd put on the floor next to it. "I'll take these for the laundress to clean. She comes in tomorrow."

"Francis said he had a visitor tonight."

"Aye, James Munro. He's below now. Him and Francis have been friends for years. He's a stubborn man, awfu' infirm now, and canna get out as much as he did. He willna take any advice from Francis about his health. But he makes the effort to come and play chess, when he's able. He's a magistrate, or was. I'm no' sure if he still is. Anyway, Francis has already tellt him that ye've just arrived today and that ye'll likely be wearing this," she waved at his attire, "for your bag was on top of the coach in the rainstorm. Ye're Alex Drummond, heading back from visiting friends." Alex laughed. Maybe they were better liars than he'd thought. "He didna say where the friends were, so if James asks that's up to you. He's a fine man. And a Jacobite," she added.

"A Jacobite? But ye said he's a Munro! The Munros have always been for Hanover, and Orange before that," Alex said.

"That's likely why he's no wi' his clan then, and has nothing to do wi' them. He makes no secret of his love for the Stuarts, at least no' wi' his close friends, although Francis refuses to let him toast the King Over the Water when he's here. Most of his servants are Jacobites too, or at the least have left clans that were for James, but are no longer. But ye'll no' be speaking of that at supper, for Francis remains impartial, as ye ken. And it's very informal. In truth, he'll be so concentrated on his chess that ye could likely walk in naked and he wouldna notice!"

When they arrived in the library Alex saw at once that Susan was right; it *was* very informal, as both men had removed their frockcoats and had a plate piled high with food next to them, which they picked at while pondering their game. As Mr Munro was next to move he remained frowning over his pieces, seemingly unaware of Susan and Alex's entrance. Francis looked up.

"Ah! I trust you slept well?" he said brightly. "You must help yourself to food. We are always very informal on evenings such as these."

"Aye, when ye're trouncing me," Mr Munro grumbled.

Francis smiled.

"You will ignore the bad manners of my friend," he said jovially. "It is not anything you have done. He is always thus when he's losing."

Munro made a guttural sound of disgust, then moved his piece.

"Good evening, Mr Drummond," he said then, looking across at Alex with merry brown eyes. "Francis tells me you are a close friend to both himself and Susan, which predisposes me in your favour. Hopefully you will forgive me not rising," he added, waving at his foot which was encased in bandages and propped on a footstool. "And my bad manners," he finished.

"I will indeed," Alex replied. "I'm delighted to meet any friend of Francis's. And chess is a serious undertaking, requiring deep concentration. I understand entirely."

"Do you play yourself, Mr Drummond?" Munro asked.

"I used to, but it is a long time since I've played, I'll admit."

"If Susan had taken my offer to teach her, perhaps you could have played each other," Francis put in. "I have another set, not as fine as this one, but perfectly serviceable."

"I've no interest in the game," Susan said from the sofa where she'd seated herself, a plate of food and a book on the table in front of her. She picked up a piece of sewing, after casting a longing look at the book then changing her mind. "I'm quite happy to sew quietly here while ye move wee pieces of wood around a board and curse each other."

"I beg your pardon, madam!" Francis cried in mock horror. "My pieces are of the finest ebony and ivory!"

"Ebony's wood, is it no'?" she replied. "So I'm half-right."

"If you'd like to play," Mr Munro said, "perhaps we could call my footman. I believe he's eating in the kitchen at the minute. I taught him to play and he's not only proficient but eager. I'm sure he'd be delighted to play someone other than myself."

"I'm no' certain I'm worth him giving up his meal for," Alex said. "As I said, it's many years since I've played. But if he wishes to I'll oblige him, and gladly. And then Susan can read her book in peace for a while."

Susan shot him a look of gratitude, and that, accompanied by her speedy departure to fetch the servant told Alex that she did not have much time to herself to read, which she did love doing. He resolved to choose a book himself and join her, if the chess match did not take place.

A few minutes passed, during which Alex watched Francis and James, refreshing his memory about the pieces and their moves, and then Susan returned, accompanied by a tall, extremely thin young man, dressed in a dark blue livery.

"Ah! Gordon! I assume Susan has told you why I've sent for you?" Mr Munro asked.

"She has indeed," Gordon replied, his accent unmistakably Highland Scots. "I'd be happy to oblige ye in a game, Mr…"

"Drummond," Alex replied.

Francis made his way to a cupboard and produced a chessboard and a box, and the two men seated themselves at a table a short distance from the others. Susan sat down on the sofa and picked up her book.

Gordon offered to set up the board, while Alex poured glasses of claret for them both.

"It's a long time since I've played," he said when he returned to the table. "I'm no' sure how much of a challenge I'll give ye."

The other man smiled.

"Let's play a game and get the measure of each other," he suggested.

They played a game and got the measure of each other, which, in Alex's view at least, was that Gordon was a far superior player.

"I'm thinking ye're just out of practice, as ye said," Gordon commented as he set up the pieces for a second game. "I play wi' Mr Munro a great deal, so I'm seeing more moves ahead than yourself."

"How many moves ahead can ye see?" Alex asked.

"I dinna ken, in truth," Gordon replied.

"I've estimated he can see about ten moves ahead," Mr Munro called from the other table. "But he's improving all the time. He has a mathematical mind, which helps."

"My sister would have been good at chess, then," Alex said. "She was a mathematical genius, my da said."

"She probably would then. Is she no' in Edinburgh with ye, Mr Drummond?"

"Alex," Alex replied. "No, she died when she was still a bairn. She never learnt the game at all."

"Oh, I'm sorry to hear that, Alex. I'm Iain, by the way."

"Ah, Gordon is your clan name then."

"Aye, although I'm no' wi' my clan any more," Iain said. "Take as long as ye need to plan your move. That will help."

They settled to play again, Alex resolving to try to see more than the two or three moves ahead he suspected was his current limit, and only observe his opponent when it was not his turn.

Iain Gordon. The Gordons were one of the largest clans in Scotland, and Catholic, but the clan was split in its allegiance to the monarchs. The flower Iain wore pinned to his breast was a clear Jacobite symbol though; a white open rose, with a bud. Mr Munro sported the same flower, also with a bud. James and Charles, then. But Iain could be wearing that because his master had told him to.

It doesna matter, he told himself, trying to focus back on the game and work out why Iain had just moved his bishop unexpectedly. *I'm no' about to discuss politics wi' the man.*

"The rose grows in my master's garden. He planted it to celebrate White Rose Day," Iain murmured, seeing the direction of Alex's gaze.

"Ah. So your master finds the tenth of June worthy of growing a rose for," Alex replied, forgetting the game entirely for a moment.

"His admiration for the rose is no secret," Iain said softly.

"So ye wear it because your master tells ye to?"

"Maybe, although I'm no' renowned for doing things just because someone tells me to. Do ye like roses then?"

"Aye, I do," Alex replied. "And the bud will hopefully open soon, as the open rose fades."

Iain smiled then, and in that moment was transformed. He would never be handsome, but his delight was genuine and lit up his whole face, making him almost attractive, a man to be trusted.

Maybe. Instinctively liking someone did not make them trustworthy. Alex sighed inwardly, wishing momentarily that Duncan was still here, and then remembering why he wasn't. This man's trustworthiness was irrelevant. Charles Edward Stuart's had not been.

"Let us hope it does," Iain agreed. "Hopefully before the open rose fades. Your move, I believe."

For the rest of the game they spoke of innocuous subjects, Iain giving Alex some thoughts on how to improve his game, after which a general discussion on chess between all the males followed, until Alex noticed that Francis was starting to look very fatigued.

"He's weary," Alex whispered to Iain, watching as the man instinctively looked to his master, and then to Francis. Then he nodded.

"It grows awfu' late, sir," he said then, bowing. "Will I bring the coach round?"

"Good God! Yes," cried Munro, looking at the clock on the wall. "Time passes so quickly when you are having fun, does it not? You are looking fatigued, Francis, and I must admit, I am also a little tired. We must do this again, and soon. What did you think of Gordon, Mr Drummond?"

"I like him. And he is, as you said, a fine player," Alex replied.

"He is a fine everything," Munro declared. "He's employed as my footman, but he can perform almost any role I need him to – as you can see, for he will bring the coach round, and then will drive me home, after which he will act as my valet so as not to wake any of the other servants, as the hour is so late. He even replaced my steward for a short time when the man was ill. Utterly reliable, utterly trustworthy. I would be lost without him, I admit it! He is a treasure! How long do you intend to stay, sir? Perhaps my man can play you again."

"I would like that, but I only intend to stay for a couple of days," Alex said.

"Ah. Unfortunate. But you and I must arrange another evening, Francis."

"Indeed. I am to start seeing patients again next week, though, so Susan tells me that I must arrange nothing else until I know how much that tires me," Francis told his friend.

"Ah! Very wise indeed. A fine woman!"

"Indeed she is. I would be lost without her," Francis replied, echoing his friend's words about his servant.

"Aye, men in general would be lost without women, even if they willna admit it," Susan replied from the sofa, putting her book down on the table.

"I cannot dispute that, Mistress MacIntyre," Mr Munro said, bowing courteously. "Indeed, without the fair sex, none of us would exist at all! If I ever find such another as my dear departed wife, I will snap her up without hesitation!"

He glanced at Francis, who coloured, which told Alex that he still loved Susan in a romantic way. A glance at Susan told him she still did not. Even so, they were doing well together, and both seemed happy.

Hopefully that situation would continue for many years.

Loch Lomond, August 1740

Alex stood, looking at the assembled clanspeople. Absolutely every member of the clan seemed to have come to his summons, even the women with babies and toddlers and those who had been in the middle of a complex task. This told him that they had probably spent much of the time he was away discussing where he'd gone, and now expected him to satisfy their curiosity.

That he was about to do, although he was not sure what their reaction would be. Duncan and Angus had had time to come to terms with his intentions, and so last night the brothers had mainly discussed how Kenneth had managed as temporary chieftain.

"I think he was awfu' good," Angus said. "He hasna got the natural authority you have, and he was awfu' nervous, particularly at first. But once he realised that everyone accepted he was in charge, he was a lot better."

"Did he ask ye for advice?" Alex asked.

"Aye, in a manner of speaking," Angus replied, grinning. "That is he'd ask me what I thought *you'd* do in the situation, and I'd tell him as best I could. No, I wasna offended," he added. "I'm thinking he kent better than I do both what ye'd do and what should be done, for he's old, and he's kent ye since ye were born, and Da too, before he lost himself."

"Dinna let Kenneth hear ye think he's old," Duncan commented.

"Christ, no! I enjoy the use of my limbs too much to do that," Angus said, laughing.

"So he did a good job."

"Aye. Everyone tellt me that he listened to them if they had a problem, and though he wouldna always have an instant answer as you would, he'd go away for a wee while and think on it. And his suggestions were good," Duncan put in.

"We dinna ken what he'd be like, what he'd do if something happened, though, like wi'—" Angus broke off suddenly, glancing nervously at his brother.

"Ye can say her name, Angus. It's three years now. I'll always miss her, but it's no' as sharp," Duncan said.

"Like wi' Màiri, then," Angus finished.

"I didna ken what to do either, as I showed too well," Alex said.

"Aye, but after the first mistake, ye did everything else well, or as well as ye could," Duncan commented.

"It was Kenneth who made me see my error," Alex said. "Without him I dinna ken if I *would* have done everything else well. I think he'd make a good decision, and he'd listen to advice. And if anything happens, I should be able to join ye in a few days, once I ken."

"Ye really *do* mean to do this, then?" Angus said.

"Aye, if I can. We havena worked through all the details, but if I need to come back quickly I'll be able to do it without raising suspicion, for I'll be a bachelor wi' no obligations, and a butterfly, a man of fashion, who dashes off to places in the hope of buying a wee bit of lace or some such foolery. We thought that up in case I need to go to Rome, if I find out something urgent, or too crucial to trust to a letter. But it would also work if I'm needed here," he told them.

"Or if ye're missing home," Duncan added.

"I'll try to resist that, for I'll be missing home the whole time. I did when I was in Paris," Alex admitted.

As he stood now, looking round the eager faces, every one of them familiar, every one a trusted part of him, he felt, just for a moment, the absolute enormity of what he was about to do, that he was teetering on the edge of a great pit, and once he leapt into it he might never find his way out.

He was being ridiculous. This was the chance to fulfil his destiny.

He shook his head, dismissing the fear, and focussed on the clansfolk instead, who were chatting quietly to each other while waiting for the meeting to start.

"Everything I'm about to tell ye is serious enough that I'll be asking ye to swear on the iron no' to ever disclose it to *anyone*," Alex began. The crowd instantly fell absolutely silent. "If any of ye dinna agree to that, then ye leave now."

He waited a moment as though expecting an exodus, although in truth he'd have been astonished if anyone *had* walked out.

"Most of ye will ken that my da always hoped I might one day be able to influence those in power to raise the proscription on our clan. It's why ye all sacrificed to send me to Paris," he continued.

"Among the things I learned when I was there was that no matter how educated I am, no matter if I can speak the usurper's language, I'll never be able to get close enough to those I might impress, for I'm no' of noble birth. My da didna ken that, but the nobles are like a clan. They have their rules and their customs, and they dinna accept *anyone* who isna of their clan. So three years ago, after Da died and I came home, I intended to forget that dream and just lead the clan, which is what I was born to do, really.

"But then in June everything changed. For I found out that I have an opportunity to become a member of the nobility. No' really, but to take on the identity of a laddie who died when he was a bairn. I'll no tell ye all the details of how I ken it's safe to become him, but I can. There's a man wi' wealth who can ensure my entrance into society, and once I'm there, then I'm hoping to become part of the noble clan."

He stopped for a moment then, thinking of how to formulate the next part of his speech. The silence was profound; no one coughed, or moved. Even the children present were absolutely silent.

"I still canna do what my da hoped, which was to show those in power how educated the MacGregors are, how civilised, for I willna *be* a MacGregor. But what I'm hoping to do is to become a spy for the Stuarts, so that one day, hopefully soon, James will take his rightful place again, and if he does, then his son has promised me he will lift the proscription immediately."

A collective gasp came from the clan then.

"I went wi' Duncan to Rome to talk wi' the prince, for I didna want to do this unless it was necessary, for it puts no' just myself, but all of ye at risk if I do," Alex continued.

"We're all at risk anyway, as MacGregors," Gregor commented.

"Aye, that's true. More at risk, then. Duncan sees the depth, as we all ken, so I wanted his viewpoint of the prince before I decided. And Duncan was impressed wi' him too, and thinks that one day, wi' an army at his back, he's likely the best chance there's ever been to restore the Stuarts to the throne and make us legal again. So I've made my mind up to try it. If it doesna work, and I canna get close enough to anyone who can give information, then I'll abandon it, and come home. But I'm thinking I need to try, for a lot of men can fight, but there's no' many who can mimic others as I can."

"And if ye're caught?" Barbara asked.

Alex shrugged.

"If I'm caught then the wealthy man will write to ye urgently, and ye'll disappear until it's safe to come back. And Duncan will be your chieftain. But if I'm careful I shouldna be. And I intend to be very careful.

"So then, I'm home now until everything's done for the winter, and then I'll away down to England to learn to be Sir Anthony Peters, for that's the laddie's name. The 'season' starts around January – that's when all the people wi' nothing better to do than gossip and dance go to London from their big houses in the countryside. But it doesna really become busy until about April. I'll need time to perfect yon Anthony laddie, for I've no' just to play the role for a few days, I've got to invent him from nothing and then *become* him, and that willna be easy. Both myself and my sponsor dinna think I'll be ready to take part in the season next year, for I canna afford to make a mistake.

"So next spring I'll likely come back again, to make sure everything is well here, and...well, in truth, to see everyone. I'll stay until autumn and then I'll go down to England, spend the winter making any final adjustments, then go to London in January, so I can ease myself into the nobility before everyone arrives. Duncan will be the chieftain while I'm away. I'm thinking that's the main part of what I've to tell ye. D'ye have any questions for me?"

"Do ye really *want* to do this?" Kenneth asked. "Will ye be happy, d'ye think? If ye willna, I dinna think ye should go."

There was a murmur of approval of the question from the others, and to his surprise Alex felt his throat tighten and his vision mist. God, he was so lucky to have such a clan behind him.

"Ye deserve the truth," he replied, swallowing back the lump in his throat. "No, I dinna really want to do this. I want to be your chieftain. But I ken I have a unique gift – my da was right in that – and I would never forgive myself if I didna take the chance to make a *real* difference to the cause."

"Did the prince command ye to do it?" James asked.

"No. He isna such a laddie. He tellt me that it would be a priceless thing, to have someone at Court who he could trust, for it seems most spies do it for the money, and so will give false information if they think to profit. But he also tellt me it must be my decision, for it's a huge one. So the decision is mine. I'm accustomed to doing things I dinna want to do. I didna want to go to university. So I can do this. But my heart will always be here, wi' all of ye, and your support will give me strength when I need it. And when I can, I'll come home."

There were no more questions for the moment, although he could see from the expressions on the faces of many of them, that once they'd recovered from the shock of what they'd just heard, he would be bombarded.

"I have other news. Susan is staying wi' Dr Ogilvy, for he's sick and she's helping him a lot, although he canna be cured. It seems to be helping her too, for she's struggled wi' being here since Màiri died, and being in Edinburgh but needed is good for her.

"The doctor taught Duncan to ride a horse so we could get to Rome faster than we would have done walking or in coaches. I've asked him to teach Angus too, and he's agreeable to it. If two of ye can ride well, then ye'll be able to get to London quickly should I be needed urgently. So when I leave to go to England, Angus will come wi' me as far as Edinburgh, and spend the winter there, learning to ride. Dr Ogilvy isna my sponsor, in case any of ye think that. The man who is none of ye ken, nor ever will, and I willna tell anyone his name, no' even my brothers, for I've sworn an oath no' to.

"And now I'll ask ye all to swear an oath to me, never to speak to anyone outside the clan of what's been said tonight. And then ye can all go to your beds, for it's late and there's a lot to do. I'm sure ye'll have a lot more questions, but I've time to answer them, for I'm going nowhere until October or November. Kenneth, I'm wanting to talk wi' ye tomorrow, for I've heard ye've done a wonderful job, but I want your thoughts on it."

It took a little time for everyone to swear their oath, but when they had they all made their way back down to the settlement by moonlight, some talking together, but the majority of them silent as they absorbed what they'd learnt tonight.

"I've a question for ye," Duncan asked as the three brothers walked down the slope, having waited until the rest of the clan were partway down the hill.

"What is it?" Alex asked.

"When ye were away in June, I stayed in your house for much of the time. Angus wanted me to and I was glad to do it." He stopped for a minute then, but neither Alex nor Angus spoke, knowing from Duncan's tone that whatever the question was, it was hard for him to ask it.

"Seeing Susan in Edinburgh made me think more on it," he continued after a while. "Ye ken I need a lot of time alone, but staying in the house I lived in wi' Màiri is bringing me more grief than comfort. It's as if she's there, but in the shadows. I canna see her and she canna see me, and we canna communicate. I used to find comfort in it, in having all her things around me, and thinking she was still wi' me, in a manner of speaking. I hoped that one day I might see her, talk wi' her, for I saw Alpin that time, ye remember.

"But it hasna happened, and now I realise that I have to move on, and I think she'd want that too. I'm feart that maybe she's waiting for *me* to move on so that she can, and when I do she'll be happy. Susan wouldna have done it without Francis needing her, but it's helping her. I never want to leave Lomond, but I'm thinking I need to leave the cottage."

"So ye're wanting to move in wi' me and Angus?" Alex asked.

"Aye, if ye've no any objection," Duncan said. "If it doesna work then I'll move out again."

Alex stopped then, which brought the other two to a halt.

"I canna believe ye think I'd have any objection," Alex said then. "I'll be overjoyed if ye come back, and I'm sure Angus will be too."

"God, aye," Angus replied with heartfelt sincerity.

Duncan smiled and Alex caught the shimmer of tears in his eyes, reflected in the moonlight, and his own eyes misted over again.

"Come here, ye wee gomerel," he said, gripping both his brothers' shoulders and pulling them into him. "It'll be wonderful for the three of us to be together again, in the same house. But I'll no' let anyone else use your cottage until you're ready for it," he added. "So when ye need to, ye can still go there."

The tightening of Duncan's grip gave Alex the answer he needed.

"I'm thinking MacGregor might want to move in too," Duncan said a little shakily, as the three of them embraced.

"Aye, well, he's a cat. He'll decide for himself. He's welcome if he does," Alex replied, smiling.

They stood for a few minutes, taking comfort from each other as they had so many times, and surely would for many more.

And then they separated, but on Angus's insistence still held hands as they continued down the hill.

"I'm no' sleeping in the bed wi' the two of ye tonight, though," Duncan said after a minute. "Ye couldna fit two of us in there now, never mind all three."

"But we have to!" Angus protested. "It's a tradi—"

"No it isna," Duncan countered. "Ye invented it. We've done it twice...three times. That isna a tradition. And even if it was, it's an impossible tradition now."

Alex laughed, and the three of them went home, Duncan and Angus bickering good-naturedly, while Alex wondered how the hell he was going to be able to leave the brothers he adored, the clan he adored, to live a false life in London, maybe for years.

Right now the idea was almost unbearable.

He thought then about a young, handsome, eager prince, eyes burning with the desire to fulfil *his* destiny, to finally, after over fifty years of exile, return his family to the throne. And then he thought of the looks on the MacGregors faces as they walked openly about the Highlands, using their name, carrying their weapons, and knowing their lands belonged to them not by the sword, but by a warrant of the king.

It has to be worth it, he told himself desperately.

It would be worth it. He would make it worth it.

CHAPTER FOURTEEN

Durham, England, November 1740

For six days Highbury and his new 'valet' discussed Sir Anthony Peters in great detail every time they were alone together, which was a lot, partly because of the skeleton staff at the house and partly because it seemed the earl needed a lot of time to train the man to his exact specifications.

They started by working out the logistics of bringing him into society, and by the end of the first week had agreed that when Anthony had been perfected, they would travel to London.

"Hopefully we can travel in February," the earl said. "It might be difficult, but after crossing the Alps winter travelling does not hold the same terrors for me. In London we can look for a suitable house to rent for you. You can visit tailors, milliners, mantua makers, and whoever else you want and learn all about fashion, and we can also have some perfectly tailored clothes made for you. The outfits I've commissioned are adequate for everyday wear – in fact the man has done a remarkably good job, but they will not be suitable for Court wear, or for balls and such horrors, when all eyes will be on you."

They had also discussed Sir Anthony's personality, his background story, his purpose in coming to England and how and where he had met the earl, and had practised their stories until they almost believed them to be true.

Now they were standing in the earl's bedroom, sharing a bottle of claret and preparing for the next phase of Sir Anthony; the physical appearance he would have.

Anyone happening to actually see this training session between the earl and his valet may well have been somewhat bemused, for the Earl of Highbury had never been one to wear either paint or brightly coloured outfits embroidered with flowers, and yet there were now three such outfits spread out on his bed, while his nearby toilet table was covered with pots of cosmetics.

Fortunately no one did see this, because the earl, who was renowned for his altruism, had excelled himself by giving all his household staff an extra day's pay, as well as enough money for lodgings at a nearby inn and two full days off, telling them on no account to return until tomorrow evening. Cold collations had been prepared for the earl, fires had been laid in the hearths, and he had told all his staff that he could manage perfectly well for such a short time. He did after all have his valet, he assured them, who was a most versatile man, and could turn his hand to many things.

At the moment the most versatile man was about to turn himself into another person altogether, and was eyeing the three exquisitely tailored outfits, clearly uncertain of which one to wear for the baronet's first appearance in the world.

"You did ask for them to be made in the brightest colours possible," Highbury pointed out.

"Aye, I did, and they certainly are," Alex replied, eyeing the peacock-blue, bright yellow and scarlet velvet outfits with disgust. "I'm thinking I'll apply the makeup first though. That's what I did as Foppington, then I put the outfit on carefully so I didna smear it."

He took a sip of claret, then sitting down at the table picked up a brush and swept his hair back, tying it at the crown of his head with a piece of green ribbon, then deftly plaiting it before securing the ends with another piece.

"If I do it like this, then it shouldna fall out of the wig later as it did on stage," Alex explained. "And I'm thinking I might use pins to keep the wig in place."

Highbury sat on the end of the bed as Alex picked up the pot of white paint and a brush and began to mix it.

"I can't believe that this is finally happening," he said. "I thought we'd be planning it forever!"

"Aye, well, we still are planning it," Alex said, starting to brush the white onto his face and neck, leaning forward so that he could see himself better. Highbury took out his watch and noted the time. "There," Alex said, when he'd finished.

"I've never seen anyone wear paint that thick!" the earl exclaimed. "I mean the ladies, and the French men I've seen with it."

"This is the way I wore it as Foppington," Alex explained, turning his head to make sure he hadn't missed any skin. "Ye wear paint thicker for the stage than in real life, Francois tellt me. He was one of the actors, played Young Fashion. If I wear it as thin as the lassies do I'll still be recognisable." He took another mouthful of claret, then picked up the pot of vermilion. "I need to be your valet one day and Sir Anthony the next, and be sure that *nobody* kens I'm the same person. If I canna do that, then I willna do this at all." He turned his face to the side and began painting his cheeks with the red paste.

"But you won't be my valet when you're not here," Highbury pointed out.

"No. But I'll be wanting to be other people as well," Alex told him.

"Other people?"

He finished his cheeks, then put the pot down and turned to Highbury.

"Aye. Because London isna too far from Stockwell, is it?"

"Stockwell? No, only a few miles. Why would you want to go there?"

"When I found out my da had died, I had to come home as quickly as possible, but there was a gale at Calais and no one would risk bringing me across, except for some disreputable men who were expert seafarers," Alex explained. "I paid a goodly amount for them to bring me, and then I helped them to unload some goods near Dover.

"On the way we had a wee blether about politics and such things, as ye do, and we found out we shared a number of opinions about certain matters. In between being this creature," he waved a hand down his body, "I'm hoping also to be purchasing things that might be of use in the future. To do that I'll need to be Alex MacGregor, although I willna use that name, and I have to be sure that no one sees the remarkable similarity between myself and the baronet.

"For my sanity, I'll likely also need days when I'm no' the fool and can just go out anonymously," he added, before turning back to the table and picking up a smaller pot of red and a finer brush to outline his lips.

"You mean you're going to smuggle arms into the country for the Jacobites?" Highbury asked, after a short silence. "Isn't that a very dangerous thing to do?"

Alex laughed.

"Aye, but no' as dangerous as what I'm about to do, if I can make Sir Anthony work. As *we're* about to do," he amended. "So ye still need to think on it, William. If ye want to do it, I mean." He stopped speaking then, so he could paint his lips.

"Yes, I want to do it," Highbury said. "I know the danger, and you're right. I've just been thinking about this day for so long, the thought of Sir Anthony the spy has become almost commonplace, and so lost some of its danger to me. Or it had until now," he added, as Alex finished his lips and opened a jar of cloves, taking one out and holding it to the candle. "What do you need cloves for?" he asked. "Will that be a scent? It smells wonderful."

"No. I was tellt the lassies use them to paint their eyebrows black," he said. "If I do, no one will ken the true colour of my hair. I need a scent, but no' one that smells wonderful. I'm wanting something that smells nauseatingly sweet. There," he finished, turning round. "What d'ye think?"

"I think you look absolutely grotesque," Highbury replied candidly. "The paint is horrible. You look like a clown."

"Good," Alex said, as though he'd just been given a compliment. "If anyone asks why my paint is so thick I can become emotional and mention smallpox. And if they're amused by my appearance, then they'll no' look beneath it. Or that's what I'm hoping."

He stood then, pulled his shirt very carefully over his head to ensure it didn't touch his face, put a pair of white silk stockings on, then made his way over to the bed to examine the outfits again. He picked up the scarlet breeches and pulled them on, followed by the waistcoat.

"I'll feel like a damn redcoat if I wear this," he remarked then, picking up the frockcoat, then replacing it on the bed and putting on the peacock-blue one instead.

"Dear God," the earl commented. "Now you *really* look like a clown!"

Alex examined himself in the mirror.

"What do ye think," he asked, "if we have some outfits made wi' the breeches one colour, the waistcoat another, and the coat a third? And all of them clashing, but wi' complementary embroidery, perhaps?"

He took the coat and waistcoat off, replacing them with the yellow waistcoat and blue frockcoat. "So wi' this, for example. If the coat had yellow and scarlet embroidery, and the waistcoat the same pattern, but in blue and scarlet, then it would seem like one outfit, and no' part of three different ones, would it no'?"

"Er...well, I suppose it would, yes," Highbury agreed, looking as though he was about to vomit.

Alex nodded.

"Aye," he said to himself. "The wig, then."

It took a few minutes to arrange the wig properly, then insert a number of pins into his hair, after which Alex jumped up and down, bowed jerkily and shook his head vigorously, without it moving. Then he slipped his feet into the shoes, which were black with silver buckles. "Now do ye recognise me?"

"No," Highbury said immediately. "Not by your appearance, at least. If you want to seem ridiculous, you've succeeded. Everyone will think you an absolute fool. Whether they'll discuss politics in front of you is another matter. I can't believe you really intend to appear in public looking like that."

"How many men think the lassies are fools?" Alex asked then. "That they canna understand serious subjects, like war and politics?"

"A good number, unfortunately," the earl said. "I find such men odious."

"But they still talk in front of them, do they no'? They just dinna ask their opinion, because they ken it'll be stupid and no' worth listening to. And the men who are the most like that are the pompous ones, who have a great need to prove their importance to the silly fragile creatures? And then there are the others who think the lassies are completely absorbed with their embroidery, so canna hear what they're saying to others."

Highbury burst out laughing.

"You have just summarised a number of noblemen of my acquaintance perfectly," he agreed.

"So they'll want to prove their importance to the frenchified fop, I'm thinking. Especially as he's going to appear very impressed by their influence. Or very oblivious, as the situation requires. My shoes are too plain," he added. "I'm wanting brocade ones, wi' embroidery and paste buckles. Ones that ye wouldna want to walk outside in."

Highbury sat down again, and eyed his friend with a mixture of admiration and horror.

"We'll order some in London," he said. "I cannot wait for you to appear in public. I will be convulsed."

"No, ye willna," Alex told him, his face serious now. "While I'm perfecting Sir Anthony in the next months, ye'll be growing accustomed to him. By the time I appear in public ye'll no' think he's amusing at all. In truth, ye mustna. No one must guess I'm anything but what I seem to be. Ye can pity me a wee bit if ye want, for that would be in keeping with your personality and Sir Anthony's tragic background, but ye canna find him laughable. Or no' at first, anyway. This will be a training for you too."

"You're right," Highbury said, sobering up now. "Of course you are." He took out his watch. "Thirty-five minutes," he said, "from when you started painting your face."

"I'll grow faster wi' time," Alex said. "So I need my stock, and as well as the shoes I'm wanting more lace on the front of the shirts, and at my wrists."

"I think you need shoes with no heels," Highbury noted, examining Alex seriously now. "You're already very tall, and don't want to add to it. That could be a distinguishing feature. And your hands won't do at all."

"That's why I'm wanting more lace," Alex explained.

"No, that won't work. You have a...well, a soldier's hands, or a labourer's at least. A nobleman's hands are paler, the skin soft, see."

He held out his hand, which was indeed pale, the fingers long and slender, the nails clean and perfectly manicured. Alex put his hand next to it, tanned, scarred, the fingers long and strong, the nails clean but rough, some of them ridged from being damaged during fighting.

"*Ifrinn,*" he cursed. Highbury was right.

"There are aristocrats who are as tall and broad as you are, for that's God-given. As long as you never undress in public, no one will suspect you to be the warrior you are. If Sir Anthony were a hunting, athletic swordsman, maybe your hands would not attract notice. But then you could not wear all the cosmetics and ridiculous clothes, which I agree you do need to be unrecognisable. If people see that your hands do not match your appearance and personality at all, they'll become curious. And you...we do not want that."

Alex put his hand up to scrub it through his hair, then stopped himself.

"You could wear gloves when outside," Highbury suggested. "Maybe even at a ball, or concert. But they would not be acceptable at dinner. And dinners are where a lot of important conversations take place."

Alex sighed, then sat for a moment, looking at his hands and thinking. Then he raised his head and smiled.

"Then, my dear William," he replied, in the falsetto voice Highbury had last heard coming from the mouth of Lord Foppington, except then he had been speaking French, not English, "I shall have to set a *new* fashion, shall I not?"

"Dear God," Highbury said. "Please tell me that is not the voice you intend for Sir Anthony."

"Aye, I'm thinking it will be. It suits his appearance, does it no'?"

"Well, yes. But will you be able to maintain it? Will it not strain your voice terribly? After all, it's nothing at all like your natural voice."

"Good," Alex said. "I'm thinking I'll be able to maintain it, once I grow accustomed. It's the voice I used for Foppington, after all, and I played him for a few nights wi' no problems. Now we have to perfect the personality to go wi' the appearance." He lifted his glass again and took a sip of wine, very delicately so as not to smear his lip paint.

"That's a good start," Highbury, observing this, said.

"What is?"

"You're drinking like old ladies who wear a lot of paint to try to conceal their age. They sip like that."

"Christ," Alex said. "Maybe I should wear a gown, and change my sex too!" He glanced at Highbury then, and seeing the look of absolute horror on his face as he tried to imagine the burly Highlander in a mantua, started laughing.

"I'm jesting wi' ye, man," he said.

"Oh, thank God for that," the earl replied. "My heart can only take so much."

"Aye. I couldna become a friend of the Elector if I was a lassie, could I?" Alex continued, winking. "Now, as I've got all the makeup and clothes on, shall I practice walking and bowing and suchlike, and ye can give me some advice?"

Several minutes followed in which Alex pranced up and down, leaving and then re-entering the room, bowing and so on, becoming increasingly effeminate as he did, during which time Highbury alternated between laughing until the tears rolled down his cheeks and giving useful comments.

"Please stop for a minute," he begged eventually. "I don't think I've laughed this much since I saw you as Foppington."

Alex took pity on his friend and stopped, but when he came to sit down again, he still fussily arranged the skirts of his frockcoat so they would not crease before sitting.

"You're already transforming yourself into Anthony, aren't you?" Highbury said. "The way you sat down. Alex would never do that," he added when Alex cast him a quizzical look.

"Aye, I suppose I am," he agreed, smiling. He leaned back in the chair, without fussiness. "If I'm going to be him for whole days at a time, and wi' lots of people I dinna ken but need to make an impression on, then I really will need to *be* him. When I did the wee scenes in Paris I didna become Geordie or the fop, because I invented what I thought they'd be like. When I was Beauregard I tried to *think* as the wee shite would have, because that made it a lot easier to be him. Now I dinna ken Anthony, so I have to invent what he *needs* to be to allow me to enter society but no' be recognised if everything goes wrong and I have to flee. But to do that I'll need to immerse myself in him completely.

"So I'm thinking that once we've perfected his mannerisms and gestures, and his basic personality, then the minute I put the makeup on, I'll have to *become* him. No' what I'm doing now, being myself one second and Anthony the next. If I do that I'll end up speaking Scots in the middle of a dinner or some such mistake. And when I'm no' Anthony, then we need to think and speak of him as a separate person. For if Alex MacGregor isna Sir Anthony Peters, and never can be, then Sir Anthony Peters can never be Alex MacGregor."

"So you need to keep a distance between the two, in your head, to ensure you never accidentally become the one while you're being the other," Highbury said.

"Aye, that's it exactly," Alex agreed. "But you need to do that too. Even when it's just the two of us together, like now. We must speak of him in the third person. And when I *am* him, ye must *always* be wi' him, and forget me entirely. If we can both do that, then there's much less chance we'll make a stupid mistake, and we'll feel more at ease wi' each other, and behave more naturally when we're wi' others."

Highbury sighed.

"This is going to be a lot more difficult than I realised," he said.

"Only at first. It'll become easier wi' time. And we've got the winter to do it in," Alex told him. "If we canna get it right by then, I think we should abandon the whole thing, for all our sakes. The prince will have to manage without an honest spy."

Highbury nodded.

"Let's do our utmost to get it right then," he said. "But today let's mould the baronet enough so we can both believe in him. Now, walk up and down again, because there was something not quite right, but I couldn't quite ascertain what it was."

Alex pranced up and down the bedroom a few more times.

"You're too erect," the earl said finally. "Your legs are taking tiny steps like a fop would, but your stance is proud, confident. Your upper body is still that of a Highland chieftain. You need to be more...I don't know exactly. Limp?" he suggested.

"Limp." Alex stood for a minute, pondering this. He cast his mind back to when he'd been standing in the wings of the theatre in Paris, watching Francois, and contemplating how Foppington would act. And then he remembered how he'd prepared himself. "Aye," he said softly, to himself.

Then he rotated his neck, rolled his shoulders backwards and forwards a few times, stretched and then slumped his shoulders and spine, before relaxing his arms completely so that they became almost boneless.

He stood then for a moment longer, focussing intently on his posture, clearly oblivious to the presence of the earl, who sat watching in fascination as Alex, physically at least, transformed himself completely into the baronet. The slumping of his shoulders made him shorter somehow, although that was surely impossible. His movements became languid, his wrist bent slightly, his fingers, still tanned and scarred, now graceful. Then he sighed, and in that moment was back, Sir Anthony now, turning to smile ingratiatingly at the earl.

Then he minced across the room, and this time he was utterly effeminate, without a single trace of the Highlander he had still been until a few moments ago. At the doorway he turned and then bowed, gracefully, perfectly, just a touch too elaborately, as someone who wore such ridiculous clothes and paint surely would.

"My dear Lord Highbury!" he gushed. "I cannot tell you how utterly honoured I am to make your acquaintance!"

Highbury stood up then, returned the bow, and started clapping.

"You are remarkable," he said. "Yes, that is perfect. You even seem shorter by a few inches."

"Excellent!" Sir Anthony trilled. "Now may I suggest we go down to our formal dinner? I am so looking forward to the delightful cuisine and exquisite company! And I shall remain in character for the next hours," he continued, still in the baronet's falsetto voice.

"I'm afraid you may be a little disappointed by the food, Sir Anthony," Highbury replied, making his first attempt to forget Alex and see only the baronet. "We will be dining informally tonight."

"Oh, how exciting!" cried Sir Anthony. "But I am sure that such a high-ranking nobleman as yourself eats nothing but the most tender morsels. I must admit my constitution is delicate and I a mere baronet, so how much more so must yours, as an earl, be? I am confident the food will be unsurpassable, and the informality will only allow us to become acquainted with each other far sooner than would otherwise be the case."

The evening continued in this manner, the baronet acting as though they were eating the most formal of banquets, rather than an assortment of bread rolls, sliced meats and cheeses, followed by almond cakes. He kept up a smooth and continuous flow of vacuous conversation as he did, and after a short while, in spite of having believed it impossible, Highbury began to respond appropriately, and even to half-believe he was in the presence of the gossipy, somewhat feeble-minded but friendly person the baronet appeared to be.

So when, several hours later, after they'd eaten all the food, the baronet delicately and fussily, the earl in his normal manner, had played the card game Mariage for a time, and then had repaired to the drawing room for brandy, on Alex's voice suddenly emerging from Anthony's mouth, Highbury actually jumped.

"I'm thinking ye'll have no problem forgetting Alex when ye're wi' Anthony, once we've practiced him a wee bit more," Alex said. "Ye did well tonight."

"In truth you made it easy," Highbury told him. "I felt a bit silly at first, but you were so unrelentingly the baronet, after a while I think it would have been more ridiculous to have treated you as Alex when you so clearly weren't."

Alex smiled then, his eyes, the only recognisable part of him, lighting up.

"You have a dimple," the earl commented. "Is that something you wouldn't want people to know about?"

Alex reached his hand up automatically to the side of his mouth.

"*Bàs mallaichte!*" he cursed. "Aye, I'd rather there was *nothing* recognisable about me. I canna do anything about my height and build. I can get the finest leather gloves possible for my hands, but if I fill the dimple wi' paint it'll draw more attention to it than if I leave it."

"You could wear a patch," Highbury suggested. "If you don't want people to suspect there's something underneath it, you could maybe wear a shaped one, like a heart, or a cat. They're very fashionable, for ladies at least. People would maybe just think you're hiding a particularly deep smallpox pit."

"Aye, that's a bonny idea," Alex said. "Can we buy them in Durham?"

"I would imagine so, but I'm not certain. They're not something I've ever felt a need to purchase."

Alex reached up then and pulled out the pins holding his wig on, then took it off, before taking the ribbons out of his hair and scratching his scalp vigorously.

"Wigs are awfu' hot. And itchy," he commented, kicking off his shoes and relaxing back in the chair. Highbury looked at him.

"Go and remove your paint," he said. "You've clearly finished being the baronet for tonight, but the last thing I need to remember when we're doing this in reality is the sight of you sitting there with the face of a clown and your hair looking as though you've just been charging across the battlefield, sword in hand."

"I dinna wear my hair loose on the battlefield. Ye dinna want it blowing in your face when ye're fighting for your life," Alex said matter-of-factly. "But aye, ye're right. It'll be easier for both of us if when I stop being Sir Anthony I take his disguise off too. Unless I canna, if I'm expecting someone else to call soon, in which case, if we need to discuss something as Alex and William, I'll stay in character as much as I can. I'll come back down as quickly as possible."

He stood up and went to the door, then turned back to his friend.

"I'm thinking we can maybe do this after all," he said. "Wi' a wee bit more practise."

He went out then, leaving Highbury to sit and think that although he wouldn't have believed it a few short hours ago, now he thought that it was actually possible they *could* do this extraordinary thing.

As long as he could work out a way to both remember and not remember the likely horrendous consequences that would follow if they failed to do it perfectly.

Edinburgh, December 1740

"Damn!" Angus cursed, eyeing his toppled king with irritation. "I really thought I'd beat ye this time."

The two men were sitting in Francis Ogilvy's library, a cheery fire crackling in the hearth and the lamps already lit, although it was only early afternoon. Outside the sleet pattered against the window, but indoors it was warm and cosy, as it always was at the doctor's.

"Ye're improving," Iain said, collecting the pieces together. "Are ye wanting another game?"

Angus glanced longingly outside.

"Aye, go on, then," he said, shifting restlessly in his chair.

"It isna obligatory," Iain replied good-humouredly. "Ye can say no."

"It isna that I dinna want to. I'm just no' very good at sitting for such a long time," Angus admitted.

"Well ye canna practise your riding in this," Iain replied.

"Aye, I suppose so. Although I'll need to ken how to ride in bad weather as well as good, will I no'?" Angus asked.

"There isna much difference, no' on roads, at any rate, although ye'll likely no' be wanting to gallop if it's slippery underfoot. Ye'll get wet, and the rain drives more into your face than it does when ye're walking," Iain told him. "But ye get there quicker, there is that. And then ye have to dry the horse so he doesna catch a chill, and tend to the saddle and suchlike too, unless ye're at an inn that has stableboys to do it for ye, which I'm thinking ye likely will be. If ye're travelling across the Highlands wi' such a mount as Apollo though, ye'll be walking anyway, for he isna designed for such terrain. Dr Ogilvy canna teach ye in such weather, though."

"No, I wouldna ask him to teach me. Susan would kill me if I even suggested it!" Angus replied, grinning. "Maybe I'll just away out for a wee stroll."

"Aye, ye could," Iain said, putting the chess pieces back in their box. "Or if ye want I could show ye some of a servant's duties. Ye were asking me about them the last time I was here. Or I'll come out wi' ye for the walk. Mr Munro'll no' be needing me until he's wanting to dress for dinner later."

"Ye'd come out wi' me in this?" Angus asked.

"Are ye thinking it doesna rain in the east of Scotland?" Iain asked.

Angus laughed.

"No. I forget sometimes ye're a clansman like myself. Ye've the ways of the city people about ye."

"Aye, well, I had to learn them, when I moved to Edinburgh," Iain said. "It makes life a lot easier if ye learn to fit in wi' your surroundings."

As Alex is learning to do now, Angus thought, but did not say. He was Angus Drummond, brother to Alex Drummond. They had met Dr Ogilvy years ago when they'd been in Edinburgh and had needed medical assistance, and had become friendly. That was all Mr Munro's servant needed to know.

In fairness Iain had shown no curiosity regarding the background of Dr Ogilvy's friends. They were here, they behaved in a friendly manner towards him, and that was all he seemed to care about. He had been equally reticent about his background when Angus had mentioned it, saying only that he used to live in the Huntly area of the north-east, and now didn't.

"D'ye miss it?" Angus asked then.

"Miss what?" Iain said.

"Clan life. Home."

Iain was quiet for so long that Angus was just about to apologise, when he suddenly spoke.

"Sometimes. There are some things I miss. But I'm different to you. I had good reasons to leave. I chose to come here, to be a servant. Your brother tellt ye to come and learn to ride, did he no'? It's a different thing."

"Aye, he did. But I dinna mind that. I'm enjoying learning new things. We wouldna be doing a lot at home this time of the year anyway," Angus said. "Ye'll ken that yourself."

"Aye. Well, then, are ye wanting to learn what else I do, apart from playing chess wi' the master? Or are ye determined to get cold and wet?"

At that moment the sleet became hail, battering the windows like gunshots. Angus opted for learning what else Iain did.

"So when Mr Munro employed me, it was as a footman," Iain explained. "In most houses the footman does a lot of stupid duties, and a few necessary ones. So the necessary ones are cleaning the glasses, knives and suchlike – ye do that before ye dress, for a large part of a footman's role is to look as though his employer's wealthy and powerful. That's why I wear a livery, like this," he added, gesturing at his blue velvet outfit, liberally embroidered with silver. "The silver and the quality of the velvet tells everyone who sees me that my master is a man of importance. Footmen are usually tall and handsome as well. I'm no' handsome, but Mr Munro was more concerned wi' my discretion and versatility than my looks. He doesna insist I wear a wig all the time, either, although if he's hosting an important dinner or evening, then I do."

"He invites you to his dinners?" Angus asked.

"No' as a guest! I set the table out beforehand, and I serve the guests, then stay in the room in case any of them need their glasses refilling, that sort of thing. Ye have to stay alert, for ye can be standing there for hours, but need to watch everyone in case they need something."

"So it's a wee bit like being on watch for enemies coming?" Angus asked, that being the only thing he'd done that seemed anywhere near as boring as what Iain was describing.

"Aye, a wee bit. There are usually a few footmen at dinner, depending on how many guests there are. I'm the only one Mr Munro employs – if he has a large dinner, which he rarely does now, then he hires some, and I have to watch them as well as the guests, to make sure they behave as they should and dinna steal anything."

"But ye can listen to all the conversation the nobles are having over dinner. Some of it must be awfu' interesting," Angus said, thinking maybe Alex would be better being a footman than a nobleman, if he wanted to be a spy. Although he wouldn't be able to go to other houses then, maybe. Or meet the usurper.

"Christ, no. The most of it's awfu' tedious, all nasty gossip and lies. There are some gems of conversation though, especially if there are lords there, or yon political men. And that's why my discretion's important, for Mr Munro kens I'll no' repeat anything I hear anywhere else. In my experience most footmen dinna do that. They canna wait to join the other servants to share what they've heard, and complain about how ill-used they are."

"But ye dinna do that."

"Never. I usually get away when I can, eat my food outside if possible."

"Ye mustna be very popular then, if ye dinna share things and they're expecting ye to," Angus said. "Is it no' lonely?"

"I've never cared much what people think of me, particularly people who canna keep a confidence, when they've promised to," Iain replied, somewhat surprised. "Ye dinna seem a man who does either."

"Oh no! I didna mean it in that way. No, if someone tells me a secret, then I treat it as though I've sworn on the iron no' to tell, even if I havena. I meant wi' no clan. Do ye no' need to make friends among the servants, so ye willna feel lonely?" Angus asked.

"Ah. No. I'm no' a person who feels the need for people round me all the time. I like good conversation sometimes, but I'm happy wi' my own company too."

"Ye're like Duncan then," Angus said. "He's our middle brother. He spends a lot of time on his own, and doesna care much what people think of him. I miss him, and Alex."

"Ye're awfu' close to each other," Iain remarked.

"Aye, we are. It's a bonny feeling," Angus agreed. "So, what else do ye do?"

"A footman often rides on the back of the coach, to watch out for highwaymen, and shoot anyone who tries to rob the master. But I usually drive the coach, for I ken how to do that too, and I also ken how to shoot and use a sword. Most of the footpads in Edinburgh ken that, and that Mr Munro willna hesitate to shoot either, so they leave us alone. The ones who dinna soon find out. We rarely travel outside the town.

"As well as that, I do things footmen dinna usually do, such as help the master to dress and undress, keep the books, take care of the horses, and watch over the other servants," Iain finished.

"So everything that requires a person he can trust," Angus said. "And ye keep him company too."

"Aye, that's about the way of it. So, if ye want I can show ye how to lay a table for a formal dinner. There's a way of doing it. It isna as simple as ye think. I dinna think Dr. Ogilvy'll mind, if we put everything back. He'll likely be at his game for a wee while yet."

"Aye, that'll be bonny!" Angus said. "I'd like that."

"Really? I canna think why ye'd find it interesting. But I suppose if your chief gives an important dinner for other chiefs he needs to make a good impression wi', ye'll be able to teach his servants how to do things, if they dinna already ken."

Angus laughed at the thought of Kenneth, Allan, Gregor, Barbara and the like, sitting round the little table in Alex's house, with powdered wigs and velvet kilts, drinking out of crystal glasses. He was about to share this amusing image with Iain when he suddenly remembered that he was a Drummond, not a MacGregor.

The Clan Drummond chief was a duke, if he remembered rightly. Iain would be suspicious if he reminisced about the clan chieftain's modest home, and he'd be more likely to make a mistake too, say something he shouldn't. Mr Munro might value Iain Gordon's discretion, and Angus instinctively liked the man, but that was not enough to let his guard down. Also, Angus realised, knowing how to set a table for chiefs and nobles to eat at might be useful to his brother, who was even now learning how to be such a person.

Angus very much wished to help his brother, in any way he could.

"I canna imagine the chief asking me to help at a dinner," he said then, to explain his sudden snort of laughter, "but I love learning all manner of new things, useful or no'. And then later, if we've time, maybe we can have another game."

"Aye, maybe, although I daresay we'll visit again soon. There isna much happening in the winter, so they tend to play a lot more chess together then. Right, so first of all, let me show you how to fold napkins so they look fancy. Ye can make them into wee roses, which the lassies love, or swans."

"Will we set the table anyway? For even if Mr Munro doesna stay for dinner, me, Susan and Francis usually eat in here. Mrs Ferguson sets the table, but she doesna fold napkins like roses. I'm thinking Susan would like that!" Angus suggested

"Aye, that's a good idea! We'll set it for the four of ye, just in case," Iain replied.

"Five of us," Angus amended. "For if Mr Munro stays, you will too, and I'm thinking ye should have dinner wi' us. The cook always makes too much anyway. There'll be plenty for you."

Iain, who was laying out a napkin ready to demonstrate the fold, looked uncertain about this.

"Ye're my friend," Angus said impulsively. "I'm inviting ye to dinner, for I'll certainly be coming. Mr Munro doesna seem a man who'd object to that. It would be good to have someone closer to my own age to blether wi' too," he admitted. "But I'm relying on your discretion to keep that secret."

Iain laughed then for the first time since Angus had met him, a surprisingly rich, infectious laugh for a man who until now had seemed a very sober person, as though he was weighed down with something, perhaps whatever had made him leave his clan. Angus could not imagine *anything* that would make him do that. He would die first.

But in that moment it was clear that there was a whole other side to this quiet, sober man. He was interesting, worth getting to know better, Angus thought.

He was here for the winter, as the weather now made it unlikely he'd be able to go home for a while yet, and apart from perfecting his riding skills and raiding Francis's library for books, he had plenty of time on his hands. It would be good to spend part of it drawing this man out of his shell a little, maybe making him less lonely.

For he certainly *was* lonely, Angus decided. He did not seem to be like Duncan, who was relaxed and happy to be alone much of the time. Iain had a sort of sadness clinging to him, as Duncan had had just after Màiri died. Angus felt no need to find out what had happened to make him sad – he respected the privacy of others. But he did feel a great wish to make people happy, if possible. And here was a man in need of such a service.

It would be a great winter project.

CHAPTER FIFTEEN

February 1741

"Ah, we're entering London now," Highbury said, with no enthusiasm whatsoever. "This is St John's Street. We should arrive at my house soon."

"You don't like London?" Alex asked, who had travelled south with the earl as his valet, and intended to retain the role for much of his time in the capital.

"This is your first time here," Highbury replied. "Open the blind and decide for yourself. Do not open the window at this point. You will know why anyway, soon enough."

Alex opened the blind to be greeted by fields, which, although not beautiful, to him did not seem to warrant the earl's response. When he looked forward as best he could without opening the window, he could see in the hazy distance many buildings.

"Ahead is Smithfield," Highbury told him. "We're fortunate that it isn't market day. If it was we would be here until midnight, although the driver would certainly have taken another route. It's the animal market," he added somewhat unnecessarily as the stench from the place began to pervade the interior of the coach as they grew closer.

"Ifr...dear God," Alex exclaimed, the smell having almost made him forget he was an English valet. "That's disgusting!"

Even with the windows firmly closed, it was indeed disgusting. The smell of stale urine, manure and decomposing blood and flesh was horrendous. Highbury took a cotton handkerchief from his pocket and handed it to his friend.

"Inhale," he said, taking another out and bunching it over his nose. Alex followed suit, gratefully allowing the scent of citrus, cinnamon and other sweet spices to fill his nostrils, although nothing could obliterate the smell entirely. He looked out at the huge area filled with pens in which he assumed the animals were kept on market days, trying to imagine what the smell must be like then. And in summer. It was winter now, yet the stench was sickening!

"In the Highlands, the houses have a byre, and in the winter the animals are kept there," Alex said, still keeping his English accent, but confident that the growing noise of traffic and people as they travelled further into the city meant that his words would not be heard from outside. "It's convenient for the milking, keeps them safe and also warms the house. But it doesn't smell like that! We slope the floor a bit so the piss runs out, and it's cleaned out regularly."

"Cleaning things out is harder to do when there are over half a million people living in the town," Highbury said. "No, keep it," he added when Alex made to give the handkerchief back. "You will need it until your nose becomes accustomed to the city smells. I will get you a bottle of the scent. I find it very useful. And it might be a good affectation for Sir Anthony, too. Not plain cotton though. I think lace-edged handkerchiefs for him."

Alex smiled at that. Sir Anthony was on both their minds constantly now, and one or other of them would keep thinking of a possible gesture, turn of phrase or affectation that might suit the man, now they had fixed his physical appearance.

They had turned away from the market now, down Cow Lane and then along Holborn.

"There have been a lot of complaints about the smell of Smithfield," Highbury continued, "but as you can imagine, half a million citizens require a great deal of food, and if the meat market was not there, it would have to be somewhere else. This whole area is very insalubrious. Chick Lane, which we passed a few moments ago, is full of the worst taverns, brothels and molly houses you can imagine. Well, maybe not worse than you can imagine," he amended, remembering where Alex had lodged in Paris, "but I would not advise you to go there, either as my valet or as Sir Anthony. Even as yourself you would be in danger, unless perhaps with your clansmen around you.

"The same could be said of the area we're now approaching. To the left is St Giles. As you can see even from the window, it's massively overcrowded, and many of the buildings are in a ramshackle state. The Irish labourers live here, and they're resented by many for taking jobs from the local workers. There's a lot of gang warfare because of that, and gin has made the whole situation much worse. I think even with your clan you might have problems here," the earl finished, smiling at Alex. "If you want to go out alone while you're in London, you must tell me, so I can advise you of the parts to avoid at all costs."

"How do you know all this?" Alex asked, finding it very difficult to imagine the man he knew wandering around a street full of molly houses, or a gang-infested hellhole.

"I don't know a great deal about such areas. I've never visited them, nor do I wish to, but it's necessary for anyone with a son such as mine to know these things exist and their locations. He would never have reason to go to St Giles, but he might be foolish enough to seek sexual adventures in places like Chick Lane, particularly at times when I refuse to advance his allowance or pay his gambling debts."

"I'm sorry you have such a son," Alex replied, not knowing what else to say. "Will he be in London?"

"No, he will not. I will take great pains to ensure the two of you never meet, although once you enter society alone as Sir Anthony I won't be able to prevent it, of course."

"You're worried that I may harm him," Alex said.

"Yes, I am," the earl admitted, giving Alex his full attention now. "Because he is foolish enough to challenge you to a duel, and if not that, will certainly mock you unmercifully if he meets you as Sir Anthony, and possibly insult you if he meets you as you are now. In truth, I'm not afraid of you provoking him, for you're an honourable man. I'm more concerned that he will put you in a position where you have no choice but to defend yourself from an idiotic challenge. Ah, here we are," Highbury continued, his face brightening as the coach turned down a narrow street lined with tall buildings, which then opened out to become a large open square, in the centre of which appeared to be a garden, although it was walled and fenced, so Alex couldn't be sure of what was inside. Around the edges of the square were many houses, most of them three stories tall, but all slightly different from each other.

The coach drew to a halt outside one of these, and Highbury prepared to get out, once the footman had lowered the steps.

"You will enter with me, and I'll introduce you to the staff," he said. The house door was already open, and a number of people were coming out to line up. "Do not offer to carry your own baggage. You're my valet, and your bedroom will be next to mine, so that I can call you at any time. You can't eat with me here as you did in Durham though, unfortunately. You'll eat with my gentleman of the horse, and the gentleman usher. They're both quite reserved, so I doubt you'll be bombarded with questions. But you can still spend a deal of time in my rooms, so we can continue our planning."

He opened the door then and walked down the steps, becoming as he did completely the aristocratic Earl of Highbury, making Alex realise that until now he had never seen this side of the man. He had seen the nobleman completely out of his depth in Paris, the philanthropist, the noble tourist, and the relaxed casual wealthy man in his country retreat. Above all he had seen the warm, friendly, open-minded and caring, if somewhat shy and introverted human being William truly was.

But he had never seen the formal face of the Earl of Highbury, greeting his servants, introducing his new valet Mr Drummond and informing them all that the man would be spending a good deal of time with him both in his rooms and visiting his tailor, as he intended to completely replace his city wardrobe, and Drummond was fortunately an expert in the latest fashions, and that he would eat with Mr Rood and Mr Ingles, as befitted his position.

And then they swept upstairs and in a few minutes were sitting in his private suite, in which a fire had been burning for some time, candles were lit, curtains drawn, and their luggage brought up to their rooms.

"No, don't unpack now," the earl said, as three footmen began to do just that. "I am weary after such a long and arduous journey, and wish to rest for a while. Indeed I'm sure Drummond is also. He can unpack my clothes when I am a little refreshed, and perhaps we can discuss what should be replaced.

"I see there is brandy. Tonight, Drummond, you may also have a brandy, as you have shared the rigours of the journey with me and must also be weary. I trust you will not take advantage of my generosity and can be trusted not to help yourself when I am absent. Nor to lounge on my sofas, as you are now being allowed to do. This is an exception, not the rule."

"Indeed not, my lord," Alex replied, immediately sitting forward, spine erect. "In fact I rarely imbibe strong spirits, although I will be most grateful for your kindness this evening, as I am chilled to the bone."

"I'm glad to hear it. You may relax for now, though. It has been a difficult few days."

"So you're a strict master then," Alex said, once he had filled two glasses and resumed his seat, the footmen having left a minute or two ago.

"Not at Skelthorpe Hall, no," Highbury said, kicking off his shoes and putting his legs up on the sofa. "But in London, yes. Servants here are quite a different thing to country servants. Most of the ones at Skelthorpe have been with me for years, and we have a mutual respect for each other. I trust them, mostly, know their families, most of whom are my tenants. They see me more as a paterfamilias. Here it's very difficult to keep servants for years. It's impossible for me to know their backgrounds – I have to rely on characters, which can be bought or forged, and I cannot trust anyone. The ones you will be dining with have been with me for years and are reliable and trustworthy – at least I've always found them so. But of course you must be very careful what you say to them, as blackmail is a wonderful way for an ambitious servant to procure an annuity for life, and power over his or her master too.

"So I am fair, but I have to be strict. If I was not they would take as many liberties as they could. As it is I'm sure they take a few, but they are careful, for they know that if I find out I'll at the least dismiss them, and at worst prosecute them."

"Interesting. I've not seen this side of you before, the privileged aristocrat, if you like. It seems you too act a part, as I am and will be doing in a different way next year," Alex said.

"I never thought of it like that," Highbury replied after a moment. "Yes, I suppose you're right, although I don't take on a completely different identity as you'll be doing. I behave as I was brought up to, as an earl is expected to. I'm just a more formal version of the person you've known for a few years. In fact you've seen me as no one else has, when we were travelling."

"So finding servants for Sir Anthony is going to be more of a problem than I thought," Alex said. "Although anyone who attempts to blackmail me will only do it once."

When Highbury had absorbed the implication of this sentence, he blinked.

"Alex, you cannot kill people here as you might in the Highlands," he said.

"I don't see why not," Alex replied matter-of-factly. "I've done it in Edinburgh. And Paris, although you're the first person I've told that to, about Paris, that is. You just have to be more careful about disposing of the body. Otherwise it's actually easier than in the Highlands."

"Is it?"

"Yes. Because there are a lot more people here. You said yourself on the way here that it wouldn't be safe for me to go to Smithfield or St Giles alone. I'm assuming from that there are a lot of people in the city willing to kill. People must go missing all the time. No one would suspect a foppish baronet, when there are so many more likely suspects all around us. At home my clan is the equivalent of the gangs of St Giles. Every MacGregor is suspected. Of everything."

Highbury passed his hand over his face.

"I'm not intending to murder my servants," Alex reassured him. "I'm just thinking finding the right ones is going to be one of our biggest problems. And I will need some at least. It will be too suspicious if I have none. I'm not intending to murder your son, either," he added, "no matter how much he provokes me. As your valet I could not, and as Sir Anthony I will be too afraid of bloodshed, probably inept with weapons. I see you're not reassured."

"You have not met Daniel. He could provoke a saint. It's a miracle Harriet hasn't killed him, on more than one occasion. I will admit that it's one of my greatest fears – not that you will kill him, but that someone will, and with justification. Indeed, if he calls you out in company then you will have to answer."

Alex leaned forward then, seeing the depth of the fear in Highbury's eyes.

"I'm no' going to lie to ye," he said then, forgetting his Englishness in his sincerity and need to reassure this man he loved. "If the wee gomerel taunts me, I'll be sore tempted, no' to kill him, but to teach him a lesson, as I did wi' yon Joseph laddie. But I willna. No matter what he does. I willna respond to him. Ye ken I've a bad temper, but ye also ken the weight of an oath sworn on the iron to a Highlander." He reached into his inside coat pocket and withdrew his dirk, which he unsheathed and laid his hand on. "I swear to ye now, that I will never physically harm your son, unless it's to protect him from worse harm if I dinna."

Highbury sat up then.

"You are serious!" he exclaimed.

"Aye, deadly serious. For whatever I may think of the son, I respect the father. Ye've earned my trust and my loyalty, and that's no' an easy thing to do. Does that reassure ye?"

"Yes. Yes, it does," the earl replied. "More than you can imagine, although you do not know what you are promising."

"Maybe," Alex said, sheathing his dirk again and replacing it in his pocket. "But I'll hold to it anyway."

"Thank you," Highbury replied simply, a world of gratitude in his voice. "Have you been carrying that all the time we've been travelling?"

"Aye, of course," Alex said. "I never travel without some means of defence. I canna carry a sword in England, but if no one kens ye've got a weapon unless ye need it, then no questions are asked. I've a wee pocket inside my coats for the purpose."

"In all your coats?"

"Aye. Well, no' the ones that Sir Anthony will wear. But I can carry a sword as a baronet, can I no'?"

"Yes. We must have one made for you. For you certainly cannot carry that fearsome thing. If it was somehow discovered on you..."

"Aye. I'm wanting something wi' a lot of silly jewels, paste and suchlike on the hilt, so it seems a mere decoration, and an ornate sheath. But I need to be able to draw it smoothly, and it be razor sharp, no' an ornament. Let's not think of that tonight though, or any more about Anthony," he added, seeing the weariness on his friend's face, and feeling a heaviness in his own limbs and eyelids as the warmth of the fire penetrated his bones.

They did not think of that tonight. Instead they drank their brandy, then unpacked the earl's clothes together, after which Alex ate supper with Mr Rood and Mr Ingles, both of whom were not the sort of men he would ever want to have more than a passing acquaintance with, being humourless and dull, but who, on the positive side, showed a spectacular lack of interest in knowing any more than the basics about him.

The earl ate supper alone in the large and somewhat chilly dining room. It was the first time he had eaten alone since November, and although he had thought he would enjoy the novelty, he found himself feeling lonely instead, and wishing he had told his staff that his valet would dine with him after all.

But even as he did he realized he could not do anything that might arouse suspicion. While it might be considered a mere eccentricity at the moment, once Sir Anthony exploded onto the world, as Highbury was sure Alex intended him to do, nobody could ever have the slightest suspicion that Mr Drummond had ever been more than a servant, and an unsatisfactory one at that, as he would soon have to prove to be.

"So, tell me then, why is it that this delightful rose pink fabric is so much more expensive than the yellow?" the inquisitive young man asked, who had expressed a desire to buy a beautiful mantua for his betrothed and a fine new suit for himself, in the hope of being presented to the king in the spring. As the silk mercer had cast an expert eye over the gentleman's current outfit and judged him to be a man of wealth, and even better, from his ignorance of materials, a foolish one, his patience was endless as he answered the myriad questions posed by his potential customer.

"The price depends not so much on the colour, my lord," the mercer explained, "but on the complexity of the weave structure, the pattern, or on the weight of the fabric. If you feel the weight of the pink, you will note that it is much heavier than the yellow," he added, inviting the man to hold a piece of each material. "In addition, as you can see by the sparkle of the fabric – so enchanting when worn in candlelight, as it appears as though the gown is sprinkled with tiny stars – it is delicately woven with silver thread."

"Oh, that would be delightful to see!" the lovestruck fool cried. "You are right, it is very much heavier. And with the silver as well, I can certainly understand the additional expense. Would it not be perhaps wearying, though, for my beloved to wear such a weighty gown? I do want her to enjoy rather than endure the occasion, you know."

"Oh no, my lord! She will hardly notice the difference in weight, as it will be distributed across the whole gown, and the panniers take a deal of the burden from the legs," the mercer lied smoothly. "I am sure she will find the exquisite effect of the silver thread far outweighs the slight difference in weight. She will feel like a princess!"

"I am sure you are right," the young lord said, holding the fabric close to his face. "The weave is very even. But what about that fabric? The purple," he asked, pointing to a roll on the top shelf. "That is glorious!"

The mercer, his counter already covered in fabrics, suppressed a sigh.

"Oh, what excellent taste you have!" he exclaimed, as he called his young assistant over to fetch it down. "Now that is indeed a silk a princess, or indeed even a queen, would not be ashamed to wear! It is from Lyons, in France. Their brocades are justifiably admired. That one has wide bands of silver thread which will sparkle beautifully as with the pink silk, and is also woven with coloured silk threads, which form the most delightful floral pattern, as you will see in a moment."

"Oh, it is not embroidered then?" the tiresome young man asked.

"No, it is brocade, which means the decoration is woven into the fabric. Embroidery is usually done on completed garments. Here," he added, rolling the fabric across the only remaining empty part of the long counter.

"I do indeed think that will be the one I choose for her. Although...could that also be made into a suit for a gentleman?"

"You mean for yourself?"

"Well, yes. I am quite enchanted with it. Perhaps we will have matching outfits! That will surely announce our love to the world, will it not?"

"Er...yes, it certainly would convey a message indeed," the mercer said, watching anxiously as the idiot's companion, possibly his father, abruptly exited the shop.

"Well, I think I will call with my betrothed for her opinion on this before I buy," the lord replied. "But I shall certainly want an outfit for myself, even if she does not approve of it for her gown." He smiled warmly. "I am quite decided|! What a delightful man you are, so patient. It will be a pleasure to do business with you."

"And with you, my lord," the mercer replied, wondering if the likely profit to be made would be worth the vast amount of time spent answering stupid questions.

"Dear God, but you really try me, at times," Lord Highbury said when his friend emerged from the mercer's clutching a business card a few minutes later. "The thought of you, or rather the baronet, flouncing into St James's Palace with an unfortunate woman on your arm, both attired in identical purple flowery outfits almost undid me."

Alex laughed.

"It's good practice for when I do become the baronet," he said. "I'm sure I'll be uttering far more outrageous comments than that when I do. It's difficult today, I know, because I'm a new person. You've become really adept at reacting to the valet and the baronet now, though. I think if I'd trilled all that nonsense as Sir Anthony, by now you'd have just seemed bored, or be rolling your eyes to heaven. We've both had two months to become accustomed to him, after all."

"I suppose that's true," Highbury agreed. "I'm still astonished by how effortlessly you can change not just your voice and accent, but your mannerisms too. If you ever take to the stage properly you could make your fortune."

"I've no wish to make my fortune. Just to go home, and be happy," Alex said as they began to walk back to the coach, which was at the end of the street, outside a button-maker's they'd earlier spent an hour at.

"You still intend to go back in the spring? I thought you might decide to stay and take up your new position immediately. You seem ready to me, once we find a house. There are two I'd like to show you, once you've finished taxing the patience of clothing merchants."

"I'm thinking that Sir Anthony should have a suit in the purple brocade though," Alex said, ignoring the earl's question. "All in the one colour, for more sober occasions."

"That will be a sober outfit?" Highbury laughed.

"It will. The purple was not too bright, and the flowers complemented it, rather than clashing. And the material looked very expensive to me at least."

"It will be. It would certainly tell everyone you were a wealthy man. Very well. Where do you want to go to next?"

"Are you not weary yet?" Alex asked as they climbed into the coach.

"No. You're the one doing all the work, well, you and the poor assistants. And we've set aside this week for you to learn all you can about fashion, so I'm resigned to it."

"Perhaps a lace-man then. I never knew there were so many fabrics before. Today has been an enlightening experience. I've spent most of my life dressed in linen and wool. But now I know a lot about the different materials and buttons, I need to learn about trimmings, lace, embroidery. I know a great deal about tailoring now from being fitted for the suits we have so far. But I want to know as much as possible about all the other aspects. Shoes and wigs too. And stays."

"Stays?" Highbury asked. "You won't be wearing stays!"

"No, but the ladies do. The stays form the body shape that the garments hang on. The mercer told me that. Part of the reason I'm learning all this nonsense is to perfect Sir Anthony."

"And to have a legitimate reason to disappear to France periodically," Highbury added.

"Yes. But a lot of the reason is to ingratiate myself with the ladies. Men talk in front of women. And they confide in them in their private chambers, when the servants aren't listening. You told me that," Alex said.

"Yes, that's true. I used to confide in Annie. But she would never have divulged any of my confidences."

"I'm sure she wouldn't. But not every wife is like yours. I want to be able to mix with the ladies so well that they almost forget I'm not one of them. I'll look so ridiculous that no man will worry about their wife's virtue with me. I think it could be a rich seam of possible information."

Highbury looked at his friend, now sitting opposite him, deep in thought about what he needed to learn, and considered this. Alex MacGregor was certainly one of the most handsome men he'd ever met. As he'd spent the last two days trailing round various merchants, then merely observing as Alex played the part of the lovestruck young fool to perfection, he had observed how the ladies reacted to him. All the ladies, both young and old. They couldn't take their eyes off him. And although they reacted in different ways, according to their ages and personalities, it had been quite obvious to Highbury that they all found him compelling. And one of the most attractive things about him was that although he was almost certainly aware of their reactions, because he noticed everything, he seemed completely indifferent to them.

"Are all the Highlanders handsome?" Highbury blurted out. They were in a closed carriage now; their conversation would not be overheard.

Alex came back from wherever he was.

"Handsome? No, they're like everyone else, I think. Some are, and some are not. Same with the lassies...the ladies. My da was a handsome man, everyone said that. I haven't really thought about it. Why do you ask?"

"I think it was what you said about Sir Anthony not being a threat to wives. I agree with you. He does look hideous. It would be a very different matter if they could see under the paint though."

"Maybe. But they won't. And the last thing I want is to attract women, so that's a good thing. I'm thinking I maybe need to spend a whole day learning about trimmings and suchlike," Alex said, still focussed on the task in hand, "because the basics of the garments, men's and women's, don't seem to change quickly. But the trimmings do. They're what set the fashion for the season."

"Yes, that's true. Even for the wealthy, clothes are an expensive item. Trimmings can be removed and replaced, as they are less costly."

"So I'll need to know all about those. And I'll need to refresh that knowledge regularly, when I'm Anthony. Maybe I will be ready. But I want to, just one more time. Because when I become Sir Anthony, I've no notion of how long it will be before I see home again," Alex continued, answering the question that Highbury had almost forgotten he'd asked.

"It's not like when you were in Paris, you know," the earl said then. "If you want to go home for a time, I'll be only too happy to pay for you to. No one will know whether you're in Paris, Rome or the Highlands, after all."

Alex sighed.

"I do need to make sure the clan are well prepared," he said then, "and that Kenneth can take on the responsibilities of chieftain for a longer time. And we need to prepare a way for me to be notified as quickly as possible if I do have to go back.

"But also, when I went home from Paris – before I met you - and then had to return, I was truly amazed by how difficult it was to readjust. I'd accepted student life, thought I was happy, even. But then when I went home for a few weeks I realised I'd been fooling myself, and how deeply unhappy I really was. Going back to that was torture. It took me a long time to settle in again."

"You really think you will be that unhappy here?" the earl asked.

"I don't know. It will be different, I suppose. I never wanted to study at all. But then I don't really want to prance around the Court as a scented fop either. We must buy scent," he added. "I'd forgotten that. So I think it will be easier if I stay here for as long as possible, as hard as that might be at times. It will be easier than going home, when I know I have to return in a few days or weeks."

"I'm still not sure you should be doing this at all," Highbury said. "I'm sure the prince will understand."

"Maybe he will, although I'm not sure of that. But I've never turned away from a challenge. And this could be such an important one. No, I'm determined. Are the houses you're thinking to rent on the way home?"

"Almost. A slight detour. I can show you the outside, at least. Then if you think they're suitable, we can arrange to view the interiors," Highbury said, taking the hint.

"Yes, I like this one better than the other," Alex said, still in the guise of the young lord, as he stood at the window of the drawing room, Highbury at the fireplace examining the marble surround.

"Really? I far preferred the other," Highbury replied. With the exception of the room they were standing in, all the rooms in the other house had been better proportioned and more beautifully decorated. "Why are you so attracted to this one?"

Alex turned away from the window, which he'd been looking out of, and beckoned the earl over.

"You see," he said softly as they stood together looking down at the garden below. "The stable is at the back, not the side of the house as the other is, and the wall at the bottom of the garden is very low. The last house had a high wall. And there were buildings behind the garden. Here it's just fields."

"Ah. So you want to see the open countryside, not more houses, and breathe fresher air," Highbury said. "I can understand that. But these rooms are really far inferior to those of the other property."

"I won't be entertaining," Alex said then. "I'm a bachelor. Entertainments are for ladies to arrange. Fresh air is good. But I'm thinking more of being able to leap out of any window on the ground floor and, with or without a horse, be over the wall and gone before they've beaten down the door, and with no witnesses to see which way I went."

Highbury turned back to the window, looking out of it with completely fresh eyes.

"But wouldn't the neighbours see you from their windows?" he asked after a moment.

"No. What would you do if there was a sudden commotion in the street?"

"I'd go to see the cause of it."

"Exactly. So while all the neighbours are enjoying the excitement of watching the authorities at the door, I'll have disappeared across the fields. This one is perfect."

"You think of everything," the earl said then.

"I have to. My life could depend on it one day. Yours too. Hopefully it won't. But you're right of course, Lord Highbury. The views are refreshing to the eye. I'm sure your friend will appreciate your consideration," Alex added.

Highbury knew without turning round that the man assigned to showing them around the house was within earshot.

"I will have it furnished for you before you come back in September," Highbury said as they drove home.

"You're spending a lot of money on this," Alex commented. "I know it's not a problem, but don't spend money furnishing rooms unnecessarily. The library, dining room and drawing room maybe. No one will be admitted to the rest. I don't intend to encourage callers at all. But I see I will need servants. I can make my own food if I buy oatmeal and flour, or I can send for it, so I don't need a cook. But I'll need someone to clean the house, and a footman to open the door, at the very least."

"And a coachman and groom." Highbury added. "We could hire one, and he could live over the stables, so you wouldn't have to worry about him suddenly appearing in the room when you're not in disguise. But then if you tell everyone you're travelling to France, the coachman will expect to take you to the coast, not wherever you might really want to be heading. And you will need a cook, because otherwise your maid and footman will tell everyone that Sir Anthony lives on oatmeal, and cooks it himself. Which will create a lot of gossip. There is a limit to how much eccentricity people will accept."

Alex cursed under his breath as Highbury banged on the roof of the coach with his cane.

"Why are we stopping?" Alex asked. "I thought we were going home. You look very weary."

"I am. But I just remembered there's a perfumer's here, and as we're passing, we might as well call in."

Two minutes later Highbury and the resuscitated foolish lovestruck lord were wandering around the shop, being invited to inhale from various slender glass bottles.

"It would help, my lord, if you had some idea of the type of scent your betrothed might like," the perfumer was saying. "Because you can only sample a very few scents before your olfactory senses are overwhelmed, after which you will not be able to distinguish between them."

"Ah! This! This is perfect! The very one!" the foolish lord cried, dabbing the cologne on his wrist and inhaling deeply. A strong, intensely sweet powdery fragrance permeated the air. "What is this?" he asked.

"That is a violet cologne, my lord," the perfumer said. "It's a very feminine scent."

"Violet! Oh, that is fitting. I'll take it. My beloved's name is Violet, after all. She will adore it, I am sure."

"Then I'm sure she will. How much would you like to order for her?"

"Oh, just a small bottle for the moment, in case I am wrong. It's delightful!" the lord enthused.

"It's nauseating," Highbury said later, when he and his valet were safely ensconced in his bedchamber. "The whole room smells of it. How much did you pour on yourself?"

"A good amount," Alex admitted. "I wanted to see how long it will last. Nauseating is perfect. It will fit the baronet's intense sugary personality exactly. You'll grow accustomed to it, like we both have to the smells of London after being here for a few weeks. Others won't, because they won't see me every day. It will be like those ridiculous huge panniers that ladies wear at Court."

"In what way?"

"It will keep people at a distance," Alex said. "So, I think we have everything we need now for the final stage of Sir Anthony before I go home. Can you think of anything we've missed?"

"No," the earl replied after a moment of thinking. "Your final outfits will arrive tomorrow, but you don't really need to wait for those, as they're Court outfits and you won't be wearing them until September at the earliest. I'll rent the house you preferred and furnish the rooms that others might see appropriately, so they're ready for you...for Anthony to move into in September. Ah, the sword. That arrives tomorrow too. Do you want to wait for it before I dismiss you from my service?"

"Yes, because as you said I can't carry my dirk. Well, I can, but if I draw it I'll attract suspicion, so when I reappear in a few days as Sir Anthony, I want more than a sgian achlais to defend myself with, should I need to."

"A what?" Highbury asked.

Alex reached into the arm of the coat that was on the sofa next to him, drawing out a small knife with a handle made of horn, and handing it to Highbury.

"It's in another pocket in the arm," he explained. "You can carry it strapped to your arm if necessary, under your shirt. Only another Highlander would expect you to have one, so no one would suspect Anthony to. If I draw it it's small enough to conceal in my hand, and harmless as it looks, if anyone attacks me in the street they won't be in any position to tell anyone where I keep it. Or anything else, for that matter."

It looked anything but harmless to Highbury. The blade, although only a few inches long, was razor sharp and pointed enough to stab or slash.

"The lassies carry them too," Alex continued. "They're useful for a lot of things, practical but easy to conceal, and can be used by them for defence, if necessary."

"You intend to carry this as Sir Anthony?" Highbury asked, handing it back.

"Yes. It's always useful to have more than one weapon. And I can carry a pistol if I go out as well without attracting attention, you said?"

"You can. We don't need to order those, I have a set that I will gift to you."

"If you're sure you want to. Gift them to me when I return then, openly. That way if I am ever discovered, people will remember you doing it, and it will not seem suspicious," Alex told him. "I'm glad I can carry weapons openly though. I can't imagine being defenceless."

"I think you will probably be the least defenceless nobleman I know," Highbury replied, remembering the ease with which Alex had disabled Joseph. He would never forget that. "Now," he continued, shaking his head to dismiss the memory, "when Sir Anthony arrives, he will be lodged in the room on the other side of the valet's room. That will be convenient because there's a narrow passage that leads between the walls from that room directly to mine. So we can visit each other without anyone knowing."

"Why would you have a secret passage like that?" Alex asked.

"I think it was so that the original master of the house could ensure his wife would not know if his mistress or a prostitute was entertaining him. The secret passage would ensure the servants didn't find out and tell her. Worth it to avoid the blackmail we spoke of previously. Not everyone is as adept at disposing of corpses in cities as you seem to be," Highbury said dryly.

Alex laughed.

"I'm hoping not to have to," he said. "After all, I may well faint at the sight of blood."

"It's finally happening," Highbury said suddenly.

"As long as none of the servants recognise me, yes, it is," Alex agreed. "This will be a good rehearsal, because I'll only have left a few days before. The memory of me will still be fresh in their minds, so if none of them have any suspicions, then we can be sure that nobody will. And it will be a good rehearsal for you to treat me as Sir Anthony continuously, and forget Alex completely."

"I will miss you when you go," Highbury said, then flushed. He hadn't meant to admit that openly.

"I'm not going yet. When I'm Anthony we can use the secret passage and have a drink or two in the evening. No one will come into my room, will they?"

"No. I will tell them how eccentric you are. But another reason I've chosen that room for you is that it's the only bedroom apart from mine that has a lock on the door."

"The first owner really didn't want his wife to find out about his adultery, did he?" Alex said, grinning.

"It seems not. I'm glad of it now."

The next morning the Earl of Highbury, with regret, dismissed his valet as just not being suitable enough for the responsibilities he would have to take on, although he did give him an excellent character, telling him that he was sure he would be a fine valet for a knight or a baronet, but was not quite up to serving an earl yet. Perhaps when he had more experience he might wish to reapply.

The valet left, sadly, his trunk slightly heavier than it had been on arrival, containing as it did a couple of new outfits, including gloves and shoes, a wig, and a sword with a jewelled hilt, which at the moment was sharp enough for a gentleman to defend himself with if forced to it, but would soon be sharp enough for a Highlander to effortlessly eviscerate someone, should the need arise.

It was kind of the earl to give the use of his coach to his now former valet to take him to the Angel Inn to catch the stagecoach, the servants thought. It was a shame he had not been suitable, they all agreed. Drummond had seemed a pleasant, if somewhat shy man. Hopefully he would find a suitable post soon.

When the coach drew up outside the house in Grosvenor Square, Highbury, who had been surreptitiously peeping out of the library window, shot across the room, threw himself into his chair near the fire, and picked up the book he had not absorbed one word of in the last hour he'd been looking at it. He could feel his heart banging against his ribs, and his mouth was dry. He had felt like this since his coach had set off an hour ago to collect Sir Anthony Peters from the Angel Inn.

You're being ridiculous, he told himself sternly. Get a grip of yourself, or the servants will suspect something even if Alex is perfect.

Alex would be perfect, he was sure of that. He stared at the book and took some deep breaths, and just thought he'd mastered himself when the knock came on the door and his heart was instantly hammering again.

"My lord, your visitor has arrived," a footman announced.

"Ah, thank you, Seymour. Show him into the drawing room. I will be there directly," the earl said, closing the book and taking a large gulp of brandy the moment the servant had gone.

He stood and made his way to the door, stopping with his hand on the knob when he heard the high-pitched tones of the baronet in the entrance hall.

"Yes, yes, please convey my luggage to my room. I would be quite unable to carry it up all those stairs! You seem a strong fellow though. Please take great care of it. What an utterly delightful entrance hall! And the flowers! In March! How divine! The drawing room you say? Where is....ah! Oh! Such exquisite gilding! I swear I have not seen the like outside the Palace of Versailles! Yes, that would be wonderful. I do so..."

The baronet's voice was cut off, presumably by the closing of the drawing room door. Highbury rested his forehead on the library door, wondering what had possessed him, what had possessed the pair of them to attempt this lunatic endeavour. They would certainly be discovered. The servants were astute. They would scrutinise him, see the similarities between this simpering fool and the valet who had departed only three days previously.

We have already agreed that if they do then we will state it was a bet between a group of noblemen, which we have now clearly lost as you did recognise him after all. What gave him away? Relax.

He stood for a moment longer, then raised his head, squared his shoulders and opened the library door, as though going into battle.

"Oh my dear William!" Sir Anthony trilled when the earl entered. He was standing by the window, looking out onto the lawns below. "What an extraordinary house you have! I cannot wait to see the rest. And such extensive grounds too, in London! It is so kind of you to invite me to reside here for a few days on my way to the coast. What conversation we will have!"

Highbury moved forward then, smiling a little rigidly.

"You are most welcome, Anthony," he said. "Are you fatigued from your journey?"

"Oh, most terribly!" the baronet cried dramatically. "I have quite the headache from all the jouncing of the coach. Really, I would have expected the roads of the capital to be in better repair. But no matter, here I am!"

He moved forward then, taking the earl's hand in both of his, and squeezing it.

"I am overjoyed to see you again! It has been too long!" he said.

"It has only been four months," Highbury replied.

"Really? So short a time since we met in Hartford? It feels like an age. Such an unlikely place to meet, but how fortunate, for myself at least."

"Did you meet with success regarding your dear father's property?" Highbury asked.

"No, no, all gone! Such sad memories for me. I have sworn never to return to the place, indeed to the county of Cheshire. I must move on with my life, as my dear mama and my sisters would have wished me to. But it is so hard to be alone! With the exception of your dear, dear self, William. I am overwhelmed with gratitude!"

So saying, the baronet released dear, dear William's hand and sank down onto a nearby sofa, closing his eyes in utter weariness.

Highbury turned, to see the footman who had opened the door a few moments ago and was waiting to see if anything was required.

"Ah. Thank you, Seymour," the earl said, his voice shaking a little from the effort of not bursting into laughter at the footman's expression of utter astonishment at what he had just witnessed. "If you will instruct the maid to bring some light refreshments and wine, we will allow Sir Anthony to refresh himself a little before you show him to his room."

"You are kindness itself!" came the voice from the sofa.

The footman left, closing the door quietly behind him, and High-bury sat down opposite his friend, who now opened his slate-blue eyes, the only recognisable part of him, which were currently sparkling with laughter, although otherwise he remained utterly the foppish baronet, as they had agreed he would when anywhere but his or the earl's private rooms, and then only late at night when the servants were in bed.

Highbury shook his head.

"Magnificent," he murmured.

"Indeed! It is a delightful house. Or at least the part of it I have seen so far is. I own, I cannot wait to see your country home, which you tell me is so much grander," Sir Anthony enthused.

"Yes, it is my main residence," Highbury replied, his heart slowing a little now as he determined to play the role of benevolent earl as well as Alex was playing the baronet. The footman at least had certainly not recognised him, which was a good start. "Such a shame, though, that you will not be able to see it for the first time in the summer months, which are so delightful."

"Ah, but I am sure the autumn will be glorious too! Are there trees, many trees on your property?"

"Well, yes. There is a woodland that borders my land and that of my neighbour, the Marchioness of Hereford."

"Ah, how exquisite! Then when I arrive it will be in time to see the foliage at its most beautiful. Gold, orange, red...every tree like a sunset! I must have an outfit made to honour the season, in autumnal shades!" Sir Anthony cried as the maid entered with a tray of pastries and cakes, and a footman with a decanter of wine and two crystal glasses.

"Oh, how thoughtful!" Anthony said. "Is there tea as well?"

"You would like tea?" Highbury asked. Tea was more of a ladies' drink.

"Yes, if it is no trouble. Tea is such a refreshing beverage! Do you not think so, my dear lord?"

"If you wish it, then of course we shall have tea. Thank you. If you will bring tea for the baronet," Highbury instructed.

"I am covered in gratitude! Yes, it is unfortunate, but as you know I must return to the continent to finalise everything, and then I can move to England permanently, and start my new life. I am so looking forward to it!" Anthony continued as the servants left the room. The maid's shoulders were shaking.

"You will be the death of me," Highbury said that night, as the pair of them sat in his room, Anthony having trilled and exclaimed his way through the afternoon and evening, during which Highbury had shown him around the house and given him a tour of the garden, which was not at all extensive. Then he had fluttered his way off to bed, declaring he was almost prostrate with fatigue.

An hour later, his makeup and wig removed, he had made his way by candlelight along the somewhat dusty adjoining passage to the earl's room, where the two of them now sat enjoying a nightcap, dressed in silk banyans.

"You were superb," Alex said softly, keeping the aristocratic accent, but not the high-pitched tone of the baronet. "A little shaky at first, but by the time we'd had the tea, you'd settled into the role. As had I. I was very nervous at first."

"You were? I would never have known it," Highbury said.

"Yes. It's the first time I've been the baronet with anyone other than you," Alex said. "I was sure that at least one, if not all of the servants would see through me immediately. They certainly observed me when I was Drummond the valet. They were deliberating on whether I was a man who they could speak freely in front of, or whether I would report everything back to you. But although they've really struggled at times to remain impassive, especially when I was being particularly flowery, none of them have shown the slightest hint of recognition, or even suspicion that I might be anything other than this ridiculous idiot."

"You're right, they haven't. I was watching for that too, as best I could between fighting not to laugh at times. And I know them better than you."

"I think we can really do this," Alex said, sipping at his brandy. "Even Ingles and Rood didn't suspect anything, and they saw me as the valet more than the others, with us eating meals together."

"How on earth did you come up with so many flowery phrases, anyway? It seemed effortless to you," Highbury said.

"Some of them are from poems I've read over the years, others I just invent. And I do repeat myself a lot, which will make me even more tedious. I must have some regular phrases. My dear will certainly be one of them, but I'll need a few, I think. Did I make any errors?"

"In etiquette? Well, clasping my hand fervently at the start was not correct, but it suited your ridiculous personality completely, so I think you will be able to get away with such overblown gestures," Highbury commented. "Otherwise, no. Your behaviour at dinner was perfect.

"Of course the real test will come when you attend a dinner with a number of aristocrats, but we can't really do that at the moment. It would seem strange for you then immediately to disappear for months. It would give people time to maybe investigate you, as a brief appearance in society of such a creature would certainly raise a lot of questions, and interest. Better you be there continuously, to let slip tasty snippets, and in fact to be questioned. Otherwise they will start to speculate and look elsewhere for information, and to believe ridiculous rumours if you're not there to counteract them. And we don't want that, even if we don't believe there's anything to find."

"No, we really don't. I've divulged a little of my background to the servants, so if word spreads as you think it will, then you can confirm them. I don't think they'll be that curious until they actually meet Anthony," Alex said.

"You were truly ridiculous, you know," Highbury said.

"I know. It was actually fun. Much more than I thought it would be," Alex admitted.

They looked at each other then, and suddenly, like small children, they started giggling, then found they couldn't stop. After a few minutes of this both of them had tears running down their faces, and had to stop catching each other's eye, which would set them off again. It seemed they had both been very nervous, and this was a great release.

"Let's enjoy it while we can, then," Highbury said, when he was capable of speech again. "I think the novelty will wear off after a while."

Alex, or rather Anthony, stayed for four days in the end, after which he made a tearful, fluttery farewell, waving a lace-covered hand at Highbury until the coach drove out of the square and disappeared.

Highbury went to the library and poured himself a large brandy, then sat by the fire staring morosely into the flames. In spite of having been dreadfully nervous when the baronet had arrived and wishing the four days would pass quickly, now he felt utterly bereft and unspeakably lonely, because it was over, and he would not see Anthony or Alex for over six months.

He could not remember the last time he had laughed so much in his life as he had over the last four days, even though he had done his utmost to behave in the tolerant, sympathetic way they had both agreed the earl should when in company. Alex had blossomed over the four-day period he'd been almost consistently Anthony, refining aspects of the idiot's character and developing more elaborate hand gestures, phrases, and flowery compliments.

And then at night, in the safety of Highbury's bedroom, they had relaxed, two conspirators united in the same endeavour, aware of the dangers but accepting them, laughing and joking about the events of the day, knowing that they would support each other through whatever happened in the future.

He could not remember the last time he had bonded with someone so completely, either. Not since his wife had died, anyway. He prayed that everything would go well, and that Anthony would never be discovered to be a fraud.

Because although Highbury had promised he would do nothing if that happened and Alex was arrested, already he knew that he would not be able to keep that promise, would do anything he could to save him, if it was even remotely possible to do so.

CHAPTER SIXTEEN

Loch Lomond, July 1741

IT WAS A BEAUTIFUL day, and Alex sat on his favourite rock by the side of the loch, watching the children playing and contemplating what still needed to be done before he set off for London to take up his new identity as Sir Anthony Peters.

In truth, when he thought about it, everything that could be done had been. Anything else depended on the vagaries of the weather or on sudden events, about which he could do nothing in advance. Kenneth would be a good deputy chieftain, if Duncan had to go away for any reason. Over the years he had earned the respect of the clanspeople, and had conducted himself very well during the time Alex and Duncan had been away visiting Prince Charles and Francis Ogilvy. He had grown in confidence too, so no longer hesitated before making decisions. Since Alex had been home he had discussed every decision he'd made with the giant, explaining why he'd made it, after which Kenneth would say what he would have done in the same situation, and they would discuss any differences honestly.

Yes, he was ready. And he would have the support of Angus, who although not mature enough to be chieftain himself still had many useful suggestions.

Almost everything was ready for the simpering baronet to make his appearance in the world – the house in London had been rented and furnished, a number of costumes purchased, and Highbury was preparing to head to London himself at the start of September to welcome Alex when he arrived, which would enable them to make any final adjustments before he was introduced to noble society.

The only thing that was *not* ready were the servants who would take care of the baronet's house. The two men had decided that he would need at the very minimum a maid-of-all-work, a cook, a footman, a coachman, and a groom. The house had a small garden, so one part-time gardener would suffice, and a laundress could visit weekly. Even if he never entertained it would be impossible for him to manage without *any* staff. It would be remarked on if he always opened the door to callers himself, did not have a coach when he was so obviously wealthy, and somehow cleaned the house himself.

Which meant that if he could not solve the problem, he would have to be Sir Anthony Peters from when he rose in the morning until he went to bed at night. In fact such an overtly wealthy man would really be expected to have a good number of servants. If he did not, the few he did have would spread the word, which would raise suspicion.

Alex sighed. He had wrestled with this issue for weeks, and this morning had finally come to a decision, and had decided that Kenneth rather than Duncan would, initially at least, need to act as chieftain, and without the support of Angus, because Alex intended to take both his brothers to London with him.

As well as learning to ride a horse in Edinburgh, Angus had struck up a friendship with Iain Gordon, who, on his frequent visits to Dr Ogilvy's with his master, had taught him a good deal about being a footman. He could wait at table, open doors, fold bits of cloth into silly shapes…all essential duties, it seemed. And Duncan would be able to act as gardener and groom at least, and possibly double as a footman if necessary.

It was not ideal, and they would have to cook for themselves and somehow manage to clean the house, or at least the rooms visible to visitors. Alex may well have asked Susan to act as his maid, if she had not been engaged in such important work in Edinburgh. Francis Ogilvy was very dear to Alex: if he stole Susan from him, the man would die very much sooner, and he would never forgive himself. And then there was still the problem of a coachman.

They would manage somehow, would have to. Alex would break the news to his brothers tonight, get their reaction and then tell Kenneth tomorrow. On a positive note it would be wonderful to have his brothers' support until he settled in, for as the date of departure drew closer, Alex grew more and more apprehensive, wondering what had possessed him to attempt such a venture. He would have to make sure Duncan at least returned home as soon as possible though. Angus would probably enjoy the city, initially at least.

One of the objects of his rumination suddenly shot past him, shedding his *féileadh mór* and shirt as he did before running headlong into the loch, to the cheers of the children, who were taking turns to have Kenneth pick them up and throw them a distance, before watching them swim back. Now there were two adults to play this latest game with!

God, but Angus was growing fast! At seventeen he was almost as tall as Alex, although not as broad, not yet, but still well-muscled. He must talk to Highbury, make sure that his youngest brother only visited the higher class of brothel, and had condoms with him when he did.

Once Angus had been told the nature of the game and had entered into it with his customary enthusiasm, Kenneth came out of the loch for a little respite. He donned his shirt, then joined his chieftain on the rock.

"Some of yon laddies are no' exactly bairns any more," he said as he sat down and helped himself to a drink from the leather flask Alex had brought. "If I'd thought, I could have played that game before throwing the *clach cuid fir*, instead of hiding in the woods to lift and throw rocks!"

Alex laughed.

"I remember the time you threw me into the loch," he said then.

"Aye, well, the action may have been the same, but the intent wasna," Kenneth replied. "I couldna do it now."

"I'm thinking ye likely could," Alex replied.

Kenneth thought.

"Maybe. No' as far though. I dinna need to, anyway. Ye've been doing some powerful thinking. Are ye wanting to tell me anything?"

"Is it that obvious?" Alex asked. "No' the now. Maybe tomorrow. It feels like years since I've played in the loch," he finished wistfully.

"Ye're the chieftain. No one can stop ye an ye want to," Kenneth said dryly. "It's a good cure for powerful thinking."

This was true. He grinned boyishly and stood, and was just unbuckling his belt when Robbie Og came running through the trees towards them at full pelt. As Robbie Og never ran *anywhere*, Alex froze and Kenneth stood up, waiting impatiently as the boy fought for breath.

"Redcoats!" he gasped when he could speak, freezing the blood in the bones of both men. Alex grabbed the boy by the shoulders.

"How many?" he asked urgently. "How far away?"

"Duncan sent me," the boy said, before a fit of coughing stopped him saying any more. Alex resisted the urge to shake him, while Kenneth ran into the loch to tell Angus and get the children out. "About twenty," Robbie continued in a choked voice, when he could speak. "One on a horse, the rest walking. Less than two miles, Duncan said. He asked me to warn ye while he tellt the men."

Less than two miles. The ground was reasonably even. Half an hour, maybe a little more.

"Ye did well, laddie," Alex said, then turned away immediately to the dripping group gathering at the lochside. Angus and Kenneth were carrying the smaller ones out.

"Dinna dress now," Alex told them. "Away to your mothers, immediately. Tell them to go to the cave, wi' all the bairns under fifteen. Now!" he shouted when they all hesitated. They grabbed their clothes and ran.

Alex tore his fingers through his hair, then looked to the two adults.

"Help Duncan tell the men to arm themselves, fast, and come to my house. No questions," he added, seeing Angus's mouth open. "We've no time for that."

They followed the children, and then he stood there for a moment, breathing deeply in an attempt to calm himself, gather his thoughts.

Twenty. One officer, the one on horseback. Not a planned attack then. Although that didn't mean they wouldn't take the opportunity, if the settlement appeared vulnerable. If the whole clan met them, armed to the teeth, only a lunatic would attempt to fight them.

But then they would likely report back to Inversnaid or Fort William, or wherever they were from, which might provoke a full-blown attack from an entire regiment. Alex did not want that, could not have that, especially as he intended to leave the clan in two months.

He closed his eyes for a moment, thinking furiously. Then he turned and ran back to the clearing outside his house.

When he got there the men were already gathering, while the women and children were snaking up the hill to the cave, carrying babies and whatever provisions they'd been able to grab as they left.

"Robbie tellt ye then," Duncan said as he arrived.

"Aye. Thank ye for this. Ye saved time," he said.

"Will we fight?" Duncan asked.

"No' unless we have to, no. Twenty, aye?"

"Aye. No' more, anyway. They'll be a good few minutes reaching us. They're walking, no' marching."

Alex nodded, waiting impatiently as the final stragglers dashed into the clearing before speaking again.

"Does everyone ken what's amiss?" he asked.

Some nodded, others said 'aye'.

"We havena much time," Alex said then. "Angus and me will be on Allan's roof, mending it. It's the one closest to the loch, so we'll see the bastards as they come. I'm wanting all of ye to hide, no' in the houses, in the heather. In earshot if either of us shouts, but dinna let them see ye. Go."

They went, none of them asking what they were to do if he shouted, for they all knew. Alex glanced up the hill. He could see the women, but only because they were moving. They were bent as low as possible, almost hidden by the bracken and gorse. They had practiced this countless times. Any of them who didn't reach the cave before the soldiers were visible would drop to the ground and freeze. Thank God for scarlet. The enemy would be visible long before they were even aware there was a settlement here.

"Right," he said then, turning to his youngest brother. "Let's away on to the roof. Hide your sword in the thatch, we're repairing it. Dinna say anything. Let me speak. Ye're an idiot, and canna speak the English. I'm no' much better. Can ye do that?"

"Aye, I can do that," Angus said, his eyes sparkling at his brother's trust in him, at the chance to prove it was justified.

Ten minutes later the soldiers appeared, heading south on their way along the track. Alex gave no sign of having seen them until they were a few yards from the hut, upon which he stopped what he was doing, stuck his dirk in the roof and sat back on his haunches, brandishing nothing more dangerous than a handful of heather as he greeted the intruders. The officer reined in his horse, his men halting behind him, looking around at the handful of huts.

"*Madainn mhath,*" the officer said, smiling across at the two High-landers from his horse. It was not morning but late afternoon, which told Alex the soldier likely had only a few words of Gaelic. Even so, it was an unexpected friendly gesture, and showed the man had made at least a basic effort. Alex amended his original plan.

"*Madainn mhath,*" he replied, smiling somewhat inanely. Angus continued to wrestle with an apparently difficult piece of thatch, seemingly oblivious to the visitors. "It's a fine day to be travelling."

"Ah, you speak English!" the soldier said with obvious relief.

"Aye, a little. Have ye far to go?"

"We're on our way to Dumbarton," the redcoat replied, causing his men to look at him in surprise.

"Dumbarton. If ye're from Inversnaid, would ye no' be better going round the other side of the loch? The ground is better. Shorter too," Alex suggested.

"Have to follow orders, I'm afraid," the soldier replied, his tone friendly. He looked around intently. "I had no idea there was a village here, Mister…"

"Aye. The lassies are away to the shielings," Alex replied, his tone equally friendly. Some of the redcoats had taken the opportunity to sit down on the grass. "The laddies are working. If the chief'd kent ye were coming, he could have offered hospitality, but it's just myself and my idiot brother and we canna without the chief telling us to."

"No, I understand. Well, we'll be on our way. Captain Hutchinson at your service, sir," the captain said, waiting a moment for Alex to return the compliment and offer his name.

"A good day to ye, Captain," Alex said.

The captain spurred his horse forward, and the men, looking some-what disgruntled, stood, reshouldered their arms and fell into line behind him.

Alex bent back to the roof.

"Shift your position and watch them, but keep your head down so they dinna ken," he murmured. Angus knelt up, moved around, and then settled again, his hands working busily doing nothing, his head bent, apparently concentrating on his task.

"They're continuing," he said after a minute. "Slow pace, no' hur-rying. A couple of the soldiers are looking back, but the captain isna."

"When they're out of sight, ye climb down. Follow them, see where they're heading. Dinna let them see ye. Dinna get too close."

Ten minutes after the redcoats were out of sight, Angus following, Alex stood and raised his hand. MacGregors materialized as if by magic all over the hillside, and began making their way down to him. He stayed on the roof until they were all congregated round the cottage, then jumped down.

"That was well done," he said to them. "Robbie, will ye away up and tell the lassies to stay in the cave tonight, until we ken what the redcoats are up to. If they need bedding and food, some of them can come down now to fetch it. Angus is away after them, to find out which way they're headed. The captain laddie tellt us Dumbarton, but he was lying. We'll post extra sentries, and ye'll all sleep wi' your weapons tonight, in case ye need to use them suddenly."

"Are ye thinking they intend a night attack?" Kenneth asked.

"In truth I dinna ken what they intend," Alex admitted. "I'm thinking yon captain's been in the Highlands for a while. He greeted me in our tongue, and he was watching the heather closely while he talked to me, so I'm thinking he kent there might be men hiding there. If they intended a night attack, I'd expect them to bring more men, but I canna be certain, and I'd rather be cautious. We'll see if Angus finds anything out."

The redcoats continued for a couple of miles, after which the terrain became more rocky and the subdued grumbling of the men increased in volume. Captain Hutchinson sighed, reined in his horse and dismounted. He had made them walk a good way, and it was a hot day.

"We'll have a short rest here," he told them. "Only a short one. Don't get too comfortable."

The men sat down, leaning against rocks or trees, and began to unpack their rations. As was his custom Captain Hutchinson sat a short distance away from them, far enough for them to relax a little, and for their voices to be a soothing murmur rather than an irritating noise. He leaned back against a tree and closed his eyes, feeling the unfamiliar warmth of the sun on his face, wishing he could take off his woollen jacket as some of the men were doing. But he was a captain, and that would never do. Sweat trickled uncomfortably down his back.

Damn Colonel Walker, sending him on this pointless escapade on the hottest day of the year! For it *was* pointless. He'd tried to explain politely to the man that there would be no purpose in building a road along the side of the loch, as they had along Loch Ness. The road along that loch linked Forts William, Augustus and George. It had a purpose. A road along either side of Loch Lomond would only link Inversnaid barracks to Dumbarton and the Lowlands, which were generally accessible anyway, and the Lowlands were not heaving with accomplished and ruthless warriors who obeyed no law except their own.

But Walker never thought about his men, or about practicalities. All he thought about was himself. If a government minister, or General Wade himself wanted to know whether it was feasible to build a road along Loch Lomond, or any of the other damn lochs that he'd sent his captain and an ever-changing group of recruits to check in the last months, Walker wanted to be able to reply immediately and knowledgeably.

It was only a matter of time before one of the clans whose lands they intruded on took offence and slaughtered the lot of them, Hutchinson thought sourly. Although so far, he had to admit, no one had shown him or his men actual violence. They had, however, shown their disapproval and thinly veiled antagonism to the sudden appearance on their lands. Hopefully this would be the last such venture he was sent on before returning to England in the autumn.

The men's voices were louder now, which told Hutchinson that they thought he was asleep. Until now they'd mainly been voicing aloud what he was thinking.

"Is that all you've got?" one soldier asked of his neighbour.

"Yes. I didn't know the bloody lake was so long!" came the reply. "I ate most of it on the last stop. Hopefully we'll get more provisions at Drummakill."

"We should have seen whether there was anything better worth eating at that place we passed just now," a third man grumbled. "Or anything worth selling."

"Worth selling?" another laughed.

"We could have burnt the rooves, saved the two idiots the job of fixing them," the first suggested, to laughter.

"Do you think the women really were up at that place he said? I think they were hiding in the hovels. We could have warmed them up before we burnt the rooves. They'd be glad of a man who washes himself."

"You were just going to watch us then?" a wag shot back, as the man who'd suggested checking the hovels was renowned for his insanitary habits. A roar of laughter greeted this.

Hutchinson sighed inwardly. Enough. He opened his eyes and turned to them, watching with satisfaction as they all fell silent.

"Let me remind you we're here to check the terrain's suitability for road-building. We're surveying, not trying to bring half the Highlands down on Inversnaid," he reminded them.

"It was only a joke, sir," the unhygienic soldier replied.

"There probably wasn't anything or anyone in the huts anyway," another muttered.

"There was certainly nothing worth dying for, that's certain," the captain stated coldly.

"Dying for?"

"You think those two were there alone? How long have you been in the Highlands?"

"Just a week, sir," the young man admitted, flushing uncomfortably at having his officer's undivided attention. "I didn't see anyone else, sir."

"No, of course you didn't. Neither did I. But that doesn't mean that at the slightest hint of aggression the hillside wouldn't have erupted with enraged clansmen, armed to the teeth," the captain explained icily. "We are not here to fight. Remember that. If we were, I'd want a lot more than twenty raw fools with me.

"That applies when we return up the west side of the loch tomorrow. I don't care if the huts are thatched with gold and the women all look like duchesses. You stay silent. Not even so much as an aggressive look. Highlanders are prickly. They take offence easily. Finish what you're eating. We leave in five minutes."

The men, silent now, stood, putting on their coats and wrapping up any remnants of food they had. Captain Hutchinson went to his horse.

God, he hoped he *did* get a posting back to England. This heat, which would be mere pleasant warmth back home, was making him irritable. He'd been in the Highlands too long, was growing to actually *like* the colder weather! He glanced longingly at the loch. What he would give to soak his feet in its icy waters. That would cool him down.

But it would also show a softer side of him he had no wish to let the soldiers see.

Sighing once again, he mounted his horse.

Having overheard most of this conversation from a proximity that would have given his eldest brother an apoplexy had he known, Angus fell back a good way, but still followed them, until they actually reached Drummakill House and it was clear they were going to stay there for the night. Then he headed home.

When he got back it was dark, and when he opened the door of his home the three men sitting there looked across at him in surprise.

"I didna expect to see you back until tomorrow at the earliest," Alex said.

"Aye, well, I overheard yon captain laddie telling the men everything we need to ken when they had a wee stop. Then I followed them until they stopped for the night, and it was where he said they were going. They didna ken I was there, so he wouldna have any reason to lie," Angus explained cheerfully.

He came closer then to pour himself a cup of ale, and in doing so saw the expression on his brother's face. "Are ye wanting me to go back?" he asked uncertainly then. "I can an ye want. They'll still be asleep when I get there."

"Tell me what ye overheard first, then I'll decide," Alex told him.

Angus pulled up a stool and sat down, explaining what he'd heard to Alex, Duncan and Kenneth in between taking gulps of ale. It was still warm outside even though it was night, and he was thirsty.

"Road-building?" Kenneth interrupted when Angus got to that point.

"I canna imagine why they'd take the trouble to build a road past us," Alex mused. "It isna as though there's anywhere they'll be wanting to go south of the loch."

"England?" Angus suggested.

"No. There are other, easier ways to get to England already. Building a road is a lot of work. Are ye sure they said that?"

"Aye, I was only...I wasna too far away," Angus amended rapidly.

"How close were ye?" Duncan asked.

"Er...it was good. Nobody saw me. I was very careful," Angus reassured the three sceptical faces.

"No, I dinna want ye to go back," Alex said, determining to go and ask Allan to instead. He wanted to make sure they *did* return along the western bank, and where they returned to. Then he would keep a closer eye on the north of the loch until he left for England.

If Angus found out he'd sent Allan, he'd say he'd changed his mind but needed someone fast. He had no wish to hurt his brother's feelings. In one way he *had* done well. But he would take risks again if he followed them back, and Alex could not have that.

When he was in England both he and Duncan could keep an eye on their little brother. Hopefully the experience would make him learn to be more cautious, Alex thought hopelessly. And speaking of that...

"I've decided to take you and Duncan wi' me when I go to London," Alex told him. "I've already tellt Kenneth and Duncan. Kenneth will act as chieftain in my place, and I'm confident he can manage well while I'm away. Once I'm settled I'll send Duncan back, in the spring."

"Oh, that'll be bonny!" Angus cried delightedly. "I didna want to lose ye again!"

"Ye'll no' lose me again, laddie," Alex said softly. "Ye didna lose me last time. I thought of ye all the time."

"Aye, I ken that, but it was awfu' hard, no' seeing ye for so long," Angus said. "Now I'll see ye every day!"

"Ye'll see Sir Anthony every day, no' me," Alex amended.

"No' when we're alone though."

"No. But all the rest of the time."

He went on to explain about the servant problem, and that at the moment he couldn't think of any alternative to taking his two brothers with him.

"For ye can both ride well now, and ye learnt a lot from yon Iain laddie."

"I did! I can be a servant!" Angus said excitedly. "Duncan hasna learnt though. Are ye wanting me to teach him too?"

"Aye, but that can wait until we're in London," Alex said, sensing Duncan's utter misery at the thought of going at all, although he was hiding it well. In fact he wasn't showing it at all, but Alex knew his brother well enough to know he couldn't be as happy as he was appearing to be at the prospect. He would talk to him when they were alone.

Right now he needed to be sure Kenneth was confident enough to do what he wanted him to.

Allan returned four days later, confirming that the redcoats had indeed stayed overnight at Drummakill House, which made sense, as the resident, Archibald Buchanan, was a supporter of the British government. The next day they'd set off along the west side of the loch.

"It took them an awfu' long time," Allan said. "They stopped every few minutes, it seemed. Buchanan had given them a lot of victuals, so that's likely why. Yon horseback mannie wasna happy, ye could see that. They arrived back at Inversnaid last night, so I slept in the heather for a wee while and then observed the barracks for a day, but there was nothing much happening, and they didna continue north, so I'm thinking they're billeted there, no' at one of the other forts. So I came back. Are ye still wanting me to go to Glasgow for the post?"

"Aye," Alex said, "but no' today. Away home and rest yourself. Take a bottle of claret wi' ye. Thank ye. I'm feeling a wee bit happier now."

Only a very wee bit though. Later he called Kenneth round, to discuss what to do next.

"I'll likely no' be here if anything does happen, for it seems Angus was right and they *are* thinking to build a road, for some unfathomable reason. So I'm wanting ye to tell me what ye'd do now, if I wasna here, and what ye'd do later, if it's clear they *are* going to build a road," Alex said.

Kenneth sat back, sipping his cup of ale and thinking for a while.

"Why would they want to build a road at all?" Angus asked after a couple of minutes of silence. "It doesna make sense, as ye said a few days ago."

"A lot of what the redcoats do doesna make sense," Duncan put in. "Wearing heavy woollen coats in hot weather, wi' all the useless bits of rope on. Smooth-soled boots. Standing outside in all weathers at yon barracks, then walking around in wee patterns for hours."

"I'm thinking I'd bring the lassies down from the cave now, for there isna any immediate danger," Kenneth said suddenly, having made a decision. "They'll no' just come and start building a road, after all, will they? It's a mighty thing."

"No, they'll have to come back and measure things, look at obstacles," Alex agreed.

"Aye. So if they do that, then we'll ken they're serious. So I'd send men up to watch the barracks, watch for soldiers starting to measure or whatever they do from there. If they do, then we've plenty of time to prepare, for they'll no' do that in a few days."

"Prepare for what?" Alex asked.

"In truth, that's when I'd come to London and tell ye, for I'd be wanting to kill them, but ye tellt me that wouldna really be an option," Kenneth admitted.

"Well, it might stop the road building, aye, for a while, but they'd no' just give up. They might have no sense, but they're awfu' stubborn," Alex said.

"If they do the measuring, does that mean they'd be definitely building a road?" Duncan asked.

"I dinna ken. They went all the way round the loch, so they might measure both sides to see which would be easiest to build on. I'm thinking that's the likeliest option," Alex said. If they were going to measure, would they do it soon, or wait for a time? He had no idea. Damn them! He had enough to worry about, without this!

"So I need to keep men up there observing until the winter comes, and if they start to measure both ways, just do what we did today? Let them do it?" Kenneth asked. "If we dinna want a battle wi' them, I canna think of another way."

"I'd love a battle wi' them, the invading bastards," Alex said. "But we canna risk it. No' without raising all of the MacGregors, and that would just give the government a reason to send a whole army up to wipe us out. So aye, if it happens, do what ye did today and let them do it. Ye'll have time to get everything and everyone up to the cave. But if they do, have men shadow them along both sides of the loch, see how many problems they find. It should be easy to discover which side of the loch they favour. Then send for me. But ye canna come, Kenneth. Send someone who doesna look so fearsome. Alasdair Og, maybe."

"Alasdair's fearsome enough," Angus commented.

"Aye, but he doesna look it, which is what matters. I'll have a suit of plain clothes made for him, or Allan, for they're a similar size. If they have to come to England, they canna wear the *féileadh mór*. But if it isna urgent, send letters instead, using the codes we've discussed," Alex said. "So aye, ye're thinking right, Kenneth. I've no qualms about leaving ye as chieftain when I'm away."

"In September," Angus said. "Two months."

"Aye. Dinna remind me," Alex replied sourly.

When Allan came back from Glasgow a few days later, he had two letters, one of which was from Highbury telling him that everything was in place for Mr Drummond to attend a further interview, this time as a footman, and that he was expected in the latter part of September, when his current position ended.

So everything was ready. He would go to Highbury's house in Grosvenor Square, while Duncan and Angus would go straight to the house which had been rented for the baronet. While Alex settled into his role as Sir Anthony and they ironed out any final issues, Duncan and Angus would work out how to run the house when he arrived.

Alex felt a surge of mingled excitement and terror, even as his stomach curdled. Now, finally, it was real. He closed his eyes for a minute, felt his mood start to plummet, then opened them again and unsealed the second letter, which was from Susan.

This would take his mind off his worries. He settled down to read it.

Dear Cousin,

...it began, which told him that it was a letter only with innocent news in, and that she was imparting nothing that would cause problems if the authorities opened it. Good. No more issues for him to concern himself with then.

He took a sip of wine and continued. Perhaps he would call the clan to the house later, tell them her news. They all loved Susan and asked after her regularly. When he replied to her letters he would include snippets of news the various clansfolk asked him to write, as his da had when he'd written to him in Paris.

All is well here. Francis is in good health, or at least is no worse, and enjoys treating his patients for two days in the week. It does tire him somewhat, but I feel the fatigue to be overridden by the joy he feels at being useful, so I have not raised any objections. It also gives me pleasure to assist him when I am able to.

Whenever I can I go out of the Netherbow Port and spend a little time walking in the fresh air among green things, which lifts my spirits when they are a little low. Francis insists on sending a footman with me to ensure my safety, but Brian is a considerate sort who does not intrude on my solitude when I am walking. I miss all of you greatly, but I am needed here, and that along with the peaceful walks means that I am content with my life. I will remain here for as long as I am needed.

I have to tell you that Mr Munro, who you will remember was Francis's chess companion, died some weeks ago. In truth his death was not a great surprise to us, as he was in very poor health and would take no advice which may have extended his life from either Francis or any other physician. In truth I think he had little in life to cause him to strive to remain in it. He was in constant pain, although he tried to conceal it, and had no family or responsibilities to give him the will to live.

Even so, Francis has taken it badly, as they were friends for many years, and he misses his companionship very much. Mr Munro's servant Iain Gordon, who asks me to send his greetings to yourself and Angus, kindly visits twice a week in the evening to play chess with Francis, which alleviates his grief a little. If Francis is sleeping, Mr Gordon will sometimes stay for a time and we will converse a little of other matters respecting gardening, and roses in particular, of which we are both fond.

Iain married recently. I have not yet met his wife, who is a maid in another household. It is clear that he is very much in love. He has of course not divulged that to me, but his whole being is uplifted and he smiles more often than he used to, even though he must be suffering financial hardship, as he lost his post on Mr Munro's death and has not yet succeeded in obtaining another. Francis offered to employ him, but he has gently refused, stating he knows well that Francis does not need his services, and will not accept charity. He is a very proud man.

Because of this they are keeping their marriage a secret, as his wife is still employed as a servant, but would certainly be released should her employer discover she was no longer a spinster. It is hard on them I think, as they can only meet occasionally until he secures another post, when they could seek to set up home together. I respect his high principles, although I could wish he would bend a little in this instance, and allow Francis to invent a post for him. He would not even accept Francis's offer of a room here, saying that at the moment he has accommodations, but at least eats with us on the evenings he calls to play chess, which is something.

The letter continued, commenting on the news he'd sent in the previous letter and asking questions of clan matters, in as discreet a manner as she had informed Alex that her and Mr Gordon discussed the Stuart cause when Francis was not around. Which meant that Susan trusted Iain Gordon. Who was now unemployed.

Interesting.

Perhaps it was time to pay a call on his dear friend and his clanswoman in Edinburgh.

CHAPTER SEVENTEEN

Edinburgh, July 1741

ALEX STOOD IN THE dark narrow wynd, hoping that at some point Iain Gordon would appear. He had been here for two hours and was aware that people were now eyeing him with suspicion, because no one in their right mind would loiter in such an insalubrious place, unless they were up to no good.

It was his second day in Edinburgh. The first had been spent in Francis Ogilvy's house, eating fine food, drinking fine wine and passing the time enjoying pleasant conversation in luxurious surroundings.

Seeing Francis had warmed his heart. The doctor looked so much better than he had done the last time Alex had seen him. If it wasn't for his swollen ankles and laboured breathing on exertion, he would have seemed cured of his affliction. Susan had worked wonders, it seemed.

At ten o'clock Susan had gently reminded her friend that he needed to go to bed, and then had gone with him, assisting him up the stairs and making sure he had everything he needed, before returning to the library and throwing herself down onto the sofa opposite Alex.

"It's good to see him so," Alex said. "Ye're doing a wonderful job, Susan. I ken his health is worsening, but he's happy. His eyes are sparkling, and he's...he's *alive* again."

"Aye, he is. It's no' me, though. Seeing patients again has given him a reason to live. He needs purpose," Susan replied.

"I'm sure he does. But you being here has given him the energy and interest to want to find that purpose."

She blushed then.

"So, ye havena come here just to embarrass me," she said. "Is it something in my letter that brought ye? Ye tellt us earlier there's nothing amiss at home, excepting the road-building laddies. Is there something else, that Francis mustna ken about?"

"It's to do wi' the thing I dinna want ye to ken about, in case it miscarries," Alex said. "But aye, it was your letter that made me come. Iain Gordon. Tell me about him."

She had told him about him. They had sat up long into the night discussing the man in detail. And now Alex was standing in one of the filthiest wynds in Edinburgh, dressed in the ragged and faded *féileadh mór* he had worn to walk from Loch Lomond to the outskirts of Edinburgh, hoping that his appearance would reassure people that whatever he was, he was nothing to do with the authorities.

Susan only knew that Iain was lodging in this wynd, but not the exact address. His wife lived in as a servant at one of the houses on the other side of the Netherbow Port, which meant they had to spend precious coin to meet each other on Sundays.

"It seems even then they're taking a risk, because her master is a churchgoing man and expects his servants to spend their precious time off in church or praying, whereas she's slipping away to see her husband," Susan said.

"Is she of the Protestant faith then?" Alex had asked.

"No. She's a Catholic, as is Iain. Her master doesna ken that either. Iain tellt me she's miserable, but her wage is the only money they have until he finds work."

Tonight was one of the nights Iain visited Francis to play chess, so Alex was sure that he would appear at some point. For the twentieth time he strolled slowly up and down the wynd, trying to avoid stepping in anything too obnoxious. Susan had suggested that he talk to him at Francis's house, but Alex wanted to be able to talk with him alone. Completely alone, and on neutral territory if possible, without worrying that a servant might be listening.

He had just turned round at the bottom of the wynd and was making his way back up it when a tall thin figure came out of a door halfway along the alley, carrying a bundle. The figure headed away up the wynd then turned left. Alex followed him at a distance, deciding to greet him on the high street and ask if there was a place they could talk together, later or maybe tomorrow.

To his surprise, instead of turning off the high street onto Niddry's Row where Francis lived, Iain carried straight on, passing through the Netherbow Port then heading out of the city altogether. Alex changed his mind about accosting Iain in the street. If he was going out of the city then they would have ample opportunity to talk together without risk of being overheard, unless he was meeting his wife. If he was, Alex would turn back and wait at the Netherbow Port for his return.

Iain did not meet his wife, or anyone else for that matter. Instead, once away from the city streets, he slipped off his shoes and stockings and, carrying them, headed across the heather for a way then down a short slope, at the bottom of which was a burn that ran over the rocks.

Once there he took off his tattered shirt and breeches and knelt down in the icy water to wash himself. Then he washed his shirt and breeches as best he could with no soap, stretching them out on the heathery slope to dry, before sitting down, arms wrapped round his knees, staring morosely toward the distant hills. Alex lay in the heather at the top of the slope, watching him.

There would not be a better time than this, he thought. The man was a clansman, or had been; he would not be mortified by being caught naked. Or at least Alex hoped not. It would be interesting to see his reaction, at any rate.

He stood and made his way silently towards the seated man.

"Good afternoon to ye, Mr Gordon," he called when he was a short distance away.

The man's reaction was instantaneous. Before Alex had finished his sentence he was on his feet, dirk in hand, unconcerned about his nakedness, ready to defend himself if necessary. Still a Highlander then, no matter how long he'd been away from his clan.

"Mr Drummond!" Iain said in astonishment as Alex drew close enough no longer to be a burly silhouette against the sun, but to be recognisable. He bent to his pack then, clearly intending to dress himself, become the servant he had been last time they'd met. Alex held up his hand.

"Dinna fash yourself, I'm no' here as Dr Ogilvy's friend, and ye're no' Munro's servant. I'm wanting to talk to ye Highlander to Highlander. Jacobite to Jacobite. Alone. Can we sit together a while? I've bread and cheese, and yon sweet cakes Mrs Henderson makes."

Iain regarded him intently for a minute and then straightened, looking away from Alex to scan the countryside.

"I'm alone, man. It isna a trap," Alex assured him

Iain relaxed, just a little, but kept his grip on the dirk, indicating with his other hand that Alex could sit down next to him.

He did and unpacked the promised food, spreading it out on the grass between them. They ate in silence for a while, Iain using his dirk to cut the bread and the cheese, filling the leather flask he had with him with water from the burn for them both to drink. Alex resisted the urge to fill the silence with words as Angus would, as he would have done before he became the chieftain. It was a thoughtful silence, not a hostile one.

"I canna believe I didna see ye following me," Iain said then. "Did ye track me all the way from the city?"

"Aye, from the high street. But I'm a Highlander, we're skilled at such things."

"So am I. I should have seen ye, or sensed ye at the least."

"I'm thinking ye've been away from your clan a good time. I was away from mine in Paris for three years, and when I returned I was shocked by how soft I'd become. It's natural."

"Maybe. Even so, I'm no' happy to realise it," Iain replied. "What is it that ye're wanting to say to me, that ye canna say in public?"

Here it was.

"I'm thinking to offer ye a position, in a manner of speaking," Alex said carefully.

"A position. As a servant?"

"A servant would be a part of it, aye. There would be other duties."

Iain was silent again for a moment.

"Jacobite duties. Ye tellt me ye wanted to speak to me Jacobite to Jacobite, so I'm presuming ye're active in your support for the Stuarts."

"I am."

Iain nodded.

"So ye're wanting a servant ye can trust no' to betray you?"

"I am. Would ye be interested in such a position?"

"How would I ken that ye'd no' betray *me*, if I said I was?" Iain replied.

Alex laughed then and relaxed a little. Instinctively he liked the man. Susan liked him, thought him trustworthy, had told him Iain reminded her a little of Duncan. Angus liked him very much.

He would have to rely on his instincts a lot when he became Sir Anthony. Take chances from time to time, as Highbury had with him. As Francis Ogilvy had with him, and with his father before him.

Decided, he turned his body, so he was facing his companion.

"I'm no' wanting to talk in riddles for an hour," he said then. "But I can only tell ye a certain amount, until I ken if ye're interested."

"I'm interested enough to listen to what ye have to say, and no' to tell anyone else ye've said it, whatever it is, and whatever I decide," Iain replied. "I give ye my oath on that."

Alex nodded.

"In a few weeks there will be a man in England, a wealthy man, who will be in great need of a servant. In fact he will be in great need of a number of servants, but due to his...ah...interests, he will only be able to have a very few. So he'll need a man who is experienced in many roles, who can teach others, and also be flexible in the duties he performs. And who can be trusted completely. Susan tells me you're married, and your wife is a servant too."

"Aye, she is."

"So then, if she shares your interests and is equally trustworthy, there would be a position for her too. It would be well paid. It would be interesting. And beneficial to the cause. Possibly crucial."

"And dangerous."

"If the interests were discovered by those who dinna share them, aye."

Silence fell again. Iain reached into his pack, pulled on a clean shirt, then got up and went down to the burn to refill his flask.

"So, I'm guessing yon wealthy friend of yours is a spy, who needs servants he can trust who willna gossip, as servants do."

"Aye, that's the outline of it."

"And why d'ye think ye can trust me?" Iain asked.

"Susan and Angus both believe ye to be trustworthy. My instincts tell me the same. I ken ye're a Jacobite, no' just because Munro was, but of your own accord. Ye're quiet and thoughtful, intelligent, and can plan ahead. And ye're accomplished in a variety of servant duties. I'm thinking it's worth taking the risk of telling ye a little. If ye're no' interested, then I'll say no more. Ever."

"Is yon wealthy man a Sasannach? Iain asked then.

"No. He's a Highlander, like us."

"And a clansman. Of a Jacobite clan?"

"Aye."

"So if I agreed, and yon plan failed, would we be abandoned in England, or would we have the protection of his clan if we escaped to Scotland?"

Whatever questions Alex had expected Iain to ask, this was not one of them. He ran his fingers through his hair.

"That's a difficult question to answer."

"Can ye ask yon wealthy man if that would be the case? He can ask his chief, if his chief is a fair man."

"This is important to ye."

"It is. I canna go back to my clan, and my wife willna go back to hers. Freedom has its advantages, but it can be lonely if ye've kent another life. We've both lived in Edinburgh for years, and we're missing the feeling of belonging to a clan. But we're no' missing the feeling of being ruled by a tyrant. So aye, it would be a consideration to ken we've a place to go and protection, if the worst happens."

"The worst that could happen would be to be caught and executed as a traitor," Alex said.

"Men die every day. We all have to die. It's what ye live for that's important. I'd want to have an answer to the question, and the name of the clan. Once I ken that, then I'd be interested enough to talk to my wife, and see if she's agreeable. If she isna, I willna do it. If she is, then we will. I trust her wi' my life. She's a rare woman, and a good one. A loyal one. Are ye still wanting to offer me the position?"

Now it was Alex's turn to fall silent and think for a while. Up to now he hadn't told Iain anything too incriminating. He was Alex Drummond, his brother was Angus Drummond. Iain did not know that Susan was of his clan. She used her husband's name, MacIntyre.

He had spent enough time with Highbury and observing other aristocrats to know that he could not become Sir Anthony without trusted and experienced servants. His brothers would not suffice. And if he hired servants in London he would have to remain in character every minute of the day. He would not be able to do that, not even to fulfil his father's wish, not even to fulfil Prince Charles's wish. Being Sir Anthony for a length of time would be dreadful, but bearable if he could be Alex MacGregor at home. Being Sir Anthony *all* the time would destroy him.

So he either had to trust Iain and his assessment of his wife, or abandon the whole idea. He took a deep breath and then turned to Iain.

"I dinna need to ask the wealthy man," he said. "I'm the chieftain of the clan, or my branch of it, and my word is law. I would offer ye the protection of my clan, and gladly. But when ye hear my name and what that protection would mean, then ye'll maybe no' be interested anyway."

"Ye're no' a Drummond, I take it?"

"I'm no' a Drummond. My name's Alex MacGregor."

"Have ye taken leave of your senses entirely?" was Iain's wife's response when he told her of Alex's offer the following Sunday. They were sitting by the same burn but a little further along, where there was a copse of pine trees under which they could make love with little risk of being discovered. It was not ideal, especially when it was raining as it was now, but it gave some shelter and was the best they could manage until Iain found work and a place they could live together. They had joked that if he could not they would move here and build a home out of pine branches.

At least six months ago they had joked about it, but did not any more, because time had passed and there was still no sign of him finding another place, which seemed incredible considering his skills. Iain thought it was probably because his former master had been a known Jacobite supporter, and while no one had acted against him, they were reluctant to employ the man's servant, assuming that he was also a Jacobite. Supporters of the Hanoverian cause would not even consider him, and closet Jacobites would not either, in case it brought them under suspicion.

In the last weeks they had begun to wonder whether Iain was maybe being watched by the authorities, and had seriously considered moving away from the filthy overcrowded city which they both hated anyway, and go to another place where they were not known. The only thing stopping them was the lack of money to do it. At least while they were here she was earning, which meant they both had a roof over their heads, even if his was a filthy damp cellar room which he shared with ten other men.

"It's the first offer I've had, Maggie, and it's an interesting one," Iain said.

"Dr Ogilvy offered ye a place," Maggie pointed out.

"That wasna a real place. It was kindly meant, but it was done from pity. And if I am being watched I wouldna want to bring him under suspicion. He's a good man. I wouldna do that. But this was a genuine offer. The man needs my skills, and yours too. Neither of us want our bairns to grow up in the city as Lowlanders. We'd be away from Edinburgh, could start again, live together. And we'd have a clan."

"The MacGregors are no' a clan. They're broken, desperate men, outlaws. When I was a bairn my da used to warn us about them, that they were children of the devil, and if they met ye they'd kill ye just for pleasure, and drink your blood when they had. It's a crazy offer! Ye're thinking to accept it from a man ye barely ken, chieftain of an outlaw clan, who's *tellt* ye it's dangerous! Christ, if a MacGregor thinks it's dangerous, then it'll be suicidal!"

Iain waited patiently until she'd finished, knowing this extreme reaction was inspired by fear for him because she loved him more than life itself, as he did her.

"Your da, who tellt ye the MacGregors were of the devil, tried to marry ye to his brother when ye were ten, Maggie," he reminded her then, gently. "I dinna think he was a man to judge who's of the devil and who isna, somehow. I never met your da and hope never to, for if I do I'll kill him, but I'm thinking he was speaking of himself rather than the MacGregors. I'm doubting he ever met one. Why would ye take any heed of him, the man who forced ye to abandon your clan and make your own way in life when ye were still a wee lassie?"

Iain and Maggie were well matched. They were both hard-working, proud, honest and trustworthy. She was fiery, passionate, brave, impulsive, fiercely protective of those she loved, and outspoken. He was patient, thoughtful, taciturn, slow to anger, sometimes hesitant to take chances due to his propensity to weigh up every possible risk. She fired him up to want to try new things; he calmed her soul, helped her think before acting on impulse.

He found it amusing that in this they seemed to have swapped roles, and when he pointed that out to her she laughed too, and the atmosphere lightened.

"He's no' a complete stranger to me, Maggie," Iain said then. "I've played chess wi' him many a time. I spent weeks wi' his brother, teaching him the basics of being a servant. Susan and Dr Ogilvy both speak very highly of him.

"When he tellt me today that he was a MacGregor, I was shocked too, and for the same reasons as you. No' because my da threatened me wi' them, but because I've heard about how brutal they are, how ruthless, barbaric. But since I've lived in Edinburgh I've heard similar tales about the Jacobites, as have you, and they're nonsense, just stories to frighten people into acting against us. The MacGregors are proscribed, and the king and various clans have tried to exterminate them for over a hundred years. And yet they're still here. I'm thinking there's something admirable in that. There's certainly something admirable about this Alex MacGregor, and about his wee brother."

"Admirable enough to risk your life for? My life for?" she asked.

The fact that he paused for a while before answering this told her that his opinion of this MacGregor man was very high indeed.

"I'll no' risk your life," he said finally. "It isna for me to do that. Ye must make your own decision. I've tellt him that if ye dinna want to then I willna either, and he didna question it, or try to make me change my mind."

She nodded, touched that he valued her opinion so highly. Most men would just tell their wives what they were going to do, regardless of what she thought. God had blessed her, the day he brought them together!

"Then before I decide, I'm thinking I need to meet the man," she said, and stood up.

"Now?" Iain asked.

"If I dinna meet him today, we'll have to wait until next Sunday. I dinna want to be worrying on that for a week. Come on."

She had no intention of letting her wonderful husband be talked into joining an outlaw clan, just because he was desperate to get work, for his life to have meaning, for them to live together. She was desperate for that too, but not desperate enough to watch Iain be persuaded into a ridiculous venture that would certainly get them killed. It was not just her da who thought the MacGregors ruthless, untrustworthy killers, *everyone* thought it. Or almost everyone, anyway.

"Good Lord!" Elspeth exclaimed when she opened the door to see the soaking wet couple on the doorstep. "Mr Gordon! Is there something the matter?" She ushered them into the hallway and closed the door on the wild rainy evening. Before Iain could answer, she led them down a passage and some steps to the kitchen.

"If ye're here to see the master, he's away to his bed, as he's a wee bit tired. He'll no' be playing chess the night. He had a man come to his door earlier who was fearful sick, and insisted on tending him, so Mistress MacIntyre tellt him he must rest, and rightly so. Here now, sit by the fire and dry yourselves a wee bit.

"I'm sorry, mistress," she continued then, addressing Maggie, "I should have introduced myself. I'm Elspeth Henderson, housekeeper to Dr Ogilvy."

"Maggie Gordon," Maggie replied. "Pleased to meet ye." She pulled the dripping cap off her head and wrung it out in the hearth. A profusion of wet auburn curls tumbled over her shoulders, causing Elspeth to start at the lack of modesty.

"Maggie's my wife, Mistress Henderson," Iain explained, noting this, and knowing how straitlaced Elspeth was.

"Ah," Elspeth said, slightly mollified. "I'm making a hot drink for the master, will I make yourselves one too? Will I give him a message?"

"It's actually Mr Mac—"

"Drummond," Iain said, rudely interrupting Maggie. "We're wanting to see Mr Drummond about something, if he's at home."

Maggie flushed scarlet as she realised her mistake, but Elspeth, busy sending a footman to see if Alex was at home to visitors, didn't notice. In fact if she had noticed she would probably have put it down to the heat from the fire, which was burning fiercely as Elspeth had been cooking all day.

By the time Alex appeared in the kitchen about ten minutes later, Maggie and Iain were both drinking a delicious posset made with hot spiced wine, their faces flushed, clothes steaming. They both looked up when he appeared.

"Iain!" he said. "I didna expect to see ye until Tuesday. Good evening to ye, Mistress," he added politely. "Alex Drummond at your service."

"This is my wife, Mr Drummond," Iain said. "I tellt her of your proposal, and she was wanting to meet ye herself."

"I apologise for disturbing ye on the Sabbath," Maggie added, with a glance at Elspeth, "I canna come any other day but Sunday, and I wished to meet ye. My *husband* holds a high opinion of ye."

Her slight emphasis on the word husband, along with her astute assessment of Elspeth Henderson intrigued Alex, who found himself warming to her immediately.

No, he told himself. *Think like Duncan, no' Angus.*

"As I do of him," he replied politely, his mind racing. They could certainly not talk here, with Elspeth listening and other servants likely to come and go. Nor anywhere in the house, not about something this sensitive.

"I was thinking ye might like to see the gardens," Alex said. "They're beautiful at this time of year, full of flowers. You wouldna think ye were in Edinburgh at all."

"Ye canna go in the gardens in this weather!" Elspeth protested. "It's pouring with rain! If ye go to the library, or the drawing room, I can bring refreshments."

"Ah, but the gardens would be bonny," Maggie put in. "I miss green spaces and flowers awfu' bad."

"Ye'll love them, *a ghràidh,*" Iain agreed, standing and politely holding his hand out to her. She picked her cap up from the hearth, screwed her hair up in her fist and put her cap on, pushing her hair under it as best she could before tying the ribbon at the top of her head. Then she stood, took Iain's hand, and the two of them followed Alex from the kitchen.

Elspeth went to the kitchen door and watched them as they strolled down the garden, looking for all the world like three gentlefolk having a casual stroll on a sunny summer's day. At one point Alex bent and plucked a rose, handing it to Iain's wife with a slight bow. Meanwhile the rain poured relentlessly from the dark grey sky.

As much as Elspeth liked Alex, and Susan, she had to admit that she would never understand Highlanders. They were all insane.

Alex had casually cast back a comment to the effect that they would certainly be observed until they were at the bottom of the garden and out of sight, which had led to the casual stroll. He led them to a summerhouse, where they could talk in private. No one would disturb them in this weather.

They sat down.

"At least it isna cold," he said.

"I wouldna care if it was," Maggie responded. "I thought I was going to faint in the kitchen, it was so hot."

"Aye, Mrs Henderson is a good woman, but a wee bit over-protective at times," Iain said. "She's very loyal to Dr Ogilvy, though, and no' a gossip."

"That's true, but I wouldna trust anyone wi' what I'm thinking ye're wanting to talk about," Alex said.

"I tellt the truth about Sunday being the only day I can come out of the house," Maggie told him.

"Aye, but the rest was because ye saw what Elspeth is directly," Alex added. "And ye dinna approve of me, or my proposal."

Maggie looked at him.

"Ye're a MacGregor," she said after a minute.

"I am," he replied. "And proud to be. Iain's proud to be a Gordon, are ye no'?"

"I am," Iain said. "Although I'll never return to my clan, I'm no' ashamed to be a Gordon."

"I'm no' ashamed to be a Menzies, either," Maggie put in. "That isna what I'm meaning. I'd think less of ye if ye *were* ashamed, for no man should be ashamed of his clan. But ye're proscribed. Everyone kens that ye dinna pay heed to the law, that ye're dangerous, ruthless. And ye're wanting us to join ye?"

"Maggie," Iain began. He loved his wife dearly, but her directness made him wince at times.

"Ye've just described every clansman, lassie," Alex replied. "You tell me of a clan that follows yon silly laws, that isna dangerous and ruthless when needful, and I'll tell ye of a clan that's extinct."

Maggie opened her mouth, then closed it again, because he was right.

"I understand why ye wouldna want to join the MacGregors, for just being one puts ye in danger. But in truth I didna make that a condition, nor did I offer it. It was your husband who brought up the subject of clan protection. I tellt him that as chieftain I'd offer him the protection of my clan, and gladly, but then I tellt him my name, so he'd ken that might no' be what he's wanting.

"If ye're a Menzies, then I can understand why ye hate the Mac-Gregors more than many, but I didna steal your lands, although I canna say I wouldna have done if the alternative was to starve. We're no' the only clan that's stolen lands from others, but we've more reason to do it than many."

She sat back then, considering this, her anger subsiding.

"If ye accept my proposal, then we'll no' be MacGregors in London," Alex continued. "The name MacGregor will never be mentioned. There are no' many people in Scotland who ken I'm a MacGregor, for that matter. Those who need to ken, ken."

"Will ye be Drummond in London?" Maggie asked.

"No. Dinna ask me who I will be, for I'll no' tell ye that unless ye agree to the proposal. If ye dinna then I'll be Alex Drummond, Iain will be the laddie who plays chess twice a week wi' myself and Francis, and ye'll be Iain's wife, servant to a lascivious bastard who's swived half his maids then thrown them out. I'm thinking he's likely no' swived you. Yet," Alex added.

Maggie flushed, her expression one of utter shock. Iain looked at her.

"Ye never tellt me—" he began.

"Ye're right," she interrupted. "He's no' swived me, because I'm ugly. I'm safe from him."

"Ye're no' ugly, lassie," Alex said. "I'm no' flattering ye. I wouldna flatter to make ye accept my offer. Ye come willingly and freely, or no' at all. He hasna seen your hair, has he?"

"No," she said.

Alex nodded.

"Ye're no' beautiful, but ye're no' ugly. And your hair is a glory to ye. Ye're no' safe from him. The reason he hasna tried yet is because he hasna seen it, and because he likes his lassies a lot younger than you. And likely because it's clear ye've a fierce temper on ye, and ye'll no' be easy to subdue. But in time he will, because his reputation is spreading, and the younger lassies willna work for him any more. And when he does, if ye dinna kill him, Iain will. Have I the right of it?"

"Aye, ye have," Iain said. "Maggie, is this true?"

"I thought it was because I'm ugly," she said softly, her anger vanished. "But aye, now I'm thinking, ye likely do have the right of it. How do ye ken all this?"

"I ken a lot of things. It's what I do. It's how I survive. I wouldna have tellt Iain even what I have unless I kent enough about him to be sure he wouldna just run off to the authorities, tell them I'm a Jacobite, and an active one, and a MacGregor too. And before I did that I had to learn a wee bit about you too, for ye're his wife, and he'd tell ye about the offer, of course."

"Tell me about the offer," she said then. "Iain has tellt me, but I want to hear it from you."

So he told her what he'd told Iain.

"If ye agree, then ye'd be a kind of maid-of-all-work. Ye'd clean the house and cook. Or rather ye'd clean the rooms we'd be using, or that callers might see, and cook just for us. That's yourself, Iain, me and two others."

"Yon wealthy mannie willna have dinners and parties?" Maggie asked. "I canna cook English meals, nor yon stupid things the gentry call food."

"He willna have dinners," Alex said. "If he did for any reason, ye wouldna be expected to cook them."

"And Iain will be a general servant."

"Aye. He'd need to be the coachman and a footman, and teach Angus more, and my other brother how to be a servant. It's a big house, so ye'd have your own rooms, a bedroom and a room for sitting in, to be alone in."

"In the attic."

"Christ, no. Ye'd be in the main part of the house. If ye agree to this, then I'm no' expecting ye to become MacGregors, but in London, in public ye'll be the wealthy man's servants, and ye'll treat him wi' respect and deference. In private we'll be a wee clan of our own, like family. Ye'll no' be in attics or cellars. We'll be equals."

Maggie thought. It sounded very tempting. But this man was dangerous. He could probably talk anyone into anything. She had to resist his force of personality, the attraction she felt for him. Not a sexual attraction, although he was very handsome. She loved Iain, and would never love another, would never be interested in another.

In that moment she realised that whatever they did, she could not remain in service where she now was, because Alex was right. If her master raped her, then he would die one way or another, either by her hand or Iain's.

Iain was saying nothing, allowing her to find out what she needed to know to make her own decision. He did not want to influence her into agreeing with him against her will, and she loved him for it. But she could see now why he wanted to join with this man.

Even so, she needed to keep a cool head.

"What would the wealthy man think of this? Is he a member of the gentry, or a nobleman? I canna imagine such a man treating us as equals."

"I canna tell ye about the man, no' yet. If ye agree, ye'll meet him in London. But I ken him very well. We'll all be equals. He'll be a wee bit like a chieftain, for he'll be taking the greatest risk, and ye'll have to follow him. When I'm at home," Alex continued, "I'm the chieftain, and my word is law. But when I can, and there's time, before making a decision I listen to my brothers' opinions, and other clansfolk, men and women. For my decisions affect all of us, and so I let the others speak. He holds a similar view."

"Have ye ever changed what ye were going to do on account of their opinions?" Maggie asked sceptically.

"Aye, many times. It's easier to plan a raid or go to battle if your clan feels they've had a part in the decision making. They'll follow ye wi' a willing heart. And it's fair, for their lives are at stake too. At times I have to make an unpopular decision, but if I do I'll explain why I'm making it, unless there isna time to do so. It wouldna work wi' a huge clan, I'm thinking, but the MacGregors are fragmented, so my clan is smaller, and it works well. It'll be the same in England, if ye agree."

Not only Maggie, but Iain as well were now looking at him incredulously, because he hadn't explained in this depth to Iain before.

Holy Mother of God, but he meant it! Maggie realised. She'd never met a chieftain like him before. Certainly the Menzies chief wasn't like this, and although she didn't know why Iain had left his clan, she knew his chief wasn't, either. If they joined him they would have a family, a sort of miniature clan in London. And if he ran his clan like this too...

She smothered the urge to agree to his venture immediately. He was a MacGregor.

"And yon wealthy man is a spy?"

"Aye. He'll be finding out information that might help the Stuarts regain the throne. Which means he'll need trustworthy servants, and a trustworthy coachman, for he may be going to places that would raise suspicion, and doing things that no man of his status would.

"The danger to you would be if he was caught. If he was, then he'd be tortured, and if he was tortured he would like to say he wouldna betray ye, but no man can guarantee that. What he *would* promise is to hold out as long as possible, to give ye time to escape. It's less likely that ye'd be arrested first, but if ye were, he'd ask that ye try to do the same. He would rescue ye, if he could, but wouldna expect the same from you."

"I'm thinking yon wealthy man has promised ye this," Iain spoke now, for the first time. "How d'ye ken he's no' lying to ye?"

"I ken it absolutely, but I canna tell ye why. Just as I willna tell ye which branch of the MacGregors I'm chieftain of, for there are many. Nor can I tell ye exactly what the mannie will be doing, or where his house in London is. Ye'll understand why."

Iain nodded then looked at Maggie, the question written large on his face.

She closed her eyes, trying to resist the combined magnetism of Iain's desire to do this, Alex MacGregor's compelling personality and her own impulsive desire to say yes. This was a life-changing decision. She had to think it through.

She had never thought things through, had always followed her instincts, and had usually been right. But not always. She had not been right about Iain, not at first.

Alex was watching her, observing the multiple emotions crossing her face like clouds on a windy day.

"Dinna decide now," he said then. "It isna a light decision, and once made I need ye to commit to it, at least for a good time. If at some point ye canna continue, it would make life difficult, but I'd accept that.

"But ye could *never* tell anyone *anything* about what ye'd been doing, for your own sake and everyone else's. At least no' until James Stuart's king again. So go away, think about it, talk about it together, in a place where *no one* could possibly hear ye. I'll meet ye down by the burn next Sunday, the same place we met this week, Iain."

"No," Iain replied. "Go a wee bit further down the burn, away from the city. There's a wee copse o' pine trees there we can meet in, and nobody will ken we're there. Whether we do this or no', we dinna want to raise suspicion. There isna any reason why a fine gentleman like Mr Drummond would want to socialise wi' an unemployed servant and a maid in secret. But ye're right, we canna meet in the city. We'll be careful, make sure no one follows us, and ye do the same."

"Good," Alex said approvingly. "I willna look like this, though. Nor will I wear the *féileadh mór*. Until next Sunday then."

They met the following Sunday and sat on the ground under a pine tree, deep in the copse. Alex, dressed as a working man in brown woollen breeches and a leather waistcoat, his coarse linen shirt sleeves rolled up to his elbows, hair unwashed, face grubby, had brought a bundle with him, which he spread out on the ground. It contained a selection of fine meats, white bread, cheese, hard-boiled eggs and cakes that would have got him arrested for thieving, if anyone had cared to investigate. In a sense they would have been right, as he'd raided the kitchen before setting out, although he knew Elspeth would forgive him.

He uncorked the wine, which they all drank from the bottle as he had not brought glasses with him, and they chewed in silence for a few minutes, Alex waiting with feigned patience for them to tell him whether they agreed to his proposal or not.

"I've a question for ye," Maggie said finally, just when Alex thought he was going to explode if he had to wait any longer.

"Aye?" he responded.

"At what age in your clan are the lassies expected to marry?"

What? Why was she asking such a question? She was married already, and clearly in her twenties. It had no relevance to the matter at all! He glanced at her, noted the expression on her face, and realised that relevant or not to the matter, his answer was clearly extremely relevant to her. He thought for a minute.

"The lassies are no' *expected* to marry," he said then. "Most of them do, but they're no' forced to. If they dinna want to marry then the clan will take care of them, but they'll be expected to play their part in the work, of course."

Her silence told him that she wanted examples. It was crucial then. What had the Menzies chief done?

"So, there's a lassie in the clan, Flora," Alex continued. "She's older than me, but she never married. She was due to marry a laddie called Alpin, but he was murdered a few days before the wedding. After that she said she wouldna marry again. I was just a wee bairn then, but my da thought she'd change her mind when she found her way through her grief. She didna. She lives wi' Alpin's parents now. Gregor's a weaver and has taught her his skills. My da never tried to make her take another, and nor would I.

"Now Alpin's brother is called Kenneth, and he was always like a second da to the bairns of the clan. He played wi' us and taught us to fight. He's a bonny fighter, avenged his brother's murder. There's a lassie in the clan called Jeannie, and she's awfu' pretty, kens her own mind. When she was eight she tellt him she'd be grown soon, and was going to marry him. Kenneth tellt her she was a wee bairn and him a man grown, and forgot it, for he thought she'd have another sweetheart the following week. But she didna. She never stopped wanting him, even though he said he wouldna marry her. It became the clan joke, everyone teased him unmercifully. Even when she was of an age to marry he said no, for he's a lot older than her. But she wore him down, and so in the end they married, and they're a good match, in fairness. Does that tell ye what it is ye need to ken?"

Maggie thought for a minute.

"What age is 'of age'?" she asked.

"I ken that Scots law says a lassie can marry at twelve and a boy at fourteen," Alex said, "but being a MacGregor, my da didna pay heed to the law, and nor do I. Twelve is too young for a lassie – having bairns is dangerous enough for any woman, but for one who isna fully grown – no. I follow his rule, for I agree with it. A laddie canna fight in battle until he's fifteen, and likewise canna marry. Nor can a lassie."

"So fifteen is the youngest then?"

"Aye, but I wouldna encourage them to marry that young. And the lassie would have to be agreeable. No lassie that I ken has *ever* been forced to marry, and never will be while I draw breath."

She looked at him intently for a while, and he met her gaze unflinching, for this was something he felt strongly about, as he did about many things. Then she glanced at Iain, who nodded.

"We accept your proposal," she said then.

"Ye accept my proposal because I willna let a lassie marry until she's at least fifteen?" Alex asked, thoroughly confused.

"No," Iain put in. "We accept your proposal because she didna believe ye were the chieftain ye claim to be. She tellt me ye sounded too good to be true, and I realised she was right. So she said she wanted to ask ye something ye couldna prepare for, and we'd see by your first reaction what ye truly felt, regardless of what ye said."

"I left my clan when I was ten, because my da wanted me to marry his brother, and the chief did nothing to stop it," Maggie explained.

"Your da wanted ye to marry your *uncle?!*" Alex exclaimed. "Christ. That's incest. No' just against Scots law, but every law, including God's! And he wanted ye to marry at twelve, I'm thinking?"

"No. He wanted me to marry at ten. So I left in the night, took some food and a dress and came to Edinburgh. I havena been back since, nor will I ever go."

"I willna go either, for if I do I'll kill the bastard, and his brother," Iain said.

"I'll help ye if ye do," Alex told them.

"One of the reasons I married Iain was because he respects me. He listens to my opinions, and he pays heed to them," Maggie said. "My da tried to beat my opinions out of me. Iain has never raised a hand to me, and if he thinks I'm wrong he'll explain why."

"And if I think she's right, I'll follow her."

"I'll never follow a man who doesna respect me because I'm a lassie," Maggie added. "I ken that's no' the normal way of things, but I canna be otherwise."

"I wouldna want ye otherwise," Iain said.

Alex started laughing then, surprising both of them.

"Ye'll fit in well wi' the MacGregors, should ye ever join the clan," he explained, "for I think there isna a clan in Scotland wi' so many outspoken lassies in. I blame my da."

"Your da?"

"Aye. He married for love, and my ma had a mind of her own. In public he was the chieftain, and a good one, and she wouldna question him then. Nor would anyone, as is right. But at night sometimes I'd lie awake and hear them blethering down below. He'd tell her his plans and thoughts, show a side of him to her that he never showed to anyone, no' even his bairns. And he listened to her. He loved her something fierce, and when she died he lost his way, for a long time.

"I willna ever love like that. But I was brought up to respect everyone, unless they didna deserve it, and I maintain that now I'm chieftain, for I find it fair. And the clansfolk approve of it. When I need to give an order they dinna like, they do as I say, for they ken I'm fair, and I've good reason for acting as I do.

"I might give ye orders like that in London too, if there's need. But I willna disrespect either of ye, unless ye deserve it. I can swear that on the iron, if it'll reassure ye," he finished.

"No," Maggie said. "We've accepted your offer. I'll need to work here until August, for we're paid yearly on the mistress's birthday, which is mid-August. Then I'll leave."

"Will ye no' have to give notice?" Alex asked.

"I willna be there. I'll be on the way to London, I'm assuming. I'm doubting she'll follow me," Maggie said. "Unless ye're wanting a character from her?"

"No," Alex said, grinning as a huge surge of relief washed over him. He could do this. And it seemed Maggie was as good a choice for a maid as Iain was for a manservant. "I'm thinking ye've shown me enough of your character in the twice I've met ye. I'm needing no more."

The matter settled, they sat down to discuss the practical details, finishing off the rest of the food between them. After that they parted.

Iain would still come to Dr Ogilvy's twice a week to play chess until mid-August. Then he would tell Francis and Susan that both himself and Maggie had been offered a position in another town, would explain that they needed to go where no one knew of his Jacobite connections. Neither of them would tell anyone else anything at all.

Then they would go to London, to the house that was waiting for them. Iain would be measured for and purchase a green silk livery to fit his status as footman, and some reasonable ordinary clothes. Maggie could choose her colours as long as they were suitable for a maid.

Angus and Duncan would arrive in September, when they could all get to know each other and start to learn their duties. Alex and the wealthy man would arrive a little later.

They sat talking, detailing as much as they could then, because writing was dangerous and Alex did not want anyone in Edinburgh to know that his relationship with Iain was anything other than that of a respectable gentleman enjoying a game of chess with a menial, whose wife he had politely expressed a desire to meet, which Iain had unfortunately taken literally.

Four days later Alex returned to Loch Lomond, both elated and depressed. Elated because he could finally embark on what he'd come to see as his destiny, to try to help return the Stuarts to the throne and in doing so lift the proscription on his clan. Depressed because he did not want, had never truly wanted this destiny. But if he didn't attempt it he would regret it for the rest of his life.

Iain and Maggie's acceptance had removed the last obstacle. Now he was committed and would give it his all, as he had always given to every endeavour in his twenty-five years of life.

CHAPTER EIGHTEEN

Scotland, September 1741

THE THREE MEN STRODE across the undulating terrain of the Cheviot hills, heading southward. Each of them carried a small pack containing food, some money and a change of clothes, which they would put on when they reached the border.

As the border grew closer their conversation, which had been brisk at the start of the day, grew more sporadic, finally halting altogether. Then they walked in silence, each wrapped in his own thoughts, finding themselves walking slower and slower as the English border grew closer and closer.

Finally the eldest of the three stopped, causing the others to halt as well.

"I'm wanting a wee bit of time here before we go any further," he said. "I want to say goodbye to my homeland."

"It isna goodbye, Alex," Duncan said softly. "No' for any of us. We'll all see home again, before long."

"Aye," Alex agreed, but he did not sound convinced. "Even so, I'll likely no' be home for a good while yet. I'm just needing to do this. I'll no' be long."

Angus made to sit down then, but Duncan gripped his arm to stop him.

"Come on," he said. "He's wanting to be alone for a wee while, no' have ye waiting impatiently for him and asking if he's ready to go on yet."

"I wouldna..." Angus began, and then stopped and flushed, realising that he would.

In spite of his sudden dark mood Alex grinned at this, because not only was Duncan right that he wanted some time completely alone, but he'd summed up how Angus would react perfectly.

"We'll away down the hill, and have a wee rest," Duncan said then. "Ye take the time ye need."

The two brothers continued then, Angus protesting that although he *might* have said those things, he wouldn't have been impatient, Duncan responding with jocular disbelief, and then they disappeared from view, their voices fading, until all Alex could hear was the wind blowing through the grass and heather, and the sound of a skylark as it ascended into the pale blue sky.

He breathed in, filling his lungs with the pure Scottish air, and then exhaled, allowing the peace to seep into his soul, reassuring himself that he was doing the right thing, that it would all be worth it in the end. He sat down for a minute, staring north, his fingers idly stripping the fading blooms from the heather, and felt the homesickness start to swirl through his blood.

He was being ridiculous, he knew. The air here was no different to the air across the border, although it was *very* different to the air awaiting them in London. Poor Duncan; he would hate it. He was right though; Alex *would* see home again before too long. He would make it happen, would take the baronet on a fictional journey to some fashionable place and then head north. It was not like when he was in Paris and couldn't afford to come home. Highbury would gladly finance a trip home, and if he didn't Alex could walk back, free of charge.

It *would* be more dangerous though, a different sort of danger to that he was accustomed to. But he would adapt. He always adapted. He just needed a little time to do so.

He sat for a while longer, willing himself to feel calm and accepting enough to continue, and to meet his brothers in a happier mood. When that showed no signs of happening he stood suddenly, telling himself to stop being silly. He walked along the plateau, counting the positives. He had his brothers with him, and Iain and Maggie were waiting for him in London, as was the Earl of Highbury. It would be good to see him again.

Yes, it would be dangerous, but so was everything the MacGregors did. But it would also be a challenge, which he had always enjoyed. And there would be fun to be had in making fools of the aristocracy, of mocking the usurper and all his sycophantic courtiers, while collecting information that would enable the true king to throw fat Geordie and all his family off the throne and back to Hanover where they belonged. And at night, in the house, he could be Alex MacGregor again, laugh and joke with his brothers, share the triumphs and the failures.

He could do this.

A sudden flash of scarlet caught his eye, rousing him from his thoughts and setting the adrenaline surging through his blood. In a split second he registered the appearance of a number of redcoat soldiers, recognised that there was nowhere that he could hide properly, and that they had not seen him, yet. Then he dropped like a stone to the ground, minimising the chance of them noticing movement which would alert them to his presence.

He wriggled backwards, coming to rest in a waterlogged depression surrounded by a thick patch of heather, pulled his green and brown *féileadh mòr* over his head, then splashed the muddy water over his legs and arms. And then he could do no more, for they were so close now that *any* movement would likely be noticed by them, no matter how unobservant they were. He froze, cursing that his right hand, though muddy, would be in full view to anyone who looked down. If he tried to move it they would almost certainly see it. Hopefully they would just continue past, chatting, looking straight ahead of them.

He dared not move his head to look at them so he listened, assessing from their voices how many there were. Or at least the minimum number, for there could be more who weren't talking. He hoped not; silent soldiers would be more likely to be observing the terrain and to see him.

If they did, he decided, he would run if he could, and if he couldn't would at least take as many with him as possible, and would bellow to his brothers to run. And then he forced his muscles to relax, and his mind to absorb everything, so that if an opportunity arose to fight or flee, he could take it without hesitation.

"Bloody hell, how anyone can live in this godforsaken hole is beyond me," one of the redcoats was saying. "The sooner we're called back to England the better."

"We'll be lucky if we're recalled before spring, now," a younger soldier answered, his voice high-pitched. "We'll be at Inversnaid till April at least, unless the Frenchies attack."

Good. They were heading north then, so once they passed him and moved on, he could continue south to his brothers safely.

"No chance of that, not this year," the first man replied.

They had stopped now, and were standing very close to him, mere feet from where he was lying. Had they seen him? He tensed again, ready to explode into action if he heard the slightest indication that they had; a change in voice tone, the sound of a weapon being drawn...

"There's still some fun to be had, though," an older soldier said, pronouncing his vowels with the flat tones of a northerner, Yorkshire perhaps. "Less chance of getting the pox than with the city whores, too."

There was no indication in his tone that he had any awareness of the Highlander lying so close to them. He moved closer, so that even with his face turned slightly to the side Alex could see the muddy black leather boots of the Northerner. If he'd moved his hand even slightly, he could have touched them.

He did not move his hand.

"I still think we should have buried her though, afterwards," the high-pitched young man said worriedly.

"Why? Do you think her ghost'll come back to haunt you?" the older man asked mockingly.

"No, of course not, it's just...well, it seemed wrong to just leave her there, for the animals and crows to have a go at."

"Suffering from a guilty conscience now, are you? Still took your turn though," another voice said laughingly.

At least six bastards then, or six who liked to blether.

"I'm sure her husband'll find her when he gets back from whatever thieving he was up to," the laughing voice continued. "He'll bury her. Save us the trouble."

The voices were starting to move away now, but the boots of the northerner were still in the same place.

"Are you coming then, or are you staying to admire the scenery all day?" the first man called back.

"No, I need a piss. You go on, I'll catch up in a minute," the northerner said.

The other voices receded now, moving eastwards. Not heading directly to Inversnaid then. And then the soldier stepped forward onto the Highlander's hand, the heel of the boot grinding his fingers into the heather. Alex caught his breath, commanded his brain to ignore the intense pain and let it fade into the background, to be replaced by more important considerations.

At least my hand isna visible any more, he thought, and swallowed back a sudden urge to laugh. He forced his body to remain motionless, although his mind was racing. The voices had almost vanished, and soon the owners would start to descend, upon which their friend would no longer be visible to them.

The northerner was fumbling with his breeches now, cursing softly as he tried to unbutton them. Maybe he was drunk, Alex hoped. If he was he would be less observant, and his reactions would be slower if he did see him, which could mean the difference between life and death.

Then there was the sound of a soft pattering, and suddenly Alex's back became warm as the stream of urine soaked through his plaid to the shirt below. He gritted his teeth and waited, counting. The soldiers would be a good way away now, far enough for Alex to do what he so wanted to do and still be a good distance away before the others returned to see what had happened to their companion.

The man finished, grunting with satisfaction, and then stepped back, buttoning his fly as he did.

Alex's right hand was temporarily useless, so he drew his dirk left-handed as he exploded from the heather, driving the razor-sharp blade up under the redcoat's chin before the man was even aware what was happening. He drove it through the tongue and upwards into the brain with his full strength, enhanced by his rage.

They both toppled over onto the grass, the soldier flailing weakly at Alex, pressing against his chest in a futile attempt to push him away. Alex smiled grimly, twisting the blade as he did and watching with satisfaction as the man's eyes widened, then slowly glazed over.

He crouched there for a moment, forcing his breathing to slow, and then he listened again. Silence. Or rather human silence, for the wind was still blowing through the heather. Good.

Carefully he withdrew the dirk and cleaned it on his victim's scarlet coat. Then he sheathed it and rose, looking eastwards. Nothing. The others would no doubt return at some point, when their companion failed to catch up with them, but he would be long gone by then. He looked down at the corpse, then rolled it backwards into the water-logged depression from which he had so spectacularly exploded mere seconds before. Then he spat copiously onto the man's back.

"Ye'll no' be murdering any more women, ye bastard," he said softly.

He flexed the fingers of his injured hand, watching the scar that Duncan had inflicted on him so many years ago writhe. He winced. It was painful, but nothing seemed to be broken. All his fingers moved normally and nothing was out of place.

He splashed some mud over the scarlet coat and then turned, heading south to catch up with his brothers. Before he did, he'd wash his shirt in the river. He'd never hear the end of it if he admitted a redcoat had used him as a chamberpot.

As he walked, rapidly now, his mood lifted. It had been a good omen, he thought. A miracle that the fools hadn't seen him, another that his dirk had pierced the redcoat in the perfect spot to stop him crying out. And he had avenged a woman's death.

Yes, it would all work out well, he decided. All he had to do was believe that, and it would happen. And if he could somehow manage to treat the venture seriously enough not to make fatal mistakes, but still see the humour in it, he *might* actually enjoy it, to some extent at least.

He smiled to himself and continued, whistling softly as he did. He would not wash his shirt, he decided. Instead he would tell his brothers what had happened. They would see the humour in it too. It would be good to enter England sharing a joke.

As he came over the next rise he saw them below him, sitting on the grass next to a burn, in the process of changing out of their *féilidhean móra* into the hated woollen breeches and stockings. He waved, then turned his face eastward for a moment, from where in due time he had to believe the prince would come, with his army. He nodded in silent acknowledgement of this. And then he made his way down to join Angus and Duncan, ready now for whatever the future held.

London, early October 1741

Once they reached London, Duncan and Angus made their way to the house that Highbury had rented for Sir Anthony, where Iain and Maggie would be waiting. Alex went to Grosvenor Square, where the earl was waiting impatiently for him, having received his letter a few days before   saying he would be arriving in the early days of the month.

They spent a happy final evening together as footman and master, sitting in Highbury's bedroom, the door firmly locked so that no servant could come in and perhaps wonder why the Earl of Highbury and his probationary footman were relaxing together like equals.

"The whole place is now furnished," Highbury told him. "The public rooms and four of the bedrooms luxuriously, the rest adequately. You did say that two of the servants were married to each other? I thought four bedrooms would be enough, but if I was mistaken, then I can of course arrange for more to be made comfortable."

"Aye, John and Margaret are married," Alex said. "They havena been able to live together since they wed, so it'll be a rare treat for them to have their own rooms. He wasna working, and she was a servant in a lecherous bastard's house. She'd have been dismissed if her master had kent she was married, and they hadna any other income."

"And they're trustworthy, you say."

"I'm hoping so. It'll be interesting to see what Murdo thinks of them."

"Murdo is your brother Duncan," Highbury said, "the one who sees the details."

"Aye, and Angus is Jim. I'm thinking it better if we both use their aliases from now on, so there'll be no slips in the future."

Highbury nodded.

"What if Murdo thinks they aren't trustworthy?" he asked.

Alex sighed.

"Then I'll do what I have to. But I dinna want to think on that now, for I like them both. I'll cross that bridge when I come to it. Is there anything at the house that still needs to be done?"

There was a short silence before Highbury answered, as he absorbed what Alex meant by 'do what I have to'. If he lived to be a hundred he would never be able to reconcile the kind, caring man he loved with the ruthless killer he could be when a situation called for it.

"I think so," he said then. "I haven't been to the house since you wrote to tell me John and Margaret were on their way, as it would have raised their suspicions. There's a selection of outfits in a chest in your room, several wigs, all the cosmetics you asked for, and a large bottle of that hideous violet perfume you're going to inflict on us. I think you have everything you need to transform yourself into the baronet, but if I've forgotten anything you'll have to make a return visit to beg for the position as footman again, before disappearing forever."

Alex laughed.

"I'm hoping Mr Drummond will be taking leave of ye permanently after this evening," he said. "He looks too much like Alex MacGregor for my liking. If we have to meet again, other than as Sir Anthony and the Earl of Highbury, then I'll make myself look different."

"I'll miss Alex MacGregor," Highbury said.

"So will I. Although I'll be him in private at the house."

"But I won't see him."

"No. For your safety, and mine," Alex replied. "Although there isna any reason why Sir Anthony canna come to visit you here or at one of your country houses occasionally. Everyone will ken we're friendly. After all, you're introducing me to English society."

"Because I'm gullible and naïve, and taken in by an impostor."

"Aye. But I'm hoping that a good many more people will be taken in by the impostor, and the more that are, the less suspicion will fall on you if I'm discovered. So we canna visit each other *too* much."

"Maybe if you go on one of the trips to Paris in search of fashion, as you said you might do, we could meet up at my house in Durham for a few days?" Highbury suggested, and his tone was so plaintive that Alex found himself incapable of refusing, as sensible as it would be to do so. He thought for a minute. He could change his appearance, maybe, enough that he would not look like Mr Drummond. And in truth he really wanted to spend time with this man he owed a lot to, and who he cared deeply about.

"Aye, we could. I'll need to think about another disguise though. I canna be Drummond or Sir Anthony. But aye, it would be good to relax with ye sometimes, and to discuss how everything is going."

Highbury's face lit up.

"It would! We had *such* a wonderful tour, didn't we?" he said. "I'll never forget it."

He would make it happen, Alex thought. He had always thought that wealth and power brought happiness, but now he realised that what he had with his brothers, with his clan, was worth more than any amount of material wealth. This man deserved to have love in his life. If his son could not give him that, he could.

Later that night he arrived at his new house, but as he was not yet the baronet, entered through the tradesmen's and servants' entrance, to be greeted ecstatically by Angus and with more reserve but as much love by Duncan. Duncan managed to express his approval of Iain and Maggie briefly before the two arrived, Angus having run into the drawing room to tell them of Alex's arrival.

They were initially nervous, unsure if he would approve of what they'd achieved so far. Alex, having seen how clean the place was, tasted how delicious Maggie's broth and bread were, and how much Duncan had learnt about being a footman in the few days he'd been here, reassured them that they seemed to be perfect for the job, after which they relaxed and spent a pleasant evening chatting and drinking claret in the beautifully decorated and furnished drawing room.

Although Duncan and Angus knew that Alex was also 'the wealthy man' Iain and Maggie had yet to meet, and that his name was Sir Anthony Peters, they had not divulged this information to Iain and Maggie yet. So Alex merely told them that the wealthy man was expected in a couple of days, after which the miniature 'clan' would be complete.

Alex sat at his dressing table surrounded by pots of paint, staring at himself in the mirror. It was still a novelty for him to see his own face. Angus did look very much like him, he noted. Enough that anyone seeing them together would know them as close relatives immediately. He would need to be aware of that. Perhaps if he was in London as someone other than Sir Anthony and anyone mentioned the resemblance, he could say that his cousin worked for a nobleman in the area. As long as no one connected the face in the mirror now with the face he was about to manufacture, Angus would be safe. Or as safe as any of them were.

Alex had already chosen an outfit from the dozen or so Highbury had had made for him. The earl had outdone himself. They were all exquisitely tailored and embroidered, and all in eye-wateringly hideous combinations of colours. He had chosen one of the more sober outfits to introduce himself to the four people currently occupied in various tasks about the house; a silk confection in jade green, embroidered with pink and yellow rosebuds.

He combed and deftly plaited his hair, and then opened the pot of white paint and began the transformation.

An hour or so later he leaned forward, examining himself minutely in the mirror. Yes. Everything was in place, no tendrils of chestnut hair visible, no tanned skin. A diamond-shaped beauty spot covered his dimple. Perfect. He doused himself liberally with violet cologne, and smoothed his pink leather gloves onto his hands. He went to the door, then stopped as a thought occurred to him. He grinned mischievously.

He *had* intended to introduce his alter ego to them all by going down the stairs and just appearing in the kitchen. But it would be much better if he could come from outside and knock on the front door. Iain would certainly open it in that case, because Angus and Duncan's liveries were not yet ready, whereas Iain had his. It would be interesting to see if Iain recognised him, and if not, how he reacted to the baronet. And for that matter, how his brothers would react, for although they knew he was the wealthy man, and that his name would be Sir Anthony Peters, they had never seen his disguise, nor had he described it properly to them.

Alex went to the bedroom window, opened it and looked out. There was no one in the garden. He reached under the bed then, pulling out a small chest from out of which he took a rope ladder. Every bedroom had one, and outside every window were two sturdy hooks from which they could be hung to facilitate a safe escape if the need arose. He laughed quietly. This would be fun.

A minute later he was in the garden, eyeing the locked gate that would slow down any pursuers and cursing silently. The key was on a hook in the kitchen, but if he walked in the back door that led to it now, his surprise would be spoilt. No. He was determined to do this. He would not let a gate defeat him.

To hell with it. He took off his gloves, put them in his pocket, and then eyed the metal bars, working out the best way to climb over it.

Getting over the damn thing taught him an important lesson; tight silk breeches were not designed for climbing over obstacles, particularly obstacles with spikes on the top. In fact such ridiculous impractical outfits were seemingly not designed for *anything* other than flouncing about and looking silly.

He spat on his hand and tried to wipe the black mark off his pristine white stockings, succeeding only in spreading it. Giving up, he straightened his frockcoat, put on his gloves, pulled the lace at his cuffs down so that it fell perfectly, and checked that his wig was still in place. *I must make sure that I have a suit of practical workman's clothes in the chest with the rope ladder,* he thought. *And some cloths and vinegar to get the paint off.* He would never be able to leap the wall and flee in an emergency in these!

He stood for a moment, rotating his neck and shoulders, then stretched and slumped his posture, as he had in the bedroom with Highbury when they were perfecting his disguise. He concentrated his mind, focussing totally on the person he was about to become.

Then he minced down the side of the house, up the steps, and knocked on the door.

Iain, who was crossing the hall when the knock came, froze. He could not think of anyone who would call at the front door. Well, except the wealthy man, but he wasn't due until tomorrow at the earliest.

He looked down at himself. Leather breeches, grubby shirt, hair falling tangled on his shoulders, and all of him liberally sprinkled with sawdust and wood chips, as until a few minutes ago he'd been cutting wood.

Only important people came to the front door. He could not open it dressed like this. It would give a terrible first impression. The wealthy man would be bound to find out; people talked.

"Bàs mallaichte," he growled to himself and then changing direction rocketed up the stairs, his long legs taking them three at a time. The bastard would just have to wait. Hopefully whoever it was would have grown bored and gone by the time he came down. There was no

one at home an important person would want to see, so it would save him having to politely but firmly refuse admission.

Ten minutes later, hands and face washed, hair stuffed up under a hideous powdered wig, and dressed in his grass-green silk livery, Iain ran back down to the hall, stood for a few seconds composing himself, adopted the supercilious expression all good footmen cultivated (unless they were Angus, who hadn't mastered it yet), and opened the door.

To his surprise the visitor was still there, although he had turned and was gazing down the street. But on hearing the door open he turned back.

"Ah!" he trilled. "I must admit I was beginning to fear that nobody was at home on this fair day. Is the weather not utterly delightful?"

"It is indeed," Iain replied, although at that moment the last thing he was thinking about was the weather. Who the hell was this grotesque creature? Surely not one of the wealthy man's friends? "I am sorry, my lord, but the master isna at home, and isna expected until tomorrow. If you would care to leave a card, I will of course inform him of your visit as soon as he arrives."

The grotesque creature patted its coat pockets.

"I declare, but I do not seem to have a card upon my person!" he exclaimed. "I am however aware that the master is not currently in residence." To Iain's surprise, the fop now sprang forward, placing one foot inside the doorway. "There!" he cried. "Now he *is* in residence! Sir Anthony Peters, arrived prematurely. And you must be Mr Gordon!"

For a split second Iain forgot all his training and just stared at the man in horror. *This* was the wealthy man, the *Highlander*, the final member of their little clan? And he had been stupid enough to trust Alex? He would kill him when he saw him! Then he remembered himself, and bowed to his master. His temporary master, for as soon as he could, he would tell Maggie and they would leave, take their chances elsewhere.

"I beg your pardon, Sir Anthony," he said deferentially. "You were no' expected until tomorrow, and I wasna given a description of your person."

"Oh, I understand completely! Let us think no more of it," the baronet said, smiling hideously.

"If you would care to go into the drawing room, I'll inform the rest of the household that you have arrived, sir. Is there luggage to be taken to your room?"

"A man is bringing it," Sir Anthony replied, waving a languid hand at the street. "I am sure he will arrive momentarily. It would be delightful to sit down, for I have walked a considerable distance – the whole length of the street, in fact, and find myself a little fatigued."

Iain opened the door to the drawing room and the baronet stepped in, to see Maggie sitting on a chair by the fire, darning.

"The master has arrived a wee bit earlier than expected," Iain warned.

Maggie looked up, her eyes widened, then she shot up from the chair and curtseyed. There was a strangled splutter, and then she looked up to see the master observing her, a friendly expression on his face. She flushed scarlet, her mouth convulsing as she fought not to laugh hysterically.

"I'll away and get refreshments," she managed in a choked voice, then fled the room without further ado.

If Sir Anthony noticed this odd behaviour he did not comment on it, instead moving to the chair on the opposite side of the fireplace and sitting down.

"Ah," he sighed blissfully, as though having walked a hundred miles rather than a hundred yards.

"While my wife's fetching the refreshments sir, I'll away and tell the others you're here," Iain said.

"That would be splendid! But please say only that a visitor is in the drawing room. I wish to remain incognito at the moment," Sir Anthony simpered.

"As ye wish, sir," Iain said, resolving to inform Duncan and Angus exactly who was here, before telling Maggie to do the refreshments and then pack her things. He made his way to the door and opened it, to be immediately confronted by Angus and Duncan, chatting amiably as they crossed the hall.

"...but is it no' better to dirk them in the heart?" Angus was asking. "That'll kill them directly."

"No, because ye've a high chance of hitting a rib when ye try," Duncan explained. "An ye do that, the man'll no' be too badly injured to fight, and he'll no' be waiting for ye to try again. If ye stab him in the belly, ye'll no' kill him, but he'll no' be fighting back either."

"Aye, but..."

"Ah! This must be the delightful Murdo and Jim!" a voice trilled from the chair before Iain had a chance to warn them. The brothers stopped and turned, failing to register Iain's warning look. Failing to register anything once the baronet stood and turned to face them.

"Holy Mother of God," Angus murmured, then let out a snort of laughter, before putting his hand over his mouth and swallowing it back.

Duncan had frozen for a moment, the look on his face one of absolute shock, but then he recovered himself, bowed and moved into the room.

"I apologise, sir, for our state of undress," he said then, only his eyes betraying his desire to burst out laughing. "Our master isna at home, willna return until tomorrow, so we're taking care of some necessary manual work before he arrives."

"I understand entirely!" Sir Anthony cried, clapping his hands together. "How commendable of you. I am sure you will be in perfect order when he arrives. Your consideration for his comfort is most affecting! Margaret has gone to prepare refreshments."

"Do ye wish us to attend your horses, sir?" Angus said from the doorway, pulling himself together, with some success.

"That is most kind, but will not be necessary, I assure you! The weather is so clement that I ventured to walk here – the entire length of the street! I am sure that after some sustenance I will find myself capable of making the return journey."

Duncan was standing a few feet away from Sir Anthony now, his forehead creased in puzzlement, while Angus, still in the doorway, was struggling not to laugh again at this ridiculous comment.

"Ye absolute bastard," Duncan said softly then, causing both Iain and Angus to look at him in shock. "I canna believe it!"

He picked up a cushion from the chaise longue, and to Iain, Angus and Maggie's horror, who had just appeared with a tray, smacked the visitor in the face with it.

"Walking the entire length of the street! I was believing ye, ye wee shite!" He turned to look at the three horrified figures in the doorway. "It's Alex," he said.

"Alex?!" Angus echoed, coming into the room and staring at him. His mouth opened as he recognised his brother, then he started laughing. Iain and Maggie exchanged a puzzled glance, then she came in, putting the tray down on the table with a crash that threatened to smash the delicate porcelain carefully arranged on it.

"*Ifrinn*," the baronet swore, his voice dropping an octave and developing a Scottish accent. "What gave me away?"

"Your eyes," Duncan said then.

"Aye, your eyes," Angus agreed. "But I wouldna have seen that if Duncan hadna tellt me it was you. No' for a time, anyway."

"Ah. Well, I canna change my eyes. Sit ye down," Alex said then to all of them, pulling his wig off as he did.

"So are ye telling me that there is no wealthy man?" Iain asked, coming to stand at the back of the sofa, still feeling that he and Maggie had been made fools of.

"Aye, there's a wealthy man," Alex said. "He's Sir Anthony Peters, born in Cheshire, raised in France. Sit down, man. Let me explain. Maggie too."

They all sat, Duncan still shaking his head that he had not recognised his own brother, the closest person in the world to him.

"I'm sorry," Alex said then to the Gordons. "I couldna tell ye who the wealthy man was, nor that it was me, no' until I kent for sure I could trust ye. I wanted Duncan to meet ye before I did that, for he sees what I canna, and he's an awfu' good judge of people."

"I'm no' so sure of that after today," Duncan said.

"At least ye *did* recognise him," Angus commented. "I wouldna have done for a good while, I dinna think."

"So if ye trust us, why did ye no' just tell us who ye were?" Iain asked.

"I was going to, but then I thought I'd play a trick on ye, partly for the fun of it, but mainly because I wanted to see how long it was before one of ye recognised me. If my own brothers didna ken me, then I'm thinking nobody will," Alex explained.

"But the people ye're going to spy on dinna ken ye anyway," Angus pointed out.

"No. But I canna be Sir Anthony all the time. Which is why I needed trustworthy servants," Alex said, nodding at Iain and Maggie. "When I'm at home I'll be Alex, and I'll need that respite, as ye can imagine now ye've seen me. And there'll be times when I need to do things and no' be Sir Anthony. So if even you two didna recognise me immediately, then no one will, even if they see myself and Anthony on different occasions."

"And ye're going to be this...this clown, wi' all the nobles?" Duncan asked.

"I am. Because nearly everyone will look at the costume and the paint, and the ridiculous flowery words and gestures, and they willna notice the important things."

"Like the eyes," Maggie said.

"Aye, like the eyes."

"It's the only thing about ye that *is* recognisable," Duncan said in wonder. "Everything else is completely different. I've heard ye copy people before, like the Father, but this is another thing altogether. It's incredible."

"How will ye keep it up though?" Maggie asked.

"I'm wanting ye to help me. When I appear as Sir Anthony, ye must all treat me as Sir Anthony, no' as Alex in disguise. Even if like now, we're alone. All of us, even me, need to think of him as a different person, for if we can do that, it'll increase our chance of no' being caught. And it'll help me to be him too."

"I dinna ken if I can do that," Angus said, laughing.

"Aye, ye can, for ye have to," Alex said then. "For if ye dinna and we're caught because of it, we'll all die. The punishment for treason is to be hanged, drawn and quartered, and if ye're a lassie, burnt at the stake."

Angus stopped laughing then, and the atmosphere in the room suddenly darkened as they all took this in.

"If any of ye dinna want to do it, tell me now," Alex said quietly. "Maybe ye didna ken just how dangerous it is. But ye do now."

"I kent it was dangerous, and I'm your right-hand man in this, as in everything," Duncan replied.

"And I'm your left-hand man," Angus added, his face deadly serious now.

"Ye'll be needing us too, more than we realised," Maggie said after a moment, "for I canna imagine how ye'll manage it without people ye trust, who ye can be yourself wi' when ye're here. I can do this, wi' a wee bit of practice, I'm thinking. Unless ye dinna think we should?" She looked at Iain.

He thought for a minute.

"Aye," he said. "For as I said to ye before, it's no' how ye die, but how ye live that matters. I'm wanting to die in my bed as an old man, no' at the end of a rope. But I'm wanting to ken that I've done something worthwhile wi' my life too. We'll stay."

Alex smiled then, radiantly.

"Thank ye," he said, then he stood. "I'll away upstairs and wash off this paint, put some sensible clothes on. I had to climb out of the window and then over the gate so ye wouldna see me, and I nearly castrated myself doing it! It was worth it though. I'm certain I'll no' be recognised now. Ye eat yon fop's 'refreshments'. I'll be back in a few minutes."

He went upstairs then, leaving the rest of them sitting in the drawing room, still processing what had just happened. What was going to happen. And what they had irrevocably signed up for. There was no going back now.

Over the next few weeks the five Highlanders settled into their new home. More gaudy Sir Anthony outfits arrived, livery for Duncan and Angus, suitable maid's outfits for Maggie, and several changes of clothes for all of them, especially Alex, which would be suitable for labourers, merchants or gentry, depending on what they might need to become.

They explored the area minutely, memorising all the narrow unlit streets, noting which ones were dead ends and which ones could be escape routes if necessary. Alex went to Stockwell, to the inn he'd been told about by the smugglers who'd brought him back from Calais over three years before, and although the man Gabriel Foley had not been there, he had met others, one or two of whom he'd helped to carry boxes ashore at Dover, and a business relationship which would hopefully be mutually beneficial before too long was established.

At home the training of Duncan and Angus to be perfect footmen, stableboys, and various other roles in an emergency, continued. Maggie perfected a cleaning routine, learnt to cook a few new dishes and how to curtsey and address visitors should she need to. A laundress and gardener were arranged to come in one day a week. The men, including Alex, would help with other tasks when necessary. While

Alex didn't need to be a footman, he did learn some of Iain's other skills, because the more skills he had the better. If he was going to take on multiple roles at a moment's notice, multiple skills would be very useful.

Sir Anthony would also make sudden appearances, for a few hours initially, and then whole days as the weeks passed. When he arrived on the scene everyone would immediately take on their appropriate roles, as though the whole of society was observing them.

Whilst that had been very difficult initially for everyone except Alex, who had become accustomed to being other people in his Parisian parodies, if not for such lengthy periods, now they realised the seriousness of the situation they soon managed to separate the baronet from Alex in their minds, and as time went on treated them as if they were two completely different people. Once the baronet had disappeared upstairs, returning a while later as Alex, they would sit and discuss any mistakes they'd made, refinements needed, and as time went on they all quite naturally spoke of Sir Anthony in the third person, as though they were discussing someone who was not there.

Which was exactly what they all needed to do, and not just when alone in the safety of the house, but also possibly under duress, or even torture, should it come to it, which all of them were aware it could, but then dismissed from their minds. They all knew that worrying excessively about things that might not happen was a sure way to slow down your thinking process, leading to potentially catastrophic mistakes.

To relax Iain and Maggie went to their private rooms, or for short walks. Angus, armed with condoms provided by Highbury, visited mid-range brothels, Duncan would disappear over the wall at the bottom of the garden and go for lengthy walks alone across the fields, and Alex would sit in the house reading books.

He did not go out to inns or taverns seeking company, not to relax. He had all the company he wanted in the house, in his brothers and Iain and Maggie, to whom he was now growing very close. He knew that soon, as Sir Anthony, he would have a mass of company and conversation, and would no doubt crave solitude. So he spent as much time alone as he could, as though he could store up the peace to sustain him through the months or even years to come.

Twice a week the four men would assemble in the largest room in the house for weapons practice. It would have been more practical to do it in the garden, but they had no wish to attract attention from the neighbours, who might wonder why the baronet's servants were such accomplished warriors. In the salon they could relax, giving each other advice, and teaching Iain some of Kenneth's most useful wrestling moves.

Maggie, who had not been taught to defend herself as a child, but who had learnt the hard way in the city streets, now added a number of useful moves to her arsenal in case she needed them in London, including how to load and fire a pistol.

In the evenings they would, when all together, sit in the drawing room and relax, chatting, reading, playing chess. If they could have continued in this way, it would have been a pleasant interlude for all of them except Duncan, who could never be truly happy away from his beloved Loch Lomond, although he tried his best not to show it. In time of course they would all have grown bored, for none of them had ever lived a safe, idle life.

But that was not to be, for one night, shortly after Christmas, Alex informed them that he had met with his anonymous sponsor, and that both of them now believed Sir Anthony was ready to enter society.

"In truth, I'm thinking I'll never feel ready," Alex admitted, "but there's no more I can learn without mixing wi' the nobility now, and if I wait any longer, I'll just be procrastinating, which is a coward's way.

"The social season starts in January, and there's going to be a wee dinner to introduce Anthony to some people who may be useful, and they'll hopefully invite him to occasions where he can insinuate himself into other useful circles, and become acquainted with the ladies. The laddies'll no' see Anthony as a threat to their wives, so he could learn a good deal from them. They'll likely think him a molly, if anything.

"Anyway," he continued. "We begin in the second week of January, wi' the dinner. Duncan, ye need to perfect how to be a footman at table."

"He's awfu' good now," Iain said.

"Why?" Duncan asked.

"Because Sir Anthony is going to take his own footman to the dinner, to serve only him, because he likes things done a certain way. No' for all the dinners, just the first one. After that he'll claim to feel more relaxed now, for he was so nervous before and other such flowery shite," Alex said.

"Why can Iain no' do it? He's experienced at the real thing, wi' yon Munro mannie," Angus asked.

"Because I'm needing Duncan to observe all the guests, which he'll have ample opportunity to do, because he'll only be serving me, and in any case the primary purpose of footmen is to demonstrate the wealth of the master, and the more wealthy he is, the more footmen he has standing about doing nothing," Alex said. "Aye, it's awfu' stupid. But it means ye'll have plenty of time to watch everyone and tell me what ye think about them later. For these will be my stepping stones into getting the information the prince needs to win the crown back for his da."

Duncan nodded.

"Aye, I'll do it then," he said. "I'm just hoping there isna anything I havena seen before that I dinna ken how to respond to. I dinna want them to suspect you because they think your footman's an idiot."

"Dinna fash yourself," Alex reassured him. "If ye accidentally break one of yon ridiculous rules, Sir Anthony will explain that in France they do it that way, or that this is why he wanted his own man to attend him, as he always prefers whatever ye've just done."

"Aye. Well, let's hope I dinna drop the sauce in your lap then," Duncan commented drily.

"Ye'll no' do that. Ye've never been clumsy. And if ye did, then it'd be practice in thinking our way out of a situation rapidly, which is something we'll likely need to do occasionally," Alex said.

"Christ, we're really doing this," Angus said then.

"Aye, we're really doing this," Alex agreed. "And it'll be a lot easier for me when I ken I'm leading such a bonnie wee clan into the battle. For I ken ye'll be there for me, whatever happens, and that's worth more than ye can imagine."

"If ye're going to grow maudlin, laddies, at least have the drink taken to justify it," Maggie commented from her chair by the fire, where she was finishing hemming one of her dresses.

The men all laughed, and then Alex fetched enough whisky, brought with them from home, to justify all the laddies, and one lassie too, becoming very maudlin over the next hours.

CHAPTER NINETEEN

London, January 1742

IT WAS A BITTERLY cold afternoon, the streets icy and the sky heavy with snow clouds. Even so the streets of the capital were not empty. In the poorer areas people were seeking warmth wherever they could, burning anything they could find in a desperate attempt to survive the night. In the wealthier areas people continued life as normal, except wearing warmer clothes, cloaks and coats lined with fur, travelling to the theatre, to concerts or to balls and dinners in their coaches, while the drivers and footmen travelling on the outside of the coach, often dressed in impractical uniforms, endured the cold as best they could, shivering and blowing on their frozen hands.

The navy blue coach that was currently making its way to Grosvenor Square was clearly owned by a considerate man, as the coachman was wearing a heavy coat and hat and thick gloves. There was no footman on the back of the coach, because he was currently sitting inside it, talking quietly with his master.

"So ye havena met any of the guests before?" Duncan asked.

"No. There will be fifteen in total, including myself," Sir Anthony replied, his accent English but without the effeminate trills and gestures that he would adopt once they arrived. "There are two MPs, a few lords – all members of the House of Lords, various wives. One has two unmarried sisters who are coming. A very religious man, who apparently moves in church circles. Oh, and the father of the youth whose hand I cut off in Rome. He's a regular attender at the Lords, so may be useful."

"The laddie ye had a duel wi'? Is that no' risky?" Duncan asked.

"No, for I believe that the boy will have told his father a pack of lies about what happened. Lord Joseph won't be there in any case. My sponsor will say nothing about the duel, and Sir Anthony wasn't there and knows nothing of the matter. I know a little about the guests' characters too, but I won't reveal that because it's your impression I want, unaffected by any views. It will be really useful, because I'll be putting all my effort into being Sir Anthony, and won't be able to observe them to any extent at all."

Duncan nodded.

"Are ye nervous?" he asked.

Sir Anthony looked at him then, and whatever the painted baronet felt, the slate-blue eyes that looked into his were those of Alex, the brother he adored, and Duncan had never seen him so frightened, not even when they were about to fight another, larger clan.

"Aye," he said then, forgetting the baronet for a moment. "If I make a mess of this, then I risk you, Angus, Iain, Maggie, my sponsor and the clan, and I disappoint the prince. It isna like doing a wee parody in an inn, or acting on a stage. If I'd forgotten all my lines, I'd have been laughed at, nothing more. But this...I think this is the first time I *really* realise what I'm doing. And I'll admit to you but no one else, I'm awfu' feart, Duncan."

"I'm no' feart," Duncan said then. "I've kent ye my whole life, and ye've made mistakes, but ye've always made it right. And I've watched ye in the last weeks as Sir Anthony, wi' us. We *ken* who ye really are, but ye've even had us believing in yon lacy wee gomerel, and forgetting Alex altogether! Except for your sponsor mannie, nobody in there kens ye're anyone other than Sir Anthony Peters. It'll be easy for ye."

"Ye really think so?"

"Aye, I do, as long as ye stop feeling the whole world's going to end if ye make a mistake. It willna. Ye're no' going to stand up and confess everything if ye use the wrong knife, or say the wrong thing, are ye? The worst that can happen is that someone will be suspicious of ye. But there's no reason to be. I havena the slightest doubt that ye'll be a success, and even enjoy it, once ye relax into the role. I've watched ye do it at home. Ye'll be no different here."

Alex closed his eyes for a moment then.

"Thank you," he said softly. "I needed that."

Then the coach slowed as they turned into the square and he opened his eyes again, and Duncan saw that Alex was already receding, letting the baronet take him over, so he said no more on the matter.

"Should I no' get out before we arrive, as I'm only a footman?" he asked.

"No," Alex said, his accent English again now. "Allowing you to sit in the coach is one of my eccentricities, as is having you come to the dinner at all. You will hardly be able to handle glasses and dishes if your fingers are blue with cold from riding on the outside of the coach, after all."

They stopped, and looking out of the window Alex could see that many, if not all of the guests had already arrived; the day was grey and gloomy but the salon windows were ablaze with light from the crystal chandeliers, and silhouetted figures could be seen walking across the room. He sat there for a moment, deep in thought, bracing himself for battle. Then he rolled his shoulders, flexed his wrists, curled and uncurled his fingers, and opened the coach door, waiting as the coachman lowered the steps for him.

He descended from the coach, carefully arranged the skirts of his cerise pink frockcoat, then minced up the steps to the open front door and announced himself to the butler, who was welcoming the guests to the house.

"Oh, and this is my footman, Murdo, who I always insist on accompanying me to such dinners, for I am quite new to the country, you know, and he accommodates all my peccadillos! I would not want to embarrass one of Lord Highbury's footmen, and this will quite avoid that happening!" the baronet said, beaming at the man. "If you will be so kind as to show him where he must go until the meal commences, I would be most obliged, I do assure you."

Another man was called, who led Duncan away, and then Alex moved to the door of the salon, which was opened to him by a bowing footman. He stood for a second in the doorway, observing the people already in the luxuriously furnished room, who were clustered in small groups, chatting. He lifted his arm, bent his wrist, allowing the intricate Brussels lace to fall elegantly from the cuff of his silk frockcoat, arranged his fingers gracefully, took a deep breath, then stepped over the threshold.

He bowed deeply to the group nearest to him, who had stopped talking on seeing him enter the room, and were now staring at him.

"Good evening, my dear lords, ladies!" he trilled. "What an absolutely *divine* room!" Others, having heard the unfamiliar high-pitched tones, also turned to see the newcomer, and fell silent.

Sir Anthony Peters, baronet, after a lengthy gestation period, had finally been born into London society.

The Earl of Highbury, who was on the other side of the room talking to a podgy florid man and two dowdy women, one plump, the other almost skeletal, now came across to greet his guest of honour. The baronet bowed deeply to him, an extravagant courtly bow.

"My dear William!" he cried. "I cannot tell you how honoured I am to be invited to dine with *such* prestigious people. I am quite overwhelmed with joy!"

"You are most welcome, Anthony," Highbury replied. "Come, there is a little time before dinner to show you my library, as I promised you."

"Ah! Delightful! I do *so* love a library! Please, lead the way."

As his host had made no such promise, Sir Anthony was not surprised when the moment the library door was closed Highbury led him to the middle of the room where they would not be overheard by anyone in the hall, and then turned to him, his face a mask of worry.

"Lord Joseph is here," he said without preamble.

"What? Yon laddie who lost the duel?" Alex replied.

"Yes. It seems that since he lost his hand in an unfortunate attack by a veritable army of footpads in Rome, Lord Joseph has been a virtual hermit. His idiot father decided this was the perfect event to 'persuade' his son to re-enter society."

In spite of the potential seriousness of this, Alex started laughing.

"I could almost feel sorry for him," he said, his accent English again now, but without the affectations. "I assume by 'persuade' you mean force? I cannot believe he could be here voluntarily under the circumstances."

"Yes. I wish you'd been here to see his face when Simon recited the absolute rot his son had told him about the incident. I thought the boy was going to have an apoplexy!" Highbury said. "You don't seem concerned," he added, seeing his friend's amused expression.

"I might have been, if it wasn't for the fact that when I introduced Anthony to my brothers for the first time, even they didn't recognise me immediately. If they didn't, Joseph won't. He's not the most observant person. No, I'm not worried."

"Even Murdo didn't recognise you?" the earl asked.

"Not immediately, although he was the first to. But he only recognised my eyes. He's here, by the way."

"Who is?"

"Murdo. I brought him along as my footman. It's one of my eccentricities. I like to be served by a familiar servant, particularly when I know no one of the company. I want his opinions of the people who will form my entrance into society," Sir Anthony said.

"So I'll meet him after all."

"Well, not *meet* him, but see him at least. As eccentric as Anthony is no doubt going to be, to introduce you to my footman would be a little too much, I think. Is everyone here?"

"Almost. I'm waiting for Edwin and Caroline. Mr and Mrs Harlow."

"Ah, the MP and his wife who was disowned by her family for marrying him?"

"Yes. They're not usually late, but the roads are very icy, so perhaps they've been held up a little. Once they arrive we'll go through. You will be sitting opposite them. The servants will have set an extra place for Joseph by now. He'll be as far away from you as possible. Because you're my guest of honour, you will be next to me at the head of the table. I thought that might allow us to surreptitiously warn each other of anything."

"William, relax," Alex said now. "I felt like you do now in the coach, but Murdo told me that the worst that could happen is that someone might be suspicious of me. He's right. And if they are, it'll be because of some slip in etiquette, which I will blame on France or those horrible grandparents, who were very odd. I sat in the coach and took a deep breath. Do the same now, and then let us enjoy it, as we enjoyed our time in Europe when I was your cousin John, and in the London shops when I was a lovesick young idiot. Tomorrow we can meet at breakfast and laugh about it."

"You are staying overnight then," Highbury said.

"My dear William, how could I possibly refuse your hospitality? I daresay after dinner, then music and cards, I shall be quite exhausted, and incapable of travelling home," the baronet simpered. "We won't make mistakes if we relax and enjoy it. If we're tense, we will."

Highbury sat then, and did as Alex had done in the coach. "You are right," he said, standing. "Let us do this."

They walked out into the hall just as the final guests were entering the house.

"Ah, Edwin, Caroline," Highbury said, going to greet them with a genuine smile, one of the few he had bestowed on his guests as they'd arrived, as most of them were here not because he liked them, but because they would hopefully be useful to Alex. "I was beginning to be a little concerned. I trust all is well?"

"Yes," Caroline replied. "I hope we haven't inconvenienced you."

"If you're inconvenienced, William, not their fault, but mine," a familiar voice came from behind them, and then its owner came into view.

"Harriet!" Highbury exclaimed, trying and failing to look happy to see her.

"Never have parties, do you? Enjoy them as much as I do. Caroline told me you wanted to introduce a new acquaintance to them, so thought I'd come along too. Only arrived in London this morning. Don't have to feed me. I know it's a bloody nuisance, unexpected guest," she said.

Sir Anthony, who'd been standing at the library door observing the entrance of the classically beautiful young woman and the pleasant-looking but plain man she'd abandoned her aristocratic family for, now moved forward, recognising the incipient panic in his friend's rigid stance at the unexpected appearance of this friend who, for some reason, he did not want to meet Alex, or Anthony.

"My Lady Harriet!" he cried, bowing deeply to the eccentric-looking old woman, who was wearing male attire even more expensively tailored than his, although considerably more conservative in colour and decoration. "How delightful to meet you! William has told me you are one of his dearest friends. I am honoured. Sir Anthony Peters at your service, my lady," he said to the floor, then raised himself from his bow. "And Mr and Mrs Harlow, I believe?"

"Yes," Caroline said, her hazel almond-shaped eyes bright with laughter. "Welcome to England, Sir Anthony."

"How kind you are, my dear lady! I already feel most welcome, being invited to such an exquisite house. William has been showing me the library – such a beautiful room, with volumes on every subject imaginable."

"You enjoy reading, Sir Anthony?" Edwin asked politely.

"Enjoy...I would not go so far as that," the baronet replied, "but I do so like to peruse a periodical, and to do it in such august surroundings would make me feel positively intellectual!" He beamed at the company. Edwin and Caroline were concealing their amused shock reasonably expertly. Harriet was observing him with eyes that betrayed her relationship to Caroline, but with quite a different expression.

"Harriet," she said briskly. "Not Lady Harriet. Just Harriet. Caroline tells me you've recently arrived from France."

"I have! It seems William was briefly acquainted with my dear mama and sisters," the baronet said, opting not to appear grief-stricken, at least not in front of this woman. He was already beginning to understand why Highbury had not wanted her to meet him, not at this early stage, anyway, whilst the baronet's personality was not fully developed. Her expression was one of deep scepticism. "And when he met me, he kindly offered to help me make my way in English society. I know nobody, as I left this fair land when I was only a small child, and did not return until very recently."

"Hmm. So why did you not remain in France?" she asked. "Perhaps you would be more at home there, after so long, and with no family here."

"Ah, you mean my taste in fashion!" Sir Anthony cried. "You find it French! I will admit, I *adore* fashion, and of course the centre of fashion is France – I'm sure everyone will agree on that! I feel it is so important to wear clothes that express who you are as a person! I can see you share my feelings on this topic, Harriet," he ended.

At this Caroline burst out laughing, then put her hand over her mouth to smother it.

"Well played," Harriet said softly, so softly that Sir Anthony appeared not to hear her.

"Shall we go in?" Highbury asked, having taken the time to recover himself a little, and to arrange for another place to be set for his closest friend, who he currently wished anywhere but here.

They all moved towards the salon to join the other guests and begin the evening's entertainment.

"He had you there, Harriet," Caroline murmured in her aunt's ear as they followed Highbury and the extraordinary baronet into the room.

"Hmm. Going to be an interesting evening, I think," the old lady replied.

By the end of the first course, Highbury had started to relax. Everything seemed to be going well. The ladies present, Harriet excepted, were going out of their way to make the baronet feel welcome, asking him questions about France and Geneva, but carefully avoiding any mention of smallpox or his family, which Highbury had told them the baronet was still heartbroken about.

Isabella Cunningham had mentioned that their other sister, Charlotte, had stayed at home as she was mourning the recent death of her husband, to whom she was devoted. Sir Anthony had expressed his deepest condolences, uttered some flowery phrases about death, and then sighed tragically, upon which Isabella had blushed, realising her *faux pax*, and the subject had dropped.

The gentlemen, after a short discussion on hunting further down the table, in which neither Anthony nor Edwin had participated, had miraculously abandoned the topic, and now the food was the focus of discussion. It seemed the evening was going to be bland, which would suit Highbury perfectly. He had no wish for there to be any contentious issues. He had had enough of those with his cousin John, in Italy.

Cousin John, in his new incarnation, was currently exclaiming about the subtle but delightful flavour of the orange vegetable on his plate, which his footman, conspicuous in his green livery rather than the silver-grey of Highbury's servants, observed expressionlessly.

"One would assume from the colour that it would have a strong, perhaps even a fiery taste," Sir Anthony cried, "but no – it has a quite delicate, almost a sweet flavour!"

"Have you never eaten pureed carrot before, Sir Anthony?" Caroline asked.

"No, I don't believe I have! I would surely have remembered," he said, smiling happily at her. Most of the company wondered if he was perhaps a little simple-minded. If so, it would explain why the Earl of Highbury had taken him under his wing. It was just the sort of thing the man would do. Half the guests thought the earl foolish and gullible to do so. The rest thought him good-natured. The fop seemed harmless, though.

"If you've eaten it in France, it would have been smothered in a ridiculous sauce," Lord Edward pronounced. "Can't taste anything you eat in the place. Just the damned sauces. Everything drowned in cream and spices."

"Ah, you must have travelled extensively in France, my lord, to have sampled so much of the cuisine," Sir Anthony cried. "What do you think of *cassoulet?* Such a delightful dish! Each region has its own version," he explained to his direct neighbours, "and it is very popular, but I admit I have never eaten one which was smothered in cream, or in fact which contained any cream at all. Where did you eat such a one, my lord?"

Lord Edward, who had in fact never been to France, coloured, but before he could reply, the baronet scampered on.

"Then there are the *gallettes.* Ah," he cried, kissing his gloved fingertips in a typically gallic gesture. "I believe you have tasted those, William?"

"Indeed I have, in Paris. Delightful, and, I must say, containing no cream at all, just cheese and ham," Highbury said, beginning to enjoy himself a little, if he ignored the fact that Harriet was extraordinarily taciturn.

"Murdo," the baronet called, and the footman stepped forward, bowing, as he'd been taught to by Iain. "Could you later perhaps ask the cook how she prepares such a dish? I would very much like to see if Margaret could make it. Margaret is my cook," he said to the guests, "a most excellent plain cook."

"Have you not employed a French chef, Sir Anthony?" Lady Winters asked.

"No! I am quite determined to become English in *all* things!" Sir Anthony cried. "I was after all born in this fair land, and must adapt accordingly. I am sure that she will be able to master the complexities of this, if she has the receipt."

"For God's sake, man, it's just boiled mashed carrots," Lord Simon commented, wondering how long the idiot could praise such a thing.

"I'm sure you see it as such, but for me it is new, as are so many things!" Sir Anthony said. "I think perhaps your son would prefer to be served such food as this, or perhaps the soup, which is quite delicious and requires no cutting, unlike the beef you have put onto his plate, Lord Simon," he added, smiling.

Both Lord Simon and his son flushed beetroot red, the one at his disability being drawn attention to, the other at his lack of fatherly consideration.

"Would you like my servant to cut your meat for you, Lord Joseph? I assure you, there is no shame in seeking assistance, particularly when you acquired your injury so heroically! I believe it happened in the crime-infested streets of Rome?" Sir Anthony continued innocently.

"Er...yes," the youth muttered, focussing on his plate.

"Appalling! Such a glorious city! What a privilege to visit the great edifices of a noble, classical culture, which gave us the writings of such giants as Virgil, Horace, the mighty Aristotle, and Homer! They inspired the culture and wisdom of our own enlightened age! And yet beneath it there is still such wanton violence and senseless brutality. So dreadful that you had to experience that, my lord." The baronet shuddered theatrically.

Highbury dropped his knife and bent under the table to retrieve it before the footman could do so, in an attempt to master his features.

"So how many of the ruffians did you despatch or wound, my lord? William told me that you were renowned as an accomplished swordsman before the tragedy, so I'm sure you taught many of them a much-needed lesson! In truth I am amazed they would brazenly attack you in the finer parts of the city. For I cannot imagine a gentleman such as yourself would visit an insalubrious area, where such a thing might indeed happen. There are many of those," he added to the ladies seated near him. "Such poverty and degradation you could not imagine! What did the authorities say of the matter?"

A short silence ensued while Sir Anthony waited eagerly for the scarlet-faced lord to answer his questions. Lord Simon took his son's plate and deftly cut up his meat. Highbury emerged with his knife, glanced at Harriet's raised eyebrow and incredulous expression and wished he could spend the rest of the meal sitting under the table.

"So, you have visited Rome, Sir Anthony?" Thomas Fortescue asked, when it became clear Joseph was not going to reply.

"I have. I spent many happy days there, visiting the Colosseum and other such wonders. It is quite a remarkable city, with many fascinating things to see!"

"But very Roman," Lord Winter said, sniffing.

"Well, yes. But as it is Rome, that is surely to be expected, my lord," Sir Anthony replied, clearly a little confused.

"I think Bartholomew means the religion, Sir Anthony," Caroline explained, who seemed to be enjoying herself immensely.

"Ah! But one can ignore that and marvel at the glorious art and architecture in any case! The Colosseum, as I mentioned, the Castel Sant'Angelo, and the opera! Ah, sublime! When I was there I went to see *Artaserse* with the Pretender's Son. Quite remarkable! The opera was excellent too, although I was unsure of the plot, as they sang in Italian, unfortunately. I had hoped it would be in French, or English."

"You attended the opera with Charles Stuart?!" Lord Winter cried.

"Well, yes. He lives nearby, I believe, and loves music. Or it is said he does, but he seemed to prefer dallying with the ladies and giggling than watching the performance. Quite vacuous! We do share a taste in fashion, though, I must admit!" He smiled around the room, seemingly oblivious of the shocked expressions on most of the faces, and the interested ones on the rest. "I must ask you for the name of your tailor, Harriet. I cannot help but admire your outfit. The tailoring is perfection," he continued.

"Harriet has the same tailor as myself, Anthony," Highbury said. "The one I recommended to you."

Harriet looked down, as though to remind herself of what she was wearing.

"Visiting Fred today, that's why I'm wearing this. Just got home when Caroline told me they were coming to dinner at yours, so no time to change into comfortable things. Was intrigued," Harriet finished.

"You visit Prince Frederick?" Lady Winter asked in a tone every bit as disapproving as her husband's had been a moment ago.

"I visit whomever I wish, Wilhelmina," Harriet replied coldly. "People I find interesting and intelligent. You can be reassured that I will never visit your home, in this outfit or any other."

"Lord Highbury very graciously held this dinner to enable me to become acquainted with some of the more prestigious members of society!" Sir Anthony cried, oblivious to the insult and Lady Winter's suddenly scarlet complexion. "People he thought I might share some interests with! I am most grateful to him. I am sure we will all have much to talk about, when we know each other a little better."

"You are a friend of the Pretender's son then, Sir Anthony?" Lord Edward persisted.

"Well, I would not go so far as to say a 'friend', but I am acquainted with the youth. Or rather *was*. Now I am determined to be completely English, I realise I must hate him, and so I shall endeavour to do so."

"Will you not find that difficult, if you have such a great deal in common?" Lord Simon asked.

"Oh no! For really, we share little. I am told he entertains the ladies in his rooms *every* night! I would never do that. And he is very fond of other reckless pursuits, but there are ladies present, so I will not elaborate. I have been told his father quite despairs of him ever taking his role seriously. Quite dissipated! No, I am not a lover of such dissolute behaviour, I assure you! I live a most sober, reserved life."

"So, Edwin, how goes it with the Foundling Hospital?" the earl asked, thinking it was time to introduce a political topic. After all, the Stuarts were not going to be able to take back the British crown due to an intimate knowledge of carrots or of Rome, and Anthony had given enough of a picture of the Stuart prince that he and Charles had agreed on for now.

Alex would probably have noted who was particularly interested in knowing more, and if he hadn't, Murdo, standing unnoticed in the background, would no doubt be able to tell his brother every detail later, down to how many eyelashes everyone had.

Of course a conversation about the Foundling Hospital wouldn't be particularly useful to the Stuarts either, but one political topic often led to another. At the very least Alex would hopefully get the political measure of the guests. He was certainly already gaining a reputation as a well-meaning, if indiscreet and tactless fool, which were some of the traits Alex had said might be useful. Although no one had picked him up on the fact that two of the classical Roman masters he'd referred to were in fact Greek, at least some of the company would have noted it. Caroline certainly, who was proficient in both Latin and Greek.

Not bad for two courses of dinner, Highbury thought as the desserts were brought in.

"Everything is going very well indeed, considering the complexities involved, and how short a time the hospital has been open," Edwin answered the earl. "A proper organised system of admitting the children has now been implemented, and wet-nurses employed to care for them in their first years. We are hoping to build a larger hospital, for there is great demand for the services."

"I'm sure there is," Lord Edward said in disgust.

"The Foundling Hospital is a project my husband is particularly fond of," Caroline explained to Sir Anthony. "Do you know about it?"

"I have heard the name, but I know nothing of the details," the baronet trilled. "Please, elucidate me, my dear lady."

"It's a place where any whore or other fallen woman might be rid of the evidence of her sin and just walk away without any punishment for her unacceptable, lewd behaviour," Lord Winter said, sniffing.

"Ah, as the fathers already do?" Sir Anthony asked innocently. "Well, that seems fairer, although of course the poor woman still has to carry and give birth to the child, which is most dangerous, is it not? And then it must be terrible to have to give your child away!"

"Indeed it is," Edwin agreed, smiling warmly at his unexpected ally. "The babies are given a new name, so that neither they nor the mother need carry the stigma of illegitimacy. If they *are* illegitimate, for no questions are asked, and some of the children may be legitimate, but from families who have fallen on hard times. A lot of the mothers leave a small token, to let the child know they were loved, or so that they can be identified should the mother find herself in the position of being able to reclaim the baby at a later date. We intend that once the facilities are available, the children will be returned to the hospital at the age of five, and then educated and later apprenticed."

"Oh, this is a most excellent idea!" the baronet cried, clapping his hands. "For it will make useful members of society out of likely criminals, or indeed tiny corpses. And give the mothers a second chance too. No wonder you are fond of the project, Mr Harlow."

"It is yet to be seen if such bastards can be redeemed," Lord Simon announced. "And most disturbing to think that such sinful fallen women might go on to make respectable marriages, or even to take positions in service in our homes!"

The ladies, with the exception of Caroline and Harriet, shuddered at such a horrific prospect.

"Oh, surely you are not concerned about that, ladies!" Sir Anthony cried. "I am sure that if you look around you at the servants present tonight, many of them will also have engaged in fornication. Indeed, many of the gentlemen sitting at the table have possibly fathered a few unwanted children. And yet none of you feel threatened by them, do you? Nor should you!"

A disbelieving silence fell on the company for a moment.

"It is quite a different thing, Sir Anthony, as I'm sure you are aware," Lady Winter said coldly.

"Well, no, I am not aware. Fornication is a sin, is it not, regardless of the sex of the person committing it. Did St Paul not say 'For this is the will of God, even our sanctification, that ye should abstain from fornication'? *Thessalonians I,* my dear Lady Winter," he added, smiling happily at the outraged noblewoman. "I'm sure that if the Lord had only meant that to apply to women, He would have ensured that St Paul was aware of that. And of course, the woman is the fairer sex, some might say the weaker sex. Does it not seem unfair that she then bears *all* the burden of the sin of fornication, whilst the stronger male walks away without blemish? To me this Foundling Hospital attempts to address that issue. What a noble concept!"

Both Lord and Lady Winter looked about to explode with rage. Caroline and Edwin looked about to explode with laughter. Sir Anthony looked as innocent as a newborn baby.

Highbury wondered if he could get away with dropping his cutlery under the table again. Probably not. He was not generally clumsy, after all.

"But I see this topic is embarrassing the ladies," the baronet said. "In France it would be otherwise. Please forgive me. I assure you, I meant no offence. Has His Most Excellent Majesty King George expressed an opinion on the venture, Mr Harlow?"

"Indeed, he signed the Royal Charter for the hospital to be built, Sir Anthony," Edwin stated.

"Ah! So you disagree with the monarch's decision," the baronet exclaimed, directing his gaze at the outraged faces of the Winters, Lord Edward and his sisters, Lord Simon and the religious gentleman, who had not as yet spoken a word. "Are you then Jacobites? I had no idea followers of James Stuart were as numerous and vocal in this fair land as they are in France."

Highbury dropped his dessertspoon under the table.

"Well, that was more fun than I expected," Alex said several hours later, having stolen down the secret passage to Highbury's bedroom.

"I'm not sure I will survive the baronet, if he continues in this vein," Highbury told him. "I nearly died of suppressing my laughter when you asked them if they were Jacobites! I thought you wanted to endear yourself to the nobles, not make them hate you!"

"I canna imagine the baronet ever endearing himself to them," Alex replied. "Pompous arrogant fools. Did ye see the two silly lassies wi' yon Edward? They'd faint if ye breathed on them."

"Isabella and Clarissa really are quite sweet," Highbury said. "They've been bullied all their lives, first by their father and then their brother. And they're quite dependent on him, being spinsters. They are very dull, but I feel sorry for them, in truth."

Alex absorbed this information, nodding slightly to himself.

"Anthony was awfu' reserved the rest of the evening though," he said then in his own defence.

"Apart from telling Lord Joseph how wise he was not to engage in card games, which in his view were even more iniquitous than fornication, for whole fortunes were lost that way, and cheats abounded who could rob an innocent man of his entire life."

"Ye were listening then."

"The whole room was listening. Anthony has a most penetrating voice," Highbury said, laughing openly now. "It was a masterpiece."

"Aye, well, I didna feel the need to endear myself to that wee shite," Alex said, abandoning thinking of Anthony in the third person for a time. It had been a long evening, and he was tired, mentally at least. It *had* been more fun than he expected, but he hoped it would be less tiring once he felt more at home as the baronet.

"I doubt either him or his father, or Edward and the Winters will want to see you again, somehow," Highbury said.

"Aye, they will. They'll be wanting to see me a great deal. For ye're introducing me to the German Lairdie as soon as you can, and they'll want to be certain that I dinna think they're Jacobites, in case I innocently tell Geordie that. I'm hoping that they'll maybe tell me something useful while they're convincing me they hate the Stuarts." Alex sipped at his nightcap, closed his eyes, then opened them abruptly as he realised how close he was to falling asleep where he sat.

Highbury was staring at him in shock.

"My God, I would never have thought of that! Was that why you accused them of being Jacobites?"

"Aye. That and the fun of watching them nearly have an apoplexy, but no' be able to challenge me, for it was a completely innocent question from a naïve idiot. I'm thinking I didna do too badly. The laddies think I'm a fool who kens about the Stuarts and maybe can inadvertently give useful information. And they'll be wanting to show me how influential they are, how important, so they're likely to tell me secrets. For there's nothing that makes a man more important than knowing the confidences of those of a higher station than him.

"Next I have to find a way of endearing myself to the lassies, for I didna have an opportunity tonight. I'm thinking to talk more of feminine things, fashion, embroidery, poetry...no one will think it strange for the baronet to have such interests. No' the poetry yon idiot Johnson insisted on entertaining us with after the music. It was interesting watching how they all tried to hide their boredom though."

"He's renowned for it. I'm surprised Harriet didn't eviscerate him though," Highbury said.

Highbury was surprised by most of Harriet's behaviour during the course of the entertainment. She had stayed for nearly all of the evening, even though she despised almost all the guests. And she had said nothing contentious at all, apart from her acid comment to Lady Winter about her visit to the prince. That was most unlike her. She'd had plenty of opportunities, after all.

He was too tired to think about that now. He would probably be awake worrying all night if he did.

"Did you have a chance to ask Murdo his opinion of everyone?" he asked instead.

"No. I made sure to announce he had to leave directly after dinner so that he wouldna have to deal wi' your servants' curiosity afterwards. His training is coming on well, but he hasna learned everything he needs to ken yet. I didna want your footmen to maybe suspect there was something amiss wi' him.

"Which reminds me. I'm wanting to rent a couple of rooms, in the St Giles or Drury Lane area," Alex continued.

"Good God! Why would you want to rent rooms there?" Highbury asked.

"They're no' for the baronet, although *I* might stay there occasionally. They're for my brothers, and any other clan members I need to ask to help wi'...certain things," Alex said.

"Certain things?"

"Aye. Ye might no' want to ken about them."

"I do want to. After all if I'm arrested I won't be tortured – not initially. I'll be politely questioned. And while that's happening, you'll be fleeing the country. By the time they get to torture, if I haven't convinced them I know nothing other than that I appear to have been duped by a trickster, you'll be back in Scotland. I just need a secure way to notify you if I am arrested," Highbury said. "I'm not as innocent as I was when I first met you," he added on seeing Alex's surprised expression.

"Smuggling," Alex said then.

"Smuggling? Oh, yes, you mentioned that once before. Everybody is involved in that, to some extent at least. Not the actual bringing in of goods, but certainly the buying and consuming of them," the earl told him.

"Aye. But I'm thinking yon lords and ladies are no' bringing in swords and muskets to fight for Charles wi'," Alex said.

"No. But I haven't heard what you just said. I will give you cash to rent rooms in the morning. I can hardly rent them without arousing suspicion. But now I'm going to sleep. I slept very badly last night, worrying about this evening. I realise now I had no need to."

Apart from Harriet. No. He would not think of that. Maybe he would pay Edwin and Caroline a visit tomorrow, see what he could find out about Harriet's view of Sir Anthony from them.

Once in bed, in spite of his fatigue Alex remained awake for a while, thinking about the evening. He was, overall, happy with his first appearance as Sir Anthony. The only thing that troubled him was the one observation Duncan *had* managed to make, as he had left after the dinner.

"Watch yon Harriet woman," he'd said.

At that moment Lady Caroline had come over to ask him if he was familiar with the music of Vivaldi.

"Oh yes! Is it his music which will be performed tonight?" the baronet had cried, giving her all his attention, while inwardly cursing that he hadn't had a chance to ask Duncan to elaborate on his comment.

"Yes," she replied. "Highbury is quite a lover of music. He is involved with the choir at his country estate."

"Fascinating. William is a man of many parts! Did you know that Vivaldi worked as a teacher of music at the *Ospedale della Pietà*? It is a foundling hospital as well as a convent. Perhaps we should not inform Lords Edward and Winter of that though. We do not wish to spoil the performance for them, after all!"

Caroline had laughed, and Sir Anthony had escorted her into the room where the concert was to take place.

He liked Caroline, he thought now. And Edwin too, who seemed a serious but gentle man. Harriet had not spoken to him, or anyone else for that matter long enough for him to gain an impression of her, other than that she was eccentric and did not suffer fools gladly, judging by her comment to the odious Winter woman.

He made a resolution to engage more with her, if they met again. Perhaps they would not. William had told him that she rarely participated in society events, preferring a quiet life on her enormous country estate. In the meantime, when he got home tomorrow he would obtain Duncan's views on all the guests.

In spite of lying awake Alex still woke early the next morning, and though he tried, found himself unable to go back to sleep. Instead he lay listening to the sounds of the house awakening, or the servants at least, and finally got up, put on his paint and dressed in the same outfit as he'd worn the previous evening but with a clean shirt. He was, after all, only going to have a private breakfast with Highbury before making his way home.

In the end he started his breakfast alone, as there was no sign of Highbury making an appearance. He was no doubt sleeping late; he too had been under a great deal of pressure, after all.

A short while later Alex heard a knock on the front door, and then voices as a footman opened it. He would finish breakfast, he thought, then go through to the library and pass the time reading until Highbury surfaced. He yawned.

Then suddenly the breakfast room door flew open, someone came in, turned round, said "Bugger off," to the footman who was attempting to enter the room behind her, and then shut the door in his startled face.

Harriet turned, to see the baronet frozen in the act of eating a roll, staring at her, eyes wide with shock.

"Right then," she said. "Who the hell are you really, and how did you persuade William to introduce you into noble society last night?"

"My dear L...Harriet!" Sir Anthony cried, throwing down his roll and leaping up immediately to bow. "What an unexpected pleasure! That was quite a memorable entrance, I must say! I'm afraid William is not awake as yet. Would you care to join me for breakfast? I am sure he will rise before too long."

"No, I would not," Harriet said, although she did come further into the room, until she was standing at the other end of the table. "I was hoping to speak to you alone. Are you going to answer my question, or try to wander around it until I grow weary? Because you'll grow weary long before I do. Who are you?"

"I am Sir Anthony Peters. I thought the introductions were made last night. If they were not, I can only apolo—"

"No," she interrupted. "It's too much of a coincidence, that William met your mother and sisters, and then all of a sudden he meets the long-lost son as well. Either you're an impostor trying to elicit Highbury's sympathy and obtain money from him, or you *are* Sir Anthony, but the man you are bears no resemblance to the ridiculous caricature you presented last night. In which case, why are you putting on such a show?"

"I assure you that I have no interest whatsoever in 'stealing' money from Lord Highbury, as you so crudely put it," the baronet said earnestly. "I would *never* do such a thing."

She scrutinised him for a moment. He seemed to be telling the truth, in this at least. But there was something very wrong with this man. She had watched both him and Highbury intently last night. While the painted clown had focussed his attentions on the company, it had been very clear to her, who knew the earl better than anyone else on earth, that Highbury was extremely fond of this Anthony character. But the more she observed him, the more convinced she was that while Highbury might feel pity for the man, he would never become endeared to such a creature. All her instincts had warned her there was something wrong, and her instincts were usually right.

She pulled out a chair, turned it round then sat down, folding her arms across the back of it. She glared at him.

"Maybe you would not," she said then. "But you *are* doing something. What is it?"

The footman, taking Lady Harriet's advice, had indeed 'buggered off', running up the stairs as fast as he could, tapping on the earl's door and then trying to open it, only to find it locked for some inexplicable reason. He knocked louder then, until the earl, dressed only in a nightshirt, his dark hair tangled on his shoulders, eyes heavy with sleep, unbolted and opened the door.

"Good God, man, is the house on fire?" he asked, alarmed.

"No, my lord. I beg pardon, but the Marchioness of Hereford is here. I told her you were not ready to accept visitors and she said she'd come to see the...er...your guest. So I told her he was breakfasting, and she walked past me into the breakfast room, and then told me to...go away, my lord. She was very forceful," he finished.

"Was Sir Anthony in there?" Highbury asked, wide awake now, the footman's words having acted like a bucket of icy water thrown over him.

"Yes, my lord. He's been there for some time. She shut the door in my face, so I thought you'd want to know. I'm sorry for—"

"No, don't be sorry. You did right. Help me dress, quickly," Highbury said, trying not to let his panic show on his face. He went to his chest, pulled out a shirt, and then changing his mind grabbed the silk banyan he'd been wearing last night from the back of a chair, and threw that on instead.

"Your hair, my lord," the footman said, as Highbury made to walk past him.

"Ah." Highbury turned back to his dressing table, picked up a brush, tore it through his hair, grabbed a lace and roughly tied it back, then made his way downstairs, followed by the footman.

"You did very well, James," he said then. "Now I would like you to stand at the foot of the stairs and make sure that no one comes either in or near the breakfast room."

And then he walked across the entrance hall and into the room.

"I am eating breakfast, madam. I would have thought that to be quite obvious," the baronet was saying as he entered, his voice petulant but with a touch of ice beneath, which Highbury recognised as Alex, becoming angry. The earl stopped then and both of them turned to him.

Harriet looked him up and down.

"I'm right then," she said.

"In what?" Highbury asked, coming across to the table and sitting down as though his intention had been just to eat breakfast rather than confront two of the people closest to him. He prayed that neither of them could hear his heart crashing against his ribs. His temples were pulsing with the start of a headache.

"You never dress so informally to greet a visitor, not even me, William. And you have a feather in your hair from the pillow, so you've leapt out of bed and come straight downstairs," Harriet said to him. "You were horrified last night when I arrived with Caroline and Edwin, and you're even more horrified right now. Which tells me you didn't want me to meet this...whatever he is. Which also tells me there's something wrong, although maybe not what I thought."

"Whatever did you think?" the baronet trilled.

Harriet turned her attention to him, as he'd hoped. Highbury seized the opportunity given him to take a couple of surreptitious breaths. He reached out to pour himself a cup of chocolate, and then changed his mind on seeing how violently his hands were shaking.

"I thought that you were an impostor, pretending to be the son of the tragic Peters women to illicit sympathy and money from William, as I said," she replied, then looked between them, "but I see now that whatever is going on, you are both in on it. The question is, what is it that you're up to?"

Sir Anthony seemed completely bewildered, so she turned to Highbury, who looked as though he was about to faint.

"William," she said, then, her voice losing the harsh tone it had had up to now when talking to the baronet. "Is this anything to do with the subject we've talked about on a few occasions over the years?" She watched as Highbury grew even paler. "You know you can trust me, as I trust you. I came here today because I thought this man was trying to exploit you, even endanger you.

"I will kill anyone who threatens those I love, Anthony," she added, turning back to the painted fop, "including you. I do not say that figuratively, as William will tell you. If this is to do with the subject we've talked about and you're determined to proceed, then although I won't get directly involved, I *will* look to protect you as far as I can, if it becomes necessary. I'll leave you to discuss it. I will say nothing to anyone else of this visit."

She stood then, and moved to the door. The baronet looked at his friend, who seemed frozen with indecision.

"Why did you think me an impostor?" Sir Anthony asked when she was at the door. Instead of answering immediately, she opened the door, looked across the hall, nodded to the footman at the stairs, then closed it again. She came back to the table and sat down.

"Not because of any mistake you made last night," she said. "But because I've known William since he was five. He's a kind man, and it's entirely possible that he'd take the Peters boy under his wing. But it was clear to me at least, that he is very fond of you. It was *not* clear whether you reciprocate his feelings. The person you showed to us all last night, whilst amusing, is absolutely not the kind of person William would ever grow close to.

"So I knew then, firstly that you are an accomplished actor, and secondly that the character you played last night is not who you really are, and not the character you play for William."

"So you came here today to protect him," Anthony said, his accent still English, still aristocratic, but not the high-pitched affected trill he had adopted until now.

"Yes," Harriet answered bluntly.

The baronet nodded.

"I admire that," he said then. "William, you must make this decision, for I cannot. I'll trust your judgement."

Highbury sighed then.

"Yes, this is regarding the subject we have spoken of," he said then.

Harriet looked out of the window.

"We cannot go out for a walk in the gardens this time," she said then. "I might do it for pleasure, but you would not, particularly in a banyan, and am I right in thinking the baronet would be horrified even at the prospect?"

"My dear lady, you have me to a T!" Sir Anthony trilled, reverting to character for a moment. "Shall we go to your rooms, William? We can't be sure no one will come in here, and if Harriet is a close friend and as eccentric as she seems, no one will be suspicious."

Harriet laughed then, and her whole face lit up.

"I'm not only eccentric but quite mad," she said. "Or so people think, and I don't discourage them. It keeps them away, which suits me."

Highbury stood then, suddenly decisive.

"Let's go to my rooms," he said, loading a tray with food and moving to the door.

"Before we begin," Alex said, still in his makeup and still with an English accent, but without affectation, once they were all settled around the fire, the food on the table between them. "There are some things I don't want you, or anyone to know. They include my real name, where I'm from and my background. William has always spoken of you with great affection, and I know he trusts you completely.

"There are people I trust completely too, who know my purpose here and are helping me to achieve it. None of them know William's name, and they never will. That's to protect him, in case they're ever arrested. If they were, although they wouldn't voluntarily reveal anything, they would certainly be tortured."

Harriet nodded.

"So you want the same to apply to you, in case I'm ever arrested," she said. "Yes. I understand that."

"I really did meet Lady Peters and her daughters in Paris, as I told you," Highbury said then. "What I didn't tell you was that the daughter told me her brother Anthony died when he was very young. I spent a considerable time trying to discover any information about his death. There was nothing at all."

"The Gazette speculated that the son might come back to see if there was any fortune," Harriet said.

"Yes. There isn't. But the widow's grandparents were believed to be wealthy, and they also died of smallpox. So Sir Anthony, if he was alive, could have inherited their fortune. Like the Gazette, the priest near Geneva thinks the son might return at some point to find out."

Harriet nodded.

"So you've taken on his identity in order to enter into society and spy for James Stuart," she said.

"I warned you that she was direct," Highbury mentioned on seeing the surprise in Alex's eyes.

"I see no point in beating about the bush," Harriet said.

"Yes," Alex replied. "Are you a Jacobite?"

"No," Harriet said. "Nor am I a Hanoverian. I follow no one. My only cause is to be left alone to live the way I want to, and for those I love to be able to do the same. And that cause I'm extremely passionate about."

"Which is why you saw me as a threat."

"Yes. William and clearly you, are Jacobites. I'm assuming you both know the appalling risks you're taking in this insane venture. I'm also assuming that you've adopted this hideous façade in order not to be recognised if it *is* found out you're not Anthony. You're both adults. I allow no one to stop me doing what I want to do, so it would be hypocritical of me to try to stop you from doing what you want to do.

"I won't do much to help you. What I *will* do is warn you if I hear anything that might threaten you, or anything that you need to know on a personal, not a political level. If either of you *are* arrested, I will endeavour to secure your release, if I can do so without risking anyone else I love."

"I don't expect you to do that for me," Alex said. "I don't expect anyone to."

"I wouldn't be doing it for you, but for William," she replied. "You said your friends would certainly be tortured. That tells me that they, and possibly you, are not of the nobility. For no nobleman would be tortured, at least not initially. If you are, at some point you might denounce William. That's why I'd secure your release if I could."

"There is one other thing you could do," Highbury said then. "If I am arrested, could you send a message to Sir Anthony immediately? That would give him a chance to escape."

"Yes. I would gladly do that. You were amusing last night, Anthony," she said then. "You made absolute buffoons of Winter and Cunningham. It was a delight to witness."

"Thank you," Alex said, smiling. "It made the evening worthwhile."

"Feel free to exploit them as you please. And anyone else, with some exceptions."

"Caroline and Edwin," Alex answered then. "You arrived together, and you and Caroline have the same very distinctive eyes."

"Yes," she said. "Philippa, when you meet her. Melanie, my sister, although you may not meet her, as she's almost as reclusive as I am. Oh, and don't kill Daniel when you meet him, as much as you might want to. I assume you haven't met him yet?"

"No," Alex said, highly amused. "I've not had that honour."
Harriet laughed.

"Anthony has already promised not to harm him, and I trust him not to," Highbury said, somewhat tiredly.

"You must be very trustworthy, Anthony," Harriet replied. "Although you have no idea what you've agreed to."

"I swore an oath," Alex said then. "I never break an oath. I would die first."

"I think I might like you," she said then.

"The feeling is reciprocated," Alex replied.

"Right, then. I'd better be off," she said, standing up. "Going home today. Had enough of London now. Been here a week. Bloody awful place. When are you going to see George?"

"As soon as possible," Highbury said. "It was Anthony's first appearance yesterday. We wanted to be sure he was ready before I took him to St James's."

"I think he's ready. Your bows and manners were perfect. Affected, but that's understandable. I'm assuming the slip about Homer and Aristotle was intentional?"

"Yes," Alex laughed. "Anthony hates reading. He's hardly going to be an expert in classical literature."

"Which I daresay you are," she replied. It was a statement not a question, so Alex didn't answer. "Send a message when you've been to see George, and I'll come back to London and introduce you to Fred. William can't do that, for reasons I daresay you already know. But I do what I like."

"Anthony hopes to be introduced to *everyone*," Alex said then. "He's too naïve to pay attention to family disputes and fractures, after all."

"Nice man, Fred. Not like his father and younger brother. Bloody awful creatures."

"I thought you said you wouldn't help us, Harriet," Highbury said then, as she picked up her frockcoat from the back of the chair she'd been sitting on, and put it on.

"No. I said I wouldn't do *much* to help you, not nothing. I'll do this."

"Thank you," Highbury replied.

She stood then, looking at them both for a moment.

"You know how I feel for you, William," she said then, her face and voice serious now. "I hardly know you, Anthony, but the little I've seen of you makes me think I could care for you too, in time. For God's sake, be careful. This is a dangerous venture, and if you *are* caught I doubt even I could save you from the gallows. I don't care for many people, as you know, William. Don't break my heart. I'll never forgive you if you do."

"I'll do my best not to," Highbury said then.

She left then without another word, leaving the two men sitting in silence for a minute.

"She never does that," Highbury said finally, very softly.

"Never does what?"

"Shows her feelings as openly as that. She feels *very* deeply, but she doesn't show it."

"She's remarkable," Alex said then.

"Yes. I love her more than almost anyone I know. She won't betray us. I can assure you of that."

"I don't think for one moment she will. Nor will I betray her, or any of those she loves. I swear that now, to you, for you really understand how seriously I take an oath, as she cannot, not knowing who I really am. Last night Murdo said to me, 'watch yon Harriet woman'. I don't need to ask him what he meant now."

He kicked his shoes off then, and put his feet up on the couch.

"Right," he said then. "As I don't need to rush home to find out what my brother meant, shall we discuss what we do next?"

Highbury leaned across to the table and picked up a pastry, and, as the snow started to fall outside, thwarting Harriet's hopes of escaping the capital that day, the two conspirators settled to plot the next move in their attempt to restore the throne to its rightful king.

EPILOGUE

Ardwick Green, December 1742

THE DARK BLUE COACH drew up outside the gates, stopping a little more abruptly than normal, but not enough to dislodge the passenger, who was staring morosely out of the window at the carefully constructed leech-shaped lake and manicured grass leading up to the driveway of Raven Hall.

He did not wait for the coachman to open the door, instead opening it himself and jumping down to the ground.

"Ye did well there," the coachman was saying to the figure now moving to open the wrought iron gates in order that the coach could continue along the long driveway, bordering which was more artificial scenery.

"Aye, but I stopped too quickly," Duncan said.

"Only a wee bit," Alex replied, "but no' too badly, and it was a smooth ride. Iain's right."

"I wouldna want to be driving in London though," Duncan replied. "I canna imagine how anyone does it without colliding wi' something."

"Aye, well, I've been driving coaches for years, but London's another thing altogether," Iain commented. "But in villages and on quiet roads ye'd have no problem alone now."

"Why have ye got down?" Duncan asked now, turning to his brother, who was pulling on his white kid gloves.

"I was thinking to walk up the driveway. I dinna think I've walked more than a mile since we got back to England. I'm worried my legs'll waste away if I dinna use them," Alex told them.

"Ye were using them plenty in the last weeks," Iain laughed. "We all were."

"Ye're just finding it hard, coming back after being at home for a wee while," Duncan said, with complete understanding.

Alex sighed.

"Aye, I am. Maybe it was a mistake to go back."

"No' from the clan's point of view, for they were all awfu' glad to see ye. Kenneth's doing a fine job, but ye're missed, no' just as chieftain, but for yourself," Duncan said, recognising his brother's melancholy mood.

"Aye, and it was good for Maggie and me to meet our new clan finally," Iain added.

"And we've got three good places to hide arms now, when they arrive in Scotland."

"Aye, I ken. I'll be myself again in a day or two," Alex said, realising what they were doing.

In truth, since he had become Sir Anthony he had achieved a lot, more than he'd expected to, although doing it had been mentally exhausting. If most of it was sedentary, it was starting to prove very useful.

He had managed to befriend the Elector, in as far as anyone could befriend such a boorish, dull man, due to his command of German, his knowledge of Hanover, and his willingness to listen for hours in apparently rapt attention while the man droned on about military issues and his own somewhat meagre achievements in that capacity. Although he was hoping to lead forces in Europe soon, should the current war continue, which it showed every sign of doing. George was lonely, Alex had realised, and overjoyed to speak to someone easily in a language he was fluent in about subjects dear to his heart, and find the man genuinely interested in what he had to say.

As long as he didn't find out *why* the fop hung on his every word, all would be well. So far he had succeeded in passing on a good deal of information about the strength of the British Navy and current military deployment in Europe, as well as learning the names of a couple of spies at the Stuart court, who were now ex-spies as a result.

He had also, thanks to Harriet, befriended Prince Frederick, a much pleasanter task, as Frederick had a much warmer personality than his father did. He had something of the common touch that his Stuart rival possessed, although it was a very diluted form of the compelling charisma of Charles. Frederick was a kind, if somewhat immature man, frustrated by the fact that the Elector would give him no duties, and channelled his energies into playing practical jokes on his friends, and setting up a rival court to his father's.

That was very good, Alex had informed Charles in his latest coded missive, because Frederick could be a real asset to the Hanoverians if he was used correctly. He was popular with the common people, whereas his father was unpopular with just about everybody, it seemed.

Apart from that, he, or rather his effeminate perfumed alter ego had, over the course of the year, managed to insinuate himself into almost every corner of society, and was now continually invited to musical evenings, balls, concerts, and was often the only male present at ladies' tea parties, where he would be treated as an honorary female and asked for advice on all matters regarding clothing.

As their own men were generally completely uninterested in the complexities of female fashion, it was a great joy to the ladies to have a man who was not only interested, but extremely knowledgeable about the minutiae of garments. And in spite of his hideous eye for colour in his own clothing, he had a remarkable ability to identify which colours would enhance a lady's complexion, hair or eyes.

After discussing subjects that in truth Alex had no interest whatsoever in, they would, after a time, forget he was a man altogether, as was his intention, and would then share gossip with him. Gossip which he could use to blackmail some men, should he wish to.

He didn't wish to. Not at present, and hopefully not ever. But it was always useful to know that when a lady referred to something 'a gentleman of her slight acquaintance' had said, she was talking about a man whose bed she was probably warming, and who that man was. Such information, which the lady believed was anonymous, was sometimes extremely useful.

It was all, also, driving him slowly insane. In spite of the baronet's success, and in spite of the amount of useful information he had learned and passed back, Alex didn't believe he could keep this up, if he could not go back to the house, close the door and then be Alex MacGregor for a time with his brothers and friends.

Because of that, in spite of his intention to send Duncan at least home after a few weeks, he hadn't, until, in November, when the nobility were all occupied on their country estates killing every animal that moved, Alex had weakened, closed down the house and fluttered off to his 'small seat in the north of the country', as he had told his acquaintance.

He hadn't lied. If they'd assumed he meant the north of England, that was not his fault. The painted baronet and his staff had headed north, changing along the way into different clothes, and after storing the coach and stabling the horses in Edinburgh, had travelled home for a few weeks of blessed relief.

It had been heaven.

But now, as Alex gazed along the curved driveway with its ridiculous shrubs carved into various shapes, and prepared himself to face the profound tedium he would endure for the next hour, he simultaneously wondered whether he should have gone home at all, whilst wishing devoutly that he was still there.

"D'ye need to go and visit the lassies?" Duncan asked now, reading his mind as always. "They're no' expecting ye, are they?"

"No," Alex said. "But their brother lets important pieces of information slip at times, usually when he's trying to impress me with how important he is. I only have to mention something 'the dear king' said to me at our last meeting, and he canna resist letting me know that he has important friends too, and is privy to all manner of consequential information. And I feel sorry for the lassies, in truth. They're boring, but that's because they havena done one interesting thing in their entire lives. I bring a wee bit of colour into their day."

"Aye, ye certainly do that," Iain commented, looking at his outfit.

Today the baronet was wearing a suit of lilac satin, lavishly embroidered with foliage in various shades of green, out of which bloomed unidentifiable yellow flowers.

"Are ye no' worried about your shoes?" Duncan asked, grinning. "Yon useful wee buckles might get dirty."

Alex looked down at the ornamental diamante buckles on his soft leather shoes.

"*Daingead!*" he said, and then looked along the driveway to the house. "To hell with it," he continued. "It's gravel, so I shouldna get them dirty. If I do I'll say I was being extremely adventurous in deciding to walk up the drive. I shouldna be too long. If ye wait a wee while and then drive up to the door, it'll give me a reason to leave. Say thirty...no, an hour. Well then, my dear gentlemen," he said, fiddling with the lace at his sleeve and adopting the baronet's accent in his last words, "I believe I shall perambulate the grounds of this delightful abode before partaking of the hospitality of the inhabitants. Please, make yourselves at ease inside the coach, if the weather grows inclement!"

He set off up the path, adopted a mincing step rather than his usual confident stride, pausing along the way to admire a piece of topiary. The two Highlanders watched him until he disappeared around the curve of the drive, before climbing up into the interior of the coach.

"I still canna imagine how he can go from Alex to Anthony so quickly," Iain said then.

"He always could do it. When we were wee he could mimic nearly everyone in the clan, if he wanted to. No' just the voice, but the mannerisms too," Duncan said, smiling. "This is draining his energy though. I ken he's wishing now that he hadna gone home, for he's feeling awfu' homesick, but he needed it. It's given him the energy to continue."

"He's no' the only one who's homesick," Iain observed.

"No. But my brother needs me more than I need Scotland," Duncan replied. "That's enough to give me the energy to continue."

When he was announced by the footman, Sir Anthony entered the room, noticed that there were four ladies present rather than the three he'd expected, then bowed extravagantly.

"I do declare, my dear ladies, your beauty is as always, utterly dazzling. I am quite overcome," he cried, addressing the three profoundly plain sisters and their companion, who was, in fact worthy of such a compliment.

The three sisters rose immediately to greet him, the fourth woman glancing at them before also doing so. Alex was reminded of his first meal in society, when he had observed which piece of cutlery others picked up before doing likewise.

He sat down, observing the stranger while appearing to absorb the irrelevant small talk of her companions. Who was she? He would certainly remember if he had ever seen her before, not only because of his formidable memory, but because she was incredibly, breathtakingly beautiful.

Not at all the sort of woman a Highlander would look at seriously – she would certainly shatter into a thousand pieces if she had to pick up anything heavier than a teaspoon, and High-landers had no use for purely ornamental lassies – but from an English society point of view, she was perfection. Tiny, delicate, with flawless skin, cornflower-blue eyes and the most incredible silver-blonde hair.

He had only ever seen hair that colour on one other person, but could not at the moment recall who, as his background senses were absorbing the chatter, waiting for a question to be asked, whereupon he would give the asker his full attention. Or appear to. He would remember later.

"Where have you been hiding yourself all this time?" Isabella Cunningham asked finally.

He turned away from the stranger then, wondering why he had not been introduced to her as etiquette dictated he should have been, and embarked on a completely fabricated tale about a business trip followed by a little recuperation in the countryside. All technically true, but if he'd revealed the *actual* details of what that had involved, the Cunningham sisters would certainly have fainted, and the beautiful stranger probably expired entirely.

God, but he was bored. Even the air in the icy room was heavy and dead. He should not have asked Iain and Duncan to wait a whole hour before driving up to the door.

"Oh, Elizabeth, is that not just quite the most amusing story you've ever heard?" Isabella cried, eyes sparkling.

Alex turned back to the now-named stranger, knew that the laughter in her eyes was not because of his dull tale, but because of his appearance, and smiled. Good. He had made his impression, and she would never look beneath it. No one ever looked beneath it.

"So, Elizabeth is your name," he said, smiling.

Isabella, immediately mortified by her lapse in manners, then compounded it by apologizing profusely rather than actually introducing the woman.

And then, to his surprise, the delicate woman, making no attempt to disguise her impatience at Isabella's fluttering, introduced herself.

"Elizabeth. Elizabeth Cunningham," she said, and standing, thrust out her hand in the way a man would. He also stood, took her hand in his, noted her unexpectedly strong grip, and then, remembering just in time that he was not Alex the Highlander, but Sir Anthony the foppish baronet, instead of shaking her hand as she clearly expected him to, he raised it to his lips, pressing a wet kiss onto the back of it. He felt her hand pull slightly back as she instinctively recoiled, and watched as she resisted wiping her hand on her skirt.

Cunningham. So she was *related* to the family? That seemed impossible. She was the complete opposite of them, in looks at least, and possibly in personality too. None of the sisters would have dreamed of brazenly introducing themselves to a stranger as she had.

Isabella went on then to explain that Elizabeth was a cousin whose parents had died, and who had, along with her brother, presumably been taken under their wing, and would be going to London with them when the season started.

She must be rich, Alex thought. There was no way that Edward would take in anyone, relative or not, unless there was something in it for him. Isabella would, certainly; dull and timid as she was, she had a kind heart. But her brother was interested in only one thing – himself.

Interesting. Not that this Elizabeth would be of any use to his cause, or to him, but at least she was something unexpected, and learning a bit more about her would liven up an otherwise intensely dull hour. He settled down over refreshments to let her know exactly what he was. She had seen the exterior, now he would show her the shallow interior and then forget her.

So he let her know that he was friendly with both the elector and his eldest son, and that he was dull enough to find the elector interesting, whilst certain that she would not.

"Is it not true then, that King George has stated that anyone frequenting Prince Frederick's home is no longer welcome at St James's?" Elizabeth asked.

She was interested in Court gossip at least, then. Probably little more than that. He would find out.

"Are you interested in the affairs of the Court then, Miss Cunningham?" he asked. Now she would talk about the various affairs that it was believed people were having, and then he could relegate her to the right compartment in his mind.

He had a compartment for everyone. Edward, Bartholomew, Simon, the Elector and numerous other men he had now met at Highbury's clubs, were pompous, arrogant, believed themselves to be a lot cleverer than they were, and were reasonable sources of information.

Edwin, Caroline, Philippa were intelligent, interesting, very likeable and good sources of information, if they hadn't been part of Harriet's protected circle. Any information he learnt from them he could only use if someone else also mentioned it. Harriet he had met once more, on the visit to Prince Frederick, and liked her immensely, but recognised that she was not someone who could ever be put in a compartment.

Isabella, Clarissa, Charlotte, Anne Maynard and numerous others were ineffectual, dominated by bullying relatives, and in the main, irrelevant to the cause.

Highbury, in his mind, was part of his clan, not because he bore any resemblance to the MacGregors, but because he loved him.

Elizabeth Cunningham *looked* as though she belonged in the pretty but frivolous compartment with Lydia Fortesque and others. Except for the handshake. He would find out by the end of the visit, hopefully.

"Not particularly, no, but I have an interest in politics, yes, and in the situation in Europe," she said.

Hmm. Maybe a Caroline, then, but not under Harriet's protective umbrella.

"What do you think then of the recent treaty concluded between Prussia and England?" he asked, to discover how superficial her interest was.

"I know nothing of it, I am afraid, sir," she replied. "I used to read '*The Manchester Magazine*' and also a newspaper from London, but my cousins do not take a journal. I have read no news since I arrived here some weeks ago."

"Oh, but Edward does take the papers," cried Isabella. "He takes 'The London Gazette,' and is kind enough to tell us of any news which he thinks may be of interest to us."

A furious expression crossed Beth's face like a cloud.

"I beg your pardon," she said, her voice tight. "It seems that treaties between foreign powers are of no interest to ladies, Sir Anthony."

Charlotte stood up so quickly that she almost tipped the tea table over with her voluminous skirts. She looked out of the window.

Interesting. She had a temper then, and was indifferent enough to society etiquette to show it to a stranger. It was clear she had a low opinion of Edward, and, by Charlotte's sudden action, that she made no attempt to hide it. He warmed to her.

"I cannot believe we did not hear your carriage approach, Sir Anthony," Charlotte said desperately.

Alex, as Anthony, leapt into a story about being terrified that a drop of rain might mar his clothes, after which he was pulled into giving fashion advice regarding Elizabeth's prospective outfits for her introduction to the London season. He embraced the flouncy baronet, seemingly entranced at the idea of ruffles and lace, while surreptitiously watching her.

She was every bit as bored as he had been when Highbury had ordered the tailor to measure him for his first outfits. She had no interest whatsoever in the things that almost every other society lady he'd met was enraptured by. And she made no attempt whatsoever to hide it. Suddenly the air in the room was no longer dead and heavy.

And then another stranger, this time male entered the room, this one certainly a Cunningham, followed by Lord Edward, and Sir Anthony was introduced for the first time to Richard Cunningham, brother to the delicate-looking Elizabeth.

Instinctively he recoiled from him. Had he met the man as Alex MacGregor, he would have made sure that he had a weapon within easy reach. In fact, he did, as the ornately-jewelled hilt of the sword he carried seemingly decoratively had a blade that was sharp enough to decapitate someone.

He had never decapitated someone for no reason, however, so instead he placed a limp hand in Richard Cunningham's, registered that the man gripped his tighter than necessary to show both his contempt and superiority to the baronet, resisted the urge to break the man's fingers, and then watched as Cunningham's whole demeanour changed on discovering that this foppish molly was a friend of the elector.

Irrelevant then. He knew no one important, was trying to insinuate himself into society, and seemed to be as stupid as his cousin, although probably more brutal. A soldier, certainly; his bearing and athletic build gave that away. Unlike Elizabeth, he was clearly a Cunningham; brown eyes, dark hair, with a dark gypsyish handsomeness that sloth and obesity had taken away from Edward.

Alex focussed his attentions back to the sister. There was something about her that intrigued him. Probably it was just that, like him, her appearance seemed to bear no relation to what was beneath. He found himself accepting Isabella's invitation to dinner, and not just because Edward so obviously wished him in Hell, and it was always fun to annoy Edward. Duncan and Iain would not mind waiting in the coach. There was a flask of brandy under the seat which would keep them warm.

Over the next hour he learnt a good deal about Elizabeth Cunningham, and at the end of it was as intrigued as ever by her.

She clearly disliked her brother intensely, although she seemed to have no fear of him. Indeed she seemed to have no fear of anyone. She had a mind of her own, was intelligent, well-read, accustomed to having the freedom to read what she wanted, and very capable of verbally eviscerating Edward when he began spouting rubbish about Isabella's French chef undermining the health of the English with his food.

She was clearly feeling restricted, stultified even, by the life she was now leading with her cousins. Which made him wonder why she was doing it. She must have money, or her brother must, because Edward would never accept paupers into his household. Maybe that was it. Maybe the brother was rich and she was not, so had to go along with him, or starve. If that was the case, she seemed determined not to become downtrodden. And yet she was protective of her pathetic female cousins, bristling when their brother insulted them.

He admired that, felt himself warming to her. He too was stultified by the life he was now leading. Maybe he could introduce her to the German lairdie, find out a little more about her.

If he *did* meet her in London, he thought, he would certainly introduce her to Caroline, and to Philippa and Harriet if he had a chance. They were also headstrong, forthright women.

He wondered what her political affiliations were, if she had any.

In the end Elizabeth gave him an opportunity herself to find out, by asking him where he'd been on his travels, which allowed him to mention Scotland. Not Loch Lomond of course, but Edinburgh, which it was conceivable the effeminate Sir Anthony might visit.

Of course the Cunninghams, who absorbed every item of Hanoverian propaganda they could find, thought every Scot to be a savage Jacobite, on which he dropped in a few comments about Jacobites and the Earl of Derwentwater in particular, waving his lacy hands about enthusiastically, whilst observing her lips tighten and her perfect skin flush as he seemingly dropped important secrets into this devoutly Hanoverian family. They were all lies, of course, but she did not know that.

Interesting. If she was not exactly a Jacobite sympathiser, she was certainly not a believer of the scurrilous rumours about the followers of the Stuarts, or of the barbarity of the Scots.

In the end he stayed much longer than he'd intended to, with the result that, once out of earshot he'd apologised profusely to Duncan and Iain, before stopping to buy them a hot meal from a chop house on the way back to the apartments they'd rented for a few weeks in order that Alex, not Sir Anthony, could establish deeper relationships with his new connections.

Manchester was proving very useful for that. Not only was it geographically in a good position for weapons to be stored for a time on their way from Dover to Scotland, but a sizeable number of the inhabitants were Jacobites. Not the ineffectual kind whose support was limited to waving their glasses over a bowl to toast 'the King over the Water', but active ones, who were willing to take risks, and who would almost certainly rise if Charles landed with his army.

When Charles landed with his army. For he would, Alex told himself as he scrubbed his face that evening. He had to believe that, or he could not continue covering his face every day with noxious paint and then prancing his way through most of it. He would come.

In the meantime, as Sir Anthony he would endeavour to become more closely acquainted with the enchanting Elizabeth. Not because of her physical beauty, although he'd have had to be dead not to be affected by it, but because she was interesting, and, he sensed, not only bored out of her senses, but, beneath that was deeply unhappy with her current life. As, indeed, was he. And she had a mind of her own, it seemed.

He would not grow fond of her, of course. He had grown fond of Caroline and Edwin, and had resolved to become attached to no more members of society, apart from Highbury. It complicated things if you had feelings for your enemy, after all.

No. He would remain neutral, but she would perhaps make social evenings a little more interesting – she had certainly made this dinner so, with her acerbic comments. And maybe he could make society life more interesting for her, too. Not as the flouncy baronet, of course, but by introducing her to people whose conversation would stimulate her.

He smiled at himself in the mirror, turning his head to make sure that all trace of the paint was gone. Now he would join Maggie, Iain, Duncan and Angus downstairs. He did not have to be Sir Anthony for another couple of days, after which he would certainly pay the Cunninghams another visit.

It was not until he was halfway down the stairs to join the others that he remembered where he had seen Elizabeth's unique colour of hair before. And the same, cornflower-blue eyes, for that matter.

Malcolm MacDonald. The man he had killed in Glencoe over five years ago, which had ended the feud between the clans. She resembled him as closely as her brother Richard resembled Edward. Alex had commented on Malcolm's unusual looks to MacIain later that evening, and the Glencoe chief had told him that there was a number of them, all with the same hair and eyes, and all hot-tempered and stubborn. Elizabeth Cunningham was certainly hot-tempered. Whether stubborn or not Alex had no idea, but he would not be surprised at all if she was.

No. It was a coincidence, that was all.

He resolved to put her from his mind, forcing himself to focus on the pleasant evening ahead, and the numerous meetings he intended to have with like-minded people over the next days. They were far more important than a pretty, forthright noblewoman. She would be a pleasant distraction; the cause was his life.

HISTORICAL NOTE

As always I wanted to include a historical note, in order to expand a little on some of the historical points I've mentioned briefly in the book.

The first one is in Chapter Four, when Highbury meets Lady Peters and her daughters, and she tells him they are on their way to Geneva. I mention the political situation there at the time. Today Geneva is part of Switzerland, but in the eighteenth century things were very different.

The city sits in a strategic spot in Europe, so was fought over for centuries before finally becoming independent in 1602 after it repelled an invasion from the Duke of Savoy. The people still celebrate that anniversary today. They had already declared themselves Protestant, which alienated them from the Roman Catholic Swiss cantons, and over the next centuries Geneva became a haven for Protestant refugees fleeing France's draconian policies against them, including many intellectuals and artisans.

The theologian John Calvin had a huge influence on Geneva too, and not only in a religious sense. He was also heavily involved in the reorganisation of the city, ensuring that the city became an industrial, financial and commercial success. Unfortunately he also had a severe policy of persecution of people who did not follow his version of the Protestant faith. Over time, however, the extremism died down.

In time there were a lot of changes to the original rule, and the city's population expanded dramatically. In the sixteenth century most of Geneva's males were citizens; by the 1700s the majority were not, and non-citizens did not have the same rights and privileges as citizens did. Because of this there was a lot of unrest as various groups arose protesting the unfairness of this. Eventually this unrest settled down, but at the time Highbury was meeting Lady Peters there were still a lot of problems in the city, although this would not have directly impacted the small villages scattered around the lake.

In 1798 Geneva was annexed to France and became subservient during Napoleonic times, but in 1814 was admitted to the Swiss cantons.

Foot washing – I've mentioned this briefly in the historical notes for *The Gathering Storm*, when Alex has his feet washed, but thought I'd go into a bit more detail this time. The act of foot washing does have a religious significance for Christians, following the Biblical account of Christ washing his disciples' feet, which symbolised their spiritual cleansing before the crucifixion.

On a more practical note, until recently many people did not have shoes (including Highlanders), and rubbish was not disposed of as it is today, and so after walking down the street their feet would have been extremely dirty! Washing them before you went into someone's home was a sign of respect – as is taking your shoes off today.

So washing the bride and groom's feet the night before the wedding probably originated as a cleansing before the sacrament of marriage, but degenerated over the years into a much more amusing affair, as I write about in this book. Feathers were often used, along with various sticky substances, not only on the groom, but also the bride. Eventually this became known as 'blackening', where horrible (but harmless) substances are not just poured on the legs, but sometimes the whole body, after which the victims may well be paraded through the village. It still takes place in parts of rural Scotland, and in fact one poor man was blackened and then secured to a lamppost for everyone's amusement just a couple of years ago in a village close to where I lived at the time!

I also wanted to mention the sèis. I've mentioned this a number of times in the *Chronicles*, but in this book it takes on more significance than in others, and although it's obviously a piece of furniture, I thought I'd expand on this a little. I've read that the word sèis was later anglicised into 'sofa'. I'm not sure if this is true, but it makes sense.

The sèis was basically a wooden bench seat, with arms at each end and a back. It would be made by a local craftsman, and its complexity or beauty depended on the craftsman's skill. The most basic version would just be a plank supported by stones at each end, whereas others would have carved arms and a back, and maybe even a storage box under the seat, the seat itself forming the lid. They were long enough for a few people to sit together, as we do now on our modern sofas. They were very popular, and found all over the Highlands and islands.

In Chapter Ten I mention Lord Winter giving a pompous account of his evening at the Society of Dilettanti. This society still exists today, and seems to be a far more serious thing now than it was when it started. It was set up in 1734 by a group of gentlemen who had been on the Grand Tour and who purportedly wanted to share and build on the experiences they'd had in Italy particularly, and to purify public taste in Britain. It attracted a number of wealthy aristocrats and most of the members were 'young men of rank and fashion'. You could not ask to join, but had to be recommended by a member. So it's exactly the sort of club the social-climbing pompous snob Lord Winter might aspire to become a member of.

Even in its early days it attracted scorn, with Robert Walpole (effectively Prime Minister) describing it as ...*a club, for which the nominal qualification is having been in Italy, and the real one being drunk; the two chiefs are Lord Middlesex and Sir Francis Dashwood, who were seldom sober the whole time they were in Italy.*

As with many such societies, various secret rituals were invented to bond members, which were rumoured to have religious and sexual undertones, costumes were worn, and items were purchased such as a box in the shape of the Tomb of Bacchus, in which the society's records were kept.

Although it seems initially to have primarily been an exclusive light-hearted society which devoted its time to drinking and sharing experiences, over the years it became more serious, providing financial support for the Royal Academy in 1775 by financing scholarships for students who wished to study in Italy and Greece. It also sponsored a series of Italian operas in the 1740s, archaeological trips, and paid for authors of various intellectual books about classical works to investigate and then write their books.

Also in Chapter Ten Harriet advises Caroline that Edwin, a rising politician, should watch out for Pelham and Newcastle, whilst remaining friendly with Walpole.

In March 1740 (the time the dinner is set in), Sir Robert Walpole had held the role of what is now called Prime Minister for nineteen years, which was an extraordinary achievement. He was an expert in working with the powers of the monarch and the increasingly powerful Commons, was a talented orator and very confident in his abilities. He adopted a moderate way, avoiding war, lowering taxes and increasing exports, and being tolerant of Protestant dissenters.

However in 1739, in spite of his attempts to stop it, and facing opposition from both the king and the House of Commons, Walpole reluctantly embarked on the interestingly named *War of Jenkins' Ear*. This signalled the end of Walpole's dominance in politics, allowing others to start the process of ousting him, spreading rumours about corruption, etc – the same things go on today, so I won't elaborate! In 1742 he resigned, and was replaced by Spencer Compton, Earl of Wilmington, but died the following year, after which Henry Pelham became Prime Minister.

Henry Pelham (brother of Thomas Pelham-Holles, Duke of Newcastle, who readers of the *Chronicles* will remember well), also preferred a policy of peace, and in 1744 forced the powerful Lord Cartaret out of office as Secretary of State, threatening the king that he would leave the country without a government if Carteret stayed. After this, Henry and his brother effectively ran the government together. Hence Harriet's warning to Edwin, as she's renowned for investigating and seeing everything that's going on in the corridors of power, especially things that might affect herself or those she loves.

In Chapter Twelve Alex and Duncan visit Prince Charles in Rome, and a couple of things are mentioned in passing (as they would be at the time), which twenty-first century readers won't necessarily know about, so I thought I'd explain.

Charles mentions a prospective trip to Madrid to try to elicit the support of the Spanish. By this time the prince had engaged in a number of highly successful if gruelling diplomatic trips, in which he had demonstrated his princely attributes and incredible charisma to great effect. The British and Spanish had been moving slowly towards hostilities for a number of years, but the breaking out of the *War of Jenkins' Ear* (mentioned above), in 1739, put the two into open warfare.

This gave an opportunity for the Jacobites to work with the Spanish, but although James Stuart had been trying to get an invitation from Spain in the previous years, now he became unsure. The debacle of 1719 had been engineered by Spain, but also if the Spanish were going to invade Britain in conjunction with the Jacobites, James knew it would be a Scottish invasion, whereas he wanted an English one, which only France was powerful enough to support. There were also concerns as to whether the Spanish would just use a Jacobite expedition to siphon off British troops and weaken them, rather than genuinely supporting a Stuart restoration. It was not only James who thought this, but a number of leading Jacobites of the day. In fairness, they were very likely correct in their assumption.

The winter of 1739-40 was brutal, and the combination of the Pope dying and there being no chance of Charles being able to go to Spain until the weather improved in spring led to James abandoning the whole idea.

On a lighter note, in the same chapter, when Highbury and Alex are discussing the physical appearance of the embryo Sir Anthony, Highbury suggests Alex might grow a beard as a means of changing his appearance. While anyone who has a bearded friend who's suddenly decided to shave it all off will understand what a huge difference a beard makes, as it conceals multiple facial features, it was a bit of a desperate suggestion for the 1700s, and particularly for aristocrats.

While the working-class or poor men may well have had some facial hair growth, it would mainly have been due to a lack of ability to remove it, either monetary or practical. Beards were absolutely NOT worn at this time as a fashion statement, by anyone. Wealthy men would pay a barber to come to their house two or three times a week to shave them, others would go to a barber's shop, which also did 'penny shaves' for the poorer. Over time, men began to use razors to shave themselves, and the poor probably did this earlier, to avoid spending much-needed money on anything other than necessities.

There are numerous pictures of eighteenth century men, particularly Scottish Highlanders, wearing full beards, but if you look at contemporary portraits, ALL of them are beardless. While it's highly likely that Highlanders would have had a decent growth of facial hair while on campaign, they did not seem to wear full beards. Or sideburns. This is a Victorian depiction of what they thought Scottish Highlanders *should* look like, another part of the Victorian rewriting of history to make it conform to their view of how things should be.

Yes, I have a bugbear about the Victorian rewriting of history, I admit! But so would you if you'd had so many posts from people telling you that women were not outspoken, men wouldn't wear such brightly coloured clothes, and numerous other things, all because of this phenomenon. The Victorians even went so far as to restore various historical buildings, not as they would have been, but as they thought they should have been. Infuriating to a history lover! Misinformation is by no means a modern invention.

On to Chapter Fifteen, where Alex travels to London for the first time with Highbury, who gives him a running commentary on the areas they're driving through on their way to his house in Grosvenor Square. To do this I followed the route on a fabulous contemporary map of London, and described a few of the notable places they would have passed through.

Firstly Smithfield Market, which really was as horrendous as I describe. It was an ancient livestock market, granted market status by the king in 1327. It was also used for some public executions, and was the site of the very popular Bartholomew Fair, held every year for four days in September. Calls to ban the fair due to its riotous nature were ignored, as it had become an institution – it was finally stopped in 1855.

Livestock was brought from all over England to Smithfield market, which held over five acres of pens in which they were held until they were sold. Some were sold for breeding, while a great many were slaughtered for meat to feed the ever-expanding population of the city. The noise and smell of such an enormous number of animals being driven through the streets to the market in the first place must have been tremendous, (at the time I'm writing about, around 74,000 cows and over half a million sheep per year), which would be multiplied at the market itself. To add to that, once the animals were sold, they were driven to nearby slaughterhouses, which were set up for huge numbers of animals. The cows or sheep would then be hit on the head before being bled to death, after which they were skinned and butchered.

As you can imagine, a lot of animal waste had to be got rid of. Some of this was loaded into boats and then dumped in the River Thames, some was put into 'laystalls' (a kind of boxed rubbish tip), which was then cleared by scavengers, while some was just thrown into the sewers and left to rot. You don't need much imagination to imagine the smell of faeces and urine alone from so many animals crowded together, to say nothing of the quantities of decomposing flesh in the days before freezers. It must have been absolutely horrendous, and incredibly noxious to anyone even just passing through the area as Alex and Highbury did, let alone to those who lived nearby!

Onto St Giles, and Chick Lane, which Highbury also talks about, and warns Alex against visiting. St Giles had been a very poor area for a long time, and had been a haunt of the poor Irish since the 1500's, who used to come over to England for seasonal work. Over time numbers of them brought their families and settled permanently in the area, often living in one room of a dilapidated house. While they were only working seasonally, the Irish were more tolerated by locals, but once they started living in St Giles year-round, resentment flourished, as it was said they were stealing the native people's work (some things never change). This resulted in a lot of brutal violence between gangs of Irish and of workers, particularly the Butcher-Boy gangs.

All this was exacerbated by the plentiful supply of cheap spirits. In 1750 a report claimed that up to one in five properties in St Giles was selling or making gin. Alcohol consumption was accepted in the eighteenth century, particularly in towns, where the water supply was often unfit to drink. But strong spirits were not freely available to the poor until they started being imported in quantity in the early eighteenth century. Gin was cheap, easy to make, and poor quality grain that was no use for anything else could be used. Suddenly it was possible for even the poorest people to become drunk on a daily basis.

As a result of this, alcohol-fused crime and violence exploded, causing huge concern on many levels. Hogarth's famous depiction of Gin Lane showed the destruction of the economy and morals of the poor people who sought escape from misery in the bottle. In 1751 the Gin Act was passed, which meant traders had to pay a licence, and enforced strict controls. But St Giles remained a hotbed of poverty, crime, prostitution and slum housing until the end of the nineteenth century.

Highbury only mentions Chick Lane as a place of taverns, brothels and Molly houses, this is because he is thinking of reasons his idiot son might have to go to such a place. In fact, although it *was* famous for that, it was also a den of thievery and other crime. If someone's clothes were stolen, the first place they would look for them was in the second-hand clothes shops in the lane. The taverns in the lane were frequented by all manner of criminals, from house-breakers to pickpockets and footpads, who would drink themselves into a stupor before engaging in mass brawls. A good number of the thieves and violent robbers were women, many of whom were also prostitutes.

And finally (now I've painted such an enticing portrait of the capital city of England), I return to Scotland, where in Chapter Seventeen Alex is talking about the age MacGregor women get married. Alex mentions that Scots law allowed a girl to marry at twelve and a boy at fourteen. I haven't invented this.

The marriage laws in England and Scotland were very different, in many ways. Marriage in England was considered to be a religious sacrament, and so people could not legally marry unless the wedding was conducted by an Anglican minister, although the place of marriage was not important. This did allow for illicit marriages (such as the potential one in *Mask of Duplicity)* and also marriages where one of the couple were underage. This led to the Hardwicke Marriage Act of 1753, which stated that in order to be legally binding, marriages had to be conducted by a minister in a church. In addition to this, parental consent had to be obtained if the parties were under the age of twenty-one.

Scottish law was very different. The age of consent for marriage was, (and remained until 1929) twelve for girls and fourteen for boys. In addition to this 'irregular' marriages were legal, which they were not in England and Wales.

An irregular marriage could be one of the following:

The couple declared themselves married in front of witnesses (it did not have to then be consummated to be legally binding).

A couple declared themselves married without any witnesses. Although this was legal, unless there was other evidence that they were married, it would not be recognised should there be a legal dispute later and one of the parties denied the marriage.

A marriage by 'habit and repute', which was one where a couple appeared in public as husband and wife regularly, even though no oath or declaration had been made.

Irregular marriages were looked down on by the church, and couples who engaged in them might be fined, but they were still legally recognised.

The difference in law between Scotland and England is what led to the famous elopements and marriage at Gretna Green by the blacksmith in the later part of the eighteenth century onwards. Gretna Green was the first place over the border for underage young people desperately wanting to marry without their parents' consent. Although such marriages could not be *performed* legally in England, once conducted in Scotland, the legality of them was recognised in England.

If you'd like to read further historical blogs and other information about the period my books are set in, and also learn about future book releases, please subscribe to my monthly newsletter (no spam, guaranteed) here:

http://eepurl.com/bSNLHD

I also post a historical blog on my website every month:
http://www.juliabrannan.com

You can follow me on Facebook:
http://www.facebook.com/pages/Julia-Brannan/727743920650760

Or if you like, you could join my very friendly Jacobite Chronicles Book Group on Facebook. I post there regularly and would love it if you'd join me!

https://www.facebook.com/groups/officialjacobitechronicles

If you enjoyed this book, I'd be very grateful if you could leave a review for me, on Amazon, Goodreads, Bookbub, and anywhere else you would like to. Reviews not only tell me I'm doing a worthwhile job, but also help sales, which allow me to eat so I can write the next book!

Printed in Great Britain
by Amazon

59064468R00239